THE
LOOMING
STORM

For Gina:
Jesus is
the Anchor
in every
storm!

DIANE/DAVID
MUNSON

The Looming Storm

©2016 Diane Munson and David Munson
Published by Micah House Media, LLC
Grand Rapids, Michigan 49525
All rights reserved.

    Micah House Media, LLC,
    5355 Northland Drive, NE, C-106,
    Grand Rapids, Michigan 49525.

ISBN-13: 978-0-9835590-8-5

Scripture quotations are taken from the HOLY BIBLE, NEW INTERNATIONAL VERSION®. NIV®. Copyright ©1973, 1978, 1984 by Biblica ®. Used by permission.

Cover design by Book Graphics.
Cover images from Ingimage, Stockfresh, and CanStockPhoto.
Formatting by Rik – Wild Seas Formatting

    Visit Diane and David Munson's website at:
    www.DianeAndDavidMunson.com

DEDICATION

To those who hope in the Lord.

Do you not know? Have you not heard?
The LORD is the everlasting God, the Creator of the ends of the
earth. He will not grow tired or weary, and His understanding no
one can fathom. He gives strength to the weary and increases the
power of the weak … (T)hose who hope in the LORD will renew
their strength. They will soar on wings like eagles; they will run and
not grow weary, they will walk and not be faint.
Isaiah 40: 28-31 NIV

ACKNOWLEDGMENT

Many thanks to Micah House Media and those supporting them for this story of faith in the midst of the looming storm. We give a special thanks to Pam Cangioli for her expertise in editing and great support for our endeavor.

Chapter 1

Northern Virginia

Monday began with a burst of turbulence, like many workdays did for Federal Agent Eva Montanna. Her awakening to a boisterous alarm quickly morphed into a hectic struggle to pry three sleepy kids out of bed and brew coffee before Scott left for work. A moment of calm touched her life when at six a.m. she stood on tiptoe to kiss her husband's cheek.

"Sure you can't wait for me to fix an egg with your bagel?" Eva stifled a yawn.

Scott shook his head, a lock of his brown curly hair falling loose. "I'm needed early on the Hill to fend off the media circus. A new Supreme Court nominee doesn't happen every day. The Speaker wants to keep pressure on the Senate."

He winked before stepping into the garage. Eva's heart overflowed with love as she watched him back out of the garage. His job as press secretary to the Speaker of the House kept him plenty busy. So did hers as Federal Agent for Immigration Customs Enforcement (ICE).

Eva ran to change into work attire. She flipped the light on to her walk-in closet. The bulb fizzled out in a blinding flash. Not willing to search for a spare or find the ladder, she snatched navy slacks and a white blouse off the rod using her smartphone for light. Minutes later, she was buttering toast when her youngest son ran in the kitchen.

"Mom, I banged my toe," Dutch cried.

"Let me see."

He held up his tiny bare foot. Blood squirted from a gash in his big toe. She rushed to the half-bath and found a bandage to stop the bleeding. Breakfast was hurried and at last, she corralled her children off to school. Eva had a few spare minutes to pull herself together. A quick flick of a brush through her wheat-colored, shoulder-length hair, and a dab of pale gloss to her lips completed her look.

Wait, were those new lines around her eyes?

Oh well. Scott still found her pretty; he'd told her so just yesterday. And life presented issues more important than wrinkles, though when she'd started pursuing criminals, Eva had youthful skin and clear periwinkle eyes. Under the harsh bathroom lights, her face revealed long days and nights of surveillance, car chases and foot chases, and scrapes and bruises from tackling guys bigger than her.

Myriad faces darted through her mind. Faces of international terrorists she'd arrested aboard Indian Ocean freighters, drug smugglers she collared in south Florida, and even a power-mad Chinese scientist. If Eva's neighbors knew what her job really entailed, they would be shocked. Others might avoid her totally.

She pushed a button, and up clattered the garage door. Before getting into her unmarked government car (G-car), she spotted their newspaper on the driveway. Eva walked to the street with her purse in one hand, and bent down to pick it up.

A voice surprised her by calling cheerily, "Hello! Good morning."

Eva's head jolted upward. Her new neighbor, whom she'd never spoken with, waved from across the street. He stood in the road, newspaper under his arm.

"Good morning to you." Eva lifted a hand before going up the concrete drive.

"Excuse me," he called out.

Despite needing to leave, Eva spun around and met her neighbor of six months.

He towered over her, and holding out a roughened hand, said he was sorry to bother her. "I'm Fred. Should have introduced myself before now."

"Glad to meet you, Fred. I'm Eva."

"I learned your name was Eva. That's what I'm warning you about. A bizarre thing happened a few days ago."

"Oh?"

What could occur in her stable neighborhood? Eva stepped back in precaution.

Fred clasped his paper tightly. "Day before yesterday, a man stood on tiptoe at your front door, peering in the tiny window."

"What time was that?"

He rolled his watery eyes, guessing, "Ten maybe. He walked to a car parked by your other neighbor, but didn't climb in. Instead, he came over and rang my bell."

"Did he give you a religious tract?"

"No, he asked about you. Said your name was Eva Savannah or something."

"Fred, did this man say what he wanted?"

"My daughter cautioned me not to open the door to strangers." The elderly man fidgeted with his paper. "But I did,

2

thinking something was wrong at your house. Then I wondered if he was a repo guy taking back a car you couldn't afford."

Suspicion crept into Eva's mind. "Why did you think so?"

"He asked if you drive different expensive cars. I asked why he wanted to know."

"And?"

"He said he was with the police."

"The police! Did he show you a badge?"

Fred shook his head. "No. He showed me a card."

"Was his picture on it? What police department did it say?"

"I can't recall a picture. I don't know what it said."

"How about his appearance?"

A car came around the corner, heading straight for them. Eva motioned Fred to his side of the street and let the car pass.

He raised his free hand above Eva's head. "He was about this tall, your age, a white guy wearing a windbreaker. He asked if I knew if you lived with a guy. I told him I have seen a guy around and some kids."

"I wish you hadn't told a stranger about me even if he did show you a card. By the way, the man you see is my husband and father to our three children."

Fred shrugged. "Maybe I shouldn't a' told you."

"You were right to tell me." Eva touched his shaking hands. "Anything else?"

"He asked if you were gone recently. I said I've lived here a few months and never met you. He hopped in his car and left. My daughter said I should tell you."

Eva thanked him, certain he didn't know much else about the odd encounter.

"I like seeing your kids tossing a football and such," he said. "It's kinda lonely here all day with my daughter at work."

Regret tumbled through Eva. Why hadn't she done more to reach out to her neighbors? She didn't even know Fred's daughter, simply waving a few times since she'd moved in with her father.

Eva shook his hand with firmness. "We need to look out for each other. You did good. If you recall anything, please come over and let me know."

"Okay then. I will."

Mystified by these events, Eva had a sudden thought. She reached into her purse and pulled out a pen.

"Let me see your newspaper, Fred."

When he handed it over, she wrote her cell number in black ink along the top.

"Make a note of my number when you get home. Then you can call me if you see any more suspicious things."

His eyes sparkled and he nodded with new vigor. "Now we're talking turkey."

Eva went to her G-car wondering what else she should do about Fred's strange revelations. A sense of foreboding enveloped her mind as the garage door clanged shut behind her. With renewed vigilance, she drove down the block as if seeing the parked cars and darkened houses for the first time.

Scott was already in his hearing, so Eva would have to wait until later to explain the peculiar happenings in their neighborhood.

Chapter 2

Eva wasn't the type to cool her heels willingly. Suspicion stuck by her side, prompting her to keep checking the rearview mirror during the drive to the office. When she punched in the access code, having reached the office with no trouble on the roads, she decided the day was definitely on the upswing.

The fenced-off building with secure gates was where she worked on the Joint Terrorism Task Force (JTTF) with other federal agents and local law enforcement. She hurried to brew coffee, quickly learning someone not very kind had used the last of the ground coffee. No coffee for the entire morning sure dampened her enthusiasm for the day.

She dropped her purse on the desk and spotted a brief note from her long-time friend and partner, FBI Special Agent Griff Topping.

Noon meeting at Topsy-Turvy in Alexandria where I'll brief you and Brett about a fresh lead.

Super—that meant she could sink her teeth into Griff's never-ending monitoring of Chechen terrorists. Even if his quest resulted in another dead end, Eva preferred any new case to typing boring quarterly reports that were due. She buzzed Griff's note through the shredder, wondering if he'd discovered they were out of coffee and dashed out for more. From the way his note read, she doubted it.

Eva pledged to go without her favorite caffeine-laden beverage until lunch. When she spun around in her chair, the armrest hit her key in the side drawer. The key broke off and fell to the floor. Half the key remained in the lock.

"Oh great!" she lamented in disgust.

"What's wrong?"

Eva looked up. John Oliver held a mug in his hands, and she detected the unmistakable aroma of roasted coffee. She told her boss about her busted key.

"Happened to me last week." His gritty voice held no sympathy. "Try your Swiss army knife. Mine worked."

Oliver walked away, taking his coffee with him. Because Eva often stored her gun and evidence in the side drawer, she spent the next twenty minutes using tweezers from her knife to remove the stub. She'd have the two pieces made into a duplicate key after her noon meeting.

Eva got busy typing a report, and then it was time to meet Griff. She headed out, keeping her foot steady on the accelerator of her Ford Fusion. Equipped with a police-pursuit package, her government-issued car could catapult her from zero to sixty miles per hour in seconds. Speed wasn't needed in the late-morning traffic. Besides, Eva wasn't following or chasing any felons.

She reached the outskirts of Alexandria when the radio announcer warned of high winds and hail overnight. Eva tightened her grip on the wheel. Bad weather might interrupt her daughter Kaley's class trip in the morning. She'd just rounded the corner for the grill when her cell phone rang. She pressed the earpiece button, answering the call.

Could it be her neighbor Fred with more strange news?

A voice lilted in her ear, "Eva, it's Julia. With Bo gone, I thought the rest of us could have dinner so the kids can be together. We enjoy the Greek food at Athena."

"Hold on, Julia."

Eva eased off the accelerator and veered into a bank parking lot. She'd worked for years with Julia's husband and CIA agent, Bo Rider. Their teenage daughter Glenna was Kaley's good friend, and traveling with her on the school trip to Poland.

Eva turned off the radio and told Julia the plan sounded fun. "Scott's working late. Half of the national media is prowling around the Capitol seeking interviews on the Supreme Court appointment."

"I have been mostly focused on possible inclement weather, which I hope doesn't delay their flight," Julia replied.

"Me too."

As she said this, Eva squinted through the windshield. Dark gray clouds swirling overhead brought to mind the caution about high winds. She had another suggestion for Julia.

"Let's pray the looming storm will not be an issue, okay?"

Both ladies agreed to be in prayer, and to see each other at six. Eva ended the call using the button on her earpiece. Traffic cleared, and she roared back onto the slow-going road. Light drizzle began covering her windshield.

She flicked on her wipers, glancing at the passenger seat. Where was her brown umbrella? Heavier rain cascaded down, and she remembered it was packed in her daughter's suitcase. Well, she'd better find parking close to the grill.

Griff had recently found the eclectic restaurant that played host to hushed meetings between lawyers and their desperate clients during breaks in criminal trials. With DEA Agent Brett

Calloway, their newest JTTF member, being involved in trial at the federal courthouse, the nearby Topsy-Turvy seemed a fine choice. Eva's mouth began to water thinking of its delicious southern food.

Was that a parking spot? She zoomed in the lot. It took some doing to wedge her Fusion in between a shiny black Mercedes and the man sitting in a battered Chevy. An unusual coincidence struck her. What were the chances two Florida cars would be parked at the same northern Virginia restaurant?

THE COINCIDENCE FLEW FROM HER MIND DUE to winds picking up the second she stepped from the car. Her blond ponytail flopped from side to side as she dashed along in the rain. Tempting smells greeted her inside the grill. A fresh tissue wiped across her face helped, though her slacks were still damp.

Eva pressed the shoulder purse against her side while her eyes scanned the crowded restaurant. The hard bulge of her weapon, a .40-caliber Glock 23, gave her a stark reminder she was on duty. Griff sat alone at a distant table casually dressed. He saw her and waved. Eva maneuvered past tables of animated attorneys and courthouse staffers. Griff rose to hand her a thick menu.

"You snagged the choicest seat as usual," she said without taking it.

"Eva, you know the drill. First to arrive gets to sit with their back to the wall."

"I'm always alert to trouble walking through the door. Brett's late. Let him sit with his back to the entrance."

She thumped in a chair beside him, brow furrowed and purse at her side. Griff's white teeth showed beneath his bushy moustache when he smiled. He nodded his head to the adjoining table.

"I've been eavesdropping on their conversation."

"Oh?" Eva gazed at two ladies talking with a man. "That doesn't sound like you."

"The women are witnesses waiting to testify in Brett's trial. It just recessed." He kept his voice low. "That guy is the police detective who brought them here from Florida."

"That explains the Florida plates outside."

Griff pushed the menu toward Eva. She dropped her eyes, deciding on a chicken sandwich with sliced tomatoes and macaroni and cheese, her favorite comfort food.

"Wish I'd worn a jacket," Eva said, feeling a draft on her neck. "I've hardly seen Brett since he moved from Miami. Where's our server? I need coffee."

"We won't see Brett until his Ponzi trial is done. He began working the case in Miami with the Florida detective sitting over there."

"Why is a drug agent investigating a financial case?" she wondered aloud.

Griff swiped at his chin explaining, "A defrauded victim introduced Brett as a potential investor to Holly and Carlos Munoz, the alleged scammers. It was done with Miami's JTTF, where Brett was assigned before transferring to our office."

"With the trial being held here in Alexandria, I assume Virginia investors were also scammed."

"Exactly. You and I both know Virginia juries readily dole out convictions."

Eva grinned at him lightheartedly. "So many facts at your fingertips. How long have you been eavesdropping?"

"Long enough, impeded by my growling stomach." Griff checked his watch. "We should get to the heart of why I called this meeting."

"First, I need coffee. Everything went haywire this morning with Kaley running around packing for her trip. She leaves for Poland tomorrow."

"Oh yeah. She and Bo's daughter Glenna are going with their class. My senior year wasn't so exciting."

"Mine either," Eva replied, searching for a server.

One finally arrived to take Eva's coffee order. Griff pointed to his cup for a refill. The young woman went to make a fresh pot. Eva used the interlude to share how Kaley would be staying with a family in Gdansk on the Baltic Sea.

"I've met the Sikorskis twice via Skype." She adjusted her purse strap so it would stay across the back of her chair. "I like that they're active in a vibrant church, yet I don't think my seventeen-year-old should be going so far without her parents."

Griff lifted his hands, palms up. "It's a balance, isn't it, living each day by faith? My pastor said on Sunday, 'Worry is really thinking God won't get it right.'"

"I know God's plan for her is great. Still, she's young and I don't want anything happening to her."

"Yeah, I can relate," Griff replied. "My adopted son Wally and his wife are set to begin his medical residency in South Sudan with a Christian non-profit group."

"And you're trying not to agonize over escalating violence among the tribes."

"You've nailed it as usual."

Coffee arrived, black and quite hot. Eva sipped it, turning her eyes to the detective's Florida gold badge blazoned on his belt. She disapproved of his back facing the entrance, something she avoided at all costs. He'd also thrown a suit jacket over an empty chair. And the prominent way his semiautomatic pistol shone against his white dress shirt troubled her.

"He shouldn't display his weapon so openly," she told Griff.

His eyes roved toward the detective. "Those ladies lost their savings to lying financial investors. Worse yet, the women convinced family members to invest before they ever knew it was a rip-off."

"Floridians might be used to plain-clothed officers exposing their guns. It's not seen that much here in Virginia," she intoned decidedly.

"Eva, you aren't the world's traffic cop."

"As I tell my kids, I don't apologize for wanting to right wrong behavior."

"Get the server's attention," Griff commanded suddenly. "I was up all night picking through garbage. I need more caffeine."

Eva lifted her arm when a man dressed in khakis and an open-collared shirt strolled by carrying a jacket over his arm. His unruly hair and unshaven face caught her attention. That's when she spotted Agent Brett Calloway walking by the front window approaching the entrance.

The unshaven man suddenly pulled a revolver from beneath his jacket.

"Gun! Gun!" Eva shrieked.

She jumped to her feet, grabbing her purse. The armed Miami detective stood. He turned the same instant the man pointed and fired at him.

Panicky people screamed. Diners hit the floor. Dishes and silverware crashed. The detective collapsed on the table in front of his two female witnesses. Both ladies screamed and dove under the table.

Eva seized her Glock from her purse, aiming at the shooter. So did Griff. The guy who shot his gun ran straight for Brett, who drew his weapon and fired. The would-be assassin toppled backward, sprawling onto a table.

Screeching diners raced in a jumble, piling up by the door desperate to escape. The detective looked dazed. Eva scurried to help him.

"Can you stand?" she asked, breathing hard.

"I dunno."

She jammed her gun in her pocket, and lifting him up beneath his arms, helped him to his feet. The trembling detective yanked at the front of his shirt. Buttons popped. Beneath his soiled shirt with a ragged bullet hole, he revealed his damaged protective vest. Eva saw Brett snatch the gun from the shooter's hand. Griff bent down and applied pressure to the man's neck. Brett gave Eva both guns.

The grill's manager stayed close to the agents, saying in a shaky voice, "I called 911. An ambulance is coming."

"He's lost plenty of blood," Brett said, panting as if he'd been running.

One of the weeping female Ponzi victims embraced Brett. The other woman's shoulders were heaving.

Brett pointed to the injured man crumpled in the aisle and asked the frightened lady, "Isn't that your brother-in-law?"

"Ye-es." Tears fell down her blotchy cheeks.

Brett wiped his hands on his shirt sleeves. His longish hair was streaked with sweat. He told Eva, "She's Lynette Jenkins, the one who convinced Arnold Ruckus to invest his million-dollar pension. He lost everything in the Ponzi scheme. I suspect Arnold was aiming for his sister-in-law."

Sharp sounds of sirens rent the air. Eva stared into Brett's light blue eyes, trying to imagine what he was thinking. One thought penetrated her mind. But for God's protection, she could be lying on the floor bleeding instead of Arnold Ruckus.

Chapter 3

Intense emotions gushed through Eva like water through a busted pipe. She stared at her blank office computer screen wanting to rid herself of the raw shock from the shooting. Where was her gratitude at being alive? Digging deep, desperate to find a thread of thankfulness, she came up empty. Instead, revulsion filled her spirit at the rude interrogation by the Office of Professional Responsibility, the arrogant OPR inspectors basically treating Eva and Griff like pond scum.

Sanity demanded that she get out of the office—and pronto. First, she canceled dinner out with Julia. The second call she placed to Scott. His gentle tone when he agreed to leave work early was a balm to her agitated spirit.

Eva walked over and clapped a hand on Griff's shoulder. "Go home to your wife. Celebrate Dawn. Being with family will push the OPR jerks out of our hearts and minds."

"Thanks, partner, I needed a pep talk." He shut off his computer. "I'm outta here."

On the drive home, Eva's mind didn't cooperate. She replayed the day's disastrous events, and scarcely aware of the stop-and-go traffic, she wandered into the HOV lane, which was a no-no. Without the required two people in her car, a state trooper could stop and write her a ticket. That would be all she needed.

The unnerving episode with the wounded Ruckus led her to a searing question. Brett had shot the "wannabe killer" mere inches from Eva. Did she still have what it took to be a federal agent?

She hoped for God to supply an immediate answer. More traffic, more blowing horns, yet no comforting voice soothed her angst. The exit two miles ahead, Eva longed for home, wanting nothing more than to be wrapped in Scott's solid arms.

Her foot hit the brakes a few more times before escaping the highway. Rounding the corner onto her empty street, adrenaline pounded against her veins. Wind gusts began buffeting the car. She eased off the gas.

"Yikes," she muttered, realizing Kaley's flight could be delayed.

The storm was blowing in faster than the meteorologist had forecast. Trees along the roadside swayed toward the G-car as Eva approached her home. By their rambling home she spotted Kaley dashing inside. The sight of her innocent daughter forced doubt further into Eva's overworked mind.

Even if the storm wasn't an issue, should she and Scott cancel the upcoming trip? No doubt he'd lobby for Kaley to spread her wings overseas, as did Julia Rider for her daughter Glenna. Eva knew Julia and Bo from church, and also because Eva had worked on thorny cases with Bo Rider, CIA agent extraordinaire.

His kids might not realize how courageously and secretly he served the country, whereas Kaley knew of Eva's career as an ICE agent. Recently she'd voiced a desire to follow in her mother's footsteps.

Eva turned into the driveway. Was it only this morning Fred warned her about the mysterious man asking questions about her?

She stopped her unmarked government car short of the open garage door. Strength of purpose to learn about that guy replaced her quandary. Eva bounded out of the car, fully intending to discourage her daughter from ever becoming a federal agent.

Things were too dangerous, much more than when Eva completed her basic training in Georgia years ago. Criminals and civilians were gunning for policemen these days. Eva would instead urge Kaley to become a doctor like her aunt, Scott's sister, Viola Montanna.

A turn of the key and Eva swung open the back door. How magnificent to be stepping into her kitchen. God saved her life today, for which she was truly thankful.

"Hello," she called out, trying to sound happy.

No response. Eva lingered by the fridge, breathing in cheering smells of home. Dutch's crayon drawing on the front swelled her heart with something fresh. Pure joy at being alive, to be here with her family, flooded her soul. But where were they?

She headed for the family room, stumbling on Kaley's suitcase. A pink string tied on the handle, the black case waited by the door. A deep breath steadied Eva. She decided not to tell her family about the shooting. Not yet.

Excited voices erupted from the family room, and Eva hurried to discover the reason. Her fifteen-year-old son Andy saw her first.

"Mom! You're on the news. They showed you close-up pushing away that gutsy reporter's camera."

"Did they identify me?" Eva asked, rushing into the room.

"Ah … not exactly," Andy sputtered.

Scott reached out to enfold her into his long arms. She inhaled his scent, and for a brief moment, she felt safe from the world. Tenderness seemed to flow through him as he kissed the top of her head.

He whispered in her ear, "We need to talk."

"About what?"

She pulled back. Scott glanced sideways at their youngest son Dutch, who sat cross-legged running a metal car on the carpet. Eva plunked her purse on a chair.

"Whew. I never expected you'd see me on the news. Did they say much about what happened?"

"You've had a chaotic time of it," was his reply.

Scott took her by the hand and sat beside her on the leather sofa. "The reporter claimed a Ponzi-scheme victim shot one of the defendants at the Topsy-Turvy. He ended up taking a bullet from one of several agents in the restaurant. They showed the agent's face. He looked like the new guy on your team. What's his name? Brent Caldway?"

"At least I wasn't videotaped," Eva said without correcting Brett's last name. "The news has it wrong. The guy fired at the woman who introduced him into the scheme, and hit a Florida detective instead. Good thing he wore a protective vest."

Kaley hurried into the room, her blond hair askew and arms flailing.

"My Bible's gone. I need it for Poland. Glenna and I wanna pray in our room each morning. Has anyone seen it?"

Andy pocketed his hands and meandered from the room whistling. Eva suspected Kaley's brother, a consummate trickster, was guilty of pulling another prank. How easily her eldest son had fooled Eva last year with something she'd thought was lost.

When her eyes shifted toward the doorway, Scott quickly caught on and went after Andy. Little Dutch raced after his dad. Meanwhile, Kaley perched next to Eva on the sofa, her eyebrows raised in a question mark.

"Mom, were you really in a shoot-out? I heard Andy squeal when you were on TV. I was in my room cramming stuff in my backpack."

"It's nothing to worry about." Eva brushed hair from Kaley's eyes. "You and Glenna will fly to Poland where you'll meet new people and immerse yourself in a different culture. That is, if you still want to go."

Kaley bolted upright. "Sure I do! Why wouldn't I?"

Because I don't want you facing danger like I did today, Eva thought. Rather than utter negative words, she swallowed misgivings. Faith meant trusting in God's goodness even when you couldn't see the future's twists and turns.

"Dad and I want you to have an amazing experience and not be homesick."

Kaley rolled her eyes. "Miss two brothers who pull tricks? It's getting old."

"Being away might shed new light on the family who loves you," Eva said without a trace of criticism. "I want to be sure you are sure."

"Definitely. Ms. Yost says this trip will prepare us for college. Her good friend is a teacher in Gdansk, and Austin loves traveling in Europe."

"Who is Austin?"

"A guy in my world government class who's going on the trip."

Eva searched Kaley's face for a hint of what the boy meant to her. Seeing nothing alarming, Eva asked evenly, "How come I haven't met him?"

"That's easy." Kaley wrinkled her nose, freckles dancing on the tip. "Glenna is more of his friend than I am."

"Does that bother you?"

"No way. I'm interested in what God has for me on this trip."

"I like the sound of that. You will be careful, right?"

"Ms. Yost covered all that. I won't lose my passport and will drink bottled water."

Eva stiffened her spine. "Be alert to something else. The host families may ask about us. Because you live near D.C., they may assume your dad and I work for the government. Because Poland is formerly part of the Soviet Union, some parents may have been or still are in their spy organizations."

"Do you hear yourself?" Kaley leaned away from Eva. "You sound paranoid."

"I know such things. You and Glenna must decide how to answer questions about your parents' jobs. You should both say we work for the Census Bureau or Smithsonian Museum, something innocuous."

"Oh sure! When Izabella comes here to visit us, you'll leave your gun in the office and bring home ancient oil paintings."

Eva couldn't help grinning. "Exactly."

"Ms. Yost said most parents of the Polish kids work at the port like Mr. Sikorski."

"I wonder ..."

"Okay, you win," Kaley said. "Though Glenna knows better, she'll say her dad is an international corporate recruiter who travels the world. I'll tell everyone you work at the Smithsonian. After all, you did spend lots of time in that museum."

Relief cascaded through Eva. She didn't want cross words with her daughter before she left home. They shared a hug. Kaley gripped her mom tightly, which Eva savored in the depths of her heart.

Kaley released her mother. "Promise me to stay safe. I couldn't bear something happening to you while I'm gone."

"That's how I feel toward you." Eva grabbed her daughter's hand. "I'm already praying for your safe return."

"Glenna called earlier. Winds tore huge limbs off trees in their yard. Is this storm gonna mess up our flight?"

"It should blow past, but I think I hear thunder. Want to pray about it together?"

"Good idea, Mom."

She and Kaley bowed their heads on the sofa, asking God to protect and guide her way to Poland and home again.

AFTER KALEY ROSE FROM THE SOFA, Eva hastened to wash her hands. She slid into the microwave a taco casserole she'd thrown together yesterday. Supper flew by with Andy entertaining them.

He beamed, telling his new joke, "What goes up and down, but doesn't move?"

"My eyes!" Dutch chirped.

"Wrong." Andy rolled his eyes. "See, they move."

Scott passed the salad, guessing, "Blood pressure."

"Nope."

Andy dumped two spoonfuls of lettuce and tomato on his plate before heaping taco stuff on top. The way he ate with great gusto lifted Eva's spirits. She even laughed out loud. Scott glanced curiously her way.

"These are the best of times, sitting around the table," she replied, taking a small helping of salad. Her appetite didn't match her enthusiasm over this family time.

"Okay, kids." Scott refilled Dutch's apple juice. "Which author said, 'It was the best of times'?"

"Dad, wait. No one answered my pun. Kaley didn't guess."

She looked over at Andy as if startled. "Guess what?"

Andy repeated his question. Kaley shrugged as if she had no clue.

"I know." Eva raised a finger. "Is it temperature?"

"Yeah, Mom. You rock."

Andy laughed, cleaning his plate. Scott used the interval to acquaint his children with Charles Dickens' novel *The Tale of Two Cities*.

"His opening sentence begins, 'It was the best of times, it was the worst of times.' Dickens then adds, 'It was the season of Light, it was the season of Darkness.' Kaley, what does he mean?"

"I'm too excited to eat." Kaley set down her fork. "This is my longest flight ever."

Eva scooped up bits of taco chips and ground beef from her plate before telling her daughter to save room for apple pie and ice cream.

"You're trying hard to send me off happy," Kaley said, her lips smiling. "Dad, in my paper on Dickens' novel for English Lit, I wrote how Jesus is the light Dickens refers to, and that true resurrection is possible only in Jesus. Mom read it."

"She did? Where was I?" Scott looked hurt.

Eva laid a reassuring hand on his forearm. "In the middle of a budget fight on Capitol Hill. That's what happens in government service. Who wants pie?"

They all did except Eva. She had no chance to talk with Scott until the dishes were washed and the kids asleep. In their bedroom, husband and wife sat on the puffy quilt, their legs dangling off the edge of the bed. Scott covered her hand with his.

"I'm so thankful you're all right. Want to tell me what the news didn't cover?"

She moistened her lips. "We briefed the local police who swarmed the Topsy-Turvy. We were forced to pass through a gauntlet of media. Griff and I were grilled by OPR Inspectors, though we didn't fire a shot. I'm still fuming."

"Are you in trouble?"

"Maybe. The inspector questions why I didn't fire at the assailant."

"Eva, I am sure you had a good reason. What did you tell them?"

"I asked if he would be happier if I'd shot the assailant in the back."

"Wow, you've been through the fire today."

She forced out a sigh. "Is our daughter ready for this trip?"

"I suppose not, yet it's a great opportunity before she heads to college. At her age, I flew a Cessna 172 by myself."

"When you put it like that ... I did an internship at the Richmond Police Department."

Scott's warm hand on hers encouraged Eva to tell him, "Something else happened with OPR."

"I'm listening."

Energy drained from her while explaining the inspector had shouted, "'Montanna, you saw Ruckus shoot a police officer. He turned, but was still armed. He posed a threat to everyone in the restaurant, including Agent Calloway. Your shooting him in the back might have saved lives. It's not like he was some innocent bystander.'"

Scott looped an arm around her. She leaned into his strength.

"Griff and I would have been justified in shooting the crazed guy in the back. Still, I didn't fire my weapon. Have I lost my touch?"

"No. You're my brave wife whom I love with all my heart."

"I needed to hear you say so."

She opened her lips to tell him what Fred divulged about the strange man roaming the neighborhood when Scott yawned widely.

"I'm beat," he said with a groan. "Time for shut-eye."

"Me too." She'd tell Scott in the morning, which would be here too soon.

Eva went to brush her teeth, one thing giving her solace—Brett had gotten off a clean shot. No one was killed in the process of taking down a maniac. Her newest task force member was hailed a hero instead of being investigated for a wrongful shooting.

A split-second decision made all the difference and Brett had decided correctly.

Had she?

Chapter 4

Lightning flashed outside Eva's bedroom window, startling her awake. Loud booms of thunder rattled the glass and jarred her nerves. The whole house shook, but Scott slept on through the worst of the storm. Edgy and unable to sleep, Eva rose at five a.m. to catch the weather on the family-room TV. The meteorologist predicted the storm would rumble through with no major damage. *What a relief,* Eva thought.

A flurry of activity surrounded the Montanna household for the next hour. Eva brewed coffee, fried bacon, and whipped up pancake batter. She wanted her sweet girl to enjoy a solid breakfast before boarding the plane.

Pancakes simmered on the griddle. The wafting aroma brought her clan trooping into the kitchen. Dutch rubbed his eyes as if half asleep. Andy's cowlick stood up in the back, giving him a comical air. Kaley hummed a praise tune while pouring orange juice for everyone.

"You look so grown-up in your blue slacks and pressed white shirt," Eva said.

Kaley treated her mother to a grand smile. "Thanks. Ms. Yost told us to dress alike so she can keep a close eye on us during our flight change in Amsterdam."

"Give hugs to your sister," Eva told her sons before they sat down at the table.

Andy traded high-fives with Kaley, and Dutch handed her something.

"Don't forget me," he said shyly.

Kaley's open palm revealed a glittering silver coin. "Cool! It's the Polish coin Mr. Rider gave you last year."

"How sweet." Eva put a tender hand on Kaley's forearm. "Tuck it away in your suitcase."

Dutch's gift touched Eva's heart. When Bo presented him with several foreign coins for his last birthday, his young face had glowed with youthful exuberance. Giving his Polish coin to Kaley for her Polish trip showed greatness of mind for so young a boy.

Eva served breakfast while Scott remained standing and downed his juice. He walked over and kissed Kaley on the top of her head.

"I put your suitcase in the van. You make me proud, kiddo. Remember to do what Mom always says. Watch your six."

Kaley wiped her eyes. "I love you, Dad."

"I've an early meeting with PSI," Scott told Eva as he headed for the back door.

"What's PSI?" Kaley asked in between bites of pancake. "Senate something?"

Scott called from the garage, "Good guess. Have a safe trip!"

Eva went on to explain PSI was the Senate Permanent Subcommittee on Investigations. "Your dad coordinates with them for the House of Representatives."

Dutch stuffed a pancake into his mouth, mumbling, "What's cordate?"

Eva simply laughed and drank her juice. While the bacon had smelled delicious, the grease hit her stomach with a thud. She rose to rinse off her plate. Scott peered in at her through the open back door. His eyes held a strange glint. Eva hurried over, and he gave her the *Washington Star* newspaper.

"Honey, read the front page of the metro section."

He kissed her before rushing into Eva's little Beetle. The VW was small but would suffice since she was taking Kaley and luggage in the new van. Eva checked the clock. Fifteen minutes until liftoff. She opened the damp paper, spotting the blaring headline:

Ponzi Trial Turns Bloody

The trial of a Florida couple turned violent yesterday. A victim of the alleged scheme lost his pension savings and tried assassinating the woman who persuaded him to invest. Florida resident Arnold Ruckus, age 60, entered the Topsy-Turvy restaurant near the federal courthouse in Alexandria, pulled a gun, and fired at his sister-in-law, Lynette Jenkins, also of Florida. Ruckus hit Dade County Detective Sergeant Mark Hendry's protective vest instead. As Ruckus turned to flee, he was shot and wounded by a DEA agent entering the restaurant.

Lynette Jenkins, a personal friend of Carlos and Holly Munoz, received immunity from prosecution for her upcoming testimony against the wealthy Miami land developer and his wife, alleged perpetrators of the Ponzi scheme.

Eva's fingers gripped the paper. Screams and the heart-pounding scene from yesterday careened through her mind. What a miracle no one had been killed. How many times had God intervened for her and her family when she wasn't aware of His doing so?

She yanked her mind to the present, shouting at the kids,

"Get a move on. Kaley, unplug your curling iron."

One detail caught Eva's eye. Ruckus was one of six witnesses who had already testified about losing millions. He and other victims discovered the lurid scheme too late. The couple converted money entrusted to their holding company to support a lavish lifestyle. Eva was aghast at the staggering sums. This was an important case for Brett Calloway, more extensive than she'd realized.

A Falls Church, Virginia, bank had loaned Munoz Costello Financial Holdings the whopping sum of $23 million to improve a resort in Palm Beach called The Knightbridge Sands. Rather than using the money for improvements, the couple spent the loan on costly props to entice other victims to invest. The government seized a mere $5 million in assets, including the Munoz home in Palm Beach, luxury vehicles, and yachts.

Eva snorted in disbelief at something more outrageous. Carlos and Holly whined they had zero money to pay their lawyers. Holly's attorney asserted in opening arguments that Holly deserved compassion; she was a woman who relied on her husband's business acumen and knew nothing of his finances.

Kaley sped into the kitchen with her backpack. "Ms. Yost warned us not to be late or we'd be left behind."

"Be happy it's a sunshiny morning, great for travel." Eva swiped her keys off the counter. "Find your Bible?"

"Yes, it mysteriously appeared on my bed when I was in the shower."

"Did you pack zinc lozenges? I found raspberry, your favorite. I don't want you getting a cold so far from home."

"I put some in my suitcase, and kept out a bunch." Kaley patted her jacket pocket.

The boys ran to the front door with Andy swinging around.

"Kaley, here's a joke for you to tell in Poland. Why couldn't the bike stand up?"

"You'd better tell me quick." Kaley sounded antsy about being late.

"Because it was two tired. Get it? Too tired!"

Kaley grimaced at her mom. "Brothers. I'll be glad to leave them for a week."

Eva realized Kaley was likely anxious over parting from her family, and didn't really mean it. Andy waved good-bye and caught up with Dutch. Eva watched out the window as they played tag on the way to the bus stop.

She and Kaley talked nonstop as they eased into the van.

20

They needed to be at Dulles airport by eight thirty a.m., so keeping one eye on the clock, Eva asked about Kaley's plans for her first day in Gdansk.

"You said you might tour the old cathedrals and attend an organ concert."

"Sounds fun, doesn't it?" Kaley angled her head. "Glenna is excited to ride the ferry to Sweden, and I want to dig into how World War II started. Germany first bombed Gdansk, you know."

"I'd like to know more," Eva said, flying along the highway.

Kaley fluttered her hands as she explained, "Gdansk juts out into the Baltic Sea. It housed a transit depot, and in the first battle of the war, Polish soldiers fought bravely. The town is a symbol of resistance."

"You've already learned more than I know. If only I had time to delve into history. Life has a way of demanding my attention."

"Ever since you and Dad brought us to the Netherlands to see where Grandpa Marty survived the German bombing, I've been intrigued by the Second World War."

Their talk about Polish history continued with Kaley mentioning a hero from Gdansk—Lech Walesa—who had stood up to the Soviets. With few minutes to spare, Eva pulled into the airport parking lot.

She turned off the van, tugging Kaley's hand into her own. "I'm proud of you as a person and my daughter. May your time in Poland be blessed. We'd better hurry."

They began a mad dash hauling Kaley's suitcases. Ten similarly-dressed students inside the terminal hovered around the teacher. A compact woman with reddish hair, Ms. Yost typed the names of arriving students into an electronic notepad. Eva walked over to remind her of potential dangers. Julia Rider, Glenna's mother, nodded at Eva's side.

"Not to worry, the students are under my supervision."

"Will our daughters be able to call us when you arrive?" Julia demanded.

The focused teacher consulted her device. "My notes reflect you have all communicated with the host families. You should have no concerns."

Eva spotted Kaley and Glenna giggling as they snapped pictures of a tall young man with combed hair. He slung a backpack over his shoulder and seemed polite to everyone. Glenna wore a mile-wide smile introducing him.

"Mom and Mrs. Montanna, this is Austin."

Austin's hazel eyes twinkled. "I'll take good care of Kaley and

Glenna, my two close friends."

Eva mentally filed away his neat appearance, curious if God had brought Austin into Kaley's life for a special reason down the road. She didn't want her daughter becoming embroiled with boyfriends before she graduated. A woman with a swirl of brown hair atop her head, and looking professional in a navy pantsuit, stepped toward Austin. She gave him a sideways hug.

"That's his mom," Kaley whispered.

She peeled a wrapping off a red lozenge and popped it in her mouth before handing one to Glenna. Eva snapped a picture of Kaley, Glenna, Austin, and his mom with her cell phone. The young man was taller than Eva's five-foot-seven-inch frame. His curly brown hair and serious eyes gave him a gentlemanly bearing.

Something about him reminded Eva of Scott when they'd first met, and her mind wandered, contradicting earlier thoughts. Wouldn't Austin and Kaley make a cute couple? Their children, her grandchildren, would have the same brown curly hair as Scott and Austin's.

Eva's face flushed. What in the world was she thinking? Kaley was still a teen. Here she was acting like other meddling moms. She nestled her phone into a pocket and drew Kaley into her arms for an all-too-brief moment.

"We love you." Tenderness overflowed in her heart, yet she felt obliged to add, "Do your leg exercises on the plane, and stay close to your Polish host family."

Kaley's eyes narrowed. "I wish you'd stop worrying."

Eva had no chance to utter another word. Kaley was whisked away by Ms. Yost to security. Austin's mom turned on her high heels and left. Eva wondered at her willingness to send her son off overseas without a backward glance.

"Have fun and be careful!" Eva called to her daughter.

Kaley spun around and waved. Eva treasured the joyful smile on her face.

Julia yanked a tissue from her pocket and blew her nose. "I wish I was going along. My son Gregg and the young twins need me at home."

"I'm counting the hours until Kaley calls," Eva said. "It's a long flight."

"And far away."

Julia sounded tense. Unexpected tears filled Eva's eyes. Why had she chosen to have her last words be ones of warning?

She dashed away the tears, telling her friend, "Let's arrange a family get-together after they return."

"What a lovely idea! My neighbor's watching Ricky and Annie, so I need to scoot. Those four-years-old twins are running my legs off."

Eva chuckled at the mental picture Julia painted. Seven-year-old Dutch kept Eva occupied too. She hugged Julia.

"I'll wait for their takeoff, and message you when they're in the air."

Julia began walking away, and then scurried back to Eva.

"I wish Bo wasn't in Germany. Still, he's closer to Glenna and Kaley over there."

"What is he—" Eva knew she shouldn't ask.

Julia's hand flew to her mouth. "Oops. I'm wrong to tell where he is."

"Your secret's safe with me," Eva was quick to say. "I already called a fellow ICE agent at the U.S. Embassy in Warsaw. Though they're nearly 200 miles from Gdansk, I feel better knowing someone in authority knows they are in-country."

"The more I think of it, maybe that's why Bo took this sudden assignment."

"Julia, it does my heart good to hear what you did not say."

Tissue in hand, Julia hustled away. Eva didn't leave the airport until the jumbo jet carrying Kaley and Glenna ascended into the clear blue sky. The girls were in God's hands. What better place to be?

BEFORE LEAVING THE TERMINAL, Eva typed messages on her phone to Julia and Scott. A quick jog to the van cleared her tangled thoughts over Kaley's departure. She decided to phone the office after buckling her seatbelt. Agent Calloway answered, and she asked how he was doing after yesterday.

"Griff and I were just talking," he replied. "Did you hear the latest?"

"No. Tell me."

His boisterous laugh rang in her ear. "Per standard operating procedure, DEA put me on leave after the shooting. I couldn't return to court after the noon recess."

"So?"

"So! Judge Harding went ballistic I wasn't there to testify. No bureaucrats were gonna interfere with his meting out justice. He adjourned until this afternoon. He ordered me to appear or he'll have the DEA Administrator arrested and brought before him."

"Wow, that's bold. Now you see why he's referred to as 'Heartless Harding.'"

"Eva, I've learned he tolerates no shenanigans and gives defense attorneys a run for their money. You caught me on my way out. What can I do for you?"

"You said you were talking to Griff. Is he around the office?"

"He's at ATF, tracking down the illegal gun Arnold Ruckus bought. The serial number was filed off. They're trying to figure out if he got it in Miami."

Brett went on to explain that the DEA was allowing him back in the courtroom if he didn't work on the Ponzi case until he was cleared, so Griff was helping him.

Brett added in a crisp tone, "Oh, he asked if I got a warning letter from OPM. I haven't."

"What are you talking about?"

"Didn't you hear federal employees' records were hacked at OPM? You know, the agency with all the records of our personal data."

Eva gulped. "I received nothing. What does Griff know that we don't?"

"Ask him when you see him."

After they hung up, Eva made her own call to Griff. His voicemail clicked on, and in frustration she left a message that she could help in an hour with what he was working on. She ended with, "What's up with OPM?"

Eva shoved the van in reverse, speeding home where she switched to her G-car. The Fusion was beautifully equipped for surveillance work with its two-way police radios. She pulled out of the driveway, her brain in overdrive.

Had her personnel file been one of those hacked into? Had the strange man asking questions in the neighborhood stolen her personal identity?

She made one quick decision, roaring into the JTTF office. No matter what happened to her file at OPM, this was the right time to check their credit history. And she'd ask Scott to change their passwords ASAP. They couldn't be too careful.

Chapter 5

Sunday morning dawned bright with promise. The sun sent golden beams into Eva's room, waking her. She instantly wondered if she had a message from Kaley. Not wanting to wake Scott yet, she snatched her phone and trotted into the kitchen. Her fingers typed in her passcode. Yes, Kaley had sent one overnight.

Mom … Dad … just out of sikorskis church … yesterday met ms yosts polish friend … shes different … Austin and I argued politics at lunch … izzy and family nice … LUV U all."

Every word was food for Eva's hungry soul. Picturing her daughter being cared for by the Sikorskis brought enormous relief. After speaking with Eva and Scott twice, they had sent a detailed e-mail containing their full itinerary. Delight pumping through Eva's veins, she was ready to face the day running. As she returned to the bedroom, Scott stirred.

"Are you awake?" she asked softly.

"Barely."

His reply, more like a noisy grunt, brought a smile to her heart. Though Kaley was away from home, the rest of the family needed Eva to smooth the way.

She whispered, "I'm fixing blueberry pancakes before church."

"Great." He flipped onto his side.

Eva shoved her feet into fluffy slippers. This was the day the Lord had made and she rejoiced in it. She threaded her arms into a freshly-laundered robe and ambled past Dutch's room.

Thwack! Thwack!

Eva poked her head into his open doorway. Her youngest son was yanking down his tower of plastic logs.

"You need to get dressed, buddy. Mom's making your favorite breakfast."

"Bacon?"

"With pancakes. Come get 'em while they're hot."

The way he swiped at his wavy hair made her heart lurch. He looked so like Scott, yet was decades younger. Andy also favored Scott in his looks, while Kaley's features were more like Eva's every day. She stepped down the hall.

"Cook lots of bacon, Mom!" Andy called from his room.

Eva peered into Kaley's dark and empty bedroom, her absence reminding Eva of a gloomy day with no sunshine. She sped to the kitchen. There, she slid a praise music CD in the player and beat pancake mix to its lively rhythm, dropping in fresh blueberries.

Breakfast came and went in a speedy fashion. Before long she and her family minus one arrived inside the Gatheria of their mega-church. Eva checked her watch.

"We still have time for coffee," she said, desperate for a second cup.

Scott shook his head. "You go. We'll save you a seat."

Eva strode to the café where, for a change, no one waited in line. After paying for a grande, she enjoyed the taste of hazelnut, this Sunday's featured choice. A woman with tightly-curled black hair appeared to be hunched over. Was she crying?

Eva dashed to her side, immediately recognizing her friend Thelma King. The sad woman's ebony face was streaked with tears.

"Can I help?" Eva asked, leaning over.

Thelma dashed the tears from her coal-black eyes. "It's too late for me."

"Are you ill?"

"Not in that way. They took me for every penny."

"Who did? What happened?"

"Them Munoz people stole all my money."

Eva's blood pressure skyrocketed. Another victim of Carlos and Holly Munoz right here in her church! She scooped Thelma's hand into her own.

"The agent working the case is on my team," Eva told her warmly. "We all want to see justice done."

Thelma clung to her hand. "Thank you, sweetie. How's your family?"

"We're all fine. Kaley is in Poland on her school trip."

"Ooh, that's far away. She's gutsy like her mama." Thelma seemed to rally. She wiped her nose with a tissue. "I'm sure gonna keep her in my prayers."

Eva promised to stay in touch before joining Scott in the large sanctuary. She and Thelma had worshiped together here for many years. The notion of her friend sinking into trouble made it hard to concentrate on the service.

Poor Thelma!

This theme revolved around in Eva's mind while the choir led the congregation in singing. She didn't sing a single song. An evil trickster named Carlos Munoz had wedged his way in between Eva and her worship of God.

Though the Ponzi scheme wasn't even her case, she found

herself eager to call Brett the moment she left the sanctuary. But wait. DEA had temporarily suspended his role. Eva folded her hands and tried to listen to Pastor Feldman's sermon. She rounded up her family right after the closing hymn.

While Scott drove home, Eva quietly fumed over Thelma's mistreatment. She set a pot of spaghetti sauce to bubble on the stove before phoning Griff. When he answered, she zoomed right to the point.

"Griff, do you remember Thelma, the African-American friend of Sari Jubayl?"

"Wow, Eva. We investigated Sari's husband Emile quite a few years ago."

"It's been a while. Thelma and I attend church together. She used to be Kaley's Sunday school teacher. I feel terrible. She lost all her money to the Ponzi scheme."

"Hmmph." Griff fell silent. "Why do I suspect you have a plan to right that wrong?"

Eva strode to the kitchen where she lowered the heat on her sauce. "Will you support me when I ask Brett to help Thelma receive money from recovered assets?"

"No problem. Dawn's calling me to dinner. We can talk tomorrow."

Griff clicked off the call before Eva could learn anything about the hacking at OPM. At least he sounded in favor of helping Thelma. Hopefully, Brett would also agree. Next she wanted to track down the guy who combed the neighborhood asking personal questions about Eva. With such few fragments to go on, was that even possible?

ONE MORE SURPRISE came to Eva on Monday morning. Cheri Dugan, a deputy U.S. Marshal whom Eva had never met, called her at the office first thing, asking for an urgent meeting. When Eva demanded to know particulars, "It will be worth your while," was all Cheri would divulge. Having seen the deputy around the courthouse, Eva reluctantly agreed.

Griff wasn't in yet, so she penned him a hasty note about her upcoming meeting at court, leaving out the particulars. Last week's shooting frayed the edges of her mind all the way to Alexandria. As she hustled along from the parking garage to the courthouse, her hand crept to her purse. Eva knew the Glock was at the ready if she needed to defend herself.

A uniformed security guard waved her around the scanning devices. Eva reached for her official credentials anyway. The guard shook her head.

"No need. I know who you are."

"I have testified here a bunch," Eva admitted with a smile.

She thanked the guard and made for the double glass doors leading to the U.S. Marshal's office. A small intercom button instructed visitors to 'Announce your purpose.' Eva pushed the button, gazing up at the surveillance camera, unsure if she'd made the right decision.

"Can I help you?" a voice asked brusquely.

Eva held her credentials toward the camera. "I'm with the Joint Terrorism Task Force and have an appointment with Deputy Cheri Duggan."

The door latch buzzed open. Eva entered a brightly-lit corridor, quickly making her way to the administrative area. If anything came of this conference she'd be shocked. No doubt the deputy's friend had a suspicious neighbor like Eva's Mr. Fred. Often she'd be pulled aside by other agents and friends professing to have critical information. Most times Eva could do nothing with it.

She walked with purpose into the chief deputy's office. A perky brunette, whose long hair was pulled into a braid, greeted her. Cheri Duggan appeared professional in her gray business suit. Eva also wore a pantsuit, only hers was black.

Cheri shut the door, adding to the sense of secrecy. "Agent Montanna, the chief's out today. We can talk here in his office. I hope it's not a wild-goose chase for you."

"Why did you call me here?" Eva asked, perching on a wooden chair.

Cheri sat across from Eva. "It took sleuthing on my part to find you. You were in the Topsy-Turvy during the shooting last week, right?"

"I'm curious why you should care," Eva said, prodding Cheri along.

"Someone heard a female agent had been present and asked me to find out who she was. That you're an ICE agent may be fortuitous."

On the alert, Eva folded her arms, demanding to know, "Who is this person and why is it a good thing I'm working for Immigration Customs Enforcement?"

"It's Holly Munoz, the defendant in the Ponzi trial."

"Oh no, and so no." Eva's hands flew up in protest. "Once they hear the evidence against them during a trial, these con artists will say and do anything to avoid prison. I can't help and have no interest in assisting such a thief."

"I figured you'd say so, and I told Holly no one can help her now. Last Friday, she was in the ladies' lockup and called me over. She asked to speak to the female agent present during the restaurant shooting."

"That's bizarre."

"I told her the train had already left the station and she should prepare herself for a long incarceration."

"Exactly," Eva exclaimed.

Cheri held up both hands, as if taking Eva into her confidence. "Holly piqued my interest when she whispered, 'No one can know what I'm about to say.'"

Eva was still skeptical. She decided to wait a minute to see what Cheri found so compelling.

"Listen, Eva." The deputy tugged the end of her long braid. "Holly insists neither her attorney nor her husband can know that she has information to give you about Cuba. Isn't that of vital national importance?"

"I doubt it." Eva had heard enough. She jumped to her feet.

The deputy stood slowly as if wanting to do more convincing. "I think Holly and her husband have Cuban connections. That's why I stopped Brett Calloway and asked him about the female agent in the restaurant. He said it was you."

"Did you tell Brett what Holly told you? He is the case agent, after all."

Cheri had not. "But when I told Holly who you were, she said, 'Good, this involves smuggling.' She made me promise to tell no one except you."

Eva debated. This seemed odd, yet she had few cases holding her interest. And if she ended up helping Thelma in the bargain, Eva couldn't walk away.

"I guess it won't hurt to talk to Holly once."

"Great." Cheri smiled a toothy smile. "Harding adjourns the trial at four thirty. When the marshals transport Carlos with other male prisoners, you'll have a chance to speak to Holly briefly before she's taken back to jail."

Eva raised a finger in the air. "Remember, no word to anyone."

"Agreed."

Eva left the marshal's office with a brand new idea. She'd sit in Holly's trial to glean what she could before their interview. Eva detested liars, and this woman's scheme involved dishonesty of the highest kind. Besides, Brett, Thelma, and the other victims would certainly object to Holly Munoz receiving any breaks.

Chapter 6

Eva slipped into the one empty space on a wooden pew in Judge Harding's second-floor courtroom. That it was packed with people was an understatement. She hoped Brett didn't see her way in the back. As case agent, he huddled next to the federal prosecutor who presented the case for the government. Assistant U.S. Attorney (AUSA) Patrick O'Rourke sat erect in his wheelchair behind a mahogany table, looking at a legal pad.

Federal District Court Judge Reginald Harding presided over his fiefdom from an elevated perch of shiny, walnut veneer. His jovial expression belied his reputation for being tough on defendants and their attorneys, as well as prosecutors. An ornate bronze seal with scales of justice adorned the walnut beneath him.

Slightly below and to his left a lady sat wearing an aqua sweater. Her hair was white as snow. Eva assumed the frail-looking woman twisting a tissue was the prosecution's witness.

AUSA O'Rourke addressed the judge in a rich tenor voice. "Your Honor, may I approach the witness to show her an exhibit?"

The judge peered questioningly over the top of his glasses. Eva recognized this as a standard question. Harding gave his permission, so O'Rourke rolled his wheelchair forward, handed the witness a sheet of paper, and wheeled back to his table. He never glanced Eva's way, which was a good thing.

"Mrs. Graham, do you recognize government's exhibit 102?" he asked.

"Yes, sir," she sniffed. "I wrote the check from my husband's and my joint checking account to invest in real estate."

"Did you sign it?"

She gazed at the front and back of the plastic envelope. Her hand seemed to tremble. "No. My husband did."

"Who is the check written to?"

"Munoz Castillo Financial Holdings."

"And the amount?"

"Five hundred and twenty thousand dollars." Mrs. Graham choked back a sob.

A noisy gasp rose from the audience. Eva sat back stunned. What a huge amount for this lady to invest at her age!

Eva sat straighter, listening intently. O'Rourke asked if Mrs. Graham had seen her husband sign the check. She had.

The AUSA gazed at the judge, "Your Honor, we ask exhibit 102 be put in evidence."

"Let me see the exhibit," Judge Harding said with sharpness.

He reached down to take from Mrs. Graham the exhibit. Then he examined it before handing it down to his clerk on his opposite side. The clerk made notations before returning the envelope to the judge. Harding asked the two defense lawyers if they objected. Neither did. He gave the check back to the witness.

"Mr. O'Rourke, your exhibit is admitted. You may continue."

Eva watched the entire painstaking process. Doubt washed over her about ever meeting Holly later. Wheels of justice did grind slowly. Here was living proof.

Thelma's tears blazed through Eva's memory. Her friend could be here testifying instead of Mrs. Graham. Eva needed to stick to her promise and talk with Ms. Munoz, whenever the judge ordered a recess.

O'Rourke leaned over and spoke with Brett before saying, "Mrs. Graham, you testified you wrote the check to invest in real estate. Where did you get the funds?"

"We had twenty thousand dollars in our savings account." She shoved her glasses up on her nose. "Plus we took out a five-hundred-thousand-dollar loan on our house."

More gasps and moans from the audience.

"To whom did you give the check?"

"Carlos Munoz stopped at our home."

"Did you know Mr. Munoz?"

"Yes. We were friends with him and his wife Holly for years. The four of us golfed in the same league, and once lived in the same golf community."

The AUSA straightened a stack of papers. "Mrs. Graham, is Carlos Munoz in the courtroom?"

She merely nodded, so O'Rourke instructed her to answer audibly for the court reporter.

"Yes." She fidgeted nervously. "He's in the courtroom."

"Point him out for the jury, please."

The elderly woman leaned toward the microphone. Sniffling, she aimed a long finger and bellowed, "He's the man sitting in a tan suit at that table. He's the man who swindled us out of all our money. My life is torn to shreds. My husband's still in the hospital after his heart attack. He can't accept we're dead broke."

She burst into sobs.

"Objection!" A defense attorney lurched to his feet. "The witness is testifying to things not in evidence. Admonish her to answer the question, and instruct the jury her emotions are not evidence."

"Your objection is denied," Judge Harding snapped. "Does the prosecution have more questions for this witness?"

"Yes, Your Honor. Let the record reflect Mrs. Graham has identified Mr. Munoz, the defendant."

"The record is so noted."

"Mrs. Graham," O'Rourke said from behind the table, "did Mr. Munoz ask you to invest in the real-estate account you mentioned?"

The prosecutor wrote on his legal pad while waiting for her to wipe her eyes. Eva wondered how many more victims had sunk money in the invidious scheme. Would Thelma have to testify? If so, Eva should come and sit with her. It was all such a mess.

Mrs. Graham dabbed her eyes with a tissue. "Yes, he urged us to invest."

"Tell the jury when the talk occurred, where you were, and what he said."

In beleaguered tones, she explained three years ago Holly and Carlos invited them and two other couples to their home. "During the catered dinner, Carlos told us he'd invested his and his kid's money in a low-risk real-estate investment fund."

"How did he describe the fund?"

"As giving a twelve percent return. It invested in rental complexes built in towns where new hospitals were going up. He claimed the fund was secure."

"Did Mr. Munoz give you a brochure advertising his financial company?"

"No, but he showed us a spreadsheet of expected payments."

O'Rourke examined his copy of the check. "After investing your five hundred and twenty thousand dollars, did you earn any profit?"

"Not in the end." The witness shook her head vehemently. "For a time, we got some of the promised interest payments."

"Did the interest payments stop coming?"

"Yes."

"When did you realize they had stopped?"

She blew her nose into the crumpled tissue. The judge leaned over to hand her a tissue box. After smiling at him, she took one and patted her nose.

"My husband's clever," she said, her hands gesturing wildly. "He arranged our bank account so the Munoz income checks went right into our account. Then, each month the bank paid our home equity loan."

The other defense attorney jumped to her feet, objecting,

"Your Honor, the witness is rambling. Her story is false. I want her entire testimony stricken."

"Mr. O'Rourke, your witness should be more responsive." The somber-faced judge shook his finger at the prosecutor. "The jury will not consider her last answer."

Eva sensed Harding wanted O'Rourke to limit his questioning. She leaned forward, eager to see what happened next. The AUSA consulted his pad before asking Mrs. Graham again about her loan. It turned out seven months after their investment, the bank sent the Grahams a letter advising they missed two loan payments.

"That's when I knew the Munoz checks weren't going into our account. Carlos blamed a computer snafu. He promised to correct it," she added, sniffling.

"Did the defendant ever send the missing payments?"

"Two more, then the local paper ran a story about this being a scam—"

"Your Honor!" The attorney for Holly Munoz was back on her feet. "How long must I endure aspersions cast on my client?"

Judge Harding lifted a hand, admonishing jurors to disregard Mrs. Graham's description of the business transaction. He leveled a stern glare at the witness, telling her, "You must refrain from using slang terms."

"Did your bank notify you about the home equity loan?" O'Rourke asked.

She breathed in loudly. "Right after the newspaper story, the bank foreclosed on us. We live with our son." She pulled a tissue from the box, her shoulders heaving.

"Your Honor, I have no more questions for Mrs. Graham," O'Rourke said. "I'd like her to remain subject to recall."

The judge asked Carlos Munoz's attorney if he wanted to question the witness. The slender attorney stood in his expensive-looking suit, not a single hair out of place. Eva failed to recognize him, so she thought he might be from Miami. Mrs. Graham was still trembling in tears.

"No, Your Honor," the lawyer replied. "I have no need to ask this lady a thing."

Judge Harding asked the attorney sitting beside Holly Munoz the same question. She was dressed identically to her client in a blue business suit and crisp white blouse. The lawyer bolted to her feet as if energized.

"Mrs. Graham, you testified you've known Holly for several years and that you are friends," she said in a pleasant tone. "Am I correct?"

A painful look crossed the witness' creased face. "I once thought so, but a friend wouldn't do what she's done."

"Did Holly ever tell you to invest in the real-estate fund?"

"No ... wait." Mrs. Graham narrowed her eyes behind her glasses as if searching for the truth. "I don't recall her exact words, but she did encourage us to invest."

"Come now." The attorney clamped a hand on her client's shoulder. "You said Holly never told you to invest. How can you claim she encouraged you to do so?"

"She invited us to her new million-dollar Florida home. She showed us pictures of their condo in Aruba, and their new fancy airplane."

The attorney dropped her hand. "Your Honor, will you instruct the witness to confine her testimony to my question?"

Eva caught Judge Harding's glittering eyes and slight smile.

"Ms. Ingles, the witness is being responsive. You asked how she could claim your client encouraged her to invest. She answered you."

He waved an impatient hand. "Proceed."

Oh, so Holly's attorney was Constance Ingles. From this far back in the courtroom, Eva had failed to recognize the feisty defense attorney with whom she'd had a few run-ins over the years. More importantly, Constance wouldn't like Eva meeting her client without her knowledge. She was known for making trouble.

Constance took a rapid step toward Mrs. Graham. "Did you invite Carlos and Holly to your home for dinner?"

"Yes."

"What were you hoping to get from them?"

"Excuse me." The witness squared her shoulders. "I wanted only friendship."

"Ah, now we get to the truth. So can we assume when Holly invited you to dinner in her home she was being friendly too, and not trying to influence you?"

The witness shrugged as if defeated. "I suppose."

"No further questions."

The attorney walked to her seat glowing like she'd scored big points for Holly. Eva wondered if she had, and tried sorting out what she'd heard. Mrs. Graham rose from the witness chair when she thumped back down. "I just remembered what Holly told me."

"Your Honor." Constance whirled around. "I've finished with the witness."

The judge banged his gavel. "Mrs. Graham, you may step

down."

"Your Honor, I have a question on re-direct for this witness," the prosecutor said.

Harding set down his gavel. Sounding irritated by the unruly witness, he said, "Very well. Make it brief. I am about to dismiss the jury for their morning break."

O'Rourke asked his witness, "Did Holly tell you something else about the investment?"

"Yes, sir." Mrs. Graham nodded her head vigorously. "The first time I walked into her home, she said if I liked it, I could move into one just like it down the block if I invested with her husband."

Eva tightened the grip on her purse. What else did Patrick have in his prosecutor evidence bag? The judge pounded his gavel for a recess.

Eva sped from the courtroom, her mind buzzing from what she'd heard. Besides being married to a crook, Holly was at a minimum guilty of being overzealous. Eva realized something else. It could be Holly had been the bait to entice unsuspecting lady friends to convince their husbands to fork over their life savings. Carlos was most likely the mastermind.

However it went down, poor Thelma had been drawn into their scheme.

Eva phoned Cheri Duggan, saying, "It's okay to hold Holly back this afternoon. I'll speak with her, yet make no promises."

"I'll reinforce that," Cheri replied in haste. "Gotta head to Harding's court."

Eva ended the call calculating her next move. First she needed to create something of vital importance.

Chapter 7

On the way back to the JTTF office, Eva stopped at the hardware store where a new desk key was made from her two pieces. Griff was not around when she reached her desk, and she knew Brett was still deep into the Ponzi scheme case. Mrs. Graham's compelling testimony fresh in her mind, Eva tried the key. It worked, which pleased Eva immensely.

She hefted her purse in the drawer and found Thelma's number in her list of contacts. Her friend answered, sounding out of breath.

"It's Eva calling. Is this an okay time to talk?"

"I'm packing boxes," Thelma huffed. "I can use a break."

Eva told her gently that she'd attended the Ponzi scheme trial against Carlos and Holly Munoz. "Will it upset you to tell me how they got hold of your money?"

"I can't think of it without crying."

Sounds of Thelma blowing her nose trumpeted in Eva's ear. This wasn't a good idea. She offered to call another time.

"Lord have mercy, I've been praying all morning. You must be my answer."

From there, Thelma's story burst forth, how her friend Nadine from pottery class had earned high interest on an investment. She'd taken Thelma to lunch several times, even inviting her to her home.

"My daughter's husband lost his job in Atlanta," Thelma lamented. "He works odd jobs. She cleans churches to put food on the table. They're squished in a two-room apartment with three kids. I took my savings, hoping to earn enough to buy them a place."

"Did Holly Munoz entice you to invest in their holding company?"

Thelma sighed forcefully. "I never met her. Carlos was the one who convinced me. He banked here in Virginia, so Nadine arranged for us to meet at lunch."

"What did he say to convince you?" Eva asked.

"He showed me pictures of his home in Florida and bragged I could make more money if I took out a mortgage on my house and invested in his real-estate deals. Shame on me for believing his pack of lies."

"Thelma, I am sorry you're going through this trouble. Do you see God's hand of mercy helping you?"

"Some days yes, some no. Not when my granddaughter calls me crying."

Eva hurt for her friend. "Do you have enough money for food and living expenses? How are you getting by?"

"You are kind to ask. I'm making it okay 'cause I put up quarts of soup and casseroles in my freezer."

"Scott and I want to help. A late meeting will keep me busy this afternoon. What if I pick you up tomorrow at five thirty? You'll be our guest for dinner."

"Oh my, that sounds terrific."

Thelma started weeping into the phone. Eva longed to drive right over there. That wasn't possible. Instead, she encouraged her friend to gather her checkbook and papers.

"Together, we'll map out a future strategy," Eva added.

Thelma sounded more hopeful when they hung up. Eva turned her chair to log onto her computer when Griff sauntered to her cubicle, a coffee mug in his hands.

"What's up with you?" he asked casually.

"Not much. You?"

"I finished what I could for Brett. Guess he's back in trial."

Eva smiled, not willing to divulge her upcoming talk with Holly. It might all come to nothing.

Griff sipped his coffee before mentioning his case against the Chechens. "I'm going over the evidence to see if we have enough to obtain a wiretap."

When Eva simply nodded, he agreed to keep her posted and returned to his desk.

Eva used the interlude to prepare a statement for Holly before asking her any questions. Her fingers flew across the keyboard, and she slid the printed sheet into her shoulder bag. She went out for sandwiches, buying one for Griff. They ate Italian subs at their individual desks. Before long, he came over seeking her opinion.

"My informant isn't what I'd call reliable." Griff swiped his moustache with his palm. "He claims the two Chechen brothers are connected to the Russian mafia and helping Russia to buy weapons. I have no way to corroborate him. I'm skeptical."

"What has your surveillance revealed?" Eva rolled the sandwich wrapper into a tight ball and lobbed it into the waste can.

"Heavy purchases of booze at a liquor store. Partying at nightclubs. I see no proof they have legitimate jobs, but hey, that's no crime."

Eva offered another insight. "You've seen them using their cell phones, right?"

Griff nodded.

"And what do their subpoenaed phone records reflect?"

"Calls to Russia, Kazakhstan, and Syria."

"Are any of those calls to known terrorists?"

"Eva, you know we have no way to vet these people in foreign countries."

She considered suggesting they phone Bo Rider at the CIA, and then recalled he was out of the country.

"Conduct round-the-clock surveillance," she replied, figuring Griff would dread that idea. "You'll learn a lot more."

He folded his arms across his chest. "It's ugly, but I know you're right. When Brett comes off the Ponzi case, he can help me pull some all-nighters on these guys."

Eva returned to her computer, but spun around quickly. "Oh, another thing. You told Brett about federal employees' files being hacked at OPM. Did they notify you that your personal data was stolen?"

"I've not received official notice. Have you?"

"None." She puffed out a ragged breath. "Can you believe nearly four million current and former employees have been compromised? Hackers, like modern Mongol hordes, are rampaging through our home addresses, social security numbers, everything."

"Eva, it's maddening, though I don't know anyone yet who's been hurt." He turned toward his desk.

"Someone has my info," Eva said with a touch of gloom.

Griff returned to her side. "What makes you say that?"

"My neighbor saw someone peeking in my window recently. The guy had the nerve to ask what kind of car I drive."

Griff stepped back in astonishment. "Why didn't you mention this before?"

"I was going to yesterday, when you hung up on me."

"Some experts point fingers at the Chinese government," Griff said. "Why do they care what car you drive? They're exporting cars to the U.S. now. Hey, maybe they want you to test drive one."

"Don't be funny," Eva protested. "What if they're selling our private lives on the black market? Think of this—one or more of the criminals or terrorists we arrested is out of prison and wants retribution."

Griff furrowed his brow. "We need to be more alert for sure. We should contact OPM and see if our data has been stolen."

The rest of the afternoon Eva spent dialing and re-dialing OPM's 800 number. Once, she even got into a queue to speak to a representative, having the wonderful opportunity to hear music and a computer voice for an hour. She finally hung up in aggravation.

At four o'clock Deputy Marshal Duggan called. Judge Harding would be adjourning in thirty minutes. Eva grabbed her purse, locked her desk, and waved good-bye to Griff, who was on the phone. Maybe he was having better luck reaching OPM.

Eva roared off in her Fusion, arriving at the courthouse with five minutes to spare. Deputy Duggan offered her the use of a private office and left to retrieve Holly. Eva set the typed statement on the desk. A rap on the doorjamb, and the deputy led in Holly Munoz, her hands cuffed in front.

Black roots above the part in her reddish-colored hair spoke volumes about Holly's month in custody. Her blue skirt was badly wrinkled from sitting in court all day. The woman looked bedraggled and unlike a high-rolling scammer. After Cheri's introductions, Holly raised her cuffed hands in an awkward attempt to shake hands.

Eva rebuffed the offer. She pointed to an empty chair, and the disheveled woman leaned to one side as she perched along the chair's edge. Eva asked Cheri to stay and observe what she told Holly.

Before Eva could explain the purpose of their meeting, Holly started talking a mile a minute, "Eva, thank you for coming. I asked to speak with you because …"

"Say nothing more." Eva raised her palm. "You're in custody and represented by an attorney who isn't here. This is highly unusual."

"Cheri knows I need to speak with you!" Holly insisted, tears pooling in her large eyes. "I don't want my lawyer or husband, or anyone else, knowing anything about it."

"That's true," Cheri agreed. "Just like I told you."

"Read the first sentence aloud," Eva said, pushing the statement closer. "Then go through the rest yourself and sign. Deputy Duggan will be a witness. Do you understand?"

Something akin to optimism sprung into Holly's brown eyes.

"Yes," she croaked.

Eva summarized the statement she would sign: It was Holly who asked to meet Eva. They had never met before. Holly didn't want her husband, lawyer, prosecutor, or the judge to be apprised of their meeting. Eva was making no promises to her.

Holly began to read, her voice shaking, "I, Holly Munoz, am in custody and in trial. I asked for a private conversation with Special Agent Eva Montanna from Immigration, Customs, Enforcement."

"Okay, you've proven you can read," Eva said. "Before you read the rest, be aware I may act on your information or refer it to the proper authorities. I may inform Judge Harding and AUSA O'Rourke of your cooperation; however, I make no promises about your future. There may be no benefit at all to you. Understand?"

"Yes." Holly pressed her lips into a thin line.

"Continue silently to the end, and then you can sign it," Eva told her curtly.

A blob of mascara smudged beneath Holly's left eye was a clue she'd been crying. Eva resisted feeling pity. Thelma's teary voice from her earlier call stayed close to Eva while Holly read the document.

After a long quiet minute, Holly gazed up at Eva, her lips quivering. She whispered, "Okay, I want to tell you everything."

"Sign here," Eva instructed, handing her a pen. "Remember, I promise no help."

ALSO AS EVA REQUESTED, CHERI DUGGAN witnessed Holly's signature before slipping out to let them talk. Eva snuggled a chair in front of Holly, a thought flitting through her mind. Perhaps Holly wanted to complain about how the marshals treated their prisoners.

"Why am I here?" Eva probed. "You have ten minutes. Make your time count."

Holly's shoulders drooped. "My future looks bleak. Though I tricked no one, I might be convicted anyway. Where will I go if I'm acquitted, or released before Carlos? The government seized our house in Palm Springs."

"Holly, I can only influence your future if you provide new information about an unrelated crime."

Holly's eyes bored into Eva's as if desperate to see into Eva's soul. She flicked her tongue across her lips.

"What if we owned a home before my husband started his real-estate firm? What if it wasn't bought with profits and hasn't been seized?"

Her brown eyes never wavered. At once, Eva sensed there was truth to her claim.

"I'm not here to answer questions," was Eva's only reply.

"We do have another home," Holly confessed. "Someone else could be using it to commit another crime."

"Could be or is?" Eva asked, looking at her watch.

"Ah ..."

As Holly fumbled for an answer, Eva opened her leather

folder. She wrote Holly's name and the date on the legal pad, and watched the defendant closely.

"Years ago we bought a house in Florida on Lime Key." Holly seemed to wilt making the admission. "We keep an airplane there. Do you know Lime Key?"

She stared at Eva, who stared right back.

"It's near Big Pine Key in the Florida Keys," Eva replied after making a note on her pad. "Continue on. Your time is flying by."

"Our caretaker lives in the home. He's a pilot too."

"His name?"

"Louis Clark."

"His age? Marital status?"

"Oh … ah," Holly stammered. "He goes by Louie. I think he served in the Gulf War, and is in his late fifties. He has various girlfriends. Some lived in his apartment at our home."

Eva looked up from her notes. "Why do I care?"

"For one simple reason. He flies to Cuba and smuggles back Cuban cigars, which he sells for big bucks here."

"Lots of people sneak back with Cuban cigars."

"Not airplanes full, twice a month," Holly countered.

"I see."

Eva's mind whirled fast. It sounded like a major smuggling operation, which was in her purview as an ICE agent. She didn't want Holly to realize her interest because she might reach the wrong conclusion and believe Eva would agree to help her on the spot.

"Well?" Holly said. "Are you interested?"

"I need to know a lot more."

Holly blinked rapidly, and Eva pressed on with more questions. Their discussion lasted until Eva elicited details of the house, when it was bought, and the Gulf War-vet caretaker. Holly shared how Louie and his girlfriends helped entertain Carlos' friends who vacationed at the Lime Key home.

Eva flexed her fingers and put down the pen. She'd heard enough.

"You hope by getting Louie arrested for supplying cigar aficionados, you'll stop the government seizure of your home and give you something to start over with."

"Can't blame a girl for trying, can you?"

"I doubt you've given me anything to help you."

Holly's eyes clouded in disappointment. Eva rose to open the door. Holly started walking out, then stopped. "There's something else."

Eva spotted Cheri standing in the reception area waiting to take her charge to the correction center. She quickly shut the door.

"What is it?" Eva pressed.

Revitalized, Holly spoke quickly. "One time Louie flew in from Cuba with another man. And Louie let me fly with them to Memphis to visit a college friend."

"So?"

Eva reached for the door handle, prompting Holly to talk in a mad rush.

"We stopped to refuel. They climbed out of the plane, and this man left a valise on the seat. I looked inside. It was crammed with stacks of hundred-dollar bills, maybe seven or eight cell phones, and passports. Some were Russian."

Eva hoped her eyes didn't reveal the excitement building within her. Would it be too weird if Holly's case was related to Griff's terrorism case against the Chechen brothers? Anyway, Holly was onto something. Eva just didn't know what.

She replied evenly, "Your ride is waiting. Don't tell anyone of our conversation. I'll do the research and get back to you."

"Will it be this week?" Holly's voice rose to a squeak.

"Probably not. This will take time. I will advise you one way or the other."

To Holly's groaning, Eva brought her to the deputy marshal who took Holly by the elbow without a word. Holly trudged away in her wrinkled outfit. Eva felt sorrow for Thelma, but none for Holly. Still, her tips could help prevent other crimes.

While Eva intended to follow every lead, she had an inkling Holly Munoz knew more than she was admitting.

Chapter 8

The moment Eva hopped into her car outside the courthouse, her cell phone buzzed against her waistband. She answered it promptly.

"Eva!" came Griff Topping's animated voice.

"I'm leaving the courthouse and will stop at the office," she said. "Did you reach OPM?"

"Forget that. When you get here, we need to talk."

"What about?" Eva readied her mind for the next shoe to drop.

Griff's voice softened. "Seeing how Kaley's in Poland and the Polish president just expelled the Russian ambassador, I thought you should know."

"What caused such a rash move?"

"Poland arrested Russian spies who were operating in their country for the past few years. So Russia's ambassador got the heave-ho to clean house."

"Is Kaley safe?" Eva blurted. "Will Russia retaliate?"

"The political back-and-forth shouldn't impact Kaley. You and I can do more checking."

Eva was in no mood to mess around. She swerved into a parking lane to search the web on her smartphone. Before she even came to a halt, it dawned on her. The phone would be much slower than the lightning-fast data speed at her office.

She hurried there, dodging two car wrecks along the way. In the office, Griff sat at his desk, his phone crammed against his ear. Eva dropped her purse on her desk, awakened her computer, and navigated to a news site. Her shoulders sagged. The article told little more than what Griff had already explained.

Polish citizens working in their country's industry and military were caught spying for Russia. Poland retaliated by sending Russia's ambassador packing, which Eva knew wouldn't be the final act by either side. Nations regularly spied on one another. Still, espionage being aired in public could exacerbate tensions.

She stared at disquieting images of Russian tanks tearing down a city street. Was war between Poland and Russian imminent? The hardnosed president of the largest country on earth never took humiliation in stride. Hadn't Russia recently invaded another country with little consequence?

Anxiety coursed through her. How could she protect Kaley from here in Virginia?

Then Eva's spirit stirred. She wasn't powerless.

There in front of her computer with colleagues wandering past, she bowed her head, praying silently to her Father in heaven for Kaley's safety and everyone on the trip. She and Glenna were in His mighty and omnipotent hands.

Sounds of someone walking up behind her made Eva look up at Griff.

"We'll be glad when she's safely home," he said earnestly.

"You were right to call me." She pressed her hands against her temples. "How do you think Russia will respond?"

He reached over and began hauling Brett's chair toward her cubicle.

"Wait." Eva raised her hand like a traffic cop. "Let's head to the conference room. I have other news."

Soon the duo was ensconced behind closed doors. Griff tented his hands, sitting across from her at the long conference table.

"Russia's president is pushing the old Soviet agenda inside of Poland," he said. "Because he wasn't challenged in Crimea, he realizes NATO is weak. He won't be content to simply seize the Ukraine."

Eva wiped her forehead. "That worries me. If this spy news had broken before Kaley's trip, she'd still be safely at home with her family, I can tell you."

Griff shrugged as if things would work out the way they were supposed to.

"Look at it this way, Eva. Your soon-to-be-an-adult Kaley is seeing a true glimpse of international relations." He added with a grin, "Maybe she'll join the CIA, like Bo."

"Don't even think such a thing. I'm keeping her as close to Virginia as I can."

"Eva, why are we in here? Kaley's situation doesn't warrant such secrecy."

She looked past him, mulling over Holly's admissions. "Griff, it's no coincidence we're talking in here. Do you think Russia would use Cuba as a corridor to smuggle terrorists like your Chechens into the U.S.?"

"Would they?" His eyebrows shot straight up. "There's no doubt in my mind. They've been using Cuba to service their operatives in Latin and South America. We can assume they're also sending terrorists out of Havana."

Before Eva could reply, Griff rapped the table with his knuckles. "All right, you got me. What are you keeping secret?"

Though the door was shut, Eva edged closer. This was the time to admit to Griff what she'd gone and done. It also felt right to drop her voice as she said, "I just spoke confidentially with Holly Munoz, a defendant in Brett's case."

Eyes wide, Griff jolted back from the table. "Does Brett know?"

"No," Eva hissed. "Holly told Deputy Marshal Duggan she would only talk with the female agent present when Arnold Ruckus shot the detective. Here's the request I made her sign."

Her task force partner's eyebrows quivered up and down as he quietly read the form. Then he gave her a dubious look.

"Eva, you are walking a pretty thin tightrope here."

"Not just me, Griff. I'm fixin' to pull you onto this tightrope with me."

Griff swept an open palm across his ample mustache. He began nodding. "Okay. She's willing to tell you something to help her, keeping it from her co-defendant husband. And by you not telling her attorney ..."

He whistled rather ominously.

"I hear you," Eva quipped, and finished what Griff didn't say. "Holly figures if she tells the case agent, he'll inform Patrick O'Rourke, the federal prosecutor."

"And once the AUSA knows, he's obliged to tell the judge."

Eva smiled. "What you and I know, we don't have to share with anyone."

"You gave her no promises?"

Eva tapped the signed agreement. "You just read it."

"How does this lead us to Cuba?"

"Good question."

Eva spent the next few minutes recapping Holly's claim about her house at Lime Key and how she was desperate to save that Florida home from court proceedings.

"Then there's the caretaker, Mr. big-time smuggler of Cuban cigars."

Griff grunted. "Hmm."

He leaned back in the chair, hands clasped behind his head. Silence filled the room until he dropped his chin.

"Eva, remember when I worked on a far-reaching drug case with the DEA in Miami?"

"The one when you brought cocaine in from the Bahamas?"

Griff's eyes flickered with intensity. "Yes. I flew the load from Cat Island and dropped it from the plane at night, real close to Big Munson Island. That's near Lime Key, which happens to be where

Holly's home is located."

"Did you spend much time there?"

"Enough. I made sure to land on the strip at Lime so locals would know me if I ever needed to land there."

"On the night of the airdrop?"

"No. With no landing lights, the Lime Key strip is mostly for the convenience of homeowners. Many fly down in their own planes."

"I wonder." Eva touched Holly's statement. "Do you suppose there's any fire behind her smoky claim?"

Griff chuckled in his hearty way. "Now who's being funny? Listen, Lime Key is a stone's throw from Cuba. With a huge market in the U.S. for Cuban cigars, if Russia could use such a gig as cover for their nefarious deeds, I'm sure Cuba is happy to help."

Eva tensed at a sudden rapping on the door. It opened with a rush of air. Brett Calloway stuck in his head.

"Why are you cloistered in here?" he asked. "Got a new case in the works?"

"We're talking about Russia." Eva nonchalantly slid Holly's agreement into its folder.

Griff motioned Brett to sit, telling him, "Eva's daughter Kaley is in Poland, which just nabbed a few Poles spying for Russia. They ejected Russia's ambassador."

"I didn't know your daughter was over there," Brett replied. He made no move to join them.

"How's the trial going?" Griff asked. "Is the end in sight?"

"I'm going to brush up on tomorrow's testimony, but it's impossible to lose. All those weeping victims telling how they've lost everything. There sits a greedy couple hoping to convince the jury they wanted nothing more than to prosper these people."

Brett flashed a vivid smile and was gone, prompting Eva to again shut the door. She wanted to know if Griff was in favor of pursuing Holly's information. He didn't answer right away, and when he did, it was with a vague, "Let's decide in the morning after a good night's sleep."

Eva had to be okay with that, for now. She swung open the door and whispered, "For the record, I think Holly knows a lot more."

"You saw Brett's confidence," Griff replied, tugging on her sleeve. "We should include him at the right time, if we do this thing."

"I understand the line we'd be walking." Strain grabbed Eva between her shoulder blades. "We don't want to torpedo his case and advocate for Holly, not when he's trying so hard to get her the maximum sentence."

Eva returned to her desk finding one informative update that heralded how efforts were under way in Poland to bring officials together for talks. Okay, in this instance diplomacy sounded better than war talk. The main comfort was that Kaley would be home soon. Eva locked her desk knowing all was well.

THE NEXT DAY, EVA WAS BACK AT WORK with Holly's agreement spread before her. Cheri Duggan had called again to advise that Holly wanted to talk more with Eva. No doubt, the lady was restless at the prospect of being found guilty for committing fraud and a dozen other federal charges. The answer to a question revolving in Eva's mind would determine what she did next.

The crux of her problem was that even if she and Griff launched an undercover operation posing as new owners of Holly's home in Lime Key, did Eva have a way to convince the FBI their case involved terrorism? Or were they looking at espionage? Whereas smuggling was in her scope as an ICE agent, the primary focus of the JTTF was terrorism, not espionage.

It was a conundrum, all right. The truth was neither she nor Griff knew exactly what they had beyond illegal cigar smuggling by a Floridian named Louis Clark.

Eva tapped her nails on the computer keyboard, her mind whirling in tandem to the clicking sounds. Before she could tick off a dozen other questions, Griff cleared his throat.

"Sorry to interrupt." He held large aeronautical charts in his hands.

"Lime Key?" Eva pointed to the charts. "Fill me in."

"Not here. These are too big for your desk. Join me in our new joint office."

Eva first minimized her computer screen, and they headed for the conference room. None of the other agents seemed to notice. This time, Griff shut the door before opening one pastel-colored chart on the long table. Eva spotted the northern tip of Colombia and Venezuela, and then the Dutch Islands of Aruba, Bonaire, and Curacao.

Griff pressed a finger on Florida's southernmost tip. "Look how near Cuba is to the Keys. In the joint case with the DEA, I flew in the right seat as copilot. We brought cocaine for smugglers in a DEA plane. They wanted us to drop it from the air …"

He paused while unfolding a smaller chart, which he smoothed on the table. At the bottom of this chart, his finger traced a tiny island southeast of Lime Key.

"We made our nighttime drop here at Big Munson Island."

"Yikes," Eva chimed. "That's extremely close to Holly's hideaway."

"I was a breath away from Lime, this island here. Houses are built along each side of the airstrip. Hers must be one of those."

"Carlos could be into drug running. Griff, did you land on that tiny strip?"

"No." He pointed to an airport north in the Keys. "We needed fuel, so we flew up to Marathon Key."

Eva laid her pen near Holly's Key, which was really an island connected by road. "Could you have landed at Lime Key in an emergency?"

"Not at night. That's a part of Holly's story I don't understand. Lime Key has no FBO, no lights for night landings, and no aviation fuel."

"FBO?" Eva echoed.

"Aviation talk. A Fixed Base Operator is the entrepreneur who provides fuel, restrooms, and small aircraft repairs and storage. It's like a rest area on the interstate where small private aircraft land for relief."

"So there's a gaping hole in Holly's story."

Griff crossed his arms. "I'm trying to figure what Louie Clark, Holly's caretaker, is doing. He flies in with cigars and strangers, but can't land at night. During daylight, neighbors can see what he's doing."

"Maybe they're so used to neighbors landing in their airplanes no one pays attention. Do we pursue this case?"

Griff shrugged. "Here's what I do know."

He erupted with a mini-course on the ins and outs of flying from Cuba. The U.S. Customs laws required aircraft approaching from foreign countries to go directly to an airport with Immigration and Customs inspectors to clear customs.

"Say Clark flies from Cuba in daylight, he must stay just above the water to avoid our radar. I suspect he lands and unloads his illegal passenger and contraband. Maybe he never bothers clearing customs or simply heads out to sea, then turns toward Miami and clears customs there or in Ft. Lauderdale, just in case he's picked up on radar."

Eva stepped over and shut the door with a definite click. She followed his reasoning, and needed to understand something else.

"Griff, our government's been on friendlier terms with Cuba's regime, and both have reopened their embassies. What stops the

Russians from sending their spies and currency in a diplomatic pouch exempt from U.S. inspection?"

"Right." He took a seat. "But—"

"There's always a 'but.'"

"Eva, consider this. Cuba can't hide clandestine spies or terrorists in a pouch. Handlers who control deep-cover operators in the U.S. do not work out of the D.C. Embassy as diplomats. They sneak them into the country."

Eva pointed at Lime Key on Griff's map. "We can go undercover, meet the caretaker, and see if besides cigars, he's also smuggling terrorists. I'm not sure it's in our JTTF mandate."

"Au contraire." Griff smiled sheepishly. "You're an Immigration Customs Enforcement agent. Aren't you authorized to work smuggling cases?"

"If I try that, I'll be transferred back to ICE. That's the last thing I want."

Griff's sunny smile frustrated Eva to no end. What had he realized that she didn't?

"I thought you told me," his voice held a lilt, "that Holly told you the man flying in with Louie had money and cell phones for supplying terrorists."

Eva glared at her partner. "No, I never said that."

"I distinctly recall you did." Griff flashed an exaggerated wink. "Isn't that what Holly told you? It makes sense. Terrorists get operating funds from somewhere. They use specially-equipped cell phones to detonate bombs. Check again with Holly. You said the man had more cell phones than he could use."

It was Eva's turn to smile. "I believe he did. And as an ace pilot, you'll have a major role if we go forward. Meanwhile, we should devise a plan to become proxy owners of the Munoz home in Lime Key. I'd like to meet Mr. Louis Clark and discover what illegal scheme he's involved in."

Chapter 9

Gdansk, Poland

Kaley Montanna loved everything about Poland. Lush green forests reminded her of the Blue Ridge forests back home. She and Glenna enjoyed the rollicking adventure of touring the medieval city of Gdansk with Izzy and the other students. They hadn't spent much time along the beach, but "soon," Izzy's father promised this morning in his thick accent.

The Sikorskis were wonderful people, inviting all the students to their home to meet Izzy's school friends. This evening, Kaley gathered in the kitchen where a big pot of soup simmering on the stove sent out tempting aromas. A rush of memories cascaded over her.

She missed her family terribly. Rather than dwell on how different things were, she remembered the message her mom and dad sent earlier. Their words were like receiving a piece of home in this faraway place.

Kaley wandered over to see what Mrs. Sikorski was pouring into glasses and took a whiff. Whatever the concoction was, it smelled sweet.

"Do I smell oranges?" she asked Izzy's mother.

The sturdy woman nodded sharply, which set the bun at the back of her head to quivering. "You will like *oranzada*. That and *bigos* my Izzabella choose for the party."

"Is *bigos* the soup? Did I guess right?"

"*Tak*. Polish stew with sausage, bacon, and mushroom. You like?"

Her warm brown eyes conveyed such goodness Kaley had no heart to admit she despised mushrooms. She could eat around them, she decided. Austin and Izzy were giggling in the living room so Kaley went to investigate. While listening to their banter, she tried finding her sea legs again, as her dad liked to say.

That got her recalling the new joke Andy had sent in the family's message. She walked up to Glenna, who was setting bowls on a long table, which spread the entire length of the cozy living room. Upholstered chairs had been pushed into the hallway to make room.

"Glenna, want to answer Andy's fun quiz?" Kaley asked.

Her friend set down the last dish. "Sure."

"Okay," Kaley chirped. "What is the best Wi-Fi connection in the world?"

Glenna wrinkled her brow. "I dunno."

"Prayer!"

Kaley and Glenna burst into laughter. Their engaging talk brought Austin and Izzy over to join in.

Austin's eyes twinkled. "I have a joke of my own. Who keeps the oceans clean?"

"I have no clue," she said, shaking her head. "Maybe Glenna does."

She didn't, prompting Austin to snap his fingers. "Are you ready? Mermaids."

Kaley and Glenna giggled in unison. Truth be known, Kaley missed both of her brothers in that instant.

Ms. Yost, striding up with her clipboard, ended their lighthearted moment. "Tomorrow, are you visiting Old Town with me or the concentration camp with Mr. Sikorski?"

"Glenna and I are tagging along with Izzy and her father," Kaley told the teacher.

"Me too," Austin said.

Ms. Yost cleared her throat. "Somehow that does not surprise me. The rest of the class is joining me."

She then asked Kaley to arrange fold-up chairs around the table. As she shoved chairs in place, Kaley had an epiphany. "I want to return to Poland someday. And maybe journey as far as Russia if my parents will let me."

"That is a trip of a lifetime, and you will not be sorry," Ms. Yost said. "It took me months to get used to living in Gdansk during my college years. Of course, things were different then under the Soviet Union."

Kaley resisted yawning. She'd gotten little sleep since she and Glenna had stayed up trading stories with Izzy before bedtime. Being the same age and a senior in high school, Izzy, too, was interested in international relations like Kaley.

Izzy hurried up, carrying a sheet of paper and wearing a frown. The willowy girl's light brown hair was fastened behind her head with a pretty yellow clip. Austin chose that moment to walk away, and Kaley wondered why.

"Papa should be here by now," Izzy said breathlessly. "I hope nothing happened. As head of maintenance for Ceba Ferry Line, he has much responsibility."

Kaley reminded her, "He's going to arrange for our ferry trip to Sweden."

"You are right." Izzy's brown eyes held fast to her concern. "Papa says I need to relax more, which is why he and Mama are hosting you and Glenna in our home."

"Thanks for having us. You and I sent so many e-mails, it's like we've known each other forever."

When Izzy handed Kaley a sheet of music, she did a double take. "What's this?"

"It's Austin's idea." The Polish teen wrinkled her pert nose. "He says you and Glenna will sing while he plays guitar. I did not know he played."

"You must be kidding! I've never seen this song before."

"My English is not so good," Izzy said, looking more troubled.

"It's a thousand times better than my Polish, but I'm no singer like you."

Izzy drew back. "I promised my friends we would hear American music."

"That's different. Of course you shall have your music."

Kaley didn't want to embarrass her new friend. After reassuring Izzy that she would think of something, Kaley searched for Glenna. There she was horsing around with Austin as if they shared a secret. Did they?

She hurried up to them, demanding to know from Austin, "Why did you tell Izzy that Glenna and I are singing?"

"I heard you both making a beautiful harmony at school. Don't you want to do something special for these nice people?"

Kaley considered his trustworthy face. "When you put it that way, I guess I do. My brother Andy pulls so many tricks, I thought you were joking."

"No way."

His hazel eyes sparkled with pleasure.

"We could perform this song from youth group," Glenna said, and began humming a tune, one Kaley recognized.

"It's fine with me," Kaley replied. "If Austin can play it."

Glenna sang the first stanza of the popular song about Jesus being with you no matter how deep the oceans. It seemed to fit, given Kaley and Glenna's flight across the vast Atlantic Ocean. The two girls practiced and Austin searched for the right chords on his guitar until Mrs. Sikorski hustled from the kitchen holding two trays.

The students hurried to find places around the table. Food was being served when Mr. Sikorski rushed in, his tie crooked.

In a booming voice he announced, "American friends, welcome. We say grace. Merciful Father, thank You for the beautiful children put in our care. We show them much in a few days. Thanking You for bountiful food and blessings. Amen."

Kaley opened her eyes to find Austin staring at her from across the table. What went on in his mind, she could not fathom. Izzy sat beside her after greeting her father. She began telling their plans for the next day. The bowl of soup Kaley found delicious, and she spied one sliver of mushroom, which she ate anyway.

Before long, it was time for her number with Glenna and Austin. The two American girls sang a duet about their Savior calling them out upon the waters. Austin strummed his guitar skillfully with enormous enthusiasm. It was strange, but singing about faith becoming stronger in times of testing caused doubts like powerful waves to crash into Kaley's mind.

Should she be a federal agent like her mom? Or go into journalism like her dad? She forced away these questions to concentrate on the final chorus. Kaley shut her eyes, singing with Glenna a lyrical "Amen." They sat down to light clapping.

Ms. Yost then asked each American student to briefly introduce themselves. Thinking about what to say as the others said hello, Kaley made a life-changing decision. She squeezed both hands together until it was her turn.

She smiled at the group Izzy had assembled, telling them all, "I love my family. Next fall, I plan to attend college and study international relations. Someday I want to work for a federal law enforcement agency."

Kaley decided not to mention that her federal-agent mom was her hero. She snagged her seat. Austin squared his shoulders, introducing himself as an only child living with his parents, and an officer in the school's Army Reserve Officer Training Corp. Kaley was surprised to hear his congressman had secured him an appointment to West Point, the U. S. Military Academy.

Lifting his chin, Austin sounded determined when he said, "I will become a commissioned officer in the U.S. Army. And one day, I want to serve in Europe with NATO to help defend this area against Russia's constant aggression. Maybe I'll return and visit in my Army uniform."

Mr. Sikorski and the Polish students gave him rousing applause. Austin took an exaggerated bow. Kaley found him amazing. He was so focused and grown-up for his age. It gave her reason to begin more planning when she returned home. Izzy read one of her poems and when the welcoming party was over, a deeper love for the Polish people was firmly planted in Kaley's heart.

Later in a small twin bed in the guest bedroom, as she listened to Glenna's steady breathing, Kaley replayed all she'd seen and done since arriving in the wonderland of Poland. She curled up on her bed wiggling cold toes beneath the woolen blanket.

What stayed most brightly in her mind was the memorial for heroic fighters who died at the hands of Soviet Russia. Here she was an American with freedom to dream for a limitless future. Before long she fell asleep, only to wake up frightened by a disturbing dream.

Their ferry to Sweden ran aground, and they were stranded at sea. Hundreds of passengers were forced to jump into the cold water. Kaley had struggled to keep her head above the waves.

She pushed off the warm blanket. What a ridiculous thing to dream all because she and Glenna had sung about walking out on the water. She determined right then to have loads of fun on the ferry boat to Sweden and forget all about her silly nightmare.

A full moon flamed out from behind a cloud, brightening the curtainless room. The *tickety-tock* of her heart beating wildly disturbed Kaley until Glenna's soft snores reminded her that she wasn't alone. Thinking happy thoughts for tomorrow, she closed her eyes and fell asleep.

Odors of frying bacon tickled her nose. Was it breakfast time already? Familiar smells gave her a thrill about the day. Surely it would unfold in exciting ways.

Chapter 10

Fried bacon, boiled eggs, and stewed fruit tasted delightful to Kaley. She decided to sit next to Austin during the drive to the Stutthof Concentration Camp, to see if she could figure out what made him tick. He could be funny and then turn somber without warning.

She didn't have a chance right away to do any probing because Mr. Sikorski called out various sites along the way. He jabbed to his right, and Izzy turned slightly in the front passenger seat.

"Kaley, that is our church. We go tonight if you want to come. Tomorrow we all take the ferry to Sweden, where we stay overnight with friends from our sister school."

"I can't wait to climb aboard," Glenna yelled from the last row of seats.

Kaley agreed it sounded like fun. She checked her phone, and disappointed to find no new text messages, she returned the cell to the backpack with the idea this was a good time to engage Austin.

"Your future is mapped out," she said in earnest. "It's incredible you want to be an Army commander."

He faced her with his stunning smile. "Why choose to be a federal agent? Isn't that rather limiting?"

"I don't think so. Living near D.C., I meet lots of agents that attend my church."

"You should see if any will let you do a career shadow, like when we have career days at school. Do you know any federal agents well enough to ask?"

Kaley didn't want to veer into her mom's occupation, so she simply told him, "I never thought of doing that. I'll see."

Mr. Sikorski announced they had reached the camp and should bring their water bottles. Kaley glanced out the window, never having been to a World War Two camp before. Gray clouds swirled above rows of tall, feathery pine trees lining the drive. From the roadway, the entrance seemed more like a park than a former prison. Dozens of tourists milled around a large bus. She wondered if they, too, were Americans.

Austin slid open the van door, helping Kaley out. Her spirits slumped upon seeing barbed wire running along the tops of concrete walls.

"Come, children," Mr. Sikorski said, leading them into the

compound.

Kaley peered across a gravel walkway where grim brick buildings were framed by a dark, foreboding sky. She clenched her teeth, feeling on edge. Glenna walked beside her through the barracks that had once imprisoned innocent people. Observing the gas chamber area turned Kaley's stomach. Though Mr. Sikorski believed it was vital they experience Stutthof firsthand, Kaley began to wish she hadn't come.

She pulled Glenna aside whispering, "This place is eerie."

"I agree." Glenna wiped her eyes. "All those shoes piled up, showing thousands taken captive here, is awful."

Kaley stared down at her blue athletic shoes. Was she standing where someone once cried out in fear and pain? She could almost hear lumbering trucks bringing in children. Disgust swept through her. Eighty-five thousand people died here at the hands of the German SS.

A nugget of truth lit her heart with something like lightning. She blinked her eyes and turned to tell Glenna, who began reading aloud from a plaque detailing the camp's history. "This was the last camp to be liberated at the war's end. Prior to the arrival of Allied forces, thousands of people were forced to march in snow and ice to the Baltic Sea where they were gunned down."

"Horrible. It gets worse and worse." Kaley's entire body shivered, even her toes.

She touched Glenna's arm. "I just remembered. My great-grandpa Marty arrived in the Netherlands right before Germany invaded, and was caught behind enemy lines. He risked his life hiding Jewish people. He fought the Gestapo in the Dutch Resistance, and joined the U.S. Army Monuments Men."

"Kaley, I didn't know your grandpa served with them. My dad took me and Gregg to a movie about those soldiers who saved famous art."

"Guess how old my grandpa was when he sailed to Holland by himself?"

To Glenna's shrug, Kaley proudly told her, "Seventeen, our age."

"Hey, my Grandpa Mac skippered a submarine and did secret stuff. I should ask what he did and how old he was."

The teens fell quiet. Kaley imagined she and Glenna were thinking the same thing. It had taken great courage for their grandparents to stand up against the Nazis.

Kaley's eyes locked onto a now-deserted guard tower. She squeezed her eyes shut, finding it unthinkable armed guards would shoot anyone who tried to escape. Sounds of crunching on the gravel made her jump. It was Mr. Sikorski walking up in his thick-soled boots.

"Germany is now our friend." He fingered the end of his moustache. "Keeping the past alive prevents us from repeating mistakes."

"My father says that too." Glenna adjusted her backpack. "He thinks General Sikorski, your courageous prime minister during the war, is a hero. Are you related?"

"Ah. I thought one of you bright ones would ask."

Kaley noticed the Polish man's almost-black eyes become shadowed beneath heavy brows. He explained haltingly, "His plane crashed in 1943 ... Our Institute of National Remembrance still investigates ... General Sikorski was killed by his enemies ... Those people are enemies to me."

"Who were his enemies?" Glenna probed.

He pulled an old-fashioned gold watch from his pocket. Looking at it with a grimace, he answered in a serious voice, "Twenty thousand brave Polish officers were murdered by Soviet Union ... buried in Katyn Forest in Russia ... General Sikorski demanded investigation."

"Come," he called to Izzy, who lingered with Austin by a memorial. "Time to leave this place of death. We return to the land of the living, and go visit Bird's Paradise on Vistula River."

Kaley and Glenna exchanged uncertain looks. As they walked to the van, Kaley kept her voice low, "You raised a sore subject with him. We may never find out if he and Izzy are related to General Sikorski."

"Did you know so many Polish officers were killed by the Soviets?" Glenna asked.

Kaley hefted her pack to the other shoulder. "No, but I intend to search about the massacre. I might include that and General Sikorski in my final term paper."

"I heard you talking." Izzy walked up, telling them the rest of the story in a bare whisper. "Our former president flew with his wife to commemorate the seventieth anniversary of their deaths. Their plane crashed in Russia. All ninety-six people on board died."

"How traumatic," Kaley said, wanting to dig further into the events.

Austin acted unconcerned, skipping dried acorns across the parking lot. His antics were no match to Kaley's somber mood. She began to see him as less mature than she thought.

She hopped into the front passenger seat, wanting to ask Mr.

Sikorski about Poland's current relationship with Russia. The moment she opened her mouth, she recalled Ms. Yost's caution to steer clear of political discussions. Perhaps a roundabout approach would be okay.

"I'm interested in Poland's history," she said cheerfully. "General Pulaski fought alongside General Washington in our Revolutionary War, and I wrote about Lech Walesa who started your Solidarity Movement."

Mr. Sikorski gripped the wheel as he spun out of the parking lot. "We live in Russia's shadow. When do they invade?"

"You mean like they marched into Ukraine?" Kaley raised her eyebrows. "Would Russia do that here?"

"We live strong in our faith." He thumped his chest with one hand. "Almighty God put desire in me for justice."

"Me too!" Kaley cried.

Soon thick trees parted. Dreary clouds disappeared. Sunlight winked brightly off dazzling water at the road's end. Mr. Sikorski aimed the van around a truck parked on the highway, swinging into a nearly-empty parking lot. At flashes of white, Kaley lifted her eyes in time to see a flock of birds soaring and flapping their wings. Seabirds landed on the gravel beside the van.

The four kids poured out. Breathing in salty sea air, Kaley gazed upward, thrilled to see nothing but blue sky. Izzy's father led the group to a gazebo-like building, giving Kaley a picturesque view of shore birds pecking along the river's edge. She took dozens of photos, being sure to include her friends in several.

A noisy jet rumbled overhead. Kaley shielded her eyes, staring skyward.

"The plane reminds me, we have only a few days left," she said wistfully.

Mr. Sikorski stiffened his arms. "That is not passenger plane. That is Russian plane from Kaliningrad. Their Baltic Sea Fleet is this close to our border."

With his fingers, he demonstrated an inch. Kaley tried recalling what she knew about Kaliningrad. Not much. Apparently Austin knew little either.

He hissed in her ear, "What's the big deal with Kaliningrad?"

"I wish I knew," she replied.

Izzy released her hair from the yellow clip. "Papa says Russia flies planes low to remind us they are close by. It makes me nervous."

"How close is Kaliningrad?" Glenna asked after sipping from her water bottle.

Mr. Sikorski seemed to ignore her question when he answered, "Russia invades Ukraine. No world leaders stop them. We in Poland know this, and pray for someone like President Ronald Reagan. He stood up to Russian bear, bringing down Iron Curtain."

"My grandfather met President Reagan," Austin boasted.

Before Kaley could find out when, Mr. Sikorski announced, "Time for a *festyn*."

"What's that?" Kaley asked, vowing to learn more Polish.

Izzy laughed lightly. "A picnic. We can try Mama's special donuts."

They returned to the van where Mr. Sikorski unloaded a box of apples, cheese, and loaves of rye bread, which his daughter broke into chunks for everyone at a table they found in the shade.

"These are *pacski*." Izzy handed Austin a golden cake. "I hope you like the homemade strawberry filling."

Kaley ate hers, praising the delicate pastry. "Did you make the filling, Izzy?"

Her new friend chimed, "Yes," all the while gazing shyly at Austin. At this news, Austin devoured his paczek in one gulp.

"Superb," he proclaimed, licking his lips.

Mr. Sikorski wiped his moustache and reached for another paczek. A larger bird lofted over their heads, and Mr. Sikorski pointed up.

"A white-tailed eagle. This nature preserve is for the birds," he said in jest before biting into his second donut.

"You get our American humor." Kaley grinned. "Have you been to the States?"

"We take Izzy once to see Statue of Liberty."

"Papa took me into the lady's crown. I could see the torch above us," Izzy added softly. "Your lady of freedom made a huge impression on me."

Kaley sat amazed, being forced to admit she'd never seen Lady Liberty. "Neither have my friends. You make me sorry I haven't."

"We do not take freedom for granted, not with Russia ready to pounce on us any day." Izzy's dark eyes blazed.

She gathered the remaining donuts, sliding the container into the basket. "Don't forget, Papa, we visited John Adams' home and heard the choir sing at Brooklyn's Tabernacle."

"Such music praising our Heavenly Father." His eyes misted.

He wiped them with the back of a gnarly hand. Austin prodded Izzy away from the table to the river's edge. Kaley encouraged Glenna to go along too. She was curious about a large group of stones that once had been covered with water. Izzy wandered over, telling Kaley about Poland's long-term drought. The Vistula had not recovered.

"See that stone?" Kaley pointed to one rising from the parched riverbed. "What is writing on it?"

Izzy leaned over to splash water over the etched words to see what it said. Kaley moved the stone, finding underneath a small rusted metal box. When she called Mr. Sikorski, the burly Polish man rushed over to examine the stone.

"Hmm. I see Russian lettering. We take."

He went to the van, returning with a fabric bag. He set the stone fragment and rusty metal box inside the bag, telling the students, "History comes alive. Because Vistula is low, Jewish tombstones turn up. Even Russian war plane."

"Can't we open the box?" Kaley was eager to know what she'd found.

He shook his head solemnly. "My friend at university will examine."

Anticipation rose within Kaley over what might be a spectacular find. Recently, her mom and Grandpa Marty had discovered valuable artwork. Maybe Kaley had as well. Their picnic came to an abrupt end when Mr. Sikorski called them to the van.

"Pray for good weather," he said. "Tomorrow on ferry excursion, we sit out on deck. We want no storm they predict on Baltic Sea."

"My parents and I don't attend church," Austin said. "Pray if you like for calm seas. Getting motion sickness is no fun. Not me, but my mom's the one."

Kaley forced a chuckle. "You're right. It is awful."

She'd had her own dreadful experience on the Chesapeake, only she didn't want to think of her rolling stomach ever again. The van's wheels crunched on gravel as they rolled out of the parking area. Kaley heard Glenna's soft giggle from the seat behind her.

"My dad rode on a ship on the Baltic Sea before he knew my mom," Glenna said. "That's why I want to take this ferry, to sail where he did."

Kaley tilted her head sideways to better see her friend. "I hope our ferry excursion is everything you hope for. Izzy says it's like being on a cruise ship."

"Ship is big." Mr. Sikorski's hand left the wheel as he gestured. "Easy to become lost. We stick together."

A mix of joy and trepidation stampeded through Kaley as she gazed out the side window. She wanted a last glimpse of the inspiring Bird's Paradise, by far her favorite place in Poland. A majestic bird swooped past, its long wings lifting it high in the air.

"The white-tailed eagle!" she cried.

It was electrifying to watch the eagle soaring higher and higher. That is how Kaley wanted to live her life—reaching for the stars and touching them.

Yet something gnawed at her in a dim corner of her mind. If she became seasick on the ferry, she didn't want Austin finding out. Nothing ever rattled or bothered him. There was one solution: She refused to be seasick. Kaley was like her mom in that way. Once she made up her mind to do something, she did it.

Kaley swallowed, thinking more about freedom-loving Izzy. Her Polish friend was showing Kaley how much she'd taken her fantastic life for granted. Russia bullying Poland bothered her. Couldn't they live in the same area and get along?

She was also learning peace in Eastern Europe was fragile. Relaxing against the seat cushion, she gave thanks Russia wasn't threatening America as it was to Poland. But if they did, would America be able to stop them?

BACK IN VIRGINIA WITH KALEY GONE, Saturday morning at the Montanna house was more quiet than usual. The boys played 3D checkers in the family room while Scott busily painted Kaley's bedroom a pretty Dutch blue. Eva had just finished washing breakfast dishes when the phone rang.

She didn't recognize the caller ID. Because it was local, she dried her hands and answered, her voice laced with caution.

"Howdy, neighbor. It's me, Fred. You know, from across the street."

"Of course." Eva braced herself for what came next. "Are you okay?"

"You tell me. That guy is parked down the street, sitting in his car."

Eva glanced out the window, unable to see far enough down the street. She gripped the phone. "Are you sure he's the same man?"

"Yes, ma'am. I just saw him hike back to his car. It's him."

Eva pressed her nose against the window, and peering down the street to the right, she saw it. "Is he in a black Jeep SUV?"

"He is." Fred sounded confident. "You should see the Jeep from your house."

"Yes, thanks for calling. I'll handle this."

Eva hung up without saying good-bye. She began dialing Griff before she stopped. She'd told Fred she would handle this interloper, and she would. Scurrying to her bedroom, she changed into jeans, and yanked a sweatshirt over her head. Eva slipped into sneakers, and shoved the Glock into the small of her back beneath her sweatshirt. Adrenaline kicked in big-time as she wedged the badge into her pocket.

Eva stormed into Kaley's room where Scott was on the floor painting the trim.

"I'm going outside," she said, masking her anxiety. "Fred called. A suspicious car is down the block. If I'm not home in ten minutes, check on me."

Scott rolled over, paintbrush poised in the air. "Really? Should I come with you?"

"Nope. It's probably nothing," she fibbed, eager to be on her way.

Eva hurried out through the garage service door. Crossing the street to the front of Fred's house, she veered right and walked parallel. In this way, she was in the driver's blind spot as she approached the rear of his Jeep. Certain he couldn't spot her from his rear or side mirrors, she stopped when nearly abreast of the SUV.

The man behind the wheel was peering down as if concentrating on something. With his dark thick hair, he looked Latino and in his mid-fifties. Eva strode across the street, again coming at him from behind, still staying outside the view of his mirror. From about five feet away, she moved quickly.

She drew her Glock, tapping the closed window with its muzzle. Eva held her badge up with her left hand. The driver jolted and dropped his portable computer into his lap. His eyes roved to Eva's drawn weapon.

"Put your hands on the wheel where I can see them," she ordered.

Without hesitation, he complied. Eva scanned the front seat. Instead of any weapon, she spotted an open briefcase.

She told him in her command voice, "Use your left hand to slowly open your window."

He reached for the button at a snail's pace. Down slid the window. He turned his head with reddening cheeks to stare at Eva.

"I like seeing your badge, Eva." The guy acted totally nonchalant.

"Who are you?"

"The investigator doing your background investigation for OPM."

Eva was incredulous. She kept her gun pointed at his face.

"No, that was done years ago. Show me your ID."

He nodded toward his shirt pocket saying, "If I may."

"Yes, but no sudden moves."

He reached into his pocket in slow motion. Eva waited for him to hand her a leather credential case. In one swift move, she thrust her own badge in her pocket and grabbed his credentials. She flipped it open. It was his photo, all right. Hector Chavez was indeed an OPM investigator.

Eva sighed, enormous relief flooding her mind and body. She slid the Glock into the small of her back, pulling the sweatshirt over her waistband.

"Permit me to exit my vehicle," he said. "And we'll talk."

Hector Chavez sounded reasonable. But wait. What if this guy had hacked into Hector's personnel file at OPM and faked the ID? Anything was possible. Though she hadn't seen a weapon, Eva stepped back carefully. The Jeep's door swung wide. Hector was no taller than Eva. Still, she was poised for action.

"Hector, you'd better explain. I have a top secret clearance. My background investigation was completed years ago."

"Correct."

The wiry man nodded, standing in the road beside Eva. "You should be aware every five years investigations are brought up-to-date. We call it a 'bring up.'"

"Right." Eva folded her arms. "But that never happens."

"That's where you're wrong. While 'bring ups' don't occur as often as they should, they do happen. Yours is being brought up-to-date."

"Does this have anything to do with OPM's files being hacked?"

"Strictly routine." His grin was lopsided. "I'm retired Air Force OSI. Mine was never brought up-to-date."

"Ah, Office of Special Investigation," Eva said with a tone of respect. "Good agency. My husband Scott was an Air Force officer."

"I know."

Eva realized she was in the presence of a real colleague, not some neighborhood stalker. "Sorry to startle you. I heard you were asking questions about me."

"No problem." Hector wiped his forehead. "It happened to me once before."

Eva glanced across the street, spotting Fred peering out his window. She made a quick decision. "Look, why not come in for a cup of coffee."

He accepted her invitation, and ten minutes later, he and Scott were drinking coffee and swapping military stories. Eva joined them around the table, asking Hector what she could do to assist in completing her background investigation.

"I need to talk with your neighbors. I tried a week ago Saturday and stopped by here to give you a heads-up. You weren't home."

"Yeah, I heard about it," Eva replied.

Hector arched a brow. "Really? The older gent across the street didn't know you."

"He said you asked what car I drove. Freaked me out."

It was Scott's turn to look surprised. "Why didn't I hear about this?"

"Too much happening." Eva rose to refill her coffee.

Hector spread out his hands. "We probe for foreign travel, unexplained wealth, or facts that hint a foreign government like Russia or China has co-opted the holder of the security clearance. When I see my subject is an FBI, DEA, or ICE agent, I'm aware they may work undercover. Their neighbors may have no clue they work for the government."

"That's wise." Eva settled back into her chair and sipped the roasted brew.

Hector pointed toward Fred's house. "I told your neighbor we were checking due to your employer bidding for a sensitive government contract. That's usually enough."

"Anything else you need from me?"

"Yes, developed informants. They are persons other than ones you named back when. It's delicate. I hesitate to approach people who don't know what you really do."

Eva scribbled on a pad. She tore off the top sheet and gave it to Hector. "Julia Rider and Dawn Topping are married to my co-workers. They know me and what kind of person is needed for what we do. I'm sure they'll talk to you."

Eva walked out with Hector. Her next stop was Fred's, where she assured him that he had no future worries of mysterious people in the neighborhood. Eva had taken care of everything.

Chapter 11

The Baltic Sea

Dawn had rolled away night's black edges, and the clear day dazzling with sunshine made Kaley whoop for joy. Here she was standing on the uppermost deck with no storm clouds in sight. The enormous size of the ferry, a cruise ship really, was far different from the small boat she'd pictured.

Pungent smells of the sea air tickled her memories.

"This reminds me of fishing on the Chesapeake last summer with my dad and brothers. We caught so many fish," she told Glenna, who stood beside her at the railing.

Glenna removed her cap. "I want to text my dad about being on the Baltic, but it won't go through. I've decided to follow his footsteps in the CIA."

"What are you two talking about?" Austin appeared at Kaley's elbow. "I'd give anything to know your peculiar thoughts."

Kaley cringed, hoping he hadn't heard Glenna say her dad worked for the CIA. Her mom's warning not to mention their jobs burst into her mind.

She tried distracting him. "You have nerve, calling me an oddball."

"You misunderstand me." He smiled, showing his white teeth. "I mean you are unique, quite special."

"Austin, did you come on this trip to annoy me?" Kaley snapped.

"Do I bother you, Kaley? I thought we were friends."

"We are. I guess we need to get to know each other better."

Austin's direct look into her eyes unnerved her. "I would like that," he said.

An ear-splitting blast from the ferry's horn made her and Glenna jump. A series of shorter blasts rang in her ears, and the huge ferry backed away from the dock with a surge. Kaley, Glenna, and Austin all snapped pictures with their smartphones.

"Did you know there's a game room?" Austin's voice rose in excitement. "They have five restaurants."

Kaley turned toward the glittering sea. "This is cool. Is it everything you hoped for, Glenna?"

"I'd love to see the entire ship so I can tell my dad," Glenna replied.

Austin put away his phone. "Okay, I'll go with you. Want to come, Kaley?"

She spotted Izzy standing off alone. "Maybe later."

Rather than dwell on Austin's quirkiness, Kaley joined Izzy, telling her, "Look how the sea changes into so many colors. Pink when we first boarded, now the water is bright silver."

Izzy laughed lightly. "I am thankful there is no sign of a storm."

"Looks like our prayers were answered."

The two teens snooped around until relaxing on lime-green lounge chairs on the lower deck. Kaley typed mega-notes into her phone to record events to help write her report. It would be a dilemma to decide which aspect of the trip to emphasize.

Her mind reviewed several angles. Differing attitudes toward freedom? Russian aggression?

White seabirds lofted, calling sharply overhead. Kaley gazed heavenward. She was disappointed not to see another white-tailed eagle. Glenna found them and dragged another chair close by Kaley, saying, "When we reach Karlskrona, we'll see Sweden's first submarine. Kaley, will you take my picture in front of it for my Grandpa Mac?"

"He skippered a sub, right?"

"Yeah. I want to cheer him up 'cause he's been sick."

Kaley quit looking down at her phone. "Where's Austin?"

"Oh, nosing around, taking pictures. I've seen what I want to see."

"I can't wait to find out what Mr. Sikorski's professor friend says about the relics I found along the Vistula."

"Maybe he'll know what the Russian box was used for." Glenna rubbed her bare knees. "I always said you'll make a super federal agent like your mom."

Remembering they weren't supposed to mention their parent's jobs, Kaley raised her eyebrows and glared at Glenna. Izzy's earbuds were in, so perhaps she hadn't heard Glenna. The farther north they went, the colder the air became. As Kaley stretched her legs on the chair, she was happy she'd worn jeans and not shorts like Glenna. Time passed, and though Kaley grew chilled, she refused to go inside.

As she zipped the jacket up to her chin, Austin plunked down on a vacant chair beside Izzy. The girls listened to music through their earbuds while he checked his smartphone. He came over to talk with Kaley, so she removed a bud to hear him.

"Want a raspberry lozenge?" she asked, easing one from her pocket.

He sneered. "No way. I bought a snack at the café."

"Are you seasick?"

"No."

"You look green," she replied.

"Why did you tell Ms. Yost you wanted to visit Russia?" he asked. "Don't you realize they're our adversary?"

"The country may be, but not the people."

Austin shrugged. "If you say so. I'm going to walk around."

"Oh?"

He pointed to Mr. Sikorski, who was fully reclined and snoring with a gentle rattle. "You're all into music, and he's no company. I'll be back."

"You could check out the game room," Kaley offered.

He pocketed his hands and shuffled along the deck's railing, looking out to sea. Kaley settled back in her lounge chair listening to a classical rendition of "Love Divine, All Loves Excelling" by Charles Wesley. She dozed off too.

The thunder of running footsteps awakened Kaley with a start. Passengers raced past their chairs, screaming in foreign languages. Terrified men and women pointed up at the sky. Kaley yanked the buds from her ears. She jumped to her feet.

Her heart pounded furiously. "Mr. Sikorski, what's happening?"

He ran to the rail, eyes glued upward. Earsplitting noises exploded all around. Fierce winds buffeted Kaley's face. Was a waterspout heading to smash the ship?

Then she saw it and stood transfixed. A mighty helicopter hovered above them. Was she dreaming or was this real?

She blinked, scarcely believing what her eyes were seeing. Armed soldiers descended on dangling ropes to the ship's main deck. Then she realized this might be an exercise by the Swedish Navy. From her studies, she knew they kept their base at Karlskrona, the ferry's ultimate destination.

Kaley told this to Mr. Sikorski. Rather than agree, he grabbed Kaley and Izzy by their arms and began dragging them toward a big lifeboat.

"Russians," he hissed. "Glenna, come!"

When he let go of Kaley's arm, she noticed he gaped skyward again, and then glanced furtively toward each end of the large ship. Kaley saw the last of the passengers disappear around a corner. She tried stuffing the earbuds in her jacket pocket, and all her zinc lozenges tumbled out.

Mr. Sikorski hollered to be heard above the chaos, "Girls, you come!"

He climbed three steps up to the lifeboat, beckoning for them to join him. Kaley had no chance to snatch her lozenges. He moved fast like a lightning bolt, loosening the tarp covering the lifeboat, and pushing it backward before helping the three girls over the side and into the boat.

Mr. Sikorski climbed in breathing hard. Kaley's heart hammered fiercely in her chest. Her mind careened like the tilt-a-whirl ride at the fair. They were being invaded by armed Russian soldiers! Why were they coming aboard? She forced herself to be calm.

"Mr. Sikorski," she said in between breaths. "Is this a drill by the Swedish Navy?"

"I know Russians," he barked.

He tugged on the cover from the inside. Kaley avoided asking questions, fervently hoping soldiers on the outside couldn't tell the tarp was loose. Then she remembered her lozenges. A shudder ripped through her. Would they give away their hiding spot? At least she'd dropped them some distance from the lifeboat.

Beneath the tarp, no light shone. They groped seats. Mr. Sikorski ordered them in foreboding whispers, "Be still. Be quiet."

His Polish accent made shadows more frightening. Kaley held her breath for a long moment, afraid to breathe. A terrible idea crowded past her reason. Should she and Glenna trust Mr. Sikorski? If only she could call Mom and ask her what to do!

Her ears caught hold of what he explained in a raspy voice, "The ferry keeps no manifest. Russian soldiers do not miss us if they do not know we are here."

Kaley recalled her lozenges might give them away. She was about to tell him when Izzy asked softly, "Papa, what about Austin?"

"Where is he?" he demanded in a stern tone.

"He's walking around," Kaley said. "Maybe he found Ms. Yost and the others."

"Hmmph," Mr. Sikorski mumbled.

Crunching-like sounds outside the lifeboat stopped their talking. The momentary quiet was shattered by the loud public address system, and a man pronouncing something first in Swedish and then Polish.

Mr. Sikorski held a finger to his lips. "Sshh, we listen."

The man's bellowing voice continued in English, laced with a Russian accent, "The vessel is seized for violating Russia's sovereign waters. You are all ordered to gather in the main deck lounge where you will present passports for inspection. Every guest is safe. Our quarrel is not with you, but with the nation of its registry, Poland."

"Guests!" Kaley cried. "They take us at gunpoint and claim to be our hosts?"

"You are right, but sshh," Mr. Sikorski insisted.

Then he snuck one arm out of the tarp. Kaley heard him snap their cover to the hull, which made her feel a little easier. Still, danger lurked all around. She couldn't help shivering from the cold and rising fear. Rubbing her arms did nothing to warm them.

Izzy's father urged them softly, "Pray for Austin and children to be safe."

As he said this, an idea lit Kaley's mind like light pierced through thick fog. She yanked out her smartphone, remembering Andy's earlier joke. He said prayer was the best Wi-Fi connection. She poked Glenna, pointing excitedly to bars at the top of the screen.

"Wi-Fi!" she shrieked, then shut her lips tight.

She zoomed to her mom's name in the contact list. Her fingers were shaking so badly it was hard to type. They had no cell towers, but her e-mail should go via Wi-Fi. Her heart beat wildly with each letter her thumbs pressed.

mom! russian soldiers attacking! hiding in lifeboat! help!

Kaley sent her e-mail, then powered off the phone to save battery. If Russians grabbed them, would she ever use it again? They might all be thrown in prison.

She clutched the phone like a lifeline, knowing Andy was right. Prayer was the ultimate wireless connection. With eyes squeezed tightly, she whispered, "God, please direct Mom to my e-mail. Please help us!"

Her mom would freak out when she found out what happened, yet Kaley knew one thing for sure. She trusted her to act fast.

TIME GRINDING BY SLOWLY was pure agony. Every second, Kaley worried soldiers would find them, guns drawn. She and the other three stowaways huddled beneath the tarp, the air close and clammy. Glenna's teeth chattered. She must be freezing in her shorts.

Kaley gulped for air in the stuffy confines, her eyes accustomed to the dimness. Every strange sound beyond the lifeboat caused Izzy to breathe rapidly as if frightened out of her wits. Mr. Sikorski sat mostly still. Kaley hoped his mental gears were churning to find a solution. He worked on this ferry and should know every inch. Whatever his plans, he didn't tell them.

She finally whispered to him, "Has enough time gone by to reach Sweden? Are we still heading there?"

Izzy whimpered loudly, probably because of the unknown.

"Sshh," Mr. Sikorski said, raising his hands dramatically, silencing questions and noises. Kaley sat up straighter and heard a voice rising up in the distance.

Could it be?

She heard the voice calling, "Kaley ... Glenna."

Kaley reached for the secured canvas. Mr. Sikorski caught her arm, forcing her to sit very still. Seconds ticked by.

"Kaley ... Glenna ... where are you?"

She knew it was Austin saying their names, looking for them.

"Should I answer? What if he's in danger or afraid we're hurt?"

Mr. Sikorski clutched her arm more tightly. She couldn't tell if he pressed a finger to his lips. Why shouldn't she—

Two men speaking in Russian ended her uncertainty. Their strident voices sounded threatening. Soldiers were near, and Kaley dared not even think. A long while later, the voices faded as if they walked away from the lifeboat.

Kaley leaned in toward Mr. Sikorski. "Could you hear what they said?"

"Yes!" he hissed. "Russians say you children are from Washington student exchange program."

"I thought I heard my name," Kaley moaned.

"You did. Russians say candies on deck are yours. They know we are aboard. Pray they do not find us."

Kaley whispered, "Austin's in the ROTC. That's student military training. Maybe he's trying to confuse the Russian soldiers."

"No matter, it is Gog and Magog," he replied.

Before she asked what he meant, shots rang out on the ship. Shrill screams followed. "Ahhh!" echoed inside the lifeboat.

Mr. Sikorski commanded Glenna, "Quiet!" to stop her from shrieking again.

Terror shot through Kaley like hot molten lava. She clamped a hand over her mouth to keep from screaming herself.

"What will happen to us?" Glenna's voice quivered.

Fear laced her every word, and she edged closer to Kaley on the bench seat. Glenna cowered with her arms over her head. Kaley wanted to do the same, but forced herself to think what her mom would do. Huddle in the lifeboat until their rescue?

Her mind turned blank. Who could possibly save them from

the Russians?

Once again Mr. Sikorski had the answer. "Pray."

This single word penetrated Kaley's heart and soul. She dropped her face into her hands, inwardly crying up to heaven, *Father, You see me. You hear me. Please keep the soldiers from finding or hurting us. Make Mom see my message. Jesus, help us!*

She gulped deeply, waiting for peace. Only it didn't arrive, and Kaley strained to hear every noise outside their cocoon, waiting in fear for the soldiers' return. Reality slowly sunk in. How long could they sit here without being found? What if her mom and dad failed to see her message in time?

Her faith said, "Yes, they will!"

Doubt tried smashing her faith with a resounding "No!"

Tears pooled in her eyes. She blinked them away. Hadn't her parents taught her to face trouble with strength? She could do it ... She would do it!

Her new resolve melted away when Mr. Sikorski said ominously, "My papa was in Soviet Gulag for belief in Christ. They beat and tortured him. It is miracle he lived. I know Russian soldiers will search harder for us. Pray darkness comes quick."

And Kaley did pray, like never before. Her entire life spread before the eyes of her mind. She was sorry for angry words yelled at her brothers. She grieved over the time she'd hung up on her friend Lexi because they disagreed over a boy. What was his name?

She should have read her Bible instead of watching mindless videos. Before today, she'd thought her faith in God was strong. With trouble swirling around, she finally understood her sin of worry and fear.

Kaley steadied her breathing, reciting in her mind Psalm 23: *Even in the shadow of death, I will fear no evil, for You are with me.*

In the shadowy cramped lifeboat, Kaley knew Jesus heard her cries. The God of heaven knew her every need before she asked Him. He loved her beyond measure.

What had the youth pastor told them about Joshua leading the Israelites to the Promised Land? She grabbed Glenna's hand. "What did pastor say about Joshua?"

Glenna sniffled. "Ah ... God promised no one would stand up against him—"

"Oh yes. God said, 'As I was with Moses, so I shall be with you. I will never leave or forsake you.'" Kaley's whispers grew stronger with each word.

Courage was within her reach. If only something worse didn't happen.

Chapter 12

Northern Virginia

Life had been kind to Eva the last few days. Still, a piece of her heart was empty with Kaley being in Poland. She checked e-mails using her phone before leaving the office. Scott had invited her to lunch, a rare occurrence, given their busy careers.

His typed message caught her off guard. He canceled lunch due to being stuck in a voting session on the Hill. Disappointment crept into her spirit.

Well, no use crying over spilt milk, as Grandpa Marty used to say. She tried spinning the change positively. It made sense to grab a sandwich at the deli around the corner and eat at her desk. That would give her time to write a report on Holly's allegations of cigar smuggling and suspicious passengers.

Wait … If Eva wrote a report, she'd have to send one to the FBI and the tobacco-tax unit at the Bureau of Alcohol, Tobacco, Firearms, and Explosives (ATF). They'd want more info, which Eva didn't have yet. Or the FBI would pull strings to interview Holly.

She decided to first organize her notes and thoughts before writing anything. Before Eva deleted archived e-mails, a new one popped on her screen. With the subject line blank, she lifted her eyes to the sender's e-mail address.

It was from Kaley. Eva rapidly scanned the message, her eyes widening in horror.

mom! russian soldiers attacking! hiding in lifeboat! help!

"What is this?" she cried.

Hair bristled on her neck, her arms. Eva's heart banged like a jackhammer. She needed to get a grip before anxiety stole her ability to think.

Griff hustled over from his cubicle. "I heard you cry out. You look like death."

No words came. She thrust her phone into his capable hands.

Griff stared at the message, demanding, "Who's this from?"

"It's Kaley's e-mail account."

"Is she still in Poland with Glenna Rider?"

Eva could barely muster a nod. Dread stabbed through her like a hot poker. Her mind was stuck in fear mode.

"Maybe it's a hoax." Griff studied Eva's phone screen. "Some kid grabbed Kaley's phone and sent this as a stupid prank. After all, they're probably learning about Poland's former struggle with the Soviet Union."

Eva scanned her e-mails until locating the one with Kaley's itinerary. "Look, they're taking the ferry to Sweden today. Kaley sent this SOS an hour ago."

"What time is it in Poland?"

"You tell me …" Eva's voice faltered. "My mind is mired in glue."

"It's noon here. Poland is six hours ahead of us?"

Eva glanced at her watch, trying to remember. "Okay, so it's six in the evening there. She could be on that ship."

"I'll check the news."

Griff strode toward the conference room. Eva leapt from her chair, heading after him. She should call Julia, Glenna's mom. Then she stopped short. If Griff was correct, and this was a senseless trick, she hated to worry Julia for nothing.

By the conference room doorway, Eva shut out chatter by the other agents. She uttered a silent, passionate plea for God's help. Opening her eyes, she felt the opposite of calm. What could she do from here? Her deepest fears were unfolding before her eyes.

Then she realized she needed to find out if Griff was right. He was searching channels with the remote when she entered the room. Commercials blared, hawking reverse home mortgages. Eva pressed her hands against her ears.

He muted the sound. "So far just commercials."

"I'm going to read Kaley's e-mail again."

Her eyes locked onto the phone as if a divine correction might appear on the small screen saying Kaley was happily traveling in Sweden.

"Uh oh."

Eva snapped her head upward. Griff aimed a finger at the TV. Horror consumed her mind, and she stood weak-kneed. A banner streamed across the bottom declaring breaking news.

"That's a military helicopter hovering above a ship!" Eva cried. "Soldiers are sliding down ropes. Passengers are scurrying away."

"It's fuzzy, like shot by a tourist's camera," Griff said, turning on the sound.

The reporter proclaimed, "We apologize for the poor quality of the videos, which were uploaded by passengers on a ferry en route from Poland to Sweden in the Baltic Sea."

The blood drained from Eva's face. "My dear sweet Kaley."

She punched in Scott's number while the reporter was saying, "We've compared the helicopter with photos of choppers used by Russia's military. Producers conclude these are Russian soldiers, though every marking on the helicopter is painted over."

"The ferry is huge." Eva squinted at the screen. "Is Kaley on it?"

Griff stepped beside her and clutched her shoulder compassionately with his hand. "She's hiding in a lifeboat, right? See the lifeboats along the deck?"

Eva pushed the green button to call Scott. His voicemail came on. Oh yeah, he was in a voting session. Steadying her voice when she wanted to scream, she left a terse message, "Call me ASAP. It's Kaley."

She hung up, wiping her eyes. "Russia is supposedly working with us in Syria to neutralize terrorists. Perhaps a radical terror group wants to make it look like Russia is behind the hijacking."

"I hate that idea even more." Griff glared fiercely. "God knows the truth. Maybe they're already off the boat."

"My mind says you're right, yet my heart is torn in two. I should phone Julia."

"See if Glenna sent her a message."

The male TV reporter's voice wormed into Eva's mind when he said, "Russia's presence in Kaliningrad increases tensions in the region. Experts suggest today's ferry seizure is an attempt by Russia's president, who some say acts like a tsar, to control the Baltic shipping lanes."

Eva tuned out the guy's report and phoned Julia Rider.

"Eva!" Julia wailed, sounding scared out of her wits. "Glenna and Kaley are hijacked! What can we do? I thought you were Bo returning my call."

"Julia." To further calm her friend, Eva used a steady voice. "Our daughters are in God's sights and in His care. Do you agree with me?"

Julia coughed out a tortured sigh. "Yes ... It's hard to focus on truth when fear is crawling up my throat. I almost lost it watching Russian soldiers swarm the ferry. Maybe our girls aren't on it. But I checked the itinerary."

"Me too."

Eva swallowed, choosing her next words carefully. "I wish I didn't have to tell you this. Kaley sent me an e-mail. Our girls are hiding in a lifeboat."

Julia started sobbing. Eva struggled to keep from crying herself.

"Our daughters need us to stay strong," Eva said with feeling. "Is Bo still in the area? Can you reach him?"

She hoped Julia knew how to contact Bo if he was still overseas for the CIA. Julia blew her nose. Her sobs subsided.

"Eva, I don't know where he is! I'll try sending a text. Glenna didn't send me a message."

Again, Julia's voice broke. Eva could almost read her thoughts—something had happened to Glenna to prevent her from communicating.

"Julia, let's stop imagining the worst, and hope. Perhaps her battery was low. I've been praying and trust you have been too."

"It's all too sudden," Julia gushed. "I'll let you know the moment I talk to Bo."

Eva ended the call reluctantly. Talking with Julia seemed like a connection to Kaley. Something Pastor Feldman preached on pushed forward in her mind. He had called out fear as nothing more than "False Evidence Appearing Real."

While his teaching sounded powerful at church, a feeling of being stranded nearly overpowered Eva. Wired to take command, tear after bad guys, and eliminate their threat, being in a conference room doing nothing was maddening to her.

Then a sudden brain wave hit her. Thumbs flying across the tiny keyboard on her phone, she wrote Kaley, "R U OK?"

Why hadn't Eva written back sooner? Valuable time had been lost.

Griff stared at her, his bushy eyebrows arched over troubled eyes. "Well? I heard your end and can't tell. Is Bo or isn't he near Poland?"

"When I dropped Kaley off at Dulles, Julia hinted he was in Germany. That was last week."

"Plan B then."

"We have a plan B?"

"Yes, only you and I must decide what it is."

Griff's loyal friendship through the years meant the world to Eva. She checked her phone. There was nothing from Kaley.

"What about your Pentagon contacts?" Griff asked. "After all, Scott was the DOD press secretary for many years."

"You are brilliant as usual."

Eva called the Department of Defense. The lieutenant commander on the other end answered in a huff. His brisk manner changed once she introduced herself.

"Scott's been on my mind," Commander Todd Marks said. "Can I lure him back here?"

Eva pictured him reaching out a hand to her, and she told him, "Commander, being press secretary for the new House Speaker keeps Scott busy. I know he misses the military action he had with you at DOD. We have a serious issue with our daughter that might involve the Pentagon."

"I'm listening."

"Kaley and nine students from her high school class are on an exchange trip to Poland. Her itinerary reveals she's taking a ferry to Sweden this very day."

"No!" he shouted, before backpedaling, "Perhaps they aren't on the same ferry."

"Commander, she is on it. I received her urgent message stating Russian soldiers commandeered the ferry. I sent a reply but heard nothing back yet."

"Be assured the Pentagon is monitoring the hijacking. You're the first confirmation that Americans are onboard. I'll crank a warning up through the system."

Eva gathered her courage. "Commander, Kaley's classmate on the ferry is Glenna Rider, daughter of a highly-placed U.S. intelligence officer."

"Dreadful."

His keyboard clattered in Eva's ear. Adrenaline pulsed through her system, escalating the anguish over sitting helplessly in Virginia.

At length, he said, "We don't want these kids falling into the hands of Russian interrogators. Call back when you receive more. If I'm not here, leave your info with whoever answers my phone."

Eva thanked him, and though he hung up with a click, she clung to her phone. Griff was on his cell talking animatedly with the FBI. From what Eva heard, he was trying to shake loose any information. He finally put down his phone and paced to the window.

He faced Eva, a frustrated look on his face. "The Bureau knows very little."

She called the Speaker's office where a helpful aide agreed to locate Scott right away. Eva joined Griff by the window, and the two agents traded intense looks.

Then he said something profound, "Eva, isn't one of your ICE agents assigned to our embassy in Warsaw?"

"Yes, I touched base with him before Kaley left for Poland."

"Call him and get someone working on this. Maybe they can arrange for you to fly over there."

"Of course. Plan B begins."

Eva sped to her desk, and calling her HQ, explained to the duty agent about Kaley's dire situation. He promised to contact the agent in Warsaw at home and advise the director of ICE. Eva leaned her head back. Relief touched the edge of her worry.

She was making progress and went to tell Griff, who was camped out in the conference room monitoring the news.

"HQ will have our Warsaw agent call me," Eva said. "Being in-country, he should know the right people in the Polish government."

Griff leaned his elbows on the table. "Russia is pushing back against Poland for ejecting their ambassador and spies. They are also upset we're arming Poland."

"What are you talking about?" Eva snapped. "We pulled every Patriot missile out of Poland, remember?"

"Yes, but with Russia's advance into Ukraine and becoming embroiled in Syria, we are boosting their military with Abram tanks and Bradley vehicles. And our defensive missiles went live in Romania."

"How do you know all this?"

Griff navigated on his phone and pulled up an article. Eva's eyes were focusing on the news article when her cell phone rang. It was Scott who sounded as tense as Eva felt.

"I've left the House floor and heard a ferry was captured in Poland. Is it Kaley's?"

Eva willed herself not to explode in frustration. Like a torrent, her words gushed forth. "Honey, it's bad. Kaley sent an e-mail. She's hiding in a lifeboat. I talked with Commander Marks and have a call into our agent in Warsaw. I want to fly over there!"

"Okay, we need to remember God will help us and our daughter. Our prayers don't stop at our borders."

"I haven't stopped praying!"

"Good. I'm heading to the Pentagon. Can you meet me there?"

"On my way."

Eva looked at Griff, tears hovering on her lashes. She told him where she was going. He promised to help in any way he could. Gathering all her fortitude, Eva left the conference room desperate to find a way to free her daughter from Russia's evil grip.

Chapter 13

The Baltic Sea

Kaley crouched in the stifling boat with no idea how long ago the shots rang out or when Mr. Sikorski told them to turn off their phones to conserve batteries. Thankfully, she hadn't heard footsteps outside their hideaway for a while. Kaley had a problem of a different kind. Her bladder was screaming.

She cautioned herself she couldn't leave to find a bathroom, and so squirmed on the seat. What else could she do? Every second seemed like torture.

Mr. Sikorski whispered, "We do not wait for Russians to hurt us. My papa escaped Gulag. We escape."

He unsnapped the canvas, and then raised it. Kaley held her breath, nervous for what would happen. All was still. Bright stars twinkled against the clear night sky. A slight breeze stirred her hair.

"It's wonderful breathing fresh air," she said, inhaling deeply.

Mr. Sikorski pointed to the night sky. Kaley saw a tiny sliver of moon winking down as if daring them to escape. The upper decks' faint lights cast an eerie glow.

"Russians hold ferry hostage," he said, leaning in. "The ship does not move. Time to launch lifeboat."

Kaley grabbed his arm. "Don't leave us."

"I return soon. You girls turn on phones, send message we will launch."

He climbed out without making any noise. He arranged the tarp loosely over their boat. Kaley checked her phone for Wi-Fi bars in the dim light. She blinked back tears at her mom's message.

"Mom knows of our capture!" she cried softly. "She asks if I'm okay."

"How long ago did she send it?" Glenna asked.

"I can't see the numbers."

Kaley typed a reply, though her fingers kept slipping off the tiny letters.

ferry stopped in baltic ... russian soldiers aboard ... shots fired ... haven't found us ... launching lifeboat ... send help!! kaley, glenna, mr.s & izzy

Kaley heard grinding sounds outside. She didn't know exactly what Mr. S was doing, but recalled seeing massive arms that secured their boat. A great lurch jostled them. Her head banged against Glenna's, and Kaley rubbed out pain above her ear.

He threw off the tarp, jumping aboard with a thud. He placed long oars into oarlocks and said, "We go."

"Papa, I am so frightened," Izzy crooned softly.

Kaley was afraid too as the lifeboat swung sideways to clear the ship's deck. She clamped one hand on the boat's edge, and one on the bench to keep from swaying. They began to drop to the dark water. She fought against her rolling stomach, keeping watch for soldiers as the lifeboat swung. She saw no one on the deck above.

The soldiers must be inside eating and drinking and plotting. Kaley wondered if Ms. Yost and the other students were being held. They wouldn't know how to activate a lifeboat like Mr. S.

"We hit water, row fast," he barked. "They find boat gone, they come for us."

"Oh, Papa."

Izzy grabbed Kaley's hand. Stark terror bolted through Kaley. All she could think of was the *Titanic* hitting an iceberg. When Glenna seized her other hand, and the three girls squeezed their hands, Kaley fought to stay brave no matter what happened when they hit the water. She was an avid swimmer, though Glenna wasn't. Kaley didn't know about Izzy.

She whispered, "God is for us. Don't forget!"

They plunged down further and further. Kaley gripped the railing with both hands. She wanted to keep living!

Hitting the water, the boat made a tremendous splash. Their little boat got tossed back in the air. The girls tumbled off the benches. Mr. S picked them up in his strong arms. It all happened so fast. Then he scurried to the bow and back to the rear, unfastening cables.

A terrible thing happened. Their boat slammed against the side of the ferry.

"Agghh!" Glenna screamed.

"Row!" he roared. "Row!"

He grabbed an oar and strained to push them away. Kaley's oar slipped from her hands. Mustering strength, she held onto the wooden pole. They rowed and struggled to break away from ferry's side. Kaley's arms burned and ached something fierce. Still, she pulled and pulled. At last, the boat rose and dipped between gentler waves.

"We're free!" she cried.

"Sshh," Mr. S cautioned. "We go in quiet."

Silence enveloped them except for never-ending sounds of oars splashing in and out of the sea. The quartet rowed, bobbing up and down. Kaley couldn't tell how long they toiled on the churning water. Her hands got blisters, so it must have been a long time. Still she rowed, as did they all.

One time Izzy leaned over the boat to wretch over the side. Kaley rowed with all her strength, praying she wouldn't become sick. Glenna groaned alongside her, straining against the oars. Kaley glanced up and saw the faintest of lights from the ferry.

"Are we safe here?" she asked, hoping to quit. "Will they come after us?"

Mr. S told them they were brave, saying, "God has rescue plan."

"My parents will see my message that we were launched." Kaley wiped her palms along her jeans. "They will act. They will contact our government."

"I sent one too," Glenna proclaimed.

Mr. S opened a compartment, removed some things, and then shined a small flashlight around the boat's bottom.

"We do not use radio or locator beacon."

"Why not use the beacon?" Glenna asked. "Wouldn't our rescuers find us quicker?"

He gazed over his shoulder. "Russia's naval base at Kaliningrad. Their planes and ships cover this sea. No beacon 'til our friends start search."

Kaley wondered if she should tell Mr. S and Izzy that her mom and Glenna's dad were federal agents who could influence the American government to rescue them. Then he began giving out bottles of water and crackers. Kaley decided to first sip the water. The coolness soothed her dry and scratchy throat.

He snapped off the flashlight, urging them to eat something. A bite of cracker never tasted so good to Kaley. She took a drink of water before twirling the cap back on.

"We row in dark, and not stop for long time."

Glenna coughed as she checked her phone. "Nothing from my dad."

"That doesn't mean he didn't find your message," Kaley said. "I'll check mine."

She had no bars on the phone. Despair flooded her mind. They might never be found rowing out here on the vast Baltic. Kaley lifted up another prayer, knowing in the depth of her soul it was wrong to lose trust in God. She started humming a song she'd learned from Great-Grandpa Marty. *God will take care of you ...*

"I wish we had rescued Austin," Izzy said as they all started rowing again.

"And everyone else," Kaley replied.

EVA AND SCOTT SPENT THEIR EVENING GLUED to the news. They'd made every call to Poland they could. Their various contacts assured them everything was being done to rescue Kaley and passengers on the hijacked ferry. Eva's parents called, sounding concerned. Eva so wanted to have good news, but she had none. She resisted phoning Grandpa Marty, as she didn't want to upset him.

Andy and Dutch fell asleep in front of the TV. Eva's heart was touched by their innocence. They were probably dreaming sweet dreams. At least she hoped so. She covered them with blankets and fetched their pillows.

Scott stretched out on the sofa, worn out from the struggle. She bent down to kiss his cheek and turned off the light. Her mind a battlefield where anxiety warred against faith, Eva could only stare at the flickering TV waiting for updates.

The news switched to a commercial, and she tiptoed to the kitchen. Before brewing coffee, she checked her phone. Glory hallelujah. Kaley had sent a new message!

Eva burst into the living room and snapped on the table lamp. She rushed at Scott.

"Wake up. Kaley wrote us."

He leaned on an elbow, shielding his eyes from the bright light. Eva thrust the phone at him so he could read Kaley's message.

"Commander Marks said to call with anything new," Eva said. "I'll be on the phone."

She returned to the kitchen, punched in the numbers, and tucked the handheld phone in the crook of her neck. The line at the Pentagon rang and rang. She took coffee from the fridge and filled the maker with fragrant grounds.

A voice said crisply in her ear, "Lieutenant Shaw here."

"This is ICE Agent Eva Montanna. My husband Scott is the former Pentagon press secretary. A few hours ago I spoke with Commander Marks."

"Yes, ma'am. Your daughter is on the Polish ferry. We're monitoring events in the Baltic."

"She's not aboard anymore," Eva said.

"Excuse me?"

"Kaley sent a message. She, her friend whose dad is the CIA agent, and their host and his daughter escaped in a lifeboat. Can you let someone know ASAP?"

"Of course ... ah ... I say this in confidence. Two Russian frigates confronted the *Ceba* ferry. They're now escorting the ship toward Russia's seaport at Kaliningrad. Your news about the lifeboat being launched complicates things."

"What do you mean, 'complicates things'?" Eva lobbed back. "Are you refusing to pass along my information? You could be risking the life of my daughter!"

Eva's blood pressure catapulted. Shaw fell silent. Scott hurried in, scowling. She held a finger to her lips, and Scott huddled close, putting his ear near the phone. Eva heard the distinct clattering of Shaw's keyboard.

Questions and doubt hammered her brain. Would the U.S. government do nothing to rescue Kaley and Glenna?

She didn't dare voice her disgust and jeopardize any rescue attempt. Perhaps she'd already jumped to the wrong conclusion. After all, she wasn't on a secure phone.

"What happens next?" she asked Shaw.

"Let me know if you hear anything further," was his vague reply. "I suspect the media will report the bad news of the ferry's status."

Eva wanted to shout, *You can't just do nothing! Save my daughter!* No doubt that would have the opposite effect.

"Okay." She forced out a sigh, exhaustion seeping into every bone. "You have my phone numbers. Please contact me with *any* update."

"Yes, ma'am. I'll be working on this."

Eva rammed the phone onto its base. Scott came near and said gently, "You didn't put it on speaker. What happened? You look like a thundercloud let loose."

She edged away, handed him the empty carafe, and pointed toward the faucet.

"I need hot coffee, and plenty of it. Lieutenant Shaw says Russian frigates are escorting the ferry to their base in Kaliningrad."

Scott set the glass carafe on the counter. "Hopefully minus one lifeboat."

"How can you stay so calm?" Eva demanded, her stomach twisting in knots. "Kaley is out bobbing on the Baltic Sea, a tiny speck in the vast ocean."

"Eva, we are in this together with God. He loves our sweet Kaley."

"I know, but Shaw said Kaley being in a lifeboat complicates search efforts."

Eva clenched her fists, steeling herself for another blow. Scott looked deeply into her eyes. "First, we trust her safety to God. Anger and frustration won't help Kaley. Besides, Andy and Dutch need us to remain strong."

Eva melted into his tender hug. Scott was a complete rock in times of trouble. It must be his military training. Where was Eva's own law enforcement training when she needed it? Her family being threatened was different. She never became emotional during her cases.

"As Kaley's mom, I won't sit back and let my daughter become a pawn in Russia's quest for world domination."

"And as her dad, I won't either."

Eva straightened her spine. "What if you call SecDef?"

She gazed into Scott's hazel eyes, daring him to refuse.

"I already did. SecDef's in China. Don't we have a more important advocate on our side? 'No eye has seen, no ear has heard'—"

"'No mind has conceived what God has prepared for those who love him,'" Eva said, finishing the verse in Corinthians.

"Exactly."

She pressed her lips in a fine line. This was time for faith and not defeatism. She lifted his hand to her cheek. "What would I do without you, sweetheart? You make coffee. I'm calling Julia."

With Scott talking to someone in the background—their sons must have woken up—Eva stepped into the den. She shut the door, her voice trembling as she told Julia the worst.

"Our daughters and the Sikorskis escaped in a lifeboat. The Pentagon's aware of it. Russian frigates challenged the ferry and are taking it to Kaliningrad."

"God help our daughters!" Julia cried with force.

"That is our fervent prayer. Have you heard from Bo?"

"I never heard it ring. He left a message saying not to worry, all would be well. Not worry? How can he think that? I'm beside myself with worry ..."

Julia's voice trailed away, and she blew her nose.

"We have to trust, Julia!" Eva repeated the verse she and Scott just shared.

They promised to stay in touch, and Eva hastened to the kitchen where Scott looked totally lost.

"Viola is flying in from Texas tomorrow for an interview at Ryan-Gauge Hospital as head of pediatrics. She's planning on staying with us."

Eva exhaled. "Yikes, I forgot about your sister coming."

They stared at each other in desperation until his cell phone rang.

"Yes, this is Scott Montanna," he said, listening to whoever was calling. When he hung up, he drew her into his arms. "Commander Marks wants us at the Pentagon in the morning, once we drop the boys off at school."

Eva leaned against his chest and wept. The most precious part of life was her family. Here she was unable to respond when action was needed.

"There's only one thing to do," Scott said, lightly touching her cheek.

The look they shared was loving and deep. He took her by the hand, and for a good hour, they knelt at their bedside beseeching God to protect their Kaley and her friends.

Chapter 14

The Pentagon

Hope ignited as Eva stepped with Scott through the Pentagon's main entrance. It was still difficult for her to enter the mammoth building. Her arms bristled. Her twin sister and feisty JAG lawyer had died here on September 11th , the awful day when terrorists crashed a passenger jet into the epicenter of America's military might.

Yet dark memories had no place in Eva's mind on this morning, not when she and Scott were here to save their daughter. She'd have time to remember wonderful Jillie.

Scott approached the guard station where he produced his credentials.

"You tired of Capitol Hill yet?" asked the security officer, his eyes roving to Scott's official identification.

Scott pocketed his ID. "If you only knew. Is your son still at Davis-Monthan Air Force Base?"

"He's at Spangdahlem Air Base in Germany. You know he's flying the A-10."

"That's right." Scott introduced him, telling Eva, "Kent's son flies the nasty old Warthog. They're a scary-mean fighting machine."

"Thanks for your son's service." Eva handed the officer her ID with a lackluster smile. She was impatient to confer with Commander Marks, though she understood Scott's need to reconnect.

Kent gave a cursory glance at her creds. "Go through. Commander Marks already put your names in the computer." He pointed. "His aide's waiting for you over there."

They followed the young aide down a long, gray corridor to the communications center. Eva snuck a look at Scott. His flexing jaw muscle telegraphed he, too, anticipated what would occur behind the double-glass doors up ahead. They breezed into the com center, where Marks looked imposing at the head of a polished conference table.

Several more aides were busy at laptop computers, listening through headsets. A giant TV was displayed at the table's far end, with a smaller one to its left. They all shook hands, their faces grim.

"Have a seat," Marks directed. "We're following the news feed."

A breaking news banner flashed across the small TV. Marks boosted the volume with a remote. Eva leaned in, her heart in her throat.

The reporter announced excitedly, "Our camera crew is flying above the Polish ferry. The Russian captors on the *Ceba* ferry appear to have discovered a missing lifeboat floating ten miles away. The empty hoist is dangling over the ferry's side. Our crew confirms the lifeboat was gone when they arrived on scene an hour ago."

"The Russian frigates discovered the lifeboat," Eva hissed. "Where is Kaley?"

No one answered her question. Scott's eyes stayed glued to the large screen. Eva turned her head and saw the ferry wedged in between two Russian ships, one blazing ahead, the other following. Narrowing her eyes to see better, there in the distance, she spied a small lifeboat lurching up and down in the water.

Frustration mounted. Eva had no radar vision like Superman; she could see no one on the tiny boat. The station switched screens.

Andrew Borsch, the European correspondent, said, "The lead Russian frigate is dead in the water. Now it's lowering an armed Mongoose patrol boat over the side."

Eva's hands flew to her face. "Scott, they're going after Kaley's lifeboat!"

"I feel so helpless," he said, his voice filled with emotion.

Borsch continued giving a play-by-play of all Eva and Scott were seeing. It seemed surreal and unbelievable. Eva clutched at her husband's hand.

"The tiny lifeboat and its four passengers escaped the ferry," Borsch said. "It is unfortunate they are being targeted by a powerful Russian frigate."

Eva watched her daughter's possible seizure by Russia unfold before her eyes. Her pulse boomed in her ears like thunder.

Borsch's voice rose with anxiety. "Will the armed boat snatch them from the sea? That's the question we want answered. Oh no, the Mongoose is heading full steam in their direction."

Eva chewed her fingernails, all while praying, *Save her, Jesus. Save Kaley.*

Scott grabbed her hand, squeezing so tightly she felt pain.

Marks reached over and patted her forearm. "Steady on. We've dispatched aircraft to the scene. They'll arrive soon."

"Amen to that!" Eva replied, gripping Scott's hand.

Scott bobbed his head while Borsch talked over the noise

from his feed. "The Russian frigate ordered our helicopter away. They're threatening to fire on our reporters, claiming we're in a combat zone."

"A combat zone!" Eva wailed.

The helicopter with the filming crew banked violently. The screen went dark in the com center. Scott's face turned chalk white. Eva's tongue stuck to the roof of her dry mouth. Sweat poured down her armpits.

"God, please help us!" she cried, knowing nothing was impossible for God.

Commander Marks swiveled in his chair and listened to an aide whispering in his ear. Meanwhile, Borsch scowled at the TV audience from his comfy studio chair.

"Our team was forced to turn back. The Russians are pursuing the four helpless passengers who escaped in a lifeboat."

Eva covered her mouth with both hands. She and Scott traded panic-filled looks. A technician at a corner table held a finger in the air and nodded at the commander.

"Go ahead and put it up," Marks ordered.

The technician snapped off the news feed to Eva's objection, "Wait. They'll have more news."

The commander flipped a switch. The much bigger screen began to glow. His voice even and his eyes darting from Eva to Scott, he explained, "Because of Russia's aggressive behavior in the region, we recently assigned a wing of A-10 Warthogs to the area. These planes are tank killers and superb for close ground support. They're feared for the 30-millimeter cannon in its nose."

He motioned to the technician, telling her, "Go live."

The large screen sprang alive with dramatic colors. Eva swallowed, clinging to hope. It showed the same sparkling Baltic Sea, the same hostile Russian frigates.

Commander Marks faced Eva and Scott before his eyes veered to the large screen. "These images are fed real time from our surveillance platform over the Russian frigate. Watch the side of the screen, and be amazed by what we do."

He pointed. Eva's eyes were riveted. The A-10 streaked low to the water. The super-fast Warthog passed in front of the frigate's Mongoose.

Eva called out, "The jet's climbing in the sky. Oh no, the Mongoose is still racing toward the lifeboat."

"Turn back!" Scott yelled, raising his clenched fists.

The loud squelch of radio traffic filled the room. The pilot could be heard: "Request permission to engage."

Marks spoke with confidence. "The commander of the Warthogs knows Americans are on the lifeboat and the ferry. He's well aware one is your daughter, Scott."

His comment covered up more chatter. All Eva heard was the pilot's answer, "Copy. Cleared to engage."

She grabbed Scott's hand again. They watched, spellbound.

The Warthog dove with tremendous speed toward the Russian patrol boat. Smoke belched from the nose of the jet. A straight white line of water splashed in front of the Mongoose as thirty-millimeter rounds struck the water mere yards from the bow.

Straightaway, the Mongoose began turning in a wide arc. The patrol boat zoomed back toward the mother frigate like a bear cub would to its mother.

"Yeah!" Eva screamed. "They're turning back."

Scott pumped his fists in the air. Their joy was doused by Commander Marks' cautioning, "They aren't done yet."

The surveillance camera switched to a wider angle. A second Warthog sprayed a line of cannon fire near the frigate's bow. Russian sailors were seen running along the deck of the frigate waiting to retrieve its launch.

A third A-10 came into view, streaking across the bow of the frigate and firing across the bridge where the ship's commander would sit. Behind the Polish ferry, a fourth Warthog sprayed its smoking rounds across the bow of the Russian ship that trailed the captured ferry.

Marks pointed to the screen. "In our ops center here, command officials are supervising this action in the Baltic. Their screen is like the one we're watching. Believe me, they're all over this. We're ready to risk war over captured Americans."

"Tell me Russia won't get away with hijacking my daughter's ferry," Scott growled.

"Let's see what happens." Marks folded his arms to watch.

Eva knew enough about her husband's courage as a former fighter pilot to know he'd take those Russian commandos out with his bare hands if he could. She sucked in a deep breath, her thoughts awash with visions of her precious daughter adrift in a war zone. She glared at the screen, willing the evil guys to be beaten, praying they would leave Kaley alone.

Eva made herself watch: The lead Russian frigate turned ninety degrees and headed the other way—toward Russia. The trailing frigate copied the turn.

"They're abandoning the operation," Marks quipped, his intense tone giving away his anxiety over the outcome.

"Hallelujah!" Adrenaline shot through Eva's veins. Now Kaley had to be rescued from the drifting lifeboat.

"Yes. Yes," Scott echoed. "Russian sailors won't mess with our Warthogs."

"They'll stop long enough to retrieve their launch," Marks observed.

The surveillance camera panned over the sea until it stopped near the lifeboat.

"There's a helicopter!" Eva exclaimed, her heart pumping furiously. "They're being rescued."

"It's from Sweden," Scott said, wiping his brow.

The Swedish Coast Guard helicopter hovered above the rolling lifeboat, a coastguardsman being lowered on a tether. Four A-10 Warthogs flew in a circular pattern around the ferry for protection. Russian commandos aboard the ferry lowered themselves over the side in lifeboats. Without warning, the volume erupted on the small TV monitor.

Borsch began talking excitedly, "Our news chopper is again flying over the *Ceba.* We're witnessing an incredible international scuffle. The Russians surely wanted to capture those in the lifeboat. While off-air, American fighter jets fired on the Russian frigates, forcing their retreat. Already a Swedish Coast Guard chopper is plucking four passengers from the Polish lifeboat."

The news camera focused on highly-intimidating Warthogs swooping around Russian frigates like swallows chasing mosquitoes. Commander Marks snapped his fingers and pointed to the TV. Eva gaped at the large Swedish helicopter hovering over the lifeboat. The camera telescoped to the passengers.

Eva applauded. "I see Kaley! There she is!"

Her daughter clung to the swimmer, the hoist lifting them both to the enormous chopper.

"She's safe …"

Tears overflowed Eva's eyes. Her knees turned to rubber.

Scott whispered, "Now they need to save the others."

They clasped hands while Borsch reported, "The Swedes must work quickly to retrieve the remaining survivors. The Warthogs can't stay in the air forever. They need fuel in reserve to reach their base."

"No problem," Marks interrupted. "Our tankers are nearby to refuel them."

Borsch continued, "The fourth passenger, a man, is being lifted into the chopper. We expect a hasty retreat."

Thanksgiving swelled within Eva's heart. What a difference

the last five minutes would make to the rest of her life, their lives. She watched in awe as the Swedish helicopter banked away, Kaley and her friends on board. It flew over the ferry. Former hostages on its upper deck erupted in cheers and waves at their former shipmates.

Com center technicians stood to their feet and began applauding. Commander Marks walked over and shook Scott's hand, and then Eva's.

"Good people, today we won one for liberty."

"Yes, sir. Thank you," Eva said with humble gratitude. "Where are they taking our daughter?"

Scott swiped at his chin. "Will they go to the Swedish naval base?"

"It's all arranged to bring her and the three escapees to Ramstein Base in Germany for medical treatment. State Department is sending a plane to bring your two girls home. Different arrangements are being made for other American hostages."

"Thanks be to God." Eva wiped her eyes, realizing the curse of the Pentagon was wiped forever from her mind.

Scott threw his arms around her. Heart to heart, they held each other close.

AFTER TRADING HIGH-FIVES WITH SCOTT, Commander Marks escorted him and Eva back to the Pentagon entrance. Eva wanted to call her folks with the good news right away. When she powered on her phone, the commander pulled Scott aside.

"I hate to warn you, but your reserve of goodwill is depleted here at the Pentagon."

The former DOD press secretary stepped back, stunned. "Have I done something wrong? I'd never want to do that."

Marks waved a roughened hand dismissively. "It's not you, Scott. I shouldn't tell you, and I'll deny I did. We were stoked to do what we could for the American kids aboard the hijacked ferry. The White House refused. Didn't want to escalate tensions, claiming it was a Polish-Russian problem."

"You mean they would let our kids suffer at the hands of Russian soldiers? What were they thinking?" Scott scoffed.

"No amount of reasoning would turn them. Directors at CIA and ICE insisted the military do something. Still the Administration balked."

"How'd you finally get clearance to move assets into the area?" Scott asked, hardly believing what he was hearing.

"Thank your boss, buddy. I'm told your Mr. Speaker phoned Mr. President, demanding these kids be rescued." Marks paused to let out a snort. "Then Mr. Speaker told Mr. President that if our military did not get involved, he'd remove all funds for Air Force One in next year's defense budget. He said he hoped Mr. President liked flying about in a World War II DC-3."

Scott laughed heartily along with Marks, but something didn't feel right about the behind-the-scenes power play.

Commander Marks lowered his voice to a bare whisper. "The White House thought for a while they had dodged a bullet."

"How's that?" Scott looked over at Eva, who was still talking to her folks.

"After the Warthogs were en route," Marks said, "Mr. President's lackeys discovered Kaley and the CIA agent's daughter escaped in a lifeboat. They requested the military stand down, hoping to negotiate release for the balance of the American kids."

Scott balled his fists. "You've got to be kidding."

"Nope." Marks shook his head. "Not until the Russkies put a Mongoose over the side to go after Kaley did those suits in the White House agree we should act. Even then, I'm told White House aides nearly had heart attacks."

"Sir, I'm speechless."

Marks extended a firm hand. "Scott, you know it's a circus in D.C. I'll advise when your daughter will arrive at Andrews."

Scott looked Marks square in the eye. "You guys are the best. Thank everyone for us."

He walked over to Eva, trying to shake the gritty details from his mind. Kaley's life had hung in the balance and his government was more than willing to sit on their hands. How could Scott ever tell Eva? Simple, he wouldn't.

Chapter 15

Northern Virginia

A few days later, an upbeat Eva rode with Scott in their minivan heading for Andrews Air Force Base. His eyes gazed in the rearview mirror at Bo and Julia Rider, who were ensconced in the second row of seats. The couples had taken the day off to retrieve Kaley and Glenna, who were returning from their ill-fated school trip. The four were casually dressed and in high spirits.

Her husband's splendid smile behind the wheel gave Eva pure joy. She was content to let him and Bo relive their daughters' dramatic liberation.

Scott exited the highway, telling Bo excitedly, "You wouldn't believe those Warthogs. Those courageous pilots deserve medals for rescuing our daughters."

"Your prior Pentagon service saved the day," Bo said in respectful tones. "I saw reruns of the Warthogs shooting at the Russians. Your friends at DOD made the impossible happen."

"The Agency would have done the same for you, Bo." Scott glanced in the mirror.

"It must have been incredible seeing the battle and rescue unfolding before your eyes."

"Right," Scott replied. "Commander Marks told us the A-10s had scrambled. He feared they wouldn't be there in time. The Swedish chopper was on standby to rescue the girls, but ordered to stand down until the Russian Mongoose could be neutralized."

Bo leaned forward. "So that's how the coast guard chopper got there so quickly."

"We thank God most of all," Eva told them.

Scott approached the Andrews gate with Eva explaining the girls were taken to Ramstein because DOD wasn't sure if they were injured or sick from their escape.

"And we're glad they are all right, except for mild dehydration," she said.

The sign announced they had reached Joint Base Andrews, prompting Bo to say, "I thought Andrews was an Air Force base."

Scott's eyes shifted again to the mirror. "It was, until it combined with the Naval Air Station. Now it's known as Joint Base Andrews."

Eva found herself reminiscing upon returning to Andrews. It was here that she'd been involved in a high-stakes swap of a

Chinese criminal for an American hero. That particular story belonged to her past. Eva turned her mind with great anticipation to the future, and God's plans for her family.

For one thing, Kaley should be arriving within the next hour.

Eva saw Scott hand his driver's license to a young airman dressed in a blue uniform, and telling him, "We're here to pick up our daughters from a medivac flight."

"Yes, sir."

The airman stepped in the guard shack momentarily before returning Scott's license with an exaggerated salute. The barricade lifted, and they drove through.

"Since the girls didn't need their return tickets, do you think we can get refunds from the airline?" Julia wondered aloud.

"Yeah, maybe the Air Force will charge us for flying them to Andrews. We'll need the money," Bo quipped.

Light laughter rippled through the van. Eva cherished sounds of happiness.

"Do you see what I see?"

Eva whirled her head to see what Julia was looking at. A humongous airplane was taxiing to a stop in front of a hangar.

"Feast your eyes on a giant C-17 Globemaster," Scott said, his voice edged with pride. "I suspect it's our girls' flight. They must have had a tailwind."

"Wow," Julia chimed.

Eva couldn't agree more. "Wow indeed."

Scott snugged the van into a spot near the hangar and parked. They all piled out. Eva watched him take long strides to an office where he chatted with uniformed personnel. He hurried out smiling.

"Yup, they're on the Globemaster. We can wait on the tarmac."

The behemoth aircraft dwarfed Eva. As the plane's door opened and the steps lowered to the ground, excitement climbed within her.

"Kaley will step off the plane and be back into our lives. All our prayers for her safety were answered," she whispered to Scott.

He looped a strong arm around her shoulders. "Eva, I'm so happy I could burst."

A military bus pulled up slowly behind the aircraft's tail. An oversized ramp began descending from its rear. Without fanfare, Kaley and Glenna rushed down the steps and sped to their parents.

Eva hugged Kaley tightly as did Scott. Pure elation watered

her thirsty soul.

"Sweetie, you look marvelous," Eva told Kaley. "More grown-up, I think."

"I feel like I've been gone a year."

"Kaley, where's your suitcase?"

Her daughter stepped back. "Really, Mom? It's on the ferry boat."

"Of course. How could I forget?"

Eva's mind was so absorbed in the here and now. All she wanted was to put behind her the intense struggle of the past few days. She and Kaley could talk later about what she'd endured. This wasn't the time.

Glenna finished her hugs and grabbed Kaley's hand. "Quick. Let's go."

The teens ran back to the lowered ramp. Several airmen and women were carrying litters bearing wounded soldiers, and taking them to other medics who received them into the open rear door of the bus. A pert blonde with collar-length hair joined the teens. Each girl took turns standing with the young woman, while the other snapped pictures with their phones. Hugs were shared.

Kaley and Glenna rejoined their parents with sober faces.

"My new career goal is to be a flight nurse," Kaley announced. "That was Captain Morgan. She's flown all over the world."

"Me too," Glenna said.

They sprinted to the van where the mothers pulled rank. Julia and Glenna climbed in the far third seat with Eva and Kaley snagging the middle seat. Bo went up front with Scott. Glenna and Kaley filled the drive home with tales of flight nurses and doctors helping wounded soldiers.

"The litters were stacked three high and anchored to the steel floor of the plane," Glenna said loudly to be heard above road noise.

Kaley's sigh trembled. "We sat on canvas seats lining both sides of the plane. They were pretty uncomfortable. It was hard to be surrounded by the hurting soldiers."

"It was," Glenna echoed. "The crew slept on the floor, so we tried it after a flight nurse gave us sleeping bags. The steel was so hard and cold, we couldn't stand it."

Scott looked into his mirror asking, "So your flight was a bad experience?"

"Oh no," they both yelled back.

"We saw things you'd never hear about in school or a career fair," Kaley chirped. "We can't wait to tell the class."

Eva touched her daughter's hand and held her peace. She knew that while Kaley's cheery attitude seemed a bit forced, she wouldn't delve into her daughter's emotions. Not until Kaley slept in her own bed, ate her own food, and laughed with her brothers.

EVA LET KALEY SLEEP FOR NEARLY TWELVE HOURS. She quietly opened her bedroom door every few hours, checking to be sure all was well. Kaley awoke with dark circles beneath her eyes. She ate an entire cheese and pepperoni pizza to Andy's incessant puns.

"Which tree has the loudest bark?"

"Dogwood," Scott answered.

"Da-ad, let Kaley guess."

Scott made a funny face, and they all laughed.

"Kaley, this one's for you. What music is played in the solar system?"

She drank her iced apple juice. So did Dutch, making slurping noises through a straw.

"Um ... my brain hasn't woken up yet. Let me guess. Starlight?"

Andy shook his head.

"By the light of the silvery moon?" Kaley tried again. "That's a song, right?"

She looked at Eva, who jokingly said, "That was way before my time, kiddo."

"I give up." Kaley took a few carrot sticks from a veggie tray Eva had set out.

"Want the answer?"

Everyone nodded.

Andy beamed. "Neptunes."

"Oh," Scott groaned. "You are one clever boy."

Kaley spent the evening racing cars on the den floor with her brothers. Eva and Scott sat on the couch watching and laughing. Eva never wanted to let her children out of her sight again.

The entire next week turned out to be a roller-coaster ride for Eva and family. Kaley's class received national attention since the students were taken hostage on the ferry. The media tried every tricky means to interview the students. Ever the suspicious parents, the Montannas and Riders refused to allow their daughters to be featured.

Eva delivered a letter to school officials denying permission for any reporters to come near Kaley, wanting to ensure nobody knew her daughter had escaped in the lifeboat. The other students didn't want to talk about it either, so by Saturday the crush of media attention had ceased.

In her kitchen, Eva hummed a praise tune in the kitchen while her hands sliced lemons for pitchers of lemonade, shaped ground beef into patties, rinsed lettuce, and tossed mozzarella cheese into the pasta salad. Her eyes kept watch on the clock.

A final stir to a pot of home-cooked baked beans with lots of bacon, per Scott's request, convinced Eva all was ready. Guests would arrive in about twenty minutes. She washed her hands, appreciating how smoothly everything was coming together for Kaley and Glenna's homecoming party.

Her daughter waltzed in the kitchen, looking relaxed in jeans and a T-shirt from Poland. She snagged a braided pretzel from a purple bowl.

"Can I help, Mom?"

"Make sure Dad's got enough chairs set out." Eva gestured out the large window over the sink, which gave her a superb backyard view. "See, he's tossing the volleyball with Dutch and Andy."

Kaley crunched the pretzel and threaded an arm through her mother's.

"To stand here by you watching Dad and the boys kick around on the sandy volleyball court is sweet. There were times when I doubted …" Kaley choked back tears. "Um, when I thought God abandoned me."

Eva hugged her daughter while she wept on her shoulder. This was Kaley's first sign of real emotion since she'd stepped off the plane at Andrews. Eva forced herself to stay calm. She, too, had such thoughts during Kaley's ordeal. Should she admit these?

She led her sniffling daughter to a chair at the kitchen table and sat beside her. Certain the truth would bind them close together, Eva chose her words with care.

"I want to tell you something from my heart. You are mature enough to understand. When I saw your lifeboat on TV, crashing against waves and a Russian Mongoose bearing down on you, I felt helpless. I've never been so scared in all my life because I could do nothing."

"Why did it happen, Mom? That's what I want to know."

Eva dashed away her tears. She formed her lips into a tight smile. "I said I could do nothing, but that isn't true. Your dad and I and your brothers prayed without ceasing. Glenna's parents also prayed, as did Griff, your grandparents, and many in the church. "

Kaley jumped to her feet to grab a tissue from a box on the

counter. She blew her nose before tossing the waddled tissue in the garbage can. Walking to the slider doors leading to the patio, she looked outside. Her voice grew hushed.

"Mr. S told us to pray many times. If I had been on the ferry without his guiding hand, I don't know what I would have done. Maybe died of heart failure with the Russians seizing us in the middle of the sea."

"God knew ahead of time which family to place you with, Kaley. I hope to meet him and his family someday. The Lord's eyes were upon you the entire time. You are His daughter and He will never leave you alone."

"Mom, I've read Bible verses about that." Kaley's bottom lip trembled. "Now I know His care is for real and I will never forget. At least I hope I won't."

"And I have learned no matter what trials come, our faith in God must not waver, but become stronger. We praise Him for performing a miracle right in front of our eyes."

The ringing doorbell caught them both off guard. Kaley jerked her hand away, and Eva whirled toward the front door issuing orders.

"Set flowers on the side table outside. I'll see who arrived first."

"Glenna, I think," Kaley guessed, picking up the flower vase with both hands.

Eva scurried to the door saying, "Maybe Griff. He is always early."

They were both wrong.

Chapter 16

Standing before Eva was a tall lady with a swath of flowers cradled in her arm. Her fingers clutched handles of several fabric bags.

Eva kissed her cheek. "Viola, welcome to our home. Is your hotel okay?"

"Couldn't be more convenient," she replied warmly. "It's next to the hospital. Sorry I didn't get here before this. I wouldn't miss celebrating my niece's safe return. Did my big brother tell you I called?"

"Scott said you were busy last week with the hospital board, medical director, and so on."

Viola peered over Eva's shoulder. "Where is everyone? These yellow roses are for Kaley. I want some face time with her before she's distracted by her friends. These are for her too," she lifted her bags, "and for my nephews."

"Your presence adds to our festivities. Scott's in the yard with the kids harking back to his youth."

Eva moved aside, letting Viola sweep in with her packages. "Have you decided to move here and take the job?"

"That's my surprise!"

The way Viola beamed, it was as if the sun shone in Eva's front hallway. "You're looking at the head of pediatrics for Ryan-Gauge Hospital in Georgetown."

Eva clapped with delight. She bundled the flowers into her arms and brought her sister-in-law outside. Scott gave his younger sister a hug. The kids squealed, ripping into the bags of goodies. Eva hurried inside to greet Griff and his wife Dawn when Ms. Yost arrived with several students from the Poland trip.

Being her competent self, the teacher pulled Eva aside saying, "It is nice of you to have us over. Sorry every student traveler couldn't come. We are glad to be home."

"Yeah," a student named Chelsea said. "I never was so scared in my whole life."

"At least the soldiers kept us all together ... well, not your daughter or Glenna," the teacher replied. "I guess they went off by themselves."

Chelsea curled her lip. "You think so, Ms. Yost. I wish I could have been with Kaley. The soldiers were rude, demanding our passports. They copied down our personal information. Why did they do it, anyway?"

Ms. Yost effused, "I worried when the girls and Mr. Sikorski couldn't be found."

The rumble of a Harley Davidson rocked the house, and Eva knew her newest partner, Brett Calloway, had arrived on his motorcycle. She excused herself from Ms. Yost. Soon every guest was present except for one. Well, two.

Austin had declined Kaley's invitation. His father was taking him to Disney World, and then on to Miami. Julia approached Eva on the deck with her lips pulled down in the corners.

"Bo sends regrets," she whispered. "He stayed home for one night after Glenna landed, then left again. Something about saber rattling. He took his sword and is off to slay dragons again."

"Is he in China?" Eva asked, keeping her voice low.

Julia shook her head. "I should say he's in the forest slaying a bear."

"Oh!"

Eva understood Bo was somewhere in Russia. She drew Julia into the kitchen, where she felt at liberty to say, "Russia's quest for power placed our daughters at great risk. Your husband has more courage than anyone I know. We wish him Godspeed."

"You are a true friend through the deepest valleys." Julie sighed, looking tired.

"Today, Julia, we celebrate our daughters' lives. Wherever Bo is, he is rejoicing that Glenna and Kaley are home. Will you help me make the rounds tallying who wants burgers or brats?"

"Of course." Julia bit her lower lip. "Eva, I won't forget you arranging this party. I couldn't have done it, not with the twins getting feverish a few days ago. Look at them now, diving in the sand for the ball."

Julia hummed merrily as she went outside to take meat orders. A little later, Scott brought Brett Calloway over to where Eva and Viola were setting out plates.

"Viola, meet Brett Calloway, the latest addition to Eva's task force. He's on loan from the DEA."

Scott nodded to Viola, telling Brett she was his younger sister. "We celebrate too because Dr. Viola Joy Montanna has just accepted a position here in D.C."

Brett extended his hand. "Happy to meet you, Viola."

"Likewise, Brett."

"My grill is calling if we want to eat before sundown."

Scott dashed off, leaving Eva to help them get acquainted. Brett suggested Viola call him Monk. "It's my nickname for years. I sometimes use it when working undercover."

"Monk?" Viola lifted her head and peered down her sculpted nose. "Let me guess. You attended Catholic schools where you excelled in Latin."

"Not even close. I'm not big on religion, and I didn't excel at much in school."

"I suspect you excel at your work."

"He's a great addition to our team," Eva interjected with feeling. "He's been here about two months."

Brett nodded, seeming to study Viola's face. "Viola Joy suggests a spiritual attribute. Did you attend religious schools?"

"No. You're right, though. Joy is one fruit of the Holy Spirit. I hope my love of God leaves me joyful."

"So you are a doctor," Brett replied coolly. "Are you a psychiatrist? Should I be on guard when we talk so you can't detect my psychosis?"

Viola trilled a laugh. "I'm a pediatrician. However, you should know even a kids' doctor can detect that a man who calls himself Monk has a psychosis."

"Do I presume too much in thinking you play the viola, Viola?"

"It's too much to assume that I'll share my secrets before drinking a glass of lemonade." Viola's brown eyes began to twinkle.

Eva motioned to Kaley, who was circling the yard with a tray of cold beverages. Kaley came over, and Viola chose lemonade and Brett sweet tea.

"Monk, can I phone you when I'm stuck waiting on the DEA's 800 line?"

"I get it." Brett sipped his iced tea. "You're talking about the DEA's regulatory side. You have a physician's DEA number for prescribing controlled substances, right?"

Viola smiled at Eva. "You work with a real DEA agent. I only get put on hold."

"Yeah, well, I have no contact with those suits," Brett said, stiffening. "They're neat and clean professional types. I work with the criminal underworld. Ask Eva."

"I'm curious how you came by a name like Monk," Viola probed.

"Sounds corny, but in grade school my mom packed a banana in my lunch each day. Friends started calling me monkey. Eventually it got shortened."

Viola raised her glass as if toasting. "So you've chosen to keep the name the kids gave you?"

"You are trying to psychoanalyze me."

With that, Brett stalked over to Scott by the grill.

Viola's face tensed. "Did I say something wrong?"

"I'm not sure." Eva shifted her gaze over to Brett and back to Viola. "He and I aren't well acquainted. He shot an assailant who threatened one of our witnesses and has since been cleared of any wrongdoing."

"Do you suppose the shooting has had a lasting effect on him?"

Eva swallowed, feeling thirsty herself. She wasn't up for where this conversation was headed.

"I'm not able to judge him, though it sounds like Brett has a point. You are trying to psychoanalyze him. Viola, do you do that often?"

The doctor smiled broadly. "Only with good-looking single ones. I assume he's single? I didn't spot a ring."

"He had a tragedy involving his wife."

"What happened?"

"Burgers are done," Scott yelled, interrupting their talk.

"I need to bring out the salads. Let me ask you this." Eva touched Viola's arm. "Are you ready for a relationship? You and Paul were close."

Viola sagged like a popped balloon before Eva's eyes. "His death just days before our wedding devastated me. Next month will be two years. That's one reason I'm moving to Virginia, to be near my family."

"I understand you want to make a new start," Eva said.

"Being here with you and Scott is part of my new path." Viola lifted her pretty chin. "Whether it includes a husband or not."

"We're here to launch you on your way. Help me set out the food?"

She agreed, and minutes later, Scott wielded his tongs on the brats, flipping burgers until two platters were heaped high. Eva piled her plate with salad, topping it off with a juicy burger minus the bun. She'd never shed the five pounds she needed to lose before her physical next month if she kept eating this way.

Scott slathered his burger with pickles, ketchup, and onions. Eva asked him quietly to bring Brett over before she took a seat next to Viola. Instead, Scott and Brett continued talking by the grill so Eva poured her energy into her sister-in-law. Before long, she learned Viola also loved America's patriots and heroes, and so she had found a new friend to visit D.C.'s endless historical venues.

Ms. Yost walked up with a sour expression. "Tell Kaley to clear her term paper with me. She wants to write on Russian power in the world, but after everything that happened, how can she be objective?"

The teacher's caustic attitude surprised Eva, and it took her a moment to respond. Although she tried sounding reasonable, her voice held an icy edge.

"What is the risk if Kaley isn't objective? I mean, Russian apologists circle the globe. Must my daughter be one of them?"

"Mrs. Montanna, I want my students to express their own view of the world, and not just espouse their parents' opinions."

"No worry. After what your trip has taught Kaley about Russia, I could never convince her otherwise."

"I see where she gets her stubbornness," Ms. Yost replied.

With a shrug, she left the party as did the other students, except for Glenna. Eva shook off her irritation and with a flourish brought out apple pie and caramel ice cream, Kaley's favorite. The remaining guests were eating their dessert when Eva noticed Brett angling toward the sliding doors. She quickly rose from her seat to intercept him.

"How is your Ponzi case?" she asked wondering if Holly Munoz would be convicted.

He leaned his solid shoulder against the door frame. "O'Rourke nailed the prosecution's case, portraying Holly and Carlos as the lowlifes they are. Defense counsel will try humanizing them as naïve investors. I guess I have to trust the jury will see through their pack of lies."

Eva clasped her hands together. "I'd like to be there when the verdict comes in. Will you keep me posted?"

"It won't be soon." Brett cast his eyes toward Viola, who slammed the volleyball across the net to Kaley. "Scott's sister is athletic, more than I'd expect from a doctor."

Rather than say, *Now who's psychoanalyzing*, Eva grinned at the brawny DEA agent. "You two have more in common than you think."

"Oh? She likes riding Harleys?" Brett sounded interested.

"You could find out for yourself." Eva dropped her hands to her sides. "Listen, Griff and I are thrilled you've joined the team. With your undercover experience, we can't wait for the Munoz trial to end."

Brett tossed a lingering look at Viola playing volleyball and left, his Harley stirring the neighborhood with sound. Eva could only imagine what her neighbor Fred was thinking. She stacked the unused napkins, realizing she'd better tell Brett soon about Holly's offer to cooperate.

First came D-Day. Tomorrow she and Griff would gauge the FBI's reaction to their proposal. If they lost that battle, she'd never inform Brett, aka Monk, of anything. To squeals of laughter, Eva dropped the napkins and ran to the volleyball court. It was about time she cut loose and had some fun.

Chapter 17

With paltry sleep the night before, Eva needed an extra jolt of energy for her morning drive to FBI Headquarters. She poured super-strong java into a travel mug and hit the road at six thirty. The freeway was already snarled with heavy traffic. That meant she might be late for their eight a.m. meeting. She jerked along bumper-to-bumper until making the final turn onto Pennsylvania Avenue.

Could she make it in time? Only if she ran.

Eva parked her G-car at a nearby meter, a miracle in and of itself. Her heels pounded on the hard pavement, and rushing inside the Bureau, Eva hoped she hadn't let Griff down by her lateness. She fought for breath giving her ICE credentials to a strapping security guard.

"Can't let you pass, ma'am. You need an escort."

"An FBI agent is expecting me," she replied, furrowing her brow.

At the guard's anemic shrug and sweeping motion with open hands, Eva's eyes searched for Griff beyond the gauntlet, not seeing him. The FBI was unlike the federal court in Alexandria where the guards knew Eva's work as an ICE agent.

She sputtered a sigh. Wait for Griff she must.

Eva went outside to watch for him by the main entrance, pausing by an inspiring bronze statue of three FBI agents before a rippling flag, one with his hand over his heart. The fitting words *Fidelity, Bravery, and Integrity* etched on its front in gold letters captured the most loyal of men, her partner and FBI agent, Griff.

Where was he? Standing on her throbbing feet, Eva grew concerned. She strode back inside the mammoth building, certain their sting called "Operation Stogie" would be denied. They should have just accepted their JTTF supervisor's go-ahead. But then Eva realized—they needed higher approval to make a case involving Cuba, a government hostile to the U.S.

Eva sensed FBI Assistant Director Wayne Taggart wouldn't be an easy sell. If he said no, she had one more option. ICE could approve it as a cigar-smuggling case. The ten-year sentence and $250,000.00 fine would be good for her career; however, she wanted Griff as an FBI agent to have the lead. Ultimately, the FBI stood to nab terrorists or even spies, if they could be convinced.

She checked her watch again as men in pressed suits, crisp white shirts, and knotted ties streamed by, running ID badges over a scanner while security guards looked on. This was so like the Bureau, buttoned up and professional, whereas her boss, John Oliver, kept things informal for the agents. With his laid-back style, he rarely pried into their cases, which was fine with Eva.

She tugged on her suit jacket. Here in the J. Edgar Hoover superstructure, her black pantsuit seemed a bit tired. Before she could plan where to buy a new one, Griff breezed through the main entrance.

"Let's go!" he called to her.

He cleared the security desk in no time, and she went through as his guest. He hustled toward the elevator buttoning his suit jacket while walking. She widened her eyes at the rare sight of Griff in a tailored suit.

"Are you running for president?" she asked in jest.

He straightened his white shirt collar, edging closer. "Director Taggart is the General Patton of the Bureau."

"So he'll slap us down?"

"Probably. He won't like my being tardy. No parking as usual."

He sounded agitated and out of sorts. They rode the elevator to the executive suites with a bunch of men who had the look and smell of FBI agents. Eva didn't feel outnumbered, just thankful she didn't work in the stuffy Bureau. They stepped out to absolute quiet in the hall.

"Quick. Down here," Griff said, whisking her to a forbidding door.

It made no sound when he opened it. They encountered another male agent who sat ramrod straight in his navy blue suit behind a spacious desk. Griff introduced them, and the agent consulted a computer screen.

With a brisk nod, he ushered them into a cavernous office announcing, "Agent Griffin Topping and ICE Agent Eva Montanna to see you, sir."

Taggart never bothered turning from his keyboard at a long credenza by the window. Rather, he growled over his shoulder, "I understand you want to target Cuba and call your operation 'Stogie.' Relations with Cuba have thawed. Soon you'll buy the best Cuban cigars in vending machines. Your case is a year too late."

"But, sir," Griff began.

Taggart waved him off, still without turning. "Topping, I told the Task Force Review Committee I had zero interest in your op. Here you are anyway. You've got some gall. Get out now and it won't derail your career."

Eva's blood began to boil as she stood rooted to the floor. Beside her, Griff fidgeted with his tie in front of Taggart's desk. The man's rude treatment proved he was a mean bureaucrat and no General Patton, the commander of the Third Army, who fought his way across France during WWII. She was halfway through his biography and knew an imposter when she met one.

Though she wanted to erupt in indignation, Eva kept her mouth shut. This was Griff's turf. He needed to articulate their strategy. From the corner of her eye, she saw her partner fold his arms across his chest.

Battle lines were being drawn. Who would win?

Griff cleared his throat, saying with gusto, "Sir, Cuban cigars are not our focus. The guy uses cigars as cover to smuggle individuals with currency and foreign passports, including some Russian ones."

"What?" Taggart whirled his chair around in a flurry. "Why did no one tell me? Is that in your proposal?"

"Yes, sir."

"Topping, you'd better spit it out."

Griff stepped forward, and he filled in missing details. Eva wasted no time advocating an argument of her own.

"Director Taggart, we see it this way," she said, keeping it respectful. "The brothers who set off bombs during the Boston Marathon were Chechens. Chechnya is a Russian puppet state. Agent Topping and I are concerned terrorists are being funneled in through Cuba. And they could be Chechens."

"How do you know the passports are Russian?" Taggart demanded to know.

Griff stood his ground. "From our confidential informant. We propose Operation Stogie to learn the scheme's true nature. We believe we can co-opt the pilot who is smuggling these cigars and passengers."

Taggart's nod was sharp, decisive. But what did it mean? Eva flashed Griff an intense look. His face was a portrait in patience.

The director pulled a small recording device from a side drawer. He spoke into it so rapidly Eva barely made out what he said except she discerned his final words, "Agent Topping is to have total Bureau support."

Bzzz bzzz, Eva heard.

The same tall agent hurried in, apparently to Taggart pressing a buzzer on his intercom. Back erect like he had a steel rod in his spine, the agent took the small recorder from his boss without saying anything.

Taggart leapt to his feet. "That's it. My approval's on record. Happy hunting."

The tall agent, "Super Stretch" as Eva would call him later to Scott, led them out of the director's presence on rubber-soled shoes. In the reception area, he pointed to a register. Griff signed them out, noting the time. No words were exchanged.

Eva and Griff took the elevator down with a bevy of other suits whose lips were zipped shut. No banter over football games or boat rides on the Potomac. Total quiet reigned as they descended to ground level. Griff never looked her way, and they left FBI Headquarters in complete silence.

When they reached the sidewalk, Eva burst out laughing.

"What happened in there?"

Griff loosened his tie. "We're on. Operation Stogie is a go."

"That's it? Unbelievable," Eva said between fits of laughter. "Let's grab coffee and talk strategy."

BEFORE HEADING HOME, Eva conducted surveillance of the younger Chechen brother while Griff was watching the elder brother. Eva's target had overstayed his student visa and was suspected of recruiting terrorists.

In her G-car beside a busy car wash where brother number two worked, Eva watched him sponge off cars. She snapped his photo with a telephoto lens. Then she waited for something to happen. More dirty cars, more suds. But one never knew with surveillance.

She stayed on alert, the car radio on low until she heard a news update about Russia. Eva turned up the sound. Negotiations with international oil cartels to limit production had failed, so Russia increased production to force a drop in prices.

Would the powerful nation respond to its worsening of the world economy with more saber rattling?

A movement outside her windshield snapped Eva's mind back to her target. He hopped into a red truck, which should be easy to follow. She stayed behind at a safe distance, and when he went inside a fast-food joint, she ordered a burger in the drive-thru.

Her risky move could backfire. She once had to pull out of line after ordering to follow her suspect. She knew many customers must have gotten the wrong orders.

The pause in action gave her time to phone home, and she told Scott, "Eat without me. I'll be out awhile yet."

"I ordered two large pepperoni pizzas," he said, his voice filled with love.

Her mouth watered. "Scott, you'd better save me a piece."

She imagined his grin as he hung up. From there, Eva tailed the terror suspect to a ramshackle apartment where his female friend lived. For an hour her eyes stayed glued to his red truck. Nothing happened, so she gave up and headed home.

Turning onto her street, she saw an unknown Toyota parked one house away from hers. A man was slouched down in the driver's seat. Hadn't she just assumed the same slouch while watching the Chechen recruiter? Her sensors began pinging.

She drove around the block and came back past. The driver wasn't Hector Chavez, the OPM investigator. Could he be a different government employee working on a neighbor's security clearance? Eva knew something more sinister could be afoot and made a mental note to call her Mr. Fred.

The kitchen was already tidied up. An eerie quiet in the house troubled her spirit. Scott walked in, giving her a kiss, which made everything right again.

"I'm tweaking a press release," he said. "How did things go for you?"

She smoothed a strand of hair behind an ear. "Oh, the usual. Watching and not seeing much. Where are the kids?"

"Andy and Dutch are doing homework. Kaley's creating an album from her Polish trip. Honey, I need to finish my press release."

"Scott, did you see anyone unusual outside?"

"No." He rattled a sheet of paper and sped to their home office.

Eva found Kaley perched on the living room sofa concentrating on photos spread around her. "Has anyone been soliciting in the neighborhood tonight?"

"Soliciting? What do you mean?"

"You know, selling scout cookies, or collecting signatures for a petition?"

"Haven't seen anyone," Kaley replied, sorting pictures as if unfazed by the question. "Why?"

"I spotted a strange car in the neighborhood."

"You're home, Mom. You can turn off your felon finder."

Eva sighed. "Helping you may take my mind off suspicions."

Kaley slid over, and Eva nestled beside her, ignoring cable news. She and Scott kept it on mute in case of important news events. Mixed feelings cascaded through Eva as she picked up one of Kaley's printed captions.

"Adventure on the high seas is the bitter truth."

Kaley faced her with large and serious eyes. "Mom, being caught in a lifeboat with Russian troops storming aboard is etched in my mind forever."

"And I am forever grateful to God for saving you."

This is a dear moment with my daughter, Eva thought. She selected one photo, a shot from a news aircraft flying over the ferry while it was held by Russian military.

"You were floating in the lifeboat when this was taken." A lone tear stung Eva's eye, and she brushed it away, telling Kaley, "You are my hero."

Kaley's hand fluttered over her heart. "God gave me courage from somewhere inside that I never knew existed. Is it like that for you, Mom, as a federal agent?"

"Some days are terrifying. We never know what case we'll be called out for. We never know who is after us. That's why the unknown car made me suspicious."

Kaley waved a photo. "Sorry I brought up work. Let's finish my album."

"This is a fun picture of you with Izzy and Austin."

"Nah." Kaley tossed it on the floor with others she didn't intend to include.

"What's wrong with it?" Eva probed.

Kaley bent over to pick it back up. "Our tongues are sticking out."

"I see that, but why throw it out?"

"Mom! Twenty years from now I don't want my kids seeing me looking so weird in my scrapbook."

"Good for you."

Eva had often cautioned Kaley about such poses, but didn't think it sunk in. Here she was witnessing her daughter's maturity in deciding what was important to retain. Eva glimpsed a paper that had a stamp attached with a paper clip.

She raised the stamp, spotting an address. "What is this, Kaley?"

"Dad said I could write to one of the Warthog pilots who saved me. His father works at the Pentagon."

"Your dad and I talked to Kent the morning of your rescue."

"I'm going to thank his son for Glenna too," Kaley said nonchalantly.

Eva combed through a stack of pictures from Kaley's departure at Dulles. She pointed to one of Austin and his mom standing with Glenna and Julia, which Eva had taken with her phone.

Kaley lifted her pert chin. "Do I want Austin in my album?"

"He was an important part of the trip, wasn't he?"

"I don't know." Kaley tossed the picture on the floor with the rejects. "Since we've come back, one minute he's friendly and another he's aloof. I've moved on."

"You did?"

"Sure, the ROTC has all his attention. He's studying Russian military tactics and will attend West Point after graduation so he can stand against Russia."

"The hijacking impacted him as well," Eva said. "Don't make hasty decisions."

She reached down and snatched up Austin's picture. "Save this for later."

Then Eva's head swung toward the TV. She recognized the woman holding a microphone in front of the Pentagon. The reporter stared with such intensity into the camera that Eva felt compelled to turn on the sound.

"A shake-up is due any day," the reporter said. "Sources within the Department of Defense tell us Russia is advancing in hotspots around the world. Russia's military shadows our submarines, flies their bombers in U.S. airspace, and their high-altitude spy planes are flying surveillance over our cities. Their provocations come on the heels of Americans being plucked from the ferry in the Baltic."

"Scott, come in here," Eva yelled.

He strode swiftly in the room "What's wrong?"

"Kat Kowicki is back from Chicago and is live at the Pentagon."

They both listened to Kat sign off her report, "The Secretary of Defense has no comment. I guarantee I will keep digging for you."

The reporter's confident smile matched her gutsy tone. When the network broke for a commercial, Eva muted the TV, thinking about past run-ins with the aggressive Kat Kowicki.

She toyed with the remote, telling Scott, "Kat sinks her teeth into a story and never lets it go."

"I am surprised she hasn't contacted either of us yet," Scott said.

Kaley looked up from her album. "You both know her personally?"

"We do," Eva said. "Kat is tenacious. She's dug around and nearly compromised my important cases."

"What's wrong with that if she's doing her job?"

"Nothing is wrong per se. Sometimes we agents have

insufficient evidence for an arrest and keep plugging away. When reporters like Kat disclose our efforts to the entire nation, suspects often flee the country before we arrest them."

"She sounds dangerous, Mom. But she looks nice."

"Kaley, be careful of making wrong assumptions. She is a nice person. Still, your dad and I aren't free to talk to her about what we know."

Scott folded his arms, concern framing his eyes. "Good thing she hasn't been back long, or she'd want an exclusive interview with Kaley following her escape."

"Wait, I thought the media didn't know I was an escapee." Kaley sounded worried.

"They don't," Eva assured. "Still, Kat has an unbelievable knack for news."

Scott hurried away to finish his project. After a few more minutes of picture gathering, Eva patted Kaley's hand and joined Scott in their office. He was engrossed in the newspaper, and she crinkled the top edge to get his attention.

"You should call your replacement as DOD press secretary," she said.

A bemused look crossed his face. "Why?"

"Warn him of Kat's assertive ways. If you had his job, you'd want a heads-up."

He treated her to a chuckle. "Makes sense. Oh, and I put the mail on the kitchen counter."

Eva wandered to the kitchen and removed a letter opener from the junk drawer to open a newsy letter from her folks. Her heart soared. They were moving back to Virginia after their travels abroad. But her heart beat faster as she spotted a letter for "Mr. Jon Reed" sent to him at their address. Eva knew no one by that name.

She pried open the envelope flap and was shocked to find a typed letter to Mr. Jon Reed. His request for a credit card was being denied because the bank could not establish he lived at Eva's address.

Eva sped to Scott, shoving the letter at him. "Do you know this guy?"

"Never heard of him. Who is he? From our church?"

Suspicion blazed in Eva's mind, casting a pall on her happiness.

"Jon Reed!" she cried. "The guy in the car!"

Scott dropped the letter. "Who?"

"I get it! Somebody applies for a credit card using our

address. He hangs out in the neighborhood until the mail is delivered so he can steal his card from our mailbox. I should get his license number."

Eva slipped out the back door. It took her a moment to walk around the side of the house and stare both ways down the street. The car with the slouchy driver was gone.

She walked home vowing to be more alert. Setting the security alarm, she hoped it was a coincidence. Life was becoming stranger by the day.

Chapter 18

The rest of Eva's week unfolded with a grueling schedule of surveillance where she helped Griff to track the Chechen brothers. On Friday, she followed the younger brother from the car wash all the way to Richmond. More dead ends weren't worth her lack of sleep. On Sunday morning, she rose before six worn out. Despite exhaustion seeping into every fiber, she couldn't wait to worship with her family.

In the church's Gatheria, Eva paid for a grande at the coffee shop. Pocketing her change, she heard someone calling her name.

"Eva, Eva."

Thinking it was Thelma, she whirled in the direction of the lady's voice. There stood Kat Kowicki stirring coffee at the condiments stand, beckoning Eva to join her. Eva stifled a yawn and motioned for Scott to follow. The years away from D.C. had been good to Kat. She had gained an air of sophistication, and twinkling eyes.

Kat extended her hand. "What a surprise to see you here, Eva. You haven't changed one iota. It's been too long."

"Scott, I think you know Kat Kowicki from her former time in D.C.," Eva said, shaking her hand warmly.

Kat beamed as she corrected Eva. "I am Kat McKenna now. On TV, I still use Kowicki. Do you remember my husband?"

Eva's jaw dropped. She gripped Jack McKenna's firm hand, and turned to Scott. "I met Jack years ago when he was a detective with the Chicago Police Department."

More hand shaking, with Jack filling them in on his new career. "Anticipating Kat's possible move with the network, I took an early retirement from the CPD and signed on with the U.S. Marshals Service. I remember meeting you, Eva, at the National Gallery of Art when you were there with Kat."

Eva appreciated Jack's direct gaze and wondered if he and Kat had children. She'd wait to find out.

His grin was wide as he said, "It's been too long since I've connected with Griff. Are you and he still working at the JTTF?"

"Yes, and with all the threats to our country, you can imagine how busy we are."

"You remember Griff." Jack put a hand on Kat's shoulder. "He came to Chicago to help our group. You met him when you worked on the JFK assassination story."

Kat nodded slowly as if trying to recall Griff's face. Eva asked how long they had been attending church here.

"I didn't know you were interested in spiritual matters," Eva added gently.

Kat pulled Jack's hand from her shoulder and held him close. "My life has come alive since marrying Jack. Our pastor in Chicago recommended we try this church when we moved. Our son Parker is six and already involved in the sports program."

"So is our son Dutch," Eva replied, incredulous. "Let's make sure they meet."

Kat's eyes sparkled. "Let's have lunch sometime and catch up."

Eva went even further, suggesting they get together as couples. Scott said nothing, so Eva motioned to Jack. "If you're interested in joining another JTTF, we can pull strings and get the marshals to assign you to ours."

He nodded vigorously. Sounds of music drifted their way from the sanctuary.

Kat arched her light eyebrows, asking in a hushed voice, "Did I hear right? Was your daughter Kaley on the ferry when it was taken hostage in the Baltic?"

"Nice meeting you both," Scott shot back. "It's time for worship."

He reached for Eva. She hung back, knowing full well blowing Kat off would only fuel her aggressive hunt for a story.

She took one of Kat's hands in hers. "Listen, Kat, as a mom you can relate to my doing everything I can to protect my daughter. She's been through enough. If you promise to let this go, I'll connect you to another crime victim here in the church."

"What type of crime?" Kat moistened her lips.

Lofty music swelled, and Scott acted restless by Eva's side. Still, she stayed rooted to neutralize what she deemed to be a threat to Kaley. Scott began talking to Jack.

Releasing Kat's hand, Eva mentioned the hundred-million-dollar Ponzi scheme stretching from Virginia to Florida.

"Kat, one of my close friends was scammed. I need to ask her, but your speaking to her may help my friend who lost her life savings."

"I admit it sounds doable since it's not strictly local."

"The trial is ongoing," Eva said. "Let me get right on this and see what I can do."

Eva gazed into Kat's intense eyes. Kat stared back until Eva saw what she later described to Scott as a shining light in the reporter's eyes.

"Okay, I'll wait to hear from you on the crime story. Forget the other angle I mentioned." Kat sounded earnest.

Eva took hold of Scott's arm, inwardly relieved.

"You won't be sorry," she promised Kat before walking to the sanctuary.

The music the orchestra played was "Great is His faithfulness." Eva settled into the pew knowing in her heart that God's mercy was the whole truth, and nothing but the truth.

AT TEN O'CLOCK ON TUESDAY MORNING, Eva phoned Thelma. After small talk about Sunday's worship experience, Eva got right to the crux of why she was calling.

"A zealous reporter stopped me at church on Sunday," Eva said. "She is interested in your financial loss in the Ponzi scheme."

"Eva, your call is perfect timing. Thank you for the gift cards. I used 'em to stock up on supplies and gas for my car."

"You are welcome. And you'll come for dinner again soon, right?" Eva asked, uneasy with praise.

"Sure thing, honey. Now what about this reporter?"

Eva and Thelma talked over the pros and cons, with Thelma agreeing to share her story with Kat because she "hoped to keep others from being scammed."

Griff poked his head around the corner as Eva hung up the phone.

He whirled a finger in the air. "I'm heading to the conference room to use the undercover phone and call Holly's caretaker on Lime Key. Want to sit in?"

"Yes, I'm curious to know if Louie buys your story that we bought Holly's Florida house."

The moment Eva stood up, her phone rang. She told Griff to go ahead, and she answered. The caller's identity surprised Eva greatly, and she waited anxiously wondering what FBI Agent Sabrina Nelson wanted with Eva.

Meanwhile, Eva listened to Griff's side of the conversation with Louie, but her thoughts were consumed by Special Agent Nelson's request to interview Eva. The buzzer rang at the secure entrance.

Eva hurried from the conference room to the reception area, where she squinted through the wire mesh glass window in the heavy steel door. Nelson held her official ID toward the door. The photo matched her face.

Eva let her in, greatly puzzled. Usually grads from new

agents' class did the background investigations. New agents couldn't be older than thirty-seven, and here was Nelson looking like forty-five with deep-set lines around her mouth.

"Are you Eva Montanna?"

"I am."

Nelson displayed her credentials again. "Can we talk in confidence?"

"No one will be coming in here." Eva gestured around the empty reception room.

"No." The FBI agent shook her head. "We need a private office."

Eva's mind whirled with what Nelson was up to. Griff had finished his call with Louie, so Eva ushered her into the empty conference room and shut the door.

Nelson looked Eva up and down. "I need to see your ICE credentials."

Eva's blood pressure began rising. She fought to stay calm.

"Agent Nelson, you call me at my office requesting an interview without telling me why. You show up at this secure facility where I've told you I will be. Do you think some impostor has commandeered this office in order to deceive you?"

Nelson tilted her square chin. "My interview involves Eva Montanna. To protect the privacy of Eva Montanna, I first need to see your credentials."

Eva spun around and opened the door with grave doubts. What on earth did the FBI agent want with her? She grabbed her purse from her locked desk, and returning to the room, presented her credentials to the agent, barely masking her irritation.

"Satisfied?"

Nelson looked them over. "Yes. Please sit down. This may take a while. The point of my visit is classified. Are you aware a foreign government has hacked into OPM's personnel files?"

"I am. Last Friday I received OPM's letter offering services to protect my privacy. Most folks I work with—including Griffin Topping, the FBI agent assigned here—got the same letter."

Eva paused. "Do you know Griff Topping?"

"I haven't had that pleasure." Nelson slid closer to the table. "While many files were breached, it appears there's a particular focus on you. Whoever orchestrated the breach is interested in Eva Montanna."

"Me?" Eva's cheeks blazed. She felt uncomfortable.

"They made an effort to alter your birth date and home address."

"What does that accomplish?" Eva tried not to explode in anger.

"We have no clue. I can tell you while they were unsuccessful, they did specifically examine your data. We're convinced it is a foreign intelligence service."

Eva sat dumbfounded. This was beyond believable.

"Have you had any contacts with a foreign government?" Nelson probed.

Eva chose her words carefully. "I don't know what you found in that file, or in FBI files, but Immigration Customs Enforcement is the first line of defense at our border crossings, airports, and seaports. We limit what can be sent to and what can enter in from certain countries. So yes, I've been an impediment to foreign governments."

"How about China or Russia?"

"I was the undercover agent who arrested Dr. Ye Park, a highly influential political crony of Chinese hierarchy."

"Bingo." Nelson's eyes widened with surprise. "That singles you out."

She sharply turned a page on her notepad and began taking copious notes of details Eva remembered, including the credit card rejection sent to Mr. Jon Reed at her home address.

"Do you have other cases involving China?" Nelson closed her folder.

"None that I recall." Eva leaned on the table, preparing to stand when Nelson popped another question.

"How about Russia?"

Several cases flew through Eva's consciousness. "Yes, there was a case."

"Good. Because we believe there's a better chance the incursion came from Russian intelligence services. We're inundated with them."

Eva struggled to remember details. "It involved technology transfer. A Russian company used clandestine operators to manipulate shipments to third-world countries. They in turn redirected shipments to Iran and other countries for weapon systems. I broke up the operation."

"I'm betting the Russkies won't forget you soon. Do you recall anything else?"

Eva dug deeper, their conversation continuing as Nelson wrote down minutia Eva summoned from her memory bank. The FBI agent finally shut her leather notepad.

"We're onto something here. I'll interface with agents in my group to discern which government is fixated on you. Meanwhile, have you thought of moving?"

Eva was speechless. "Do you know who my husband is?"

"Ah ..." Nelson stared blankly.

"Scott Montanna was the DOD press secretary."

"Right. I remember seeing his name in your personnel file. It didn't register."

Nelson opened her file to pen another note.

Eva wiped her face, the magnitude of Nelson's info-bomb sinking into her heart. "Scott is now press secretary for the Speaker of the House of Representatives."

"Oh, wow." Nelson scribbled. "I'll follow up this angle. The Russians or Chinese might be targeting him. This case is becoming one ugly tar baby."

"That's why I won't ask ICE to transfer me. Both my husband's job and mine are here. Our children are settled into their lives and are happy."

"For now," Nelson quipped.

Though the agent made a valid point, Eva didn't appreciate her negativity. The interrogation was about over when Eva had a sudden thought.

She leveled a direct gaze. "Agent Nelson, our daughter was on the Swedish ferry seized by Russia in the Baltic."

Nelson's eyes grew wide with shock. "No!"

"Thanks be to God, she has come home safely."

"I saw it on the news." Nelson's mouth hung open.

"Kaley was one of four lifted by the Swedish helicopter after escaping in a lifeboat. We've done everything to keep her name from the press."

Nelson's head was bobbing as she began writing again. "I saw her rescue. Could the Russians have known your daughter was aboard that ship?"

"I have no idea what they knew."

Eva decided to divulge a key fact about Kaley's trip. "A Polish man and his daughter were in the lifeboat, plus Kaley's classmate. That girl's father is a CIA agent."

"Yikes!" Nelson held her pen in midair. "The plot thickens. Who is her father?"

"I can't tell you that."

"Agent Montanna, I should talk with him. This is too bizarre for a coincidence. I want to check and see if his personal information has been accessed."

Eva tented her hands. "I will tell him of your investigation. If he and the Agency feel it's appropriate, he can contact you."

Nelson slid two business cards to Eva. She wasn't finished with her innuendos.

"You said your daughter was with a Polish citizen. Perhaps he's a Russian agent, deliberately segregating Americans onto a lifeboat so the Russians could grab them."

It was Eva's turn to sit dumbfounded, mouth ajar. She forced herself to consider Nelson's charge. She supposed anything was possible.

"No, I think not," she said decisively. "A nice family man, he's the maintenance supervisor for the ferry line. That's how they managed to escape. Kaley insists we invite Mr. and Mrs. Sikorski and his daughter to our home, and we will."

Nelson tilted her head. "Russia has many active spies in Poland."

"I'm aware several were discovered before Kaley's trip. I think it's not him. The Russians must have learned about the students from another source."

Nelson closed her folder and offered to run their names through the system before Eva issued any invitations.

"I think that is wise," Eva said, pulling the contact information from her phone for Kaley's Polish hosts.

Agent Nelson opened her folder again, with Eva sensing she was playing a part in a sci-fi film that never ended. Her mind was reeling with every perplexing possibility Agent Nelson snapped her folder shut and stood. Eva reached out to shake her hand, hoping the agent was finished.

At the door, Nelson turned, a deep scowl etching her eyes. "Except for the CIA agent, don't mention this to your boss or colleagues. We don't need panic spreading throughout the government."

"May I share your questions with my husband?"

Nelson gaped before relenting. "Downplay the repercussions. Say it's routine."

Eva remained noncommittal. Because she and Scott shared essentials in life, she refused to hide such a crucial matter from him. She escorted Agent Nelson out the door before sitting at her desk, staring mindlessly at her computer.

Reality hit her hard. Scott worked for the man third in line to the Presidency. How much danger were she and Scott in? Or the children?

Later that evening, after the children were asleep, Eva and Scott huddled in their office to dissect Agent Nelson's dire warnings. Her husband took the issue in stride as he usually did. Their prayer, asking God to protect their family and bring justice for whoever was hacking into their personal lives, brought her some comfort.

When she tried to sleep, Eva's mind wouldn't cooperate. She desired to do more, she just didn't know what.

Chapter 19

Eva's remaining workweek brought more decisions. The undercover call to Louie resulted in Griff arranging to fly with Eva to Lime Key in a few days. So she prepared to be gone, cooking extra casseroles and soups all day Saturday. Life was so busy; Agent Nelson's visit never came up between Scott and Eva again.

Well, not until Sunday. Eva was wiggling into her dress when Scott said, "I agree with Agent Nelson about one thing."

"Will you zip my dress first?" She didn't want to leave late for church.

Scott did, also helping her fasten a silver cross around her neck, proclaiming, "Honey, you are one beautiful woman."

"Thanks." Eva gazed into his eyes. "Why do I suspect you're softening me up for a blow? Are the Russians hoping to co-opt you to work for them?"

"I'd be surprised if I'm the target." He took hold of her hands. "And I took steps for everyone in the Speaker's office to be interviewed. We're adding secure measures to the computer systems."

"Does the Speaker know why you're taking these precautions?"

"No, he is absorbed in the upcoming elections. I told his chief of staff you and I received strange mail, and suggested it would be wise."

"What has you agreeing with Nelson?"

"That she should run the Sikorskis through the system before we confirm their journey here over Thanksgiving."

Eva's jaw tensed. "You make perfect sense. Still, it stinks being scrutinized by criminals when I'm supposed to be doing the scrutinizing of them."

"Honey, I meant every word I said. You are gorgeous. And I'll be missing you."

She hugged him tightly and gathered the rest of her family for church. Pastor Feldman's teaching about end times when Jesus will rapture the church had Eva riveted to her seat. Seven years of tribulation would follow. That's when the battle with Gog and Magog would erupt on the earth.

Her pastor mentioned something about Russia being involved in the fierce battle, and that made her mind wander to her doubts about Mr. Sikorski. What did Eva really know about him or his family? Kaley and Izzy stayed in touch via messages on their computers. It might be wise to discourage her from doing so.

Scott drove home with the kids quietly playing with electronic gizmos. Eva welcomed the silence and chose to empty her mind of problems. Kaley intruded upon Eva's mental break.

She leaned forward asking, "Dad, who was the pretty woman I saw you talking to in the cafe?"

That got Eva's attention. "What? Your dad was talking to a pretty woman?"

He kept driving. Eva tilted her head. "Who was the pretty woman?"

Scott's eyes shifted to the rearview mirror. He winked at Kaley.

"It must have been your mother."

"No, Dad. She wore a beige linen suit. It's like I know her, but don't."

"Okay, you got me," Scott said. "She was Kat Kowicki, but she's not that pretty."

Eva laughed good-naturedly. "Kat not pretty? Kaley is right, she is quite pretty."

"Do I know her?" their inquisitive daughter asked.

"You watched her report from the Pentagon with your dad and me," Eva said. "You know, the night you put together your photo album."

"Oh right. You complained she noses into your cases."

Glancing over at Scott, Eva said, "I didn't see Kat at church. Did the two of you fix a time for a couple's get-together?"

"That never came up." His eyes stayed at the road ahead. "She was on a fishing expedition. I learned more than she did."

"What is she angling for?" Alarm bells rang in Eva's mind. Was the reporter back probing into Kaley's escape from the Polish ferry?

Scott cranked a turn. "Her source claims Russian cargo ships are bringing Russian missiles into Cuba."

"Oh no!" Kaley cried. "Isn't Cuba our friend?"

Eva reached toward Scott, snapping her fingers to make him change the subject. From the corner of her eye, she saw the boys were still glued to their handheld games.

"Don't worry," she told Kaley. "Reporters want sensational stories for higher ratings. It's been over fifty years since Russia tried installing missiles in Cuba. We are friendlier these days."

Scott looked into the mirror again. "Cuba is Russia's friend too."

Eva glared, yet he didn't miss a beat, making a few turns and ignoring her.

Kaley wasn't deterred. "Russia threatened Poland by seizing their ferry. Why wouldn't they force themselves on Cuba?"

"What did you tell Kat?" Eva asked, hopeful Scott was attuned to Kaley's fears.

Rounding the corner for home, he glanced at Kaley in the mirror. "Don't worry, kiddo. I said I talk to Pentagon people every day. There's no evidence Russia is advancing into our hemisphere."

Kaley fell silent and Scott pulled into the garage. Andy challenged Dutch to a game of checkers. While the boys traipsed inside, Eva gathered her purse and Bible, vowing once in the house to steer their conversation away from international intrigue.

Kaley didn't wait to leave the van before asking, "Does Kat make up stories to report, Dad?"

Scott gave no answer, urging her inside with Eva so he could close the heavy garage door. Eva washed her hands in the kitchen before starting Sunday lunch.

Scott tossed down his keys, telling Kaley, "D.C. lobbyists vie for support and money from the federal government for whichever company or group pays them. They influence decisions made by the White House and laws passed by Congress."

"What does that have to do with Russia and missiles in Cuba?" Kaley lingered at the counter wearing a puzzled expression.

Since this discussion couldn't be stopped, Eva listened intently to see if she should jump in anytime. She turned on the oven and slid in her premade casserole. Scott sat their daughter around the kitchen table and opened his hands.

"Our Guantanamo Bay naval base sits on Cuba's southern coast. We lease the base for four thousand bucks a year. There's no end date. Ever since Cuba's revolution sixty years ago, their Communist regime wants to terminate the lease. We have refused."

"So what? I'm trying to understand."

"I'll tell you so what." Scott's voice grew edgy. "Just like President Jimmy Carter gave the Canal to Panama, many people are concerned the Administration will end the lease at Guantanamo, giving our naval base to Cuba's Communist government. Kat Kowicki may have heard rumors started by lobbyists trying to prevent that from occurring."

Although Eva trusted Scott's account would end Kaley's

concern, she added her two cents. "Our military will protect the lease."

Kaley shrugged her shoulders and rose from the table. "I hope so. I never want to see another Russian soldier so close again."

She disappeared around the corner with Eva telling Scott, "Sweetheart, be careful not to talk about dangerous things around Kaley. She's growing up fast enough as it is."

"That's exactly why I am teaching her," he said. "She's smart. I want her knowing what to expect. You and I aren't raising hothouse flowers. Our kids are this country's future."

Eva faced him. She might as well get her question off her heavy shoulders.

"What if Kat is right and Russia is shipping missiles into Cuba?"

"That would be devastating to America's future."

SCOTT HAD A CHANCE ON TUESDAY to find out if Kat had stumbled onto the truth. He stopped a pentagon liaison officer striding toward the House Armed Services Committee office. They once worked together at the Pentagon.

Scott grabbed his sleeve. "What's the latest on Russian missiles at Santiago, Cuba?"

"How did you—wait. What are you talking about?"

Scott sensed the lieutenant commander knew something he wasn't free to discuss. He dropped his hand from the man's arm.

"You mean how did I know?" Scott raised an eyebrow. "Any truth to the rumor I picked up?"

"Where did you hear such a thing?"

"From an intrepid reporter. Is there truth in the rumor?"

"I can say nothing to either confirm or deny such a rumor."

Scott rubbed his hands together. "That says a lot. I think the committee should ask for a classified briefing on Russian activities in Cuba."

"You guys usually do."

"Would that be smart of us?"

The officer simply shook his head. "I don't know what you might learn."

Scott mulled over the unsatisfying exchange all the way to his office. He went right to his computer, checking for messages. Most of his e-mails were routine requests from news organizations for information about a dozen pending hearings.

He shrugged those off and switched screens to read the latest

Pentagon unclassified press releases. Then he began perusing through incident reports from around the world. An incoming call on his private line interrupted his search.

It was the lieutenant commander's boss, Commander Todd Marks, who already knew about Scott's question.

"I'm in the Capitol," Marks said in gritty tones. "Can we meet in the SCIF?"

Scott consulted his watch, asking, "Does five minutes work for you?"

"Ten-four, Montanna."

Scott hung up, certainty washing over him. He and Kat Kowicki were onto something, all right. He wasted no time speeding to the Sensitive Compartmented Information Facility, or SCIF. The specially-built room protected against electronic intelligence gathering, and was where classified documents could be stored and discussed.

He turned off his cell phone before stepping inside where Navy Commander Todd Marks waited with folded arms. Scott respected the commander who had pulled out all the stops to rescue Kaley. He also knew his cantankerous side could cut like a buzz saw on steroids.

Commander Mark's lower jaw seemed locked in place as he demanded, "Montanna, where did you learn about Russian missiles in Cuba?"

"Sir." Scott noted Mark's reddening face. "I don't know of any missiles in Cuba."

"Don't play games," he roared. "You asked my assistant about classified information. You claimed you heard it from a reporter."

"So the reporter must have discovered something being kept under wraps."

Marks' jaw muscles contracted. "I'll tell you only as much as you need to know. I need to find out if we have a leak."

"It's Kat Kowicki, sir." Scott rubbed out rising stress from the back of his neck. "You must know who she is. The bold TV reporter is back in D.C. developing sources after her stint in Chicago. On Sunday at church she pigeonholed me asking if I knew about a Russian cargo ship unloading missiles at the port of Santiago in Cuba."

"What did you tell her?"

"I had nothing to say. Not wanting to appear grossly uniformed, I simply said if I knew something, I wouldn't be able to tell her."

"Any idea of where she heard such an account?"

Scott let this question sink in. "No, and I wouldn't ask her either."

Marks stared at Scott as if grasping for a way to end their conversation. Scott was not about to let him escape.

He kept his composure, telling the commander, "I'll recommend to the House Speaker and Chair of Armed Services that we seek a classified briefing."

"I'd expect as much." Marks held Scott's gaze. "I'll say this much. Some S-300 antiaircraft missiles were unloaded from a Russian cargo ship. It puzzles me how this Kowicki reporter learned of it."

"So there's a leak at the Pentagon." Scott hated even saying that aloud.

Commander Marks' left eye twitched. "About the same time, a Russian cargo plane landed at the coastal airport of Baracoa, northeast of Guantanamo Bay. It unloaded construction materials. There's building going on down there."

"For what, do we know?"

"Look at it this way. Santiago's port is west of Gitmo. You know the Baracoa airport is northeast. You can figure the result."

Scott's own jaw muscles began tensing. "If Cuba sets up a defense between the two, they've just cut Gitmo off from the rest of the island."

"You nailed it."

"With S-300 missiles, Russia or Cuba could stop supply aircraft from even flying into Gitmo."

"But the port at Gitmo would still be open," Marks countered.

"This sounds worse than President Kennedy's Cuban missile crisis," Scott said. "Russia could use the S-300s to build nuclear missile sites. How do we stop them?"

"We're alarmed, which is why I need to know where Kat got her info."

"I'm glad she did," Scott growled. "How long were you going to keep this from Congress?"

"Politicos at the White House are ringing their hands, totally invested in their pseudo-relaxed relations with Cuba. They think antiaircraft missiles are for beefing up Cuba's own defenses."

"So close to Gitmo? I don't think so," Scott scoffed.

"What about Kowicki?"

"What do you mean? I won't ask her a thing. That would only confirm she's right. I'll make sure our committee and the Speaker receive a full briefing."

Marks raised a finger in warning. "You know everything I told you is classified."

"Right. I respect that, sir."

Commander Marks looked at his watch, signaling their SCIF meeting was over. A key question percolated through Scott's mind.

"Sir, we have more Americans visiting Cuba. Does that seem like a good idea?"

Marks pressed his lips together. "No. They could be seized as spies or held as hostages to raise money from wealthy American families."

"Who are we kidding?" Scott scoffed again. "More like raising money from our government or swapping prisoners as our government now does routinely."

"If this becomes public, the State Department will restrict travel to Cuba," Marks replied.

Scott reached out his hand. "Commander, you have our gratitude for spearheading Kaley's rescue. Eva and I thank you from the bottom of our hearts."

"That mission will stay with me as a huge success for our military. We all need more of those days. Watch your six, Montanna."

"You as well, Commander."

Scott left the secret room taking new secrets with him. He saw the danger to America, to his family, and did not like Cuba and Russia's military strategy one bit.

If only he hadn't mentioned anything about Cuba to Eva or Kaley. What had he been thinking? Just because a reporter told him something didn't mean he should spout off about it. He'd caution Eva. What about Kaley? It might be she would forget what she'd heard and never mention it to her friends.

Glenna would be no problem. Her dad was a CIA agent and Scott's buddy. Scott realized, to his chagrin, he knew little about Kaley's other school chums.

Sweat dripped down his armpits. His life flashed before his eyes. Kat Kowicki was back a few weeks and already causing havoc. Not only would he insist Eva put the kibosh on any couple's shindig, Scott also would make a wide berth from the pesky reporter and ensure Eva did the same.

Chapter 20

Griff's decision to leave for Lime Key the next morning threw Eva for a loop. She needed a few more days. She tossed an annual leave request form onto her boss's desk so she could head home two hours early.

Oliver waved off her request. "You'll be working 24/7 in the Keys. Go home and kiss your kids good-bye."

If only it was that simple. Eva didn't confide in her boss, so she told him thanks. As she tore up the form, she added with feeling, "Griff and I want Operation Stogie to count for something."

"You will," he snapped, picking up his phone.

Eva blasted home. If only she didn't have company coming for dinner. The idea had arisen yesterday when Viola phoned to say she enjoyed her new position. Their van wasn't in the garage when Eva pulled in the driveway. She rushed inside, where she secured her Glock and changed into casual clothes.

When she tried becoming organized in the kitchen, Eva realized she needed help. "Kaley, please set the table. Andy, you can pour tea in glasses, the tall ones."

"Do I have to?" he complained, zooming past. "That's women's work."

Eva pointed salad tongs at him. "Son, where did you get such a strange idea? Men eat too. You should learn how to arrange a meal."

Andy banged ice into the glasses. "Gregg Rider is challenging me to an X-box battle in thirty minutes."

"No he isn't. You guys played yesterday. Once a week is our rule, remember?"

"Aw, Mom." Andy slammed the fridge shut after yanking out a pitcher of tea.

"Okay, you don't like our rule. How's this one? Starting tomorrow, you help Dad cook burgers and take over as grill master in this house."

"Aw, Mom, no way."

Scott walked in. "Hey, sport, what's all the whining?"

Andy set the pitcher on the table. Rapid-fire, he told his dad how he was letting Gregg down.

"He'll get over it," Scott said, loosening his tie. "Besides, I need your help getting something from the van. Let me change outta this suit first. Meet me in the garage."

He grinned at Eva before sauntering down the hall. For his

part, Andy sloshed the last of the tea into a glass and dashed away. Kaley, who was drying her hands on a towel, whirled around. She faced her mom.

"Dad sounds mysterious."

"He has pizzas in the van," Eva said evenly.

"Too bad. Andy will be crushed it's not something fun."

Eva stayed quiet, thinking Kaley, too, would enjoy Scott's surprise.

Ding dong!

Kaley visibly jumped at the chiming doorbell. "Who are we expecting?"

"That's probably Brett from my task force. Will you let him in? Viola is joining us too, if she leaves work on time."

"Are you trying to fix them up, Mom? He's more like a cactus and Aunt Viola is like her name—a pretty flower."

"She can be gutsy at times." Eva chuckled, lightness filling her heart. "You don't think they're suited for each other?"

The bell pealed again, and Kaley scooted to answer it. Meanwhile, Eva tossed the salad and raced against time to complete her meal, all the while reflecting on Kaley's observation. Were they a good match?

By all appearances, Brett seemed a capable agent, though his bravado sometimes wore on her nerves. But then, hadn't he shown much daring when he'd stopped Arnold Ruckus in the Topsy-Turvy? Eva refused to quibble over his tactics. No doubt, he made an excellent undercover agent.

On the other hand, Viola's temperament veered to the opposite of impulsive. Serious to the core, she exuded compassion and warmth. Was Eva mistaken in wanting her sister-in-law to begin fresh with a new friend? Besides, Brett was busy with the Ponzi trial and Viola just started a demanding job. It wasn't like Eva was throwing them together forever.

A pungent odor assailed her nose. Eva flew to open the oven door, snatching out Buffalo wings before they burned. Seconds later, Brett's southern voice reached the kitchen as he told Kaley, "Howdy. This cheesecake survived the back of my Harley. Take it quick."

All giggles, Kaley carried a tied box into the kitchen. Brett trailed in wearing baggy jeans and leather vest over a T-shirt. With his shaggy hair, the DEA agent looked every bit the biker.

"Do you need help?" he asked, snatching a raw carrot from a plate.

"I don't, but Scott—"

Bang! Bang!

Harsh sounds echoed from the garage, interrupting her.

Brett folded his strapping arms. "You've got builders working out there?"

"They like to think so." Eva grinned at her new partner. "Do me a favor."

"Name it."

"Go into the garage and tell Scott we're ready for the pizzas."

Minutes later, with Brett's much-needed help, Scott and Andy wrestled in a large foosball game. Dutch came rushing out of his bedroom, squealing, "I wanna play."

"Give me a chance to set it up in the family room," Scott grumbled.

His face beamed red. Eva's sons scurried by with Kaley hot on their heels. This should be a fun night and lessen the sting of Eva's leaving. All she needed was for Viola to appear.

She did arrive, in time for dessert. Eva fixed fresh decaf coffee for the adults. The kids rushed off to try out their foosball game. Viola downed one cup of coffee and asked for another with her piece of dessert.

She looked weary, proclaiming, "I was rushed off my feet at the hospital."

"Want to talk about it?" Brett reached for a second helping of the famous New York cheesecake.

"A severe case of cystic fibrosis blew in at four."

"CF is one serious disease."

This came from Brett. Eva flashed a look at her husband that said, "Let the two of them talk." In reply, he raised an eyebrow while finishing his creamy dessert.

"I appreciate your insight," Viola told Brett, her voice gaining strength. "The child needs a liver transplant. I spent hours juggling a myriad of details to make surgery a reality, sooner rather than later, I hope."

Brett leaned back in his chair. "My buddy's son has CF."

"Is he local? My colleague at the hospital specializes in that malady."

Eva nudged Scott's leg under the table with her foot. When he stayed put, she jerked her head for him to leave the table. He got the idea and followed like a good guy.

"Challenge you to foosball," Eva said, her eyes glittering with mirth.

"You're on."

Andy and Dutch rooted for their dad, with Kaley cheering on

her mom. Scott won easily. Eva performed a mock bow, telling him heartily, "That was great!"

Eva plunked on the sofa to recover from the excitement. Viola and Brett wandered into the family room, with Brett daring her to a match. In the end, Scott's sister couldn't compete against the DEA agent at the foosball table. She took her resounding defeat with a genuine laugh.

"Perhaps your associate can help my friend's son with CF," Brett said, catching his breath. "May I phone you about it?"

"That would be nice, wouldn't it?" Viola's lips curved into a warm smile.

Brett stared at her in silence until saying, "I need your phone number, I guess."

"Of course."

Viola blushed. She removed her business card from her purse, wrote on it, and handed it to him.

"It's my home number. There I'm freer to talk."

Brett slid her card into his wallet and walked Viola to her car. Eva resisted an urge to peek out the window. Instead, she went to the kitchen where Scott loaded the dishwasher.

"Your idea to buy the kids foosball is a winner," she complimented.

"They need to spend less time on electronic games and phones."

"Knock, knock, y'all," came a bass voice.

Brett stood in the doorway. "Thanks for a fun evening. Since moving from Miami, I've poured myself into the trial. I haven't played my bagpipes once."

"Scott and I adore 'Amazing Grace' on the pipes," Eva said. "Do you know it?"

"I enjoy playing my pipes and I've played that song at funerals. I'll bring them sometime."

"Our son Andy is one fantastic drummer," Scott added.

Eva kept her voice low. "Brett, I haven't had a chance to fill you in. Griff and I are packing our straw hats and sandals for a case in the Keys."

"Wish I could go along. AUSA O'Rourke tore into a defense witness today who had nothing but glowing praise for Carlos. By the time O'Rourke finished with the witness, Carlos looked shaken."

"What about Holly?" Eva asked vaguely.

"A CPA testified on her behalf claiming Holly knew zero about her husband's financial dealings. Evidence is stacking up against

Carlos, though."

Eva went with him to the front door where she explained, "Griff and I are working on a smuggling case that might involve terrorists. Once you've finished the Munoz case, we'll brief you."

"Maybe I can join you in the Keys. I miss the ocean and my mom's fried okra."

Eva grasped his hand. "I'm praying for a safe trip home for you on your Harley and a safe flight for us to the Keys."

"Hmm ... Eva ..." Brett seemed to fumble for a reply. "Viola seems nice."

"She's the best. I've known her almost as long as I've known her brother. Their parents are a pair of gems too."

Brett zipped up his leather vest. "I'll touch base with her after my trial concludes. My family is quite small, which is a story for another time. Thanks again, Eva. You and Scott make me feel right at home."

"You are welcome here anytime."

Brett quietly disappeared down the sidewalk. The bark of his Harley rocked the quiet neighborhood, and he prattled away. Eva double-locked the front door and set the security alarm. The night couldn't have gone better if she'd orchestrated events herself.

Much later she eased into bed. Scott climbed in beside her, reaching for her hand and pressing it into his.

"A successful evening," he said softly. "Did you set your alarm for five?"

"Ye-es." She yawned.

"You promise me to be careful in Florida, with Cuba so near and everything."

Eva gripped his strong hand. "I'm not keen on going undercover again. I'd send Brett if he wasn't in trial."

"Sweetheart, you're equipped for anything. You have courage galore. Just remember I'm here loving you and praying."

Eva leaned over and kissed his cheek. She settled onto her pillow bone tired. His support meant the world to her. In another moment, she fell asleep. Dreams of chasing an escaped felon woke her up in a sweat.

Scott was breathing soundly. Eva got up quietly, sipped some water, and tried going back to sleep. Her mind was alive going over her to-do list. Her bag was packed with slacks and blouses. The government's slim computer was stowed in her large purse. Fake ID she'd put in an undercover wallet that had no photos of Eva or family. After a week of backstopping their new undercover identities, her driver's license and credit cards identified her as

Evelyn Montague.

And Griff held his pilot license in the name of Digger Boyd. The FBI-owned Cessna was registered to a phony plane rental company. A shell company had been created as owner of the house in the Keys, complete with its own bank account. Even though Holly still owned her home, it didn't appear so publically.

One thing Eva wasn't sure of. Would Holly's caretaker, Louis Clark, be readily convinced she and Griff were the new owners of Pelican's Nest? Or would he be trouble?

She opened an eye. The lighted clock beamed it was three in the morning. She could sleep two more hours if she tried. Rolling over didn't help. Her pillow was too lumpy, the room too warm, and her mind too keyed up about flying to the Keys.

It was an ideal time to talk with her Heavenly Father with no interruptions. Eva slipped to their office. On the couch, she began with praise for God's care in their lives, and then lifted up prayers for her family, new task force partner, sister-in-law, and her flight with Griff in a few hours.

Curled on the sofa is where she awoke to Scott's tender voice in her ear, "I fixed you coffee and eggs for breakfast."

Though the room was dark, Eva reached up and grabbed hold of her husband. She didn't want to leave him.

Chapter 21

Lime Key, Florida

Eva's attention to every detail in becoming a wealthy real estate investor had paid off. Here she was dressed in her new Caribbean colors, sitting in the copilot seat with Griff ably piloting the aircraft. So far, the flight proved uneventful, except passing over the mountains had played havoc with her stomach. They were thirty minutes out from their undercover meeting with Louie Clark.

"You're dipping quite low," Eva said. "I see waves lapping against the shore."

Griff smirked. "I've been flying so long, I rarely notice what's beneath me. This Cessna 421, Golden Eagle is a good and stable plane."

"I guess Louie would expect me to know details like that."

"Right. Prepare for landing, Evelyn. And don't forget to call me Digger."

"Sounds weird, but I'll remember."

Griff's landing at a small airport in Marathon Key was smooth. While the plane was refueled, Eva refreshed herself in the bathroom at the General Aviation building. She came out in time to hear Griff engage the attendant at the service counter.

"We're on our way to Lime Key," Griff told the young man whose shirt bore the embroidered name "Shane."

"You don't have far to go then."

"We bought a place there, so we'll be buying fuel here often."

"Welcome to the neighborhood," Shane said. "Where did you buy?"

Griff rapped a hand on the counter. "On the airstrip. Do you know Louie Clark?"

"Know him? I nearly rebuilt his 310."

Shane pointed to a small, white twin-engine Cessna with red trim sitting outside the maintenance hangar. "I put new tires on, and I'm waiting for his pickup."

"We bought the place Louie manages." Griff nodded toward the 310. "In fact, I could fly him up here to get his plane."

Shane extended a hand. "Nice to know you. I'm Shane."

"I am Digger."

He introduced "Evelyn" as his business partner. Eva simply smiled and headed out the door. Searing humid air hit her face, a vivid reminder she'd reached the tropics. Although late summer could be warm back home, Virginia suffered nothing like this intense heat. It was close to scorching the top of Eva's head.

Griff beat her to the plane and lowered the steps. She climbed up, then stooped over to squeeze through a narrow aisle between leather seats in the corporate plane. She'd closed the fabric window curtains to reduce the heat. Still, as she sat down in the right seat, hot leather burned through her thin slacks.

He secured the cabin door with a thump and slid into the pilot seat.

"We need AC," she grumbled, wiping her cheeks.

"I hear you loud and clear."

Griff started throwing switches. One engine and another fired. Eva lowered the headset onto her ears and adjusted the microphone boom so Griff could hear her talk.

Static crackled in her ears as he shouted, "Can you believe the heat in those few minutes? I should have packed shorts instead of jeans."

"I am surprised Shane knows Louie," Eva observed.

"Take it as a warning. This is a tight-knit community. Folks will be watching us as we're watching them."

With a push on the throttles, the Golden Eagle rolled onto the taxiway. Griff announced on the radio he was ready to depart. With a few turns, he crept onto the runway. Aiming for its opposite end, his feet pressed the brakes, and he revved both engines using the throttles. Eva sensed the plane straining to get airborne.

He pulled back on the throttles, and through her headset came his voice, "Golden Eagle Two Lima Charlie, departing runway two five at Marathon."

Griff looked out both side windows before gazing upward at the sky. His eyes focused down the runway. He gently eased the throttles forward and the Cessna 421 began traveling fast, whizzing by parked planes.

Eva prepared for liftoff as Griff pulled back on the yoke. Their plane leaped into the air. With a loud thud, wheels collapsed against the bottom of the undercover plane. Emerald water below mesmerized Eva. Differing hues of green turned into a gorgeous sapphire blue as the water deepened. Such beauty took her breath away, and Eva wished her family could see the awe-inspiring sights.

They flew parallel to Highway One, or Overseas Highway, the main artery linking Florida's many Keys. Eva marveled as tiny and big resorts, hotels, and luxury homes with yachts at adjoining docks slipped beneath them.

"Did you know that highway has forty-two bridges," Eva said into the boom, "and goes over the Atlantic, Florida Bay, and the Gulf of Mexico?"

"No, but I'm glad I brought my tour guide along."

A few minutes later, he pointed below. "I do know that long bridge is Seven Mile Bridge. You don't want to break down or run out of gas on it. You'd have a long walk."

"Well, let's stay off of it then."

"That may be impossible. Lime Key is south of Marathon."

Eva shrugged off future issues, instead admiring the stunning beauty out her window. What a vantage point she had to God's creation. Although she'd visited Florida other times, this was her first glimpse of the Keys.

Griff lifted his hands off the yoke, smiling. "If we keep going straight, we'll be in Havana in no time."

"No thanks."

The road below turned as Griff continued a westerly flight path. He gestured to his right.

"See that stretch of islands? Big Pine Key is where I dropped the cocaine load for a smuggler who owned one of the tiny islands."

"Where is he now?"

Griff flashed a huge grin. "Doin' time."

He held a finger up for silence, then announced for planes in the area, "Cessna Golden Eagle Two Lima Charlie landing on runway three zero at Lime Key."

Griff made an identical announcement before turning sharply to the right. A short distance and he banked left. Eva felt lightheaded and wished she'd bought a granola bar in Marathon. Oh well, once she climbed out of the plane, she'd be fine.

Below, Eva spotted Highway One running through the middle of Lime Key. Wait, was that narrow strip where they were going to land? She didn't want to mess with Griff's head, but from here that slab looked teeny.

Eva decided to keep her eyes off the runway. She grabbed her purse and prepared to meet Louie Clark, smuggler extraordinaire. She and Griff hoped to reach deep into his organization and rip it apart from top to bottom.

Asphalt streets straddling both sides of the runway were lined with swaying palm trees. Many of the large homes had a canal behind them. Eva assumed the owners had instant ocean access with their luxury boats.

The fast-approaching runway made her flinch. Griff set the

plane expertly onto the concrete with a slight bump. The 421 thundered toward blue water at the other end of the runway. She thumped her feet hard against the floor. Still they raced toward the water. Her stomach churned. She could do nothing!

Griff had warned not to put her feet on the brake or rudder pedal in front of her seat. Her body slipped forward, ramming against her seatbelt. The ocean grew closer before her eyes. She slammed them shut.

Then the plane jerked to a stop. Eva popped one eye open. They were mere yards short of the runway's end.

Griff turned toward her. "Had you scared there for a minute, didn't I?" she heard him quip through her headset.

"Yes." Eva whacked his arm. "We need a smaller plane to land here. What were you thinking?"

"No, this plane is fine. I could have stopped further back, but I didn't want the wear and tear on the tires and brakes."

"I'll live." Eva wiped moisture from her brow.

Griff pushed on the right brake, and increasing the throttle to the left engine, the plane slowly turned a hundred and eighty degrees. Eva saw the puny strip where they'd just landed. She gulped.

He tugged the throttle to idle. Both of his feet off the brakes, he advanced the plane back down the runway. "See that bright yellow house with two tall palms standing like royal fans in front? That's our place. We know why Louie's plane isn't here."

"Nice flight, Digger." Eva emphasized his undercover name. "I don't see him."

"He's expecting us. Be ready for what he might throw at us."

Griff hit the brakes, revving one engine. The plane turned off the runway toward the house, and Eva looked over the yellow stucco with three stories. The second-story deck circled the house. A smaller third story penthouse had a deck around it. A sign declaring "Pelican's Nest" signaled they were at the right place.

He edged the plane so close Eva feared the propellers would suck a large patio umbrella off the second-floor deck.

"Look out!" she cried.

"We're fine."

Eva blinked back irritation at her partner. He was a master pilot and she needed to get used to flying with him.

She noted Holly's house was built high off the ground, as if on stilts. The first level was enclosed with a large overhead door that covered the plane's hangar. Through a passageway next to the house, Eva spied a small yacht moored in the backyard canal.

A slender man appeared on the third-story deck. Dressed in brown shorts and sandals, his flowered green shirt made for a perfect picture of the Keys.

The man's long wispy graying hair blew in the breeze. He watched, both hands gripping the deck railing. Propellers sputtered and spun once Griff killed the engines. Eva and Griff removed their headsets. Then Eva froze.

"Wait. I imagine Louie thinks he's losing his job with us in town. His tense posture makes me uneasy. He matches Holly's description, but is that even him?"

"Who else would it be?" Griff mopped his brow with a hankie. "He sounded friendly on the phone. Here we go!"

Squeezing again between the cabin seating, Eva launched into her first undercover role in several years. She tamped down concerns by lifting up a prayer for God's guidance. He had so often helped her in past cases.

Though her control in this situation was limited, Eva faced the unknown with a certainty she wasn't alone.

EVA BLEW OUT HER BREATH at arriving safely in Lime Key. Griff unlatched and lowered the door containing the steps. He clambered off first. She climbed down, her legs a bit wobbly. A blast of hot air hit Eva's nostrils and nearly took her breath away.

The thin man emerged from a compact elevator by the corner of the house. "You must be Digger. I'm Louis. Friends call me Louie."

Eva noticed he failed to give a last name, which wasn't unusual. Most criminals dealt with each other on a first-name basis. His voice sounded raspy, like an out-of-tune violin. After shaking hands with Griff, Louie extended his speckled hand to Eva.

"Evelyn, welcome to Lime Key, a perfect paradise. Hope it knocks yer socks off. You can't believe how glad I am that yer both here. It is fantastic meetin' you."

"It was a long flight," was all Eva said.

She wanted to wash Louie off her hand, so when he looked over at Griff, she slid it along her slacks.

The Floridian asked in his gravelly voice, "But did you have a good flight down? The weather showed you had low ceilings when you left Richmond."

His comment startled Eva. She had momentarily forgotten their undercover story was that they were from Richmond and not D.C. Being from the nation's center of power would spook any wrongdoer. She'd chosen Richmond for a good reason. It was where Eva grew up with her parents and sister Jillie.

Eva got her bearings while Griff raised the steps and latched the door.

"Our trip was great," he said. "Weather was no issue."

"I was shocked when you phoned, sayin' you talked to Holly's lawyer. I read about their problems. Holly and Carlos haven't called me lately."

The sun's sweltering rays beamed on Eva's head. Too bad she hadn't thought to bring a hat.

"Let's escape the heat, and we'll explain what's happening," Eva said.

"Sure," Louie croaked. "First, let's get yer plane outta the sun."

The caretaker punched buttons by the hangar door. It clattered and groaned as it rose. He attached a tow bar to the nose gear before he and Griff pulled the plane around, backing it beneath the house.

Meanwhile, perspiration ran down Eva's sides. Her distaste for Lime Key improved a fraction when Louie took them into the small elevator, which could lift them to the second-and third-story decks. At least she didn't have to climb steps in this heat. They crowded into the small cube, and Louie pressed the button for the third level.

His air-conditioned, one-bedroom apartment was decorated in bright corals and aqua. Someone had a flair for the Florida look. Eva figured that must be Holly. The open design had a dinette table that spanned between the living room and the corridor kitchen. The table seemed to be the hub of the open space.

"Sit and be comfortable," Louie said. "I'll rustle up somethin' to cool yer pipes. I got beer, sweet tea, and lemonade."

Griff wanted sweet tea. Eva raised the hair off her neck, and letting it fall back, she asked for lemonade.

"Good. The beer is for Carlos. Me, I never touch the stuff."

Griff snagged a chair facing the door. Eva sat so her back was to the kitchen, giving her a striking view of shimmering palm trees. A stark realization hit her with force. She was here as a real estate investor and not a federal agent about to arrest Louie. At least not yet.

Eva surveyed the room as a new owner might. Large French doors were framed with tropical plants growing tall and green on the deck. The mast of a sailboat moored against the seawall across the canal seemed surreal. In this Hemingway setting, with its floor tiles, plantation shutters folded against the windows, and wicker furniture, Special Agent Eva Montanna steeled her mind to protect her true identity.

She pushed forward her pretend self—Evelyn Montague. One other time she'd used the false name working undercover in Nashville to stop a Chinese smuggler. And hadn't that earlier case ended well? For this assignment, Eva vowed to expose the depth of Louie's criminal enterprise in the same successful way.

Talkative Louie kept a running monologue about Lime Key as he set drinks on coasters. He held a glass of tea. Sitting with his back to the canal, he stared keenly at the new owners who held his future in their hands.

"I'm curious," he said. "What's happenin' to Holly and Carlos?"

"It's pretty simple."

Eva removed a notebook computer from her purse. She folded the cover to form an easel. This she spun around so Louie had a good view of the screen.

"Holly sold this place to me and my business partner, Digger," Eva explained.

"Digger said as much. How come?" Louie grumped with a mouthful of tea.

Eva made a sweeping motion with her hands. "Obviously she needed money and had to liquidate before the Feds discovered she owned such a splendid home."

Louie's mouth fell open, but all the while he nodded in agreement.

"You're wondering what will happen to you," Griff said.

"Right on, man!"

Griff tried his tea before saying, "Holly made a recording with her lawyer. The attorney gave it to us. Go ahead, Evelyn, play it for Louie."

This was Eva's cue to switch on the video. Holly sprang to life on the small screen, appearing as if she talked eye-to-eye with Louie.

In the video, Holly wrung her hands as she gushed, "Louie, I appreciate all you've done for me and Carlos. Most of all, thanks for respecting our confidences."

Louie lifted his head, his eyes flickering from Eva to Griff. As Holly talked on, he edged closer to her in the computer.

"We need cash to fight this outrageous case. Evelyn Montague and her partner Digger Boyd are the new buyers. We've dealt with them before, so understand when I say I trust them. So can you. I told them you've maintained Pelican's Nest, doing nice things like arranging for renters. I don't know their plans for the Nest, but I bragged about you enough, so I hope they'll keep you on."

Holly signed off with a wave. "I'm going to work on my defense. Good luck!"

The video ended, and Louie gazed questioningly at Eva and Griff. An awkward silence engulfed the third-floor apartment. She let the man ponder his quandary while stowing the computer back in her purse.

"That's it?" His face contorted like he'd been sucker punched. "I'm fired and kicked out?"

Eva sipped the last of her lemonade. Griff stared out the sliding glass doors.

Louie jumped up. "Let me refresh your drinks. More tea, Digger?"

He shot to the kitchen and refilled their glasses, regaining his seat and wiping his mouth tentatively.

Before he said a word, Eva jumped in. "We asked to meet with you to explore the possibility of continuing the relationship."

He sank into his seat, his head sagging in a tired nod. "Okay."

"We can't be here all the time," Griff said in hushed tones. "We may fly down to soak up sun in winter. Someone has to manage things here. If you're willing to maintain the place and clean between visitors, we can let you stay in this cozy apartment rent free."

Louie ran a hand through his wispy hair. "I'm glad. Just so you know, Holly paid me twelve hundred a month, plus supplies in addition to free rent."

"Don't get cute," Griff growled. "Holly was paying you eight hundred a month. That seems pretty steep, but we could agree to it."

Louie looked sheepish. "Well ... what you said is fair."

Eva rose to her feet. The two men did also, with the trio sealing the deal with handshakes. For his part, Louie gaped toward the back of the house.

"Digger, that's a nice plane. What kind of business are you in?"

Griff narrowed his eyebrows to a fierce scowl. "We won't ask about your business. You don't need to know ours. Let's say we dabble in this and that. You could call us investors."

"I gotcha," Louie said, raising his hands.

It was as if he respected this type of relationship. He added to convince them, "In the words of old Sarge on *Hogan's Heroes*, I see nothin'."

Eva headed for the door. "Will you show us the rest of the house?"

"No problem." Louie bolted to the kitchen, returning with a set of keys. "You guys bought one fun place for kickin' back, island style."

Eva imagined spending time in such an island paradise with Scott and the kids. Holly owned the property for now. Eva and Griff's success would determine if she could keep it.

Chapter 22

The two undercover agents followed Louie down an outside stairway at the corner of the deck, close to the canal. Eva quickly concluded this remote hideaway, accessible by air and water, was perfectly situated for boats arriving with contraband or criminals. Also, the area by the runway was large enough to park two planes.

She carefully observed Louie as they went out on the second-story deck. Puffy white clouds floating by didn't stop Eva from questioning if she and Griff could infiltrate the man's smuggling ring. Large windows on each side of the door had tightly closed plantation blinds. Even if the sun weren't bright, she'd be unable to see in. The caretaker might be just as closed about his activities.

He pointed to the sign above the French doors overlooking the canal. "Since you're flyin' a Golden Eagle, you might change the name of yer place to the 'Eagle's Nest.'"

"No," Eva said. "I'm sure there are more pelicans around here than eagles."

"We have a bald eagle nesting on Cudjoe Key. I can show you sometime."

Eva nodded, and Griff acted as if he could care less. He was busy eyeballing the canal toward the ocean.

"Okay, let me show you the inside of yer new place," Louie said, walking them around the deck to their door a few feet from the elevator. A turn of the key, and he pushed the door open.

"What do you think?" Louie said. "Nice, huh?"

The lavish island retreat spread before Eva's eyes. It looked like crime did pay better than law enforcement. Such trappings meant zilch to Eva. She'd never trade the swanky locale bought with illicit proceeds for her clean conscience and dear family.

Still, she looked around in keeping with her undercover role. Shiny hardwood floors were covered with pale bamboo rugs the color of beach sand. Furniture in the open living area was decorated with brilliant white-and-blue-striped fabrics. Eva perched on a pretty sofa edged with light wood trim, noticing the countless seashells mounded inside of silver bowls and glass lamps.

"Digger, this place is prettier than I expected," Eva said. "What do you think?"

Griff pointed to nautical charts on the walls. "I'm up for exploring by boat."

"Evelyn, you will adore this view."

Louie sprang to open the shutters along the front of the living room. Beyond the double French doors was a vast deck, and Eva pulled open the doors. Sweltering heat almost knocked her over as she stepped outside. The view of the rippling canal and neighboring yachts was spectacular. Lofty palms provided shade for a hammock.

Griff tagged along, pointing at a concrete-terraced seawall below. "Evelyn, look—we have davits to raise our boat out of the water, a boat ramp for our personal watercraft, and a fish-cleaning station. What more could we want for entertaining?"

"It will do."

She turned on her heels to reenter the house with Griff coming behind her.

"Digger, you asked what else we want. I think we need a professional to keep it looking this way."

Louie waved his hands in the air. "Hey, that's what yer payin' me for. I clean it and rent it for however long yer gone." He faced Griff with a pleading look. "Isn't that what we've agreed to, Digger?"

"That's right," Griff replied, adding, "Not while we're here though. Evelyn and I will draw straws to see who gets to clean."

Louie gestured back toward the area opposite the kitchen. "Two bedrooms are down there. Holly used the back one as a guest room. If you've seen enough, I'll show you the storage and apartment in the hangar."

They rode the elevator to the ground level. Louie unlocked a service door, which to Eva's surprise opened to a small efficiency apartment. They walked through a small corridor kitchen and out another door into the hangar. Eva found it curious to be standing by the tail of the Golden Eagle.

"Yer plane stays nice and snug outta the sun. Back here's the maintenance area."

He showed them to the opposite side of the hangar, and bragged about having an air compressor, tools, and all stuff they needed to maintain their airplane.

"Digger, here's the two bikes Holly bought, the ones I told you about."

Eva checked out two 150cc motor bikes. A red one had a basket on its back. She swung her leg over the blue one.

"Look Gri—Digger, we can drive to the store for groceries."

"If you fly in and have no car, you won't starve," Louie said. "The red one's not runnin'. I called a bike shop to come repair it, but they haven't come yet. Things operate on island time."

Louie mentioned the apartment they'd just stepped through had a washer and dryer.

"It's everything Holly promised and more," Eva assured him.

Griff slapped him on the back. "What about the hangar?"

"The door combination is four three two four," Louie replied.

Eva longed for some ice water and a bite to eat. But Louie hadn't finished yet. He handed keys to Griff when they were back outside in the excruciating heat.

"I keep the other set of keys. I wanted to fly and see my sister in St. Augustine. Then you called sayin' you wanted to talk about Holly. I postponed leavin' today."

Eva gazed at Griff and took matters in her hands when he didn't say anything.

"I don't see why you shouldn't go tomorrow morning, but plan on breakfast first to discuss any loose ends."

"Where do you keep your plane?" Griff asked, looking around.

"My Cessna 310's up in Marathon for service. I was usin' the hangar. Now yer here, I can park mine outside."

Griff gestured at the blue Honda bike and offered an idea. "Evelyn could give you a ride to Marathon on that bike, or if you want, I'll drive you up in your car."

"Okay, I'll go with you in my car in the mornin'."

"Sounds like a plan," Griff said. "I'll get our bags out of the plane and freshen up from the flight."

Eva was good with the plan. No way she'd be scooting up Highway One over the Seven Mile Bridge with Louie behind her on that motorbike. What was Griff up to, anyway?

After Louie ascended in the elevator to his apartment, Griff pushed the button to summon it down. He and Eva grabbed their bags from the plane, and after hauling their suitcases to the apartment, Griff phoned Brett in Virginia.

"Monk, we're here," Griff said into the phone. "Call me when you receive this message. Louie's been showing us around. Bring your snorkel and gear ..."

Eva left him to finish his calls and flopped on the guest bed beneath the whirling cabana fan. She was excited to talk with Scott, and while his office phone rang, Eva switched back to her real self.

"Sweetheart," she crooned when he answered. "All safe here."

"It's great to hear your voice." Scott sounded happy, which made Eva happy.

"It may be a few days. Remember, I made taco casserole.

Heating instructions are taped on the top."

Scott's gentle laughter brought his handsome face flashing into her mind's eye.

"You know the matter I spoke to you about before you left?" he asked, fresh tension lacing his voice. "The reporter has really stirred up a hornet's nest."

"Is her info correct?" Eva sat up on the bed, alert to coming danger.

"Not sure." He sighed in her ear. "I suspect she'll dig her way to the bottom."

"Then I will be at peace for now. I love, love you!"

"Love you back, honey."

Eva checked her office voicemails after she and Scott ended their call. FBI Agent Nelson had left her a cryptic message, "No problems with the helicopter people."

Eva mulled over her meaning. The builder of helicopters was the Sikorski Company. She determined Nelson had run Mr. Sikorski in Gdansk, Poland, through FBI's computer archives, and he'd come up clean. Relief that Kaley hadn't been in the company of spies quickly twisted into unanswered questions. Would Eva find out which intelligence service was targeting her personnel file? And when might Nelson tell Eva what she'd found?

MAGGIE MOORING'S PARKING LOT WAS CRAMMED WITH CARS, so Griff and Eva pulled off Lime Key's main drag. Griff stopped the Honda in the shade of a palm tree.

"If the joint is packed, my rule is the food must be good," he quipped.

Eva climbed off, stretching her back. "Or they have coupons for something no one wants."

As he stood straddling the bike, Eva couldn't resist laughing.

"Digger, this bike is a huge step down from my G-car or your Bucar."

"Look at it this way," he replied evenly. "It is a convertible."

Griff snorted in jest and put down the kickstand. Off came their helmets, which they hung on the handlebar. Inside, locals talking boisterously filled nearly every table.

A hostess in a pink T-shirt, shorts, and flip-flops asked, "Two for dinner?"

"Do you have anything away from the door?" Griff asked.

The only open table was near the back wall, Griff's favorite place to be. Eva glanced at the plastic-covered menu and shoved it away.

She inhaled deeply. "Ocean air, seafood galore, you're gonna like this place. Me, I'd love a Reuben sandwich, but it's not on the menu."

Griff ignored her to gaze around the restaurant, seeming distracted.

"What's up, Digger?" Had something gone wrong already, Eva wondered.

He palmed his moustache. "I saw a red Porsche convertible out front. The plate said CONCH LVR. I want to know who it belongs to."

Eva surveyed the room, ready to ply her investigative skills. "Two overdressed blondes sitting by the front window are locals. Their skin looks like rawhide."

"Nah. I think it's the gray-haired guy with the ponytail and bandana. He could be an old smuggler I worked a case on. That's why I'm curious who has the car."

"This dive is probably crawling with former suspects," Eva said. "I'm famished."

Griff didn't bother checking the menu. "Double cheeseburger for me."

"That quick? You're in the Keys. Why not something authentic? The grouper sandwich comes with coleslaw and hushpuppies."

"Another time. I'm sticking to my standby, another one of my rules."

Eva shook her head. After all these years, she should have realized she and Griff shared the same quirk.

"Growing up," she said, "when my folks took me to a new place to eat, I ordered a grilled cheese and fries. Since becoming an agent, it's a Reuben."

"So Eva, are you going with the grouper? It's fresh and local."

Before she decided, the server came for their orders. Griff wanted a diet cola and double cheeseburger platter with extra fries. Eva shut her menu asking for a Hemmingway salad, a side of tomatoes, and water with lemon. The server hurried off.

"Authentic?" Griff frowned. "The Hemmingway salad is the same as any northern Virginia grilled chicken salad."

"It's served with fresh mango," Eva said over the rumbling of her stomach.

"Too exotic for me." Griff's voice dropped without warning. "Tonight we go clubbing."

"What? You're no jet-setter. Neither am I."

"Au contraire. Think again."

Eva examined his stoic face. Here he was acting weird again.

With folded arms, she pushed back. "Besides starving and heat making me tired, I will relax at the Nest talking later to Scott. You need to call Dawn."

"Already called her. Louie said he's flying to Saint Augustine tomorrow."

"So?"

The server placing drinks on the table prevented Griff's immediate reply. When she hurried away on flip-flops, Griff hissed, "Remember the court order? We have to put a GPS locator on his plane."

"Of course." Eva's eyes narrowed. "Phone Tech Ops, tell them to hustle down to Saint Augustine tomorrow and install the locator."

"Evelyn, you're smarter than that," came his sharp reply.

"What are you talking about?"

"Would he admit he's flying to Cuba? No, he'd pretend to fly to Saint Augustine. Besides, we know where his plane is at this very minute."

"We can't get the Tech Ops team down here fast enough."

"That's why we'll be clubbing." He tapped his temple. "I brought a GPS locator with me just in case."

"You'll install it on the plane? Do you know how?"

"You have forgotten, Evelyn. I used to be in the Tech Ops group."

Eva threw her head back and whooped wildly. A few folks turned her way, even Mr. Bandana.

She leaned forward, speaking to Griff in hushed tones, "This heat has melted my brain cells. You installed a tracking device on the freighter in the Indian Ocean on the Isle of Socotra. I acted as your lookout."

Their meals arrived as Mr. Bandana hurried out.

"Let's see if you're right," Eva challenged. "I believe he recognized you."

"Or you scared him off with your cackling."

The scrawny guy stomped toward the Porsche. Griff smiled widely in apparent victory. A moment later, they heard the distinct blast of a Harley firing up. With the revving of the throttle, the engine continued popping.

"Looks like my ladies are still here," Eva said with a winning smile.

Griff salted his fries, and Eva cut grilled chicken into bite-sized pieces.

"I'm serious, Evelyn. We wire up Louie's plane in case he heads for Cuba. You'll be my lookout again."

"Are we flying back up to Marathon? Louie will wonder what's up."

Griff bit into his burger. They ate in silence until he shook his head.

"Can't take off or land at Lime Key at night. The strip isn't lighted, remember?"

"You're not suggesting we ask Louie to borrow his car so we can install a tracking device on his plane? That's the ultimate insult."

"Evelyn, you missed one option. We take the motorbike."

"Are you crazy?" she whispered. "It's forty miles to Marathon. My back hurt after four blocks to this restaurant."

"Louie will think we went out to some club."

"Can't we rent a car?"

"Nope. The car rentals are all at the Marathon airport."

"A cab?" Eva held her fork by her mouth. A piece of chicken dropped into her lap, which she quickly swept into a paper napkin.

"Oh sure. We tell the cabby, 'Wait here while we break into this guy's plane. We'll only be about forty-five minutes.'"

"So much for an early night." Eva stabbed another piece of chicken with her fork. "I guess it's Marathon or bust. We install it tonight."

Griff didn't try hiding his smirk. "I knew you'd agree."

"There's one condition." It was Eva's turn to smirk.

"What's that?"

"I drive the motorbike. You ride on the back."

They finished eating, taking the pressure off by talking about future family vacations.

"I can hope this case will be finished by Christmas, can't I?" Eva asked. "I want to bring my kids to Florida to swim and play in the sand."

Griff grabbed his check. "Sounds like fun. I want to take Dawn to England to see Grandmother Topping, who is not well."

With that, they paid separately for the meals, and making for the door, they passed the two blondes sipping cocktails.

Outside, Eva raised her hands, not noticing the heat. "Looks like I win."

"Wrong again, Evelyn."

He pointed to an empty place in the gravel lot. The Porsche convertible was gone.

"Okay, Digger." Eva yanked on her helmet. "We have a

serious problem. Two ladies are inside, and the fancy car is nowhere in sight. Our instincts need to improve."

"At what?"

"Judging the predisposition of people based on their appearance."

Griff pulled on his helmet, fastening the strap beneath his chin. "Here's a question. After talking with Louie, do you believe he's a criminal?"

"You mean besides being a cigar smuggler? We don't know, do we?"

Eva pulled out the motorbike key from her pocket. She started the bike, then wiped the face shield off with an extra napkin from the restaurant. Griff climbed on behind her and bent forward.

"Which is why we install the device on his plane tonight. We get it done and find out about the real Louie."

Eva couldn't argue with his logic. She sputtered out of the parking lot, dreading the sweltering miles to Marathon.

Chapter 23

After leaving the restaurant, Eva and Griff made a quick trip to the Nest where he removed from the undercover airplane certain things he needed for their covert mission at the Marathon airport in roughly an hour.

Eva kept a lookout for Louie, not spotting him anywhere. No lights burned in his third-floor apartment. She figured the caretaker had turned in early before his morning flight to wherever he was going. Griff held up his backpack, indicating he was all set.

She grabbed a pack of gum from her purse. They hustled down to the bike and motored away in the dark with Griff perched awkwardly on the back of the undersized Honda. The pack dangling on his back gave him the appearance of a college student. Rather, it contained his secret stuff—amp meter, electronic devices, and tools.

It was nearly eleven thirty and they passed few other drivers on Overseas Highway at this late hour.

"I hope it stays that way," Eva muttered under her breath.

Griff piped into her ear, "Me too. Let's get in and out without being seen."

"The headlamp on this bike is dim," Eva complained. "It's pitch-black."

"I brought each of us a flashlight."

Both agents, being equipped with small police walkie-talkies, kept up similar chatter during their ride to Marathon. Tiny buds running from the radios to their ears worked slick. A mini-microphone in the same wire gave them the ability to talk back and forth during the forty-mile ride.

One thing Eva hadn't counted on during the trip. Bugs splattered against her body and visor. By the time she reached the airport, she could barely see. She stopped long enough to wipe the visor on her jeans, and then sped on past the airport, noting a place where she could act as Griff's scout.

Eva said in her mic excitedly, "I see Louie's plane, near General Aviation."

"Keep going," burst Griff's crisp voice in her ear. "Be alert to any activity."

She drove to a T-intersection before making two rapid lefts to enter the parking lot of a closed sandwich joint. Placing both feet on the ground, Eva used all the strength in her legs to back the bike to the airport fence. She cut the engine.

They removed their helmets in unison. Her face shield already had another squished bug right where her nose belonged. When she told Griff that she'd need to clean it before their long trip back to Lime Key, he told her he had a water bottle in his pack.

"Good thinking, Digger," Eva said, adding a caution, "Let's not stay too long."

Griff hustled off the bike, causing it to rise on its springs. "I am glad to see no signs of life along the street or by Louie's plane."

Eva gaped at high fences and shadowy side streets. "It's like I've stepped off the planet into another realm. Everything is unfamiliar. We have no idea what to expect."

"Quit worrying. I've got this," Griff said, hoisting the pack over his shoulder.

Eva's eyes searched the perimeter, and she gazed heavenward. Sparkling diamonds covered the night sky despite the low lighting around the airport building.

"I haven't seen this many stars since we pretended to be scientists on Socotra," she whispered, her spirits soaring. This was actually fun.

"Let's hope we have as terrific a result as that case." He pointed behind the sub shop. "I'm skirting behind those buildings between here and Louie's plane."

"Okay." Eva tapped her earbuds. "As your extra set of eyes, I'll be hiding in thick bushes by General Aviation and the highway."

"Keep me posted. We'll meet here when I'm done. Say a prayer all goes well."

Dressed in black jeans and shirt, her partner quickly melded with the shadows. He was gone. Eva started the bike and drove slowly down the road adjacent to the airport. Besides a car whizzing by on Highway One, the night in Marathon was eerily still.

Eva shut off the engine, coasting to the curb near the flowering bushes. She froze for a moment to listen. No sounds alerted her ears. It took some doing, but with one powerful motion, she hefted the bike over the sidewalk and into the bushes. Boy, did she feel the strain in her upper arm muscles.

There was nothing to do but shrug off the dull ache. She laid the bike on its side and peeled off her helmet. In its place, she pulled a black knit stocking cap over her blond ponytail coiled atop her head. Griff sure had thought of everything.

Through mini-binoculars, Eva's eyes searched the fenced compound. Then she scanned the grassy area east of General Aviation. The glasses were powerful enough to give her a commanding view of the area and Louie's plane. Eva soon spotted

Griff's dark shape stepping from behind the maintenance building.

She pushed the button on her microphone. "I'm concealed in the bushes and see you. No activity."

"Thanks," came his answer in her earbuds.

Eva sat down on the bike and jumped to her feet in a jiffy.

"Yikes!" she exclaimed, rubbing her bottom.

She'd made the mistake of sitting on the hot exhaust pipe. A quick flip of the bike, and she carefully perched on its other side. Moments later, she observed Griff through the binoculars as he strode across the tarmac and into the gloom cast by Louie's Cessna.

Griff planned to use his lock pick tools to get into the plane. He'd proved his lock picking was a handy skill to have. The most memorable time was when Eva locked herself out of her house. Dutch was a baby and napping. She'd gone for the mail. Being locked out, she called on Griff, who came to her rescue before Dutch awoke.

A whisper crackled in Eva's ears. "I'm in. Let's hope I find no problems."

"Gotcha covered," she answered from her perch.

A breeze blowing through the bushes not only kept mosquitoes at bay, but the lovely air brought cheerful childhood memories floating into Eva's mind. She shifted her weight from one hard spot to another, thinking of fun visits to Florida with her folks and Jillie. Eva had loved snorkeling and collecting shells with her now-deceased twin sister.

Just as she returned her thoughts to their op, a white Chevy veered off Highway One and through an open gate. Eva jolted up straight, watching the Impala drive onto the tarmac.

She keyed her mic. "Griff, white Chevy heading your way."

He pressed his microphone button twice in her ears. It was his way of confirming without a word.

"It may be an unmarked cruiser," she said. "I can't tell if it has a spotlight."

His double crackle came again. The car swung to a stop beside Louie's plane. Eva held her breath waiting for a spotlight to sweep across the plane. Were they busted?

She adjusted the binoculars in time to see the driver's door open. A husky man hustled out from behind the wheel. Eva was already on her feet when out of the passenger door stepped a shorter man. Sizing him up, she could easily take him.

Was it a crazy notion to hop on the bike and race to the tarmac to even the sides?

Prudence won out, and she stayed put, viewing the driver haul three suitcases from the trunk. Were these two guys somehow in league with Louie?

Eva memorized the passenger's face as he walked to the single-engine plane next to Louie's. He opened that door, tossing in bags one by one from the driver. It was an odd time of night for someone to fly off in a small airplane. Why three suitcases? Could he be smuggling cigars or drugs?

The engine of this unexpected plane began running. The driver eased into the Chevy, backing up to make room for the plane's departure. With a muffled roar, the plane pulled forward and headed toward the taxiway, the strobe flashing on its tail.

Griff's voice popped in Eva's ears. "Wow, that was close. Get the tail number from the plane and tag from the car."

"Ten-four. Car's coming out now. I can get it."

Eva shifted her spyglasses to the plane, memorizing the number emblazoned on the tail. She used a pen from her fanny pack to write it quickly on her palm. When the car turned on the highway, she noted the license plate too on her palm.

"Okay, I got both tag numbers," Eva reported.

"It's an oven in here. Sweat's burning my eyes. I had to stop and douse my light when the plane took off. It's installed, and I'm testing. Give me fifteen minutes."

Eva stretched her legs to relieve a cramp. Suddenly, headlights of a car pulling off the highway swept through the bushes. She didn't move. A Monroe County Sheriff's patrol car rolled slowly down the street. Eva's heart thumped wildly.

Someone must have spotted her or Griff and called the police to complain. Eva used the binoculars to sweep across the tarmac. Everything was quiet. A dazzling light pierced her bushy hideaway. In an instant, Eva was blinded.

A car came to a halt by her hideaway. She heard the unmistakable squelch of a police radio. A female voice growled, "Get out of the bushes. Keep your hands where I can see them."

Triggering her microphone, Eva warned Griff, "I'm being tossed by locals."

Her legs protested with cramps during her stroll to the patrol car. The female deputy stepped out, and Eva quickly said, "I'm an ICE agent on a stakeout."

The deputy shone a bright flashlight in her face. "You've got ID, right?"

"With your permission, it's in my fanny pack."

"Let me see it."

Eva gave her the case with the gold badge affixed to it. The deputy shone the flashlight on the ID. "Special Agent Eva Montanna, sorry to pull you from your lair. I saw a motorcycle in the bushes and came to see if it was stolen. You're a surprise."

"Mind turning off the light?" Eva asked. "It attracts unwanted attention. My partners and I received a tip our fugitive might be flying in tonight."

"Sorry to mess you up." The deputy extinguished both lights. "Can I help?"

"Not really, but thanks." Eva put away her credentials. "You might spot our other cars in the area on surveillance. We shift around to avoid encounters with your patrols. I wasn't in a position to move as I have the close-up point."

The deputy tipped her hat. "Good luck, Montanna. I hope you find your fugitive."

Moments later, another close call pulled away and Eva sighed in relief.

Eva heard from Griff, "I used the distraction you created to button up and move. I'm headed to where you dropped me off."

"On my way."

Eva yanked the bike from the bushes knowing she'd made a narrow escape and went to meet Griff. In the subtle glow of a distant streetlight, she waited, tensing when she heard feet crunching on gravel. First their operation was nearly rousted by a late flyer, and then a committed county officer nosed in. What next?

Her pulse raced, and Eva steeled herself to the unknown. Seconds later, her partner emerged from around the eatery.

"Good, it's you," she told Griff, meaning it.

"Is everything okay? I saw police lights."

"A local officer spotted my bike in the bushes. I told her we had a stakeout for a fugitive coming in on a private flight."

"Did she buy it?"

"Seemed to." Eva rubbed sweat off her forehead.

Griff climbed aboard the bike. "GPS installed. I called the Virginia monitoring group. They confirmed it's working."

"Good. And we're off."

Eva started the engine and released the clutch. As she rolled from the lot, Griff leaned in close to her helmet.

"Stop at any fast-food joint that's open. I need some relief and coffee."

AT SEVEN IN THE MORNING, Eva's phone alarm startled her awake. Her eyes flew open. A strange ceiling fan rotating above her bed was the link to her recall. She was undercover at Lime Key. In the guest bedroom decorated with an island motif, thoughts of Holly wasting away in prison flitted through Eva's mind.

She prayed to God for the right result. Her goal was always for justice, yet at times her cases ended far differently than what Eva expected. After washing up and changing into slacks, a knit shirt, and comfortable shoes, Eva made a beeline for the kitchen, tapping on the closed master bedroom door on the way.

"Rise and shine, sleepyhead."

Both she and Griff needed to be sharp before Louie flew to St. Augustine. A hectic search revealed a coffee packet. Eva tossed it in to brew. Griff still hadn't stirred, so she knocked harder on his door. Silence greeted her ears, which seemed strange. She pushed the door open to his tidy room and perfectly-made bed.

Eva spun around, going to the deck with its gorgeous view of the Gulf's green-blue water.

"Good morning," a voice called from below.

She glanced down. There sat Griff and Louie under a tiki hut on the patio, drinking what looked like coffee.

Louie waved. "Evelyn, coffee's all ready. Bring yer cup."

Rather than yell and wake neighbors so early, Eva collected a cup and the fresh pot she'd brewed. Down the steps she went wearing a smile, thinking the guys looked every bit the part of relaxed vacationers. Only, she and Griff were on duty 24/7.

She lifted the coffeepot. "I made some too."

"Good," Louie piped. "We'll have enough."

After pouring coffee for herself, Eva pulled a chair next to Griff and using his undercover name said, "Digger, I'm surprised you're up already."

Louie laughed. "You must not have partied too hard last night."

"I needed java." Griff gestured to empty davits along the canal. "Louie said Carlos and Holly used to hang their speedboat on those. We should get a boat."

Eva raised her eyebrows and sipped the hot coffee, not sure where Griff was going with his comment. Louie was all for the idea.

"See that boat bobbin' in the water?" He pointed two houses down the canal. "Theirs was like that one. A real beauty. Carlos took his boat to their place in West Palm. Prob'ly the government has it now."

"What do you have planned for today, Digger?" Eva probed,

thankful for a cool breeze blowing across her face. Must be mornings were the "get-it-done" times in the Keys.

"Digger is drivin' me to my plane in Marathon. He'll bring back my car."

"Sounds like a plan," she said. "I could use breakfast."

Apparently not ready to leave, Griff urged Louie to tell what got him flying.

"That's easy." Louie poured more coffee all round before saying, "I grew up in northern Florida by a rural airport. From the day I could ride my bike to the field, flyin' hooked me. I was a jumper for the 82nd Airborne Division for the Army—"

"The 82nd fought in Grenada. I saw it on TV," Griff interjected.

Louie's eyes bulged. "Oh yeah? Well, I was there, and in the Gulf War, Bosnia, Kosovo. I stayed in, retirin' as a sergeant major. Used my GI bill to learn to fly. I got my multi-engine, instrument, and instructor's license and headed for south Florida."

"Good move," Griff observed. "I love airplanes. No GI bill, so I paid to learn. It was worth it. Sure beats flying commercial. Done any flying to the Bahamas, Louie?"

"Yeah. Flew charter flights to Nassau where I met a well-connected lawyer. Lots of his clients were drug smugglers. They'd be arrested and jailed there."

He stopped talking when a group of divers slid by in their boat, gurgling noises and steam rising from the stern.

"You have good connections," Eva said, mentally noting details of his story.

"Yeah. The lawyer had me stand by at Lauderdale's airport waitin' for a sack of money. Then I'd fly to Nassau. When the smugglers made bail, I flew 'em back to Florida. I was flying the lawyer and politicians all over. How about you, Digger?"

"Sure." Griff guzzled his coffee. "I've flown to Cat Island, Caymans, and Turks and Caicos to, you know, relax."

"Ever been to Norman's Cay?"

"No, Louie, I've heard it was a smuggler's haven."

"Yer right. You didn't fly there uninvited. Guys with guns crawlin' all over the place. I flew there a bunch, and toward the end I hated it."

"I can imagine," Eva replied. "So you quit all that flying?"

Louie didn't answer. Instead, he looked at his watch. "We should get a move on."

They gathered up coffee and cups, with Louie walking up to his apartment for his suitcase. Eva collected her purse, and some minutes later, she sat ensconced in the backseat of Louie's BMW convertible, her hair in a ponytail. He said he'd drive. Eva conjured an awful image of him tearing across the highway, her hair a tangled mess.

Griff walked up, and after giving Eva a perceptive glance, he told Louie to put the top up, adding in a clipped voice, "I heard it might rain."

"Oh yeah?" Louie gazed at the cloudless blue sky.

"Maybe later. Put it up just in case," Griff insisted.

Louie did as asked, and they sped along Overseas Highway at fifty-five miles per hour. Eva sat back, enjoying the sparkling blue water slipping by. Louie swapped stories with Griff about past hair-raising flights.

"What are the chances Holly and Carlos will beat the case?" he asked.

Griff looked back at Eva. "I almost invested in their scam, but decided not to."

"Hey, me too." Louie's rough hands gripped the wheel. "I never sunk in a dime. I'm sorry for the suckers who lost everything."

So far so good, Eva thought. Louie acted comfortable with them with no sense he was about to be drawn into a legal quagmire of his own making. They reached General Aviation at the Marathon airport. Eva spotted the bushes where she'd hidden last night when the officer rousted her. Louie parked by the office, popped the trunk, and jumped out. He swiped his carry-on bag from the trunk.

"Thanks for drivin' me." Louie tossed Griff the keys. "See 'ya in a few days."

"We'll stay until your plane is good to go," Griff said as if Louie was a friend.

That was all they said. Being in the Keys for who knew how long didn't sit well with Eva. She started steaming as she twisted out of the backseat. Settling into the front seat, Eva watched Louie stride with purpose to the plane, and wondered what his purposes were. Soon the Cessna's propellers were spinning, and the plane headed to the taxiway.

Griff started the BMW. "You want to stop for breakfast?"

"We might as well buy groceries. Looks like we'll be in Lime Key forever. We should let our families know."

"I know you're peeved, Evelyn," Griff said, turning south. "He thinks we're here to enjoy the Nest. Let's see how long it takes Tech Ops to tell us that he's airborne."

"There! There!" she shouted.

"What?" Griff's head followed where Eva was pointing.

"Jody's Nook is packed with cars. I like your idea of breakfast."

"You startled me. I didn't know what to expect."

He wheeled into the lot, snatched his phone, and glared at the display. "This is it," he said, answering the call. "Topping here."

Eva watched him nod and listened to his side of the conversation.

"Right. We knew he left the Marathon airport. Advise when he lands. Said he's going to Saint Augustine. Thanks."

Griff popped a grin. "Our work last night paid off. Tech Ops says Louie is flying north. That white Chevy and passenger aren't on any watch lists. Isn't technology wonderful?"

"Right about now, steak and eggs would taste wonderful," Eva said to the growling of her stomach.

Chapter 24

Eva was stowing cold items in the fridge at Holly's island retreat when Griff entered the kitchen huffing from his climb to the second floor.

"I've been thinking." Eva wadded up a plastic bag. "We should apply for a warrant and search Louie's quarters. Or ask for a listening device."

Griff removed a decanter of iced tea from the refrigerator.

"I've thought about it plenty. Eva, we don't have probable cause. Not for a bug."

"You doubt what Holly told us?"

Griff set the tea down hard. "Listen to what you just said. You're generally a bigger skeptic than I am. Why wouldn't Holly lie?"

Eva marched to the window. Her eyes sought the calming waters, which helped change her mind.

"Yes," she said, spinning around. "We do need more evidence."

"We may have it. Tech Ops called while I was downstairs and had me check my app." Griff walked over and showed Eva his smartphone. "They gave me this app to monitor the tracker I installed on Louie's plane. He lied about Saint Augustine."

Her eyes rounded. "I sensed it all along. Look at him flying past Saint Augustine and going up the East Coast. What's his game?"

"The fact he lied proves Holly's info is true."

"You decide on a warrant," Eva said. "I'll let Scott know I won't be home soon."

She took a private moment out on the deck. While punching in the number and waiting for Scott to answer, she saw a majestic sight. A bald eagle swooped across the canal, its white head and tail feathers flashing brilliantly against the blue sky.

"It's Scott," her husband barked in her ear.

As her phone came up blocked, he wouldn't know she was the caller. "Hi, honey, it's me," she quickly said. "Can you talk?"

"I've a meeting in one minute. How is your trip going?"

"An unexpected twist caught us by surprise. I may not be home for a few days."

Scott proposed a twist of his own. "If need be, Viola can stay with the kids, and I'll fly down. I could use a sunshine break. Another storm is brewing."

"Like in tornado?" Eva was instantly on the alert.

"Just rain and plenty of it. A real deluge. The kids are good, though Kaley is antsy to confirm Izzy's trip with her parents. I told her to wait until you're home."

Eva pictured her family living without her, and a dull ache stabbed her heart. If only Operation Stogie could move along more swiftly.

"I just blew you a kiss," she told him with tenderness. She knew he wouldn't intrude on her undercover case, but loved him for proposing a trip down.

"Love you too," he said. "Maybe we can talk later."

Eva agreed to call him come evening. She signed off and poured a glass of lemonade before Griff joined her on the deck. He reclined on a lounge chair and stared up at wispy white clouds as if deep in thought. She perched on a rattan chair.

"Be alert and you'll see the bald eagle Louie mentioned. Have an update on his flight?"

"Not yet." Griff swatted an insect. "Once we ascertain his scheme, you head home. I'll stay here until we can arrange for my replacement."

Eva approved of his plan. "Scott will also be relieved. Brett could fly down and pose as our friend and tenant when his case finishes up."

"He called yesterday and said the judge is giving instructions to the jury."

The roar of jet engines shattered the balmy breeze. Eva and Griff leapt to their feet. Walking to the railing, they saw a U.S. military jet swooping low over the runway on the opposite side of the house. Eva set her drink on a table and plugged her ears. Griff scurried to get a glimpse of the tail.

The jet banked and circled around. A second time the giant plane blasted over the house, its thunder reverberating in the air. It was so low Eva glimpsed the pilots inside.

She stood incredulous. "Is he going to land? You barely stopped the 421 in time."

"Nah, that jet is too big. It's a Navy P-8 Poseidon."

"What do you make of his flight so near the rooftops?"

"I have no idea, but he's way too close." Griff craned his neck around. "I love seeing these babies up close and exhaust from their engines."

"Scott would love it too." Her husband would be as stoked by the jet's intrusion.

Griff kept his gaze skyward. "It's a reconnaissance aircraft, probably on a training flight. Maybe going to Key West Naval Air Station."

"That makes sense." Eva's ears popped. "Try reaching Brett and see if he can get down here in a few days."

SCOTT MONTANNA HUNG UP FROM EVA and hustled to the staff meeting, only to find it was cancelled due to a scheduling conflict. Back he sped to his cramped office at the Capitol, where he printed tomorrow's press release. His eyes shifted from piles of congressional reports to his credenza, lingering on a stunning photo of his lovely wife in her lacy wedding gown.

The way Eva gazed at him so trusting with her periwinkle blue eyes convicted him. Scott missed her, yet something else bothered him. He'd let her down, and worse, he failed to tell her so earlier. A prolonged press conference yesterday meant the kids choked down a pizza burned by Kaley with no parent being present. He hadn't gotten home until nearly dark.

Scott vowed to do a better job starting now. As press secretary for the Speaker of the House, he oversaw release of congressional news to the world's media. Still, his family came first. A small window facing west out toward the Washington Monument made him think deep and hard about the sunshine in which Eva was basking.

The falling rain gave him an irresistible urge to call his wife and tell her they were all moving to Florida. He could buy a small plane and shuttle tourists around. He was plenty sick of politics in D.C. Before he could talk himself out of the wild notion, his desk phone buzzed. Scott yanked up the receiver.

"SecDef's chief of staff is on the line," Scott's secretary Nancy said, sounding winded. "Claims it's important."

Scott punched the flashing button. "Hey, what do you need?"

"Secretary Douglas is in your SCIF with members of the Armed Services Committee. We've tried his cell phone but can't reach him."

"Everyone has to turn their phones off anywhere near or inside the SCIF, even Secretary Douglas." Scott bounded to his feet. "I can run up and ask him to call you from a secure phone."

"Thanks. Make that ASAP."

Choosing not to grill the Secretary's aide about the vital matter, Scott rushed from his office and through the Speaker's Lobby, right past the portrait of the first Speaker, Fredrick Muhlenberg, and dozens of other past speakers lining the walls. At this moment in time, the "People's House" was again absorbed by the tyranny of the urgent.

Thoughts of sunny Florida disappeared from Scott's mind as he arranged with security personnel guarding the SCIF for Secretary Douglas to call the Pentagon. Mission accomplished, he hesitated outside the special room, which prevented anyone from intercepting audible or electronic conversations. Scott's curiosity mounted as to what prompted James's call.

Within minutes, the meeting adjourned, and Secretary Douglas made phone contact with his chief of staff. Scott hung around to see what he could learn. As SecDef prepared to leave the area, Scott grabbed the sleeve of one of his four assistants. The aide, a full colonel, fumbled to turn on his cell phone.

"Why the rush?" Scott asked. "I was called to get your attention."

The colonel scowled. "Montanna, you know better. It's classified."

"Come on." It was Scott's turn to frown. "You know I am cleared. I sat in on all your meetings when I served at the Pentagon."

The colonel stared at Scott for a long moment before turning his phone back off.

"You have one minute."

He and Scott went into the SCIF. Scott pulled the door shut.

The wiry colonel arched his graying eyebrows and sounded like he had a mouthful of gravel when he intoned, "We just learned a Russian sub is lurking in the Gulf of Mexico. We're heading back for a top-secret powwow."

This news stunned Scott. A steady man filled with courage, he was rarely taken aback. But this time his concern went beyond national security. It was a given that Russian subs should never be in the Gulf. But with his beloved Eva in the Florida Keys, this was akin to war in Scott's mind. Kaley had already been too close to Russia's crosshairs.

Tough questions berated him, the main one being what kind of danger was Eva in? The intel was classified. It wasn't like he could phone her and shout out a warning.

He gulped and managed, "The same thing happened what … three years ago?"

"Yes, sir. The 'Czar of all the Russias' pushes our buttons once again. When will it stop?" The colonel reached for the door. "Remember, tight lips."

Scott promised to remain mum about what he'd just heard. Outwardly he seemed calm, but dashing to his office, his mind pushed ahead of him all the way. He wasted no time checking incoming messages on his computer. Nothing about a Russian Federation sub lurking off Florida's coast.

Next he called his wife, hoping Eva wasn't in the midst of meeting the target of her investigation.

"Welcome to hot and humid Margaritaville," she chirped.

Scott was in no mood to be merry. "Can you talk?"

"Yes. Is everyone okay?"

"We're all fine up *here*," he said, emphasizing the last word.

"Good, you sound tense and had me worried." She puffed a breath into his ear. "Griff and I are sitting on the deck beneath an umbrella talking strategy. After you and I spoke earlier, a large Navy jet flew super low over us twice."

"Hmm." That got his mind revving. "Eva, what kind was it?"

She asked Griff and Scott heard him say in the background, "Tell him it's a Navy P8."

"Griff says it's a Navy P8," Eva repeated.

"Really? Is he sure?"

"Scott, he's a pilot himself."

Griff interrupted in a louder voice, "Tell Scott the P8 is a sub chaser."

"Did you hear? Griff says the P8 is sub chaser."

"I heard. That's why I wonder if he's sure. Why is a P8 flying over the Keys?"

"Griff thinks it's a training mission."

"Maybe. Then again, maybe not," Scott mused aloud when he wanted to shout, "Get out now!" Before he could issue a cryptic warning, Eva changed the topic.

"A team member will be sent here so I should be home before long."

"Is Griff staying put?" Scott asked.

"He'll follow me home, and then run back and forth."

"Great!" Trouble rolled off Scott's shoulders. Eva would be leaving the danger zone. No need to divulge classified intelligence.

"Our kiddos miss you, honey," he said. "I'll head home early so I can have dinner with them before Andy's concert at church. He's drumming tonight."

"Too bad I didn't realize it was scheduled. Tell him for me he'll do great. What's for dinner tonight?"

"Whatever the kids select at The Athena's. Your favorite Greek place to eat."

Her laughter in his ear sounded wonderful. "Good thing I'll be home by week's end. Our budget can't endure my absence much longer. Hug the kids for me."

The line went dead. Scott set the receiver on its base and then hunted online for any hint of the Russian sub lurking near America's shores. He found nothing.

So Scott began devising a strategy while shutting down his computer and locking his desk. Come morning, he'd evaluate developments and press the House Speaker to hold classified hearings on Russia's military strength. He'd also check with Commander Marks at the Pentagon and see what he could glean about Russia's future intentions.

It was impossible to imagine their next move.

Chapter 25

Eva refilled her lemonade after ending Scott's call. Why had he phoned again so soon? She sat across from Griff on the deck, her brow flexed.

"It's hard being Mom and Dad. Scott sounded distracted, like he can't tell me something. Maybe hearing about the P8 has him nostalgic for his Air Force flying days."

It seemed Eva was talking to herself. Griff was preoccupied with his smartphone. He finally looked up. "I'm watching Louie's flight track. He landed at Lynchburg."

"We need to find out what's taking him to Virginia."

The words barely escaped Eva's lips when Griff's phone rang. He raised it to his ear, mouthing to Eva, "It's Tech Ops."

"Yes, Lynchburg," Griff said into the phone. "I watched him descend."

He paused before telling the caller, "Good. You read my instructions. Let me know if they arrive in time. Patch them through to me if anything happens. Thanks."

"Did he leave Virginia already?" Eva wondered aloud.

"He's still there. Tech Ops alerted FBI Lynchburg of Louie's flight, and requested agents be dispatched to the airport for surveillance."

Overcome by the heat, Eva fanned herself with a magazine as she told Griff, "Louie lied about his flight plans. Do you suppose he's delivering cigars in Lynchburg?"

"How could he be? I was in the 310 last night. Plus you and I saw him load his plane before he left. All he took was a small carry-on bag."

Eva shrugged. "Money or drugs then?"

"That's why we flew here. If we don't uncover his gig soon, we'll shut down."

"I'm wilting out here," Eva said, rising to go inside.

A gnawing in her stomach drove her to raid the fridge. A green apple might refresh her. Meanwhile Griff turned on the TV, muting its sound.

Before Eva took a bite, her phone beeped, advising she had a message.

It was from Brett: *... do you know kat kowicki ...*

Eva typed back: *... yes ... why*

A pause before Brett replied: *... she says you are good friends ... so i should talk with her ... jury deliberating ...*

Eva called to Griff who was pillaging in the fridge. "Brett texted me. His case is with the jury. I'll text back and fill you in."

She typed Brett a message in bold capital letters:
DON'T SPEAK TO KAT ... IS ZEALOUS REPORTER FIRST ... FRIEND SECOND!

His reply a little later was simply ... *roger that* ...

Eva munched her apple while Griff inhaled a handful of carrots.

"I'll be gaining the five pounds I lost," Eva grumbled, heading for the garbage disposal with her apple core.

Her phone chirped again. Brett sent a new message: ... *jury back ... fastest verdict I've ever seen* ...

"Jury's in," Eva told Griff as she clicked on the TV sound. "Kat Kowicki's after Brett for an interview. Oh, there she is already on the courthouse steps."

Griff sauntered in, devouring a purple plum. The camera focused on Kat.

Her eyes gleamed as she aimed a microphone in the face of a woman, and quizzed, "How do you feel knowing the jury is about to enact justice?"

The woman shook her head and held up a shaky hand. The camera zoomed on tears rolling down her face.

"Leave her alone!" Eva barked at Kat on the TV.

"Chill, Eva, she's doing her job."

"No, I saw that poor lady break down on the stand. Plus, Thelma lost everything to Holly and Carlos. Here we sit in their expensive home eating fruit and enjoying the fruits of their crime. It stinks."

"I agree." Griff finished his plum, wrapping a napkin around the pit. "If only the jury sees things the way we do."

Eva sat down, anxious to hear the verdict announced. The newscast went to a commercial. It took several minutes for Kat to speak animatedly into her microphone, "A jury of eight women and four men returned guilty verdicts on every count for Carlos Munoz. His wife Holly has been acquitted of four counts, and convicted on two related charges of taking money from investors in their Ponzi scheme."

Several boisterous people streamed by, some crying, some shouting for joy. Kat swung her microphone into the face of a woman Eva knew well.

"Kat's interviewing Thelma," she told Griff in a hushed voice.

Thelma clasped her cocoa-colored hands, telling Kat and the world, "I never prayed for my finances. I plunged ahead at the first chance to invest."

She wiped her moist dark eyes. "Anyone who hears me, please be careful trusting your hard-earned money to anyone. I waited to file my claim, and the deadline passed. God is helping me with wonderful friends, and I thank Him."

"What do you think of guilty verdicts?" Kat probed.

Thelma's hands clung to a tissue. "God is filled with mercy."

"Do you mean forgiveness? Ms. King, have you forgiven Carlos and Holly?"

"It's been hard." Thelma swung her head sideways. "Yes, I forgive them. That's what my Christian faith teaches me."

Kat looked into the camera, telling her viewers zestfully, "Two perpetrators of a multi-million-dollar Ponzi scheme are now feeling the sword of justice and will be sentenced in thirty days."

A commercial swelled across the TV screen, and Eva muted the sound. "When Louie finds out Holly is a convicted felon, it might shake him loose."

"You raise a valid point."

For the next hour, as FBI agents tried finding Louie in Lynchburg, Eva and Griff phoned their boss to arrange for Eva to be relieved by Brett along with her flight home. She stepped out onto the deck to clear her mind. Beyond the canal toward the Gulf of Mexico she saw storm clouds gathering. Winds picked up. But all Eva could think of was Thelma. Her jaw flexed with concern. Was Eva hurting her friend by helping Holly? She mulled over this dilemma to Griff banging cupboards inside.

When his noise quit, she'd made a decision. Their pursuit was for justice, wherever it led. If a convicted criminal by the name of Holly Munoz received a light sentence, so be it. Moments later, Griff joined her on the deck holding up his phone.

"I was down checking the undercover airplane. I have Tech Ops on the line."

He suggested they confer inside. They sat at the dining table, and Griff turned on the speaker before saying in the phone, "If he flies, he'll use the Cessna 310 he arrived in."

The agent on the other end replied, "FBI Agent Jethro Smith is on my other line. He's at Lynchburg General Aviation. I'll connect you both but will stay on the line."

"Go ahead, Agent Smith. You're on with Agent Griff Topping."

"Jethro, you're on speaker," Griff said. "ICE Agent Eva Montanna is with us."

"Here's the story," Jethro began. "We found the Cessna 310, but no pilot. A few minutes ago that changed. White male, six feet tall, with long thin hair stowed a suitcase in that plane. He's doing a pre-flight inspection."

"Is it a small black carry-on? That's what we saw him take from Florida."

"No siree. This bag's large and bright pink, like a lady's suitcase."

"That's odd." Griff shot Eva a perplexed look.

"Griff … stand by." Jethro fell silent, then erupted, "Your guy's heading into the terminal. He is veering to where I'm sitting, so we're in luck."

It was a quiet moment before Jethro hissed, "Griff, he's talking to a lady with a bright pink carry-on. There they go, walking to the 310."

"Description?" Griff shouted back.

"Drop-dead gorgeous! White woman, maybe twenty-five, brown hair styled behind her head. Long legs. She's as tall as your guy. Any idea who she is?"

"No clue." Griff arched an eyebrow at Eva. "Yours is the first surveillance."

Jethro kept a running commentary of action. "He shoved her small pink bag in the rear … She's in the passenger seat … I'll e-mail you a photo I snapped on my phone."

Eva heard a voice paging someone in the background before Jethro spoke in a lively tone, "Both engines are running. I didn't see her arrive, or their initial meet. It's possible her car is parked nearby. I don't know how we'd find it."

"If she flew commercial, you could get her name off the manifest," Griff said.

"The 310 is on the taxiway," Jethro told them. "Tech Ops will be monitoring his flight. I have your file number and will send a surveillance report. Happy hunting."

Griff offered to return the favor, then shut off the speaker, giving Eva a penetrating look. "Yet another twist. What do you make of Louie's friend?"

"Did he mention a wife or girlfriend to you?"

"Let me think." Griff went to fetch two bottled waters from the fridge. Setting one down in front of Eva, he said, "He bragged of his military time, but nothing personal."

"Holly inferred Louie hides lots of things."

"I want to fix the red bike," Griff said, to which Eva snapped, "Don't you care where he goes next?"

"The carburetor is dirty. I'll see if I can start it in time to go out for dinner."

"What about Louie?"

"I multitask." Griff made straight for the door. "I'll be watching his path on my phone."

Eva had another question. "Will you ask for more surveillance?"

"If I know where he's landing. Maybe he's coming here to introduce his wife."

"Griff, I have a funny feeling in my bones about Louie Clark."

He shrugged, going off to monkey with the motorbike. Eva used the interval to call home, eager to find out from Andy how his concert went. The machine clicking on gave her a letdown feeling. Still, she left an upbeat message: "Mom loves you. See you all as soon as I can."

Eva settled onto a rattan chaise lounge, opening a devotional on her phone. A few passages into the teaching entitled "Faith Building," she heard the *blub-blub-blub* of a ski boat passing by in the canal.

Pleasant memories flowed through her mind. She imagined bobbing in the water, a blue ski vest supporting her torso. Her dad's ski boat advancing, and she could feel the tug of the tow rope. Even now her breathing contracted, thinking of slaloming as a teen with Dad spinning her around the vast Smith Mountain Lake.

Happy thoughts were interrupted when Griff walked in wiping his hands on a rag.

"Let me try your phone. Mine keeps getting dropped."

His forehead was lined with perspiration. Eva handed over her phone with no questions.

"Louie landed in Columbus," Griff said. "I get no response from their JTTF."

"You're dropped because you're working in the hangar." Eva picked up his phone. "See, you have enough bars here on the second floor."

Griff lifted a finger for quiet and began talking into her phone, "It's Agent Topping again. I'm in the Keys. My earlier calls were dropped."

"Griff," she jabbed a finger at her phone, "put it on speaker."

He tapped the screen, and Eva heard a woman say, "Our group is out qualifying at the gun range. A detective on the task force finished and I diverted him to the airport."

"Did you give him descriptions of Clark and his airplane?" Griff asked.

"Yes, sir. He has your number and will phone you directly."

Griff agreed to stand by and disconnected the call, venting to Eva, "Can you believe it? The whole squad goes to the firing range?"

"So do we," Eva said, grinning. "After they finish, they'll celebrate."

"Meanwhile, Louie and his mystery lady are off in the wind."

Eva sought to soothe his ruffled feathers. "Do as you told me earlier. Chill. Louie will return eventually. My appetite for a decent meal is real."

"Okay." Griff picked up his rag. "Decide where to eat. I almost have the bike running."

He reached for the door handle when a bright flash blinded Eva. A crash shook her entire body. Griff jumped and turned his face, twisted by the horror.

"That jet crashed!" Eva screamed.

"No," Griff stammered, running to the window. "That was lightning."

Eva hurried over, seeing nothing but sunshine and palms waving in the breeze. "It can't be. It's not even raining."

"In case you didn't know, Florida is the lightning capital," Griff said. "The bolts start cracking before the rain comes. Just pray it doesn't hit the house and start a fire."

Suddenly, huge drops began to splatter on the deck. Raging winds of tropical storm strength knocked over the potted palm trees on the deck. Another blast of thunder shook the house as sheets of rain blew horizontally past the windows.

Griff sped away from the glass and Eva did too. He unmuted the TV and started flipping stations. "I'm glad I wasn't outside going down the steps when the bolt of lightning hit."

"Are we safer down in the hangar?" Eva asked to the lights flickering and the TV going off and coming back on.

"You go ahead." Griff motioned toward the door. "Me? I'm staying in here where it's dry."

Lightning sizzled and thunder rocked the Pelican's Nest as Eva and Griff were treated to a high-velocity Florida storm.

"Dinner out is a bust," Eva said. "I'm not driving on that bike in a rainstorm."

Chapter 26

Northern Virginia

The next day, Eva and Brett took crisscrossing flights, with the DEA agent taking her place at Lime Key. For her part, Eva gratefully parted company with the Pelican's Nest and soared home in blue skies to attend her own nest.

Her first day back in the office, Eva received a heartening call from Griff.

"Louie drove Brett to a marina to scope out a boat for sale," he said. "I fully briefed Brett about Holly's cooperation, and he says he'll help us nab Louie."

"I'm relieved he's finally in the loop," Eva said, deleting old messages on her smartphone. "And Louie is accepting of Brett?"

"Like they're old buddies."

"Did Louie reveal anything about his pretend jaunt to St. Augustine?"

Griff grunted. "Only that his plane handled well."

"Stay on him, Griff. We need something to justify two agents being pulled away from the task force. Our boss is acting anxious, has me on your Chechen case."

In the following days, Eva conducted surveillance on the younger Chechen brother at the car wash. The only thing she came away with was a clean G-car.

Life at home became complicated. Eva and Scott received a new denial of a credit card for a new phantom, Mr. Brian Wheatley. A serious dilemma reared its head when Kaley handed her mom a printout of Izzy Sikorski and her parents' travel plans for Thanksgiving. Eva still wasn't sure she wanted them to come before the Lime Key case was resolved.

And to add more stress, Viola wanted Eva and Scott to tour a farmhouse she'd found near Leesburg before submitting an offer. Scott also had been busy during her absence researching great destinations for next year's Easter vacation.

On Monday, Griff called Eva, his tone downcast. "Brett and I are stumped. We've uncovered nothing to support Holly's allegations that Louie is smuggling."

"So it's over? You're pulling the plug?"

"Not entirely. I come home, and Brett becomes a lazy island dweller."

"Good. The more time he spends with Louie, the better the chance Brett will sniff out something we couldn't."

Eva went her merry way enjoying life and work until receiving a brief and worrying call from CIA Agent Bo Rider.

All he said was, "Meet me by the baseball diamond at Nottoway Park this afternoon."

"How about two o'clock?" Eva asked, to which he agreed.

The line went dead. Though mystified by his cryptic tone, she also knew their connection was unsecure. Bo wouldn't tell her any more even if she pressed him. On the way out the door, she bumped into Griff, who had returned yesterday.

"I have to run out," she said, "but you can reach me on my cell."

He nodded without asking where she was going. "The moment I hear anything about Louie, I may call you for a quick trip to Lime Key. Brett just phoned and says Louie never leaves the house without Brett. We can't rationalize keeping him down there unless our folksy vet shows his true colors soon."

A second trip to the Keys? Eva shrugged off her misgivings for the time being, telling Griff, "Bo Rider wants a meeting, so I'll fill you in later."

EVA HIKED TO HER G-CAR, and before long jumped onto the highway consumed by what Bo didn't want to say over the telephone. Had he learned something bad about the Sikorski family, who were on track to visit over Thanksgiving?

She couldn't discern why that caused him to be more secretive than usual. Nearing the park, Eva passed the street leading to Griff's house. No doubt this morning he'd completed his daily run through Vienna's Nottoway Park.

As she turned in the entrance, a past event hurtled through her mind, giving her pause. Years ago, FBI agents arrested one of their own for delivering secrets to Russian spies in the same park. Eva tensed just driving along the narrow road. In the woods, former FBI Agent Robert Hanssen had marked bridges with white tape for dead drops to his Soviet spy handlers.

His acts of espionage shook many, not only in the Bureau, but also in the nation's government. To think of a respected FBI agent betraying his country in Notttoway Park where Bo asked for a secret meeting was mind-numbing. How creepy was that?

Doubts assailed Eva. Should she even be here?

Then again, perhaps her friend and CIA agent was in difficulty with the Agency. She respected Bo greatly, which is why she was here.

The Fusion rolled past shade trees turning orange and russet.

Some trees were bare, having already shed every leaf. In these same trees a former agent had committed treason. Eva shuddered at the thought.

Then she spotted Bo's family van parked near the ball diamond by a sprawling opening in the woods. Eva parked near his van, pocketed her keys, and took a deep breath. She walked slowly to the fence behind home plate, her eyes scanning the trees and her feet crunching the drying leaves.

Not seeing Bo anywhere added to the weirdness. Hairs on the back of her neck tingled. Eva leaned down, peering into the woods. A sudden movement caught her attention. There was Bo standing by a park bench adjacent to a running trail, beckoning her with his hand. Eva went toward him, her eyes skimming the vibrant strand of woods behind him.

"Is this your idea of a sick joke?" she snarled.

Bo looked puzzled. "Why?"

"Nottoway Park for a suspicious meeting? You know what Hanssen did here."

Bo didn't flinch. Rather, he turned and looked behind them. His eyes also seemed to gaze into the woods.

"We need to talk about something even worse," he said, clenching his fists.

She'd never seen Bo this edgy. Or serious. Adrenalin surged through her body.

"What kind of trouble are you in?" she hardly dared ask. This was so eerie.

"Eva, have you heard from OPM about China hacking into your personnel information?"

Her emotions blazed. "Yes. Sabrina Nelson, an FBI agent, sprung a surprise interview on me, swearing me to secrecy. Scott and I changed our passwords and banks. We've gotten letters from credit card companies for a fake Jon Reed who's using our address to get credit cards. I saw a stranger in my neighborhood doing surveillance and thought too late to copy down his plate. I've returned home from an undercover case to find another credit denial letter, this time for Mr. Brian Wheatley. What about you?"

"You can't tell anyone what I'm about to say."

"No one? Not even Scott?"

"Nobody. Nada. Not a soul. You promise or I leave. That's why I didn't ask you to meet in the Agency's SCIF. I can't risk anyone knowing what I'm about to divulge."

"Come on, Bo. What about Griff? He has the same clearance as we do."

Bo clamped his hands on his hips and glared.

"Okay, okay." Eva stepped back. "I promise. What happened?"

"Do you know a girl named Lexi Dawson?" He fixed his eyes on hers as if to gauge her reaction.

Eva grabbed his hand, her eyes widening in fear. "What happened to sweet Lexi?"

"So you do know her. How?" Bo demanded, his nostrils flaring.

"Lexi is Kaley's friend. The two of them survived a run-in last year with their government teacher."

Bo pressed his lips to a fine line. His silence prompted Eva to yank on his hand as if it were the handle to a water pump.

"Tell me! Why these questions?"

Bo shook his hand free, motioning to a park bench. Eva's mind pulsed at the speed of light as she went over and thumped down on the wooden slats. A cold wind blew across her neck, and Eva quickly zipped up her jacket. Whatever Bo was about to confide wouldn't be good. Fear that Kaley was mixed up in something terrible grabbed her throat.

Bo perched beside her and took a few deep breaths. "Eva, yesterday I was ordered into the SCIF, where I was informed the Agency is convinced a foreign government has created a dossier on me."

"Because of the OPM files they hacked?"

"Yes. Publically, insiders say it's China. We at the Agency believe the Russian Federation is behind the theft of personal data. Not only me, but you as well. The government won't tell you, so I am."

Eva studied Bo's eyes. They never moved one iota.

"Agent Nelson alluded to something similar," she admitted. "I was warned not to inform anybody. She asked me to have you call her. I am so sorry. When I went undercover, I completely forgot."

He waved off her concern. "Maybe she contacted the Agency. In any event, they've discovered the data collection on me, Julia, and our kids. Lexi Dawson is listed as Glenna's friend. As far as Julia and I can figure out, Glenna is not her friend."

"Oh, so you've told Julia," Eva exclaimed. "But I can't tell Griff, who has a security clearance. So does Scott, by the way. Last I knew Julia didn't have a clearance."

Now it was Bo grabbing Eva's flailing hand. "Wait, I didn't tell Julia. I subtly asked her to learn who Lexi was. Julia doesn't know her as our daughter's friend."

"Okay." Eva tried to think. "The bottom line is Lexi is a friend of Kaley's, who is a friend to Glenna. What does it all mean?"

She glared hard at him, her mind anything but clear.

"Here's what we at the Agency think," he said in low tones. "Once the Russians peruse the government employees and find those with the greatest intelligence or policy value, they set about creating dossiers on them and their families."

"Go on."

"As much as we've cautioned Glenna about revealing details on social media, I've concluded Russia's intelligence services have read our daughters' social media postings. They have absolutely identified Kaley as Glenna's friend."

Eva's hand flew to her mouth. "Then they targeted Kaley's account, discovering her friends include Lexi Dawson. The Russians linked her back to Glenna."

"I believe they've created a dossier on you and Scott."

"Did you hear the hackers also have our fingerprints?"

"Yes. Some of our most sensitive facilities use biotech fingerprint readers to grant access. So a Russian spy with my fingerprint affixed to a piece of vinyl can fool the reader into granting them access, thinking it's me."

"What next steps do we take?" Eva's mind raced to find a solution.

"First of all, you can't tell Scott or anyone else. They determined Kaley is one of Glenna's friends, and they know your daughter is a photographer."

"She probably listed the photography club on her social media."

Bo raised his finger into the air. "There, you see. We must prevent our kids from publicizing anything. When they do, they tell about us."

"I agree. What about Izzy and her parents visiting us? After all, Stanislaw Sikorski did help our daughters escape when the Russians hijacked the ferry."

"Could be he's a Russian agent." A deep glower etched Bo's features. "Coming to our daughters' aid puts us squarely in his debt. Poland's crawling with Russian spies, which is why I was reluctant to allow Glenna on the trip. Julia insisted I was paranoid."

Eva flicked her hand. "Been there too. Oh, I told FBI Agent Nelson of the Sikorskis' desire to visit. She checked their files and left a message he's okay."

"I'm not sure the FBI has the same data we do. And weren't they fooled by Hanssen? Course, I investigated Sikorski the best I could before Glenna and Kaley left. "

"Maybe I should call Agent Nelson again," Eva mused aloud.

"No! Don't tell her what I shared with you. She and the Agency may be working together. Our priority is getting our kids to close social media accounts ASAP."

Eva agreed without hesitation. "Scott and I will talk to Kaley and Andy tonight."

"Likewise for me with Glenna and her brother Gregg."

Bo stood up and dug his keys from his pocket. "Meanwhile, I'll see what else the Agency develops. We can meet up again if need be."

"Is Russia targeting us because our daughters went to Poland?"

"It's possible." Bo's eyes clouded. "I suspect they're compiling a list of targets, hoping to find one of us at a vulnerable moment in the future."

"So they're watching each of us."

"Yes. However, I figured they wouldn't want to risk another disclosure here at Nottoway Park." Bo forced a grin and began walking away, his shoulders hunched.

"I get your point." Eva jangled her keys. "Next time, though, not here."

He turned. "What?"

"Not here." Eva pointed to the ground. "Not this park. It's too sinister talking about spies on this ground. I feel like I am being watched, and it's not me who is paranoid."

Chapter 27

Eva left Bo edged with fury. The Russians were after her and her family. She had to stop the nameless, faceless "them." Only she didn't know why they targeted her. Worse, she couldn't tell Scott about the danger for which Bo had taken great risks to confide.

Eva wasn't one to give up without a fight. She parked next to Griff's Bucar in the task force lot, convinced to stop Izzy and her family's visit. Over the years Bo's instincts had proven to be incredibly prescient.

Yet, Stanislaw faced tremendous peril in rescuing Glenna and Kaley from a ship overtaken by Russian soldiers. Eva and Scott hailed his heroism at the time.

She went inside and powered up her computer to search for Russia's hacking into OPM computers. Griff sauntered over, and she minimized her screen.

"Hmm," he said, "I finished our report about Louie's flight to Lynchburg. From your online searching, I'd say your meeting with Bo may have been more interesting."

Eva stared in disbelief. "Forget what you saw."

"What did I see?"

"Seriously, Griff, the more I think of it, Stanislaw saved no other students, only ones whose parents worked for the U.S. government."

"Aren't you forgetting his daughter?"

"You make my point," Eva snapped. "His saving them the way he did seems convenient."

Griff folded his arms. "Confession is good for the soul. What did Bo say that has you so rattled?"

"I shouldn't have mentioned I was meeting him. Don't press me to say anymore."

"You got it." Griff swiped at his moustache. "Are you interested in what Brett did while you were out playing snoop with a spook?"

"I'll take your bait," Eva said, almost grinning.

He obliged, telling her, "Things are getting interesting at our home away from home. Brett took the blue motorbike for a ride. He simply drove around a few blocks. From the side street behind a boat shop, he watched Louie head out in his BMW."

"That doesn't sound illegal."

"Don't jump to conclusions. Where do you suppose Louie

went?"

"He flew back to Lynchburg," Eva guessed.

"Not even close."

Griff stopped talking as another agent swept by talking loudly on his cell phone. That agent stepped into the conference room, so Griff continued sharing the rest of Brett's discovery. When he finished, his smile was genuine.

"What do you think of that?"

"I begin to think Holly's information will lead somewhere. It's time for me to conduct another interview and find out what else she's holding back from us."

ALL THE WAY HOME, EVA chewed over the news that Brett had tracked Louie to a private mail center on Little Torch Key. He'd waited for him to leave the facility before going inside, asking to rent a box. He engaged the female employee in banter about a local Scottish band advertised on a wall poster. It didn't take long for Brett, who played the bagpipes, to charm the woman into mentioning the name of the customer who'd left before Brett. He was not Louie Clark, but Carlos Munoz.

Eva realized Carlos could have given Louie the key to retrieve his mail; however, her instincts screamed this was an important development. They needed to discover what mail Carlos received at the box and if Louis was using an alias. Perhaps the most disturbing aspect of Brett's discovery was that Holly had deceived Eva.

She arrived home in record time. The family van parked in the garage meant Scott arrived home before her. Eva dropped her shoulder purse on the counter.

"Sweetheart, I'm home."

"I just phoned my boss," Scott called from the den. "And may be a while."

Taking up her purse again, she stepped to the doorway of their home office, blowing him a kiss. He winked before talking into the phone. Eva shut the door quietly.

Securing her weapon and changing into comfortable clothes did nothing to clear her mind of Bo's surreptitious meet. After resolving to speak at once to her teens, Eva turned her attention to Louie's hidden agendas, wanting some answers—and fast.

Dinner came before work, so she sped to the kitchen. To her delight, Andy and Kaley were hotly discussing their social media pages. Kaley wrinkled her nose at her grim-faced brother.

"So a friend posted your photo sticking out your tongue. How professional will that look when you apply for a job next summer?"

Andy dropped his eyes. "I never saw her take the picture."

Eva couldn't have timed their conversation any better, and said lightly, "You two are bringing up the very topic we'll be discussing after dinner."

They groaned, but so be it. She and Scott were the parents. Their rules reigned supreme. After her husband finished his call, she served the salad supper with hot tomato soup. Dutch always enjoyed whatever she put before him, and she was heartened to watch him crumble crackers into his soup.

"No puns tonight?" Scott asked their oldest son.

"Nah, I have a paper to write."

"Me too," Kaley announced, sticking a fork in her salad.

Eva ate her soup, and after excusing the kids from the table she told Scott, "We need to talk about shutting down social media for the kids."

"Oh? Something new happen?" he asked, reaching for his briefcase.

Eva skirted the edges of Bo's talk by saying, "We agents decided that with the OPM hacking, it's wise."

"Can we talk later?" He hurried to their home office.

Eva set up the ironing board to blow off steam. A quick spray of starch to Scott's shirt collars, and she pressed them on hot. Her hands swayed across the fabric, her mind stuck on applying for a warrant to search the Florida postal box.

When finished, she folded the board into its cabinet and wrapped the cord around the handle of the still-cooling iron, when Scott yelled, "Eva, come quick. Kat's on."

She scooted into the family room carrying his shirts on hangers. The TV screen showed a film of a typical Cuban street, crowded with donkey carts and classic 1955 Chevys belching smoke. Eva set his shirts on an empty chair.

Kat spoke animatedly, "I've received confirmation from a second Pentagon source. As I speak, Russian cargo ships are offloading Russian antiaircraft missiles in Santiago. The port city is a stone's throw from our base at Guantanamo Bay."

"Unbelievable!" Eva gasped.

Graphics from a satellite photo revealed just how near Santiago was to Gitmo. Scott was shaking his head as if alarmed.

Kat continued reporting what else her source had confirmed. "Russian military cargo planes are landing at Cuba's airport at Baracoa. They've been unloading construction material. I asked about this at today's Pentagon press briefing. The spokesman refused to confirm or deny my source's information."

The imagery shifted to Kat, who stood reporting live at the Pentagon. Her intent gaze into the camera didn't surprise Eva one bit. She was the same intrepid reporter doggedly pursuing the truth, and in a way, she reminded Eva of herself when she confronted criminals. The fresh revelation brought a wry smile to her face.

Kat was talking about S300 missiles systems and Eva tuned her ears to listen.

"The missiles can shoot down our most sophisticated fighter jets, which would render our Gitmo Naval Air Station defenseless. The Administration remains mute. It's unusual for non-essential employees of our Havana Embassy to be sent home. The State Department says it's working to normalize relations with the Communist government of Cuba, and asserts Cuba's relationship with Russia is a balancing act."

Kat promised to persist in her quest for details. Eva's thoughts of her earlier secret meeting with Bo, and Russia's targeting of them, made gooseflesh spring on her arms.

Eva faced her husband. "Do you think Kat really has such a source?"

His eyes flickered, though he remained quiet.

"Wait." Eva narrowed her eyes. "You told me recently to back off social events with Kat and her husband Jack. You ... no you aren't ... has Kat been hounding you?"

"I'm uncomfortable talking to her. Let's leave it at that."

"Given your powerful job, it's no shocker Kat has zeroed in. It's like she's always working. She must not have any real friends."

"Her story will rile folks at the Pentagon," Scott replied with fervor.

"Will her disclosure be something the House will hold hearings about?"

"Maybe."

At Scott's noncommittal response, Eva surmised he knew more about Russia's installing missiles in Cuba than he could let on. He had his secrets, and she had hers. With pressures swirling around them, she longed to reveal her heart to him.

"I want to ask you something after I hang these up, so don't go anywhere."

"Like sneak out for ice cream when your back's turned so you don't know I'm off our healthy eating plan?"

"Don't even think about it. Unless you take me," she said in jest.

She stowed his clean shirts in the closet, then checked on the kids. Andy and Kaley were typing in their rooms. Dutch was fast asleep. His innocent brow accentuated the horror of potent missiles being installed ninety miles off Florida's coast.

Eva rejoined Scott in the living room, where he watched a twenty-four-hour news channel.

"Any reaction to Kat's breaking story?" she asked.

"The usual." He patted the couch beside him. "What did you want to ask me?"

Eva moistened her lips. "This whole Russian escapade with Cuba tells me to postpone the Sikorkis' visit."

"That caught me off guard. I thought ... well, never mind what I thought." Scott cleared his throat. "I assume you have an untold reason for delaying their coming."

"Yes. I'm glad you know me so well. Still, the reason we give them is true."

Scott tapped her temple and smiled. "What is going on in your pretty head?"

"I'd divulge classified material if I explain further."

He looped an arm around her shoulder, and Eva snuggled against him.

Scott smoothed her hair. "Even when secrets are necessary for our jobs, when we are truthful with each other, I have perfect confidence in us. Do you know what I mean?"

"I couldn't agree more," Eva said with feeling. "Bo said something to me, and I take him seriously. We need to regroup. Shut the kids down from their social media."

Kaley walked in just then. "Why should we shut down? Is it because of Russia moving their missiles into Cuba?"

"You know about that?" Eva asked, incredulous.

"The story appeared on my computer when I finished my report. When I saw Kat broke the story, I read the entire article."

They talked over the allegations with Scott adding, "Remember not to believe everything you hear on the news. It's the same with social media. Mom and I want you to take yours down for now, and your brother as well."

"I'm okay with that. Andy will be too after the goofy photo his friend posted of him. Should I tell him?"

Scott rose. "Thanks, kiddo. I want to talk with him. Besides, your mom has something else to say."

He left and Kaley took his place on the sofa.

"What else is up?" Kaley puckered her brow. "More travel out of town?"

Eva let out a sigh. "Dad and I want Izzy and her parents to visit another time."

"Ooh, that's ugly. Izzy and I are e-mailing. I think they booked their flights."

"That would be unfortunate. We hadn't yet agreed to the dates. Russia is asserting their military off our coast. We wouldn't want them to be in harm's way."

Kaley rolled her eyes. "You're paranoid again. I can't believe this, Mom!"

"Are you concerned how you'll look to Izzy or for their safety?"

"How can they be in danger from something going on in Cuba? We owe them for hosting me and saving me, don't we?"

Eva clasped her daughter's hand into hers. "We are grateful to them, certainly. There may be a time when we can host them in return. Do you trust me and your dad?"

Kaley pulled back her hand. She jumped to her feet. "You're unfair asking me that. Yes, I trust you. Do you trust me? Because there's something you're not telling me."

"Love never fails," Eva replied. "That's what the Bible teaches and is what we believe. Dad and I love you and will not fail you."

Her shoulders drooped, and Kaley sputtered a sigh. "I know."

"Then how can I help you accept our decision?"

Kaley dropped on the sofa beside her mom. "Mr. Sikorski is bringing a report about the artifacts I found in the Vistula River. I want to include my discovery in my term paper about Russia, and interview him about his father being in the Soviet Gulag."

Eva let that sink in a moment before coming up with an alternate plan. "Pastor Feldman has been teaching how Russia plays a key part in the latter days. Last Sunday he preached on Ezekiel 37 and 38. We could meet and discuss that aspect."

"Maybe," Kaley replied tentatively. Then a light sparkled in her eyes. "Yes!"

Eva squeezed her hand. "Learning the prophetic significance might give us clues about Russia's past and present aggressions in Eastern Europe and Cuba. Send Izzy a brief message explaining the situation. Ask her when I might call her father to answer any questions. He can provide me with a report of your findings."

Kaley looked into her mother's eyes. "I see your concern. After what happened on the ferry, you question his Russian connections. You warned me before I left to be alert for possible traps. We never dreamed our ship would be taken hostage."

"Never in a million years. With your reasoning ability, you'll make one fine agent someday," Eva said in praise. "Unless you decide on another career path."

"I don't know yet. You like your job, right?"

"Mostly, except when I'm powerless to stop people from be victimized."

"That describes me, I guess, which is why I want Izzy to come and really experience America. She loves freedom. So does her papa. At least they said they did. Maybe it's all made up to fool us. It's pretty confusing."

"We'll pray for wisdom," Eva said to uplift her daughter and her own sagging spirits. "The Bible tells us to ask God for wisdom, and He promises to give it to us generously."

Mother and daughter leaned their heads against the sofa. Kaley began to sing a song she was practicing for next Sunday. Her sweet and mellow voice fortified Eva, giving her confidence in her daughter's well-being in the coming days.

Chapter 28

Eva was ecstatic with Kaley's good news the following day. She'd contacted Izzy in time; her family hadn't booked their flights. The change worked well because Gita Sikorski had volunteered to nurse a lady from their church back to health from a bout with pneumonia. Izzy's papa had to be in Sweden a few days, so if Eva called him on Saturday, he'd explain the university's findings of Kaley's discovery.

The Polish family did seem nice, which gave Eva a moment's pause over canceling their trip. She had little patience for looking backward. So, in that moment, she relinquished all regret. It was go forward in life full steam ahead.

Eva kept supper light and easy, heating chicken soup and serving chef salad from the deli. Kaley drizzled ranch dressing on the salad, and her eyes darted to her mom.

"Isn't Pastor Feldman too busy? In our big church, he helps a lot of people."

"He is free after his class to talk to us about end times prophecy," Eva said.

"Would you check these questions?" Kaley handed her a folded paper. "It's what I hope he can answer."

Eva scanned the list, commending her daughter. "You've done a stellar job."

"What's *stellar*?" Dutch held a spoon by his mouth, dripping soup on the table. "Is it stars?"

"It means good job," Scott said. "Which you'll do if you keep your spoon over your bowl."

"Mom, you did a good job on the soup." Dutch smacked his lips. "I like it."

His simple expression of goodness brought a loving smile to Eva's face. "Thanks a bunch, buddy of mine."

"Okay, back to my list," Kaley insisted. "Per Mom's suggestion, I read Ezekiel 37, 38, and 39. Pastor's teaching on end times greatly interests me, but shouldn't I delete a few questions, you know, to shorten our time?"

"You're being considerate. I'll look them over after we eat."

Eva's eyes shifted to Scott, who toyed with a tomato slice as if preoccupied. She guessed some new national security issue had popped up, which led her to say, "Kaley, see how well things worked with Izzy? It's all about God's timing. He helps us figure things out when we ask Him."

Andy interrupted Eva with some new jokes, so their meal ended amidst giggles and laughter. Eva added two more questions to Kaley's list after cleaning up the kitchen. Scott had disappeared, so she went to investigate, finding him in the home office quietly reading the newspaper in the recliner, his feet up.

Eva rattled the top edge in greeting. To his vague, "Hi," she left him alone and settled into her chair thinking of Kaley's maturity. While her daughter seemed to be transfixed by Russia's global reach, she did possess acute insights, similar to what Eva observed in Bo Rider.

Except Kaley wasn't privy to the kind of intelligence either Bo or Eva had. God had certainly gifted her daughter with keen intellect. Eva's recent escapade at Lime Key awakened a new desire for Eva—to achieve a deeper understanding of God's plans for them all. Her mind looped back to Bo's revelations, and in seconds she began creating a list of her own. She hoped by concentrating on essentials, she could zero in on the fiend harassing her family. Pen in hand, here's what she knew from the past weeks:

1. Kaley and Glenna were invited to stay with Stanislaw Sikorski and family. Kaley developed a friendship with Izzy online. A coincidence?

2. Kaley and Glenna's ferry was seized by Russian soldiers in the Baltic. Did Russia know in advance the two girls were on board?

3. Sikorski worked for the captured *Ceba* ferry. His knowledge of the ship was crucial for hiding in a lifeboat with the girls. Other students were not around.

4. Sikorski also escaped in the lifeboat. They floated at sea, rescued by U.S. military due to Scott's Pentagon connections. Did that foil Sikorski's plan to deliver the girls to Russian patrol boats? To be held as hostages for ransom?

5. My background investigation is updated by an OPM inspector who claimed my time was due. It was a year early.

6. OPM personnel files of federal employees are hacked. I received a letter from OPM notifying me to protect my identity. Griff and Bo also received one.

7. I spot a strange man doing surveillance on our street, but failed to get his license number.

8. Bo's meeting with me and the intelligence he shared are disturbing: Russia compiled a dossier on him and on me, linked by Kaley's friend Lexi.

9. Lexi attends the same school. She is not in Kaley's world

government class. Lexi is linked as Glenna's friend, but doesn't know Glenna.

10. Kat Kowicki showed up in town pursuing news stories about Russia and Cuba. Scott hinted at something he couldn't tell me. What does he know besides Russian missiles and building materials in Cuba that Kat reported?

11. Odd letters arrived from credit card companies denying credit in the names of Jon Reed and Brian Wheatley.

12. Scott and I switched passwords and banks. Tonight we shut down the kids' social media pages.

13. What else should we do? What am I missing?

Eva reviewed her list a second time to find Scott standing over her shoulder.

"Eva, you will no doubt hear this, and maybe I shouldn't tell you—"

"I knew you had something on your mind." She dropped her pen and pushed back her chair. She looked him in the eye. "Tell me everything."

"An American was arrested today in Russia. You said you spoke with Bo today, right? So it can't be him."

Her breath caught in her throat. "I saw him at three o'clock. It's impossible for him to be in Russia."

"Okay … At first I thought maybe you talked with Bo on the phone. I didn't know how to tell you. The identity has not been released."

"Do you know why Russia arrested the American?"

"I think it's to retaliate for NATO announcing they're sending troops to Poland."

"I heard that news on the drive home," Eva said. "NATO is rotating four battalions to counter Russian aggression."

They shared a hug before Scott went to set their security system. Realization dawned within Eva. Yesterday she'd urged Kaley to ask God for wisdom. They both prayed and the dilemma had been resolved, for now.

Still, the underlying issue remained. Why was Russian intelligence after Federal Agent Eva Montanna? She and Bo though it might be due to their daughters' lifeboat escape. Was their harassment some kind of retribution as well?

Eva buzzed her list through the shredder and opened her Bible to Ezekiel. She began to read with a belief building that tomorrow's meeting with her pastor would shine a bright light.

IN THE DUSKY TWILIGHT, Eva walked into the cool church in McLean with Kaley. A friendly assistant ushered them into an office, its wall-to-wall shelves packed with books. She offered drinks, with Eva opting for coffee and Kaley a can of lemonade.

The assistant told them crisply, "Dr. Feldman's class has ended. He will join you soon."

"We are a few minutes early," Eva whispered to her daughter.

Kaley patted her Bible. "My list is all ready. What if he's too busy?"

"Relax. Remember Pastor Sal Feldman helped me with a family mystery after Grandpa Marty and I returned from the Netherlands a few years ago."

"I forgot he knows our family so well." Kaley's eyes grew round as if delighted.

She snapped the tab off the can when Dr. Feldman walked in, looking harried.

"Oh dear," he quipped. "Your appointment slipped my mind. Forgive me."

Kaley had been right after all. Eva tensed, offering to reschedule. He told them to be seated, and then removed his rumpled jacket. After slipping behind his desk, they became reacquainted. Yet Eva's pastor seemed out of breath.

He seemed to rally once the assistant brought him a cup of steaming coffee. A smile of gratitude lit his strained features. Eva and Kaley waited in seats across from his desk while he drank the hot java.

"With Russia's recent rise in power and incursions into Ukraine and Syria," Eva began, "Kaley and I have prophecy questions, especially about war in the latter days."

Raising thick, dark eyebrows, he replied, "I have time for you and such a vital topic."

His generous spirit exuded warmth and caring. Eva smiled at him. "You and the church were faithful in praying for Kaley's safety. God answered those prayers."

"Thank you, Pastor." Shyness laced Kaley's words.

Love for her daughter flowing through Eva's heart, she added, "We are truly grateful. The daunting experience changed her."

Pastor Feldman gazed at the teen. "How so?"

"God is changing my inner self and is moving in my life. I can't get Russia out of my mind. My friend Izzy lives in Poland. I'm afraid she isn't safe there." Kaley looked sideways at her mom. "I want the Sikorskis to visit sometime, when the time is right."

"You sound grown-up, Kaley Montanna." He lifted his heavy

brows once more. "Have you prayed for God's help?"

Eva and Kaley nodded in unison.

"My daughter's term paper will explore Russia's increasing power and America's future. She stayed with the Christian family in Poland before the hijacking."

Eva stopped, looking at Kaley, not wanting her to relive the trauma if she didn't want to. "You tell Pastor Feldman whatever you'd like."

Kaley lifted her chin as if steeling herself. "Soldiers stormed aboard. I was scared not knowing what danger lurked outside the lifeboat we took refuge in. Mr. S helped his daughter, my friend, and me to hide in there. He lowered us into the water to escape. The Russian patrol raced after us, and our Air Force saved us. I—"

Dr. Feldman interrupted, "Powerful proof God is our refuge in times of trouble."

"Yes!" Kaley's voice rose. "In the lifeboat, we prayed constantly. My fear was so huge, a giant mountain I couldn't climb over. It didn't help when Mr. S whispered, 'It's Gog … it's Magog.'"

"He said that?" Eva turned her head in surprise. "You never told me."

"I remembered last night after reading about Gog and Magog." Kaley tapped her Bible with vigor. "Since my teacher has finally agreed, I'm writing on Russia's history and want to include prophecy. But I don't find Russia in the Bible."

"Nor do you find the U. S." The Bible professor tented his hands. "Prophecy and end times are my areas of expertise. The prophet Ezekiel warns of a ferocious end times battle with the world's armies. Magog will descend upon Israel, so Russia is in the fight."

Kaley looked down at her list. "When will it happen? Could it be tomorrow?"

"Come on Sunday when I will answer all your questions."

Sal Feldman's brown eyes sparkled. His dark brown hair, sweeping away from his forehead, framed a face devoid of wrinkles. He appeared to be a man at peace with God and the world. Eva knew she'd been right in bringing Kaley here.

"Pardon my feeble joke. Let us turn to God's Word."

The leather Bible he opened was hefty. Eva navigated to a Bible app on her phone while Kaley flipped pages in her teen study Bible. Turning to the Old Testament, their pastor introduced Ezekiel, a man anointed by God and who lived 2,500 years ago.

"God inspired the prophet with insights into future events," he explained, his voice strong. "That's what Bible prophecy means. In verse 2 of chapter 38, Ezekiel says, 'Son of man, set your face against Gog, of the land of Magog.'"

He fixed his warm brown eyes on Kaley. "He warns of the coming battle where many nations swarm together to fight against Israel. Magog is a group of people. Gog is their human leader."

"Is it Russia?" Eva prodded.

"To learn where Magog is, let's examine what occurred before Ezekiel's prophecy." He opened the Bible at the beginning. "Go with me to Genesis. The entire earth was covered by the flood, and Noah's family survived. The waters eventually receded, and Noah left the ark. Look with me in chapter 10."

Kaley turned pages in her Bible, and Eva swiped to Genesis.

"Noah's descendants are found in the first two verses," he said. "His sons were Shem, Ham, and Japheth, and they, too, had sons after the flood. Three of Japeth's sons are important to our discussion. They are Magog, Tubal, and Meshech."

"Mom!" Kaley cried. "Magog is Noah's grandson. He's ancient so he can't be alive now."

Their pastor smiled. "Your point is a good one. Let's dig a bit further into Scripture. So Magog is Noah's grandson. Historians have scoured the Bible, examining where the men settled, and here's what they found. Meshech and Tubal settled with descendants in modern-day Turkey. Magog and his descendants went north, beyond the Caspian Sea into what is now Russia."

"So it's true!" Kaley gasped. "Magog is the president of Russia."

He hastened to explain. "Remember what I said moments ago. Magog refers to the place, meaning modern-day Russia. Gog will be the future leader of the northern hostile nation that battles against Israel."

"So Magog is Russia, and Gog will be a leader of Russia," Eva repeated as understanding dawned.

"Yes. I am convinced it's Russia. Here's why. The Bible teaches Gog, the hostile leader, lives in the land of Magog. Ezekiel 38:15 says Gog will come from 'your place in the far north.'"

"Is Gog alive today?" Eva wanted to comprehend if these were the last days.

He held up his large Bible. "I can't say with certainty. Gog is someone like Pharaoh who enslaved the Israelites prior to Ezekiel's time."

Their pastor reached behind him to remove a spiral notebook, opening it to the middle. "Other countries align with Russia in fighting Israel. Ezekiel states that Put, or known today as Phut, will be one of the would-be conquerors. This is ancient Libios, or Libya as we know it. Persia is modern-day Iran."

"What Ezekiel prophesied is coming true," Eva observed. "Russia and Iran have formed a strong coalition, and are fighting in Syria near Israel's northern border."

His finger reverently touched a page in the book of Ezekiel. "We could be entering the phase leading to the last days."

"When?" Eva stiffened. Had she involved Kaley in something beyond her years?

"The exact times are in our Sovereign Lord's hands. When the Bible refers to the 'latter days,' it means the time on earth after Christ's resurrection. The days before His death on the cross and His ascension are considered 'former times.'"

"So according to Scripture, we are in the last days?" Kaley wrote in her notebook.

"Certainly. And have been for two thousand years." He folded his hands. "Jesus told the disciples before His crucifixion not one stone of the Temple would be left upon another. This prophecy came true when Roman General Titus sacked the Temple in 70 A.D., collapsing every stone and stealing the gold."

Kaley creased her brows. "So is war between Russia and Israel approaching?"

His eyes softened as he lowered his voice. "The Bible reveals the epic battle will begin after the Antichrist confirms a peace treaty with Israel, which heralds in the Tribulation period. Ezekiel points to the Israelites living in peace, in unwalled cities. That isn't the case today."

"We," he made a circular gesture with his hand, "will not be here. We believers meet our Lord Jesus in the air at the trumpet sound."

"Meaning the Rapture?" Eva asked.

"Yes, the glorious time when the trumpet sounds, Jesus will call every one of His believers, His children, to be with Him in a twinkling of an eye. The church of Christ will be taken away before the most terrible times of the Tribulation."

Eva kept an eye on her watch. "To confirm, the ferocious battle between Russia and Israel comes after the Rapture and during the Tribulation?"

"And leads into the Battle of Armageddon. Most prophecy experts believe all events that will precede Christ's Rapture of His church have already happened. For example, the return of Jewish people, including my family, to their homeland in Israel occurred in 1948. Christ paid for God's wrath, and Paul writes in Romans chapter 8 there is no condemnation for those who put their trust in Jesus."

Eva faced her daughter. "So we have nothing to fear."

"Maybe not about Gog and Magog," Kaley said. "But Izzy is afraid to be living in Russia's shadow. That disturbs me."

"You say she attends a church in Poland?" Dr. Feldman asked.

"She is a Christian too." Kaley closed her Bible. "I need to pray more for her."

Eva rose to her feet, voicing a final question. "Pastor, you believe biblical prophecy about future times is going to come true, right?"

"Every word is true." He picked up the Bible, and with a glowing face said, "These pages are filled with prophecies about the coming Messiah, which Jesus the Christ fulfilled. God promised to send His Son to pay for our sins. He kept that promise. In Isaiah it says the LORD Himself will send a sign, a virgin would give birth to a son called Immanuel, which means 'God with us.' Jesus's virgin birth fulfills Isaiah's prophecy. Think of it this way. The fulfillment of past prophecies, such as Jesus's birth and the Temple destruction, give us confidence God will keep all of His promises."

Kaley got to her feet. "Your teaching gives me a lot to think about."

"Call if you have any questions for your report," Pastor Feldman said, reaching for their hands. "My family was raised Jewish as was I before finding Jesus the true Messiah. The LORD gave Moses a blessing for Aaron to bless the Israelites. Will you let me pray this blessing over you?"

They held hands, and Eva closed her eyes, listening to her pastor's melodic voice lifting up the familiar verses in Numbers: "The LORD bless you and keep you; the LORD make His face shine on you and be gracious to you; the LORD turn His face toward you and give you peace."

"Thank you, Pastor," Eva said, feeling God's goodness enriching her spirit.

Before they could leave, Kaley posed another question. "Pastor, does God use bad people for our good?"

Eva immediately understood. Kaley wondered if Mr. Sikorski had been working for the Russians, would he have saved her?

"Read the story of Joseph," he replied, opening the door. "His jealous brothers sold him into slavery, yet when they're reunited years later, Joseph graciously told them what they meant for harm,

God meant for good."

Kaley stared out the van window on the way home. "I get Pastor's teaching on the war of Gog and Magog being after the Rapture. Do you think the president of Russia knows that? I mean, he could still invade Poland, right?"

"Yes, he could. Remember, Jesus says there will be wars and rumors of wars. We don't want to live in fear and not trust God."

"That's true, Mom. As Pastor Feldman says, we should pray about these things."

Chapter 29

Eva arrived at the task force office on Monday after a fun weekend enjoying lazy family days for a change. The foosball table received a continual and vocal workout, with Andy and Scott vying for the championship. Eva was pleased the subject of Russia never came up.

That didn't mean Russian hackers and wrongdoers left her mind. As she unlocked her desk, she recalled experts warning that Russia's leader was a brilliant strategist and ruthless man. With him at the helm, anything was possible.

She gave a second look at Griff's empty chair, wondering what progress he'd made at Lime Key. He flew back down last Thursday to help Brett execute the search warrant, which would allow them to hunt through Carlos's mail daily. Whether their snooping would reveal damaging evidence was the ultimate question.

Apparently doubts plagued Griff too. Before leaving, he'd cautioned Eva, "Operation Stogie may be swirling down the drain. We haven't pried from Louie where he went in Lynchburg or the identity of the woman with the pink luggage."

"Don't be hasty," she'd replied. "First see what you find in Carlos's postal box."

Eager to hear from Griff, Eva switched on her computer, noticing a blinking voicemail light on her office phone. Maybe he'd already phoned her.

She listened to Holly's passionate request to meet ASAP. No doubt with her sentence lurking around the corner, the convicted felon wanted to ensure Eva would lobby for a lighter sentence. What could Eva advocate on Holly's behalf to the judge?

Louie's caretaking at the Pelican's Nest had turned into a disappointing dead end. Eva deleted Holly's plea in frustration and typed her travel voucher. This task done, she began to see the wisdom in having a second meeting with Holly. They were waiting to analyze Carlos's incoming mail anyway. Eva had nothing to lose.

After all, if his wife knew about the postal box and kept it from Eva, the judge would receive a bad report from the agents. Eva spent an hour writing status reports on several old cases waiting for sentencing of low-level defendants. Meanwhile, the Lime Key case hovered in the back of her mind like a bad smell.

Why didn't Griff call with an update?

Just when she decided to contact Deputy Marshal Duggan to concoct a way to question Holly, Eva's phone rang. She snatched up the receiver.

"Agent Montanna," she said.

"Eva, am I glad you're there."

The forceful voice on the other end belonged to Griff.

"And you're the agent I need to speak with," she replied with fervor.

"Has something happened on your end?"

"First I need to know if you're tired of Brett's cooking," she said jokingly. "I suppose you'd like me to fly down and whip up some fantastic meals."

"Yeah. I mean no, forget food. Louie just took off in his plane heading to Cuba."

Eva bolted upright in her chair. "That's what I wanted to talk to you about. I was beginning to think Holly had us on a wild-goose chase for some sinister reason. So you and Brett will await Louie's return?"

"We won't follow him into Cuba, if that's what you mean. And you need to come down here pronto."

"No I don't." Eva stepped hard on the brakes.

"We need you."

"No."

"Seriously, Eva. Things are breaking apart here. In his mailbox, Carlos is receiving mega-investment statements under the name of Ulises Munoz, who I believe is his deceased father. Brett and I were running that down when moments ago Louie fired up his plane and veered straight south for Cuba."

Eva heard extreme pressure in his voice. Yet her mind pulsed with needs of her family, her home. Kaley wanted Eva and Scott to take her to see a college in southern Virginia. Andy was drumming for Sunday's worship service. Dutch played a tag football game on Saturday. Plus, Scott hinted over breakfast how he planned to take her out for a special evening, just the two of them.

Here again, work cried out for preeminence like a hungry baby.

She tried dissuading him. "You and Brett call for some help. Long story short, my husband and kids need me."

"You have lots on your plate, Eva," Griff said, his tone growing mellow. "Listen, if Louie flies here with contraband, we'll grab him and apply for a search warrant. That delays uncovering what he's doing. Plus, we create a paper trail for the likes of Kat Kowicki. If he has limited time before he's to contact someone, delay in getting the warrant tips his associates something is wrong."

"Yes, those are risks." Eva stared at her smiling family in the beach photo. "How does my presence eliminate your problems?"

Griff snorted into the phone. "Have you forgotten? You're an Immigration Customs Enforcement agent. You have customs border search authority, right?"

Eva knew where her partner was going. But why couldn't they brief a customs agent from Miami? Before she could pose the alternative, Griff continued rushing his arguments at her.

"We checked Louie's previous flights. He routinely avoids flying into an airport and clearing customs on return as the law requires. He flies directly to Lime Key."

"What about Miami customs heading down to Lime Key?"

"I called the agent in charge. He's up to his eyeballs in an undocumented immigrant roundup organized from Washington. He can spare no one."

Eva sighed into the phone, her excuses fizzling.

"Okay. We'll grab Louie after he unloads the contents of his plane into his apartment. Using my search authority, we nail him dead to rights, no delays, no warrant."

"You never miss a beat, Eva. When can you get here?"

Might this be the reprieve she hoped for? She went for it, telling Griff, "Louie may fly back tonight, and I can't fly in until tomorrow."

Griff's tone turned cutting, losing sympathy to her plight. "Eva, he can't fly in tonight. The airstrip has no lights, remember? The FBI aviation team will pick you up at the Manassas airport. An FBI executive jet can fly you here before the moon rises."

"Wait, you just said we can't land there at night."

"Here's the deal. You land at the Marathon airport, which is lighted, as you recall. You meet Brett there."

Her mind whirled to the wild night she'd been busted hiding in the bushes. "Oh sure, I get to motor down to Lime Key at midnight. Me and my bag on the back of that crazy motorbike."

"Listen, Eva," Griff barked. "We're running out of time. You've run out of excuses. DEA authorized Brett to lease a car. He'll pick you up in a convertible, no less."

Eva waged a mental battle. In the end, she reluctantly agreed Griff was right. And Scott would take good care of the kids in her absence.

"Make the arrangements. I'll dash home with the bad news. Have the plane meet me sometime after eight. Scott and kids can drive me to Manassas."

"I knew you'd come through."

They hung up. Without wasting a second, Eva went to brief her boss on these fast-moving developments.

"You and Griff seem to find the best times to head to Florida," John Oliver quipped. "Tomorrow our temps dip to the low forties."

"It's a major inconvenience, but yeah, we do it for our country."

Eva cleared her desk and left a message about the hasty travel plans on the home phone. She called Scott on his cell. Once again, she reached his voicemail.

"Honey," she said softly into the phone. "Plan on early dinner. I need a lift to the Manassas airport. Can't say more."

EVA COMPLETED A MENTAL PLAN for a dinner menu from the freezer as she pulled into the driveway. Their heavy garage door was up, and what a nice surprise to see Scott's car parked inside. She rolled into the garage, noticing the house door standing open. Something seemed peculiar, all right.

She bounded out of her G-car smelling what she imagined was the aftermath of a fire in an Italian restaurant. Acrid smoke stung her nostrils. Concerned, she practically flew inside.

"Hey, Mom." Andy greeted her by waving a towel toward the open back door.

She resisted plugging her nose. "What's going on?"

Without waiting for his answer, she stepped into the kitchen, which looked like a disaster area. An empty pizza sauce jar tottered against a cutting board. Spilled sauce, plastered all over the countertop, dripped down to the tile floor. Twisted remnants of refrigerated pizza dough containers amidst cheese and pepperoni bags completed the chaotic scene.

Eva whirled toward the oven. Through the smoky glass she saw two pizzas bubbling.

"Dad says they aren't ready yet," Andy mumbled.

"Your dad made this mess, did he?"

Andy shook his head. His bottom lip began to tremble. "I heard your message. You have to leave after a fast dinner. I wanted to prove I could do what Kaley could do."

"Aw, buddy, you're terrific." She folded him in her arms. "Something go wrong?"

He slid out of her hug. "Directions said, put dough on a cookie sheet. Cheese and sauce ran off in the oven. It sure stinks. Dad says I should'a used a cookie sheet with sides."

"Let me see." Eva peered into the oven again. "I think these are ready to come out. You can help me whip up a salad."

"Whatever."

"Son, I'm thrilled you tried something new. We'll dine tonight at Andy's Eatery."

"Whatever you say."

He sounded so disheartened; she came up with another idea. She pointed to buttons on the oven panel. "Don't worry, buddy. This oven cleans itself. I'll show you how when I'm back home."

"Sweet!" he chimed.

"As we eat your delicious pizza, ask your dad about our first year of marriage. One of the biscuit tubes exploded. He and I hit the floor thinking someone was after us."

Andy sputtered a laugh, and Eva clapped him on the back. She hated the idea of leaving home again.

Chapter 30

Lime Key, Florida

Eva's eyes opened with a start. Was that a low-flying jet she heard? The rotating cabana fan in her room confirmed what her mind was trying to grasp. She was back in the undercover guest bedroom in Holly's home. The weak light of dawn seeped in around closed plantation shutters. The sun's searing rays hadn't yet broken over the horizon.

She flexed her calf muscles and kicked off the light blanket. Last night's flight from Manassas drifted through her murky mind. The FBI agent who flew the Bureau's Citation Executive Jet offered her the option of relaxing in the cabin's leather seats. She'd waved off comfort, opting for the copilot's seat, which had been a great choice.

On this early morning, Eva sat up in bed, relishing the thrust of their takeoff, multicolored cockpit lights, and thrill of seeing the ribbon of runway lights as they reached Marathon's airport. Had a plane flying overhead jolted her awake, or had she dreamt it?

Sounds of a whirling aircraft engine made her spring from bed. She raced to the window, tilting the wooden blinds. There was Louie's Cessna already rolling on the taxiway ostensibly returning from Cuba. Only one engine was running.

She changed from pajamas, wiggling into a pair of jeans. After yanking a T-shirt over her head, she sped out of the bedroom on bare feet, the delicious aroma of fresh coffee welcoming her. Griff gazed out the window overlooking the runway.

"What's going on?" she demanded. "Why did no one wake me?"

He held up his cell phone, motioning for her to join him at the window.

"Tech Ops phoned when it was barely light," he told her. "They said Louie's plane left Cuba and was heading our way."

"Right. I saw him from my window. You should have wakened me."

Griff tilted the slat, giving Eva a clearer view of Louie's approach. Throttling one engine, he spun his plane around, putting its tail in front of the hangar below their apartment.

"Brett," Griff hissed into his phone. "You got an eyeball on him?"

The DEA agent must be in the efficiency apartment in the hangar, Eva figured. She heard him say through the phone, "Louie cut the engine. He's wasting no time."

A pause, and then Brett's voice dropped to a whisper, "He's out, dragging two suitcases to the elevator."

Griff aimed a finger toward the elevator shaft, telling Eva, "Watch for him going up to his apartment."

She scurried over to look out the kitchen door by the elevator. An instant later, Griff snarled, "Brett says Louie's running back to the plane."

Eva came over and leaned her ear next to Griff's phone. Becoming their eyes and ears, Brett sounded astonished telling them, "He's hauling two more suitcases."

The mystery deepened, as for the next five minutes, the scenario repeated itself over and over again. Brett finally reported, "Louie has stuffed ten suitcases into the elevator."

Eva and Griff watched and waited as their quarry bolted up the stairs along the deck's corner. The ascending elevator's shadow crept toward the third-floor deck.

"He's got the elevator so crammed with suitcases, there's no room for him," Griff whispered, staring down at her bare feet. He cleared his throat. "Put on shoes and brush your teeth, Ms. Customs Agent. You have major searching to do in about two minutes."

"I wish I could have a cup of coffee. No time." Eva whirled around to get ready.

"You better hustle," Griff snapped. "I saw Louie's flight path on my phone app. He never flew into Ft. Lauderdale from Cuba. He never cleared customs."

On her way down the hall, she heard Griff tell Brett via the phone, "Sneak up here by the canal-side stairway so we can plot our next move."

Eva swooped together her toiletries and scurried to the guest bathroom. Face washed, teeth brushed, and hair pulled into a ponytail, she poked her hair through the back gap in her blue ICE-emblazoned ball cap. She looked in the mirror. Yes, Federal Agent Eva Montanna was ready to bust Louie and his smuggling ring wide open.

Adrenaline kicking in, she joined their confab at the kitchen table. Instead of confidence, she saw concern smoldering in Brett's eyes.

"We're debating whether to act," he admitted.

"What?" Eva adjusted her cap. "We saw him flying in from a Communist country. Those suitcases never cleared customs. I'm stoked to blow the lid off."

"And you'd blow our cover as well," Griff shot back.

"So? Wait!" Eva grunted. "You were in a mad rush to fly me down here."

"Just considering all our options," Brett reasoned.

Eva folded her arms, pondering their arguments. "We could follow him and see where he flies that bevy of suitcases. The risk of losing him is high."

"Holly claims it's cigars," Griff said. "Remember, we are on the JTTF looking for suicide belts or weapons."

"Look, you guys, I flew all the way down here with my ICE authority." Strength exuded from Eva's voice and hot glare. "Enough waiting. Let's go."

She held her ground, and so they all agreed. Within minutes, three armed federal agents clad in raid jackets bearing FBI, ICE, and DEA logos slipped from the second-floor residence. Brett stepped out on the deck, taking the stairs by the canal. Eva and Griff hiked to the opposite side and ran up the stairs to Louie's third-floor flat.

Eva jerked to a stop at his front door. Brett was covering the sliders to the canal. With her brows arching, she glanced at Griff. He nodded. Eva took the lead by knocking on Louie's door. She waited a few seconds.

Hearing nothing inside, she knocked again with a shout, "Louie, it's Evelyn."

The only sound was the breeze rustling the fronds of a palm tree.

"Hey, Louie." She pounded louder. "It's Evelyn."

Griff boomed, "Federal agents. Open the door."

No response. Eva grasped the doorknob. It was locked. She made a split-second decision.

"Griff, hit the door," she said, stepping aside.

He heaved his body against the wooden door, and it smashed open, splinters flying. The messy apartment boasted swanky Florida décor, but no Louie.

Eva and Griff raced in to find their target sticking his head out a partly-opened bathroom door. His trousers were crumpled around his ankles. Griff charged at him, gun drawn. Louie slammed the door in Griff's face. The lock engaged. The painted door of wood was no obstacle to Griff's momentum, and he crashed through it.

Eva's jaw clenched as both men tumbled into the tub, the shower curtain wrapped around them. She lurched forward, ready to assist her partner in the scuffle.

"We're federal agents. You're under arrest," Griff huffed, shoving his gun into the back pocket of his jeans.

"Whew," Eva said under her breath. It looked like Griff had things under control.

She quickly put her Glock into the holster in the small of her back. Griff dragged Louie from the bathroom, and Eva stepped out of the way. Their suspect fumbled to hitch and fasten his pants. Brett entered through the broken exterior door.

"I heard the uproar," he barked, "and knew y'all had him."

"Have you guys gone crazy?" Louie cried, sweat pouring down his face.

Griff yanked him to a kitchen chair and sat him down. Eva stepped in front of him. With resolve, she displayed her badge and credentials close to Louie's eyes.

"Louie, I'm an Immigration Customs Agent. You are under arrest for entering the country without clearing customs. Your house will be searched for contraband and your plane seized."

Griff towered over the surprised man, gruffly telling him, "You have a right to remain silent. Anything you say can be used against you in court. You are entitled to talk to an attorney. If you can't afford one, the government will appoint one for you."

"I don't have to say nothin', right?" Louie's eyes blazed, darting from one agent to another like fiery hornets.

"That's right, you're the boss," Eva replied with a curt nod. "You could help yourself."

His eyes clouding over, his lower lip drooped. "I get it. Holly set me up."

"Okay, buddy." Brett reached him with one powerful stride. "Stand up."

Louie staggered to his feet. Brett seized his wrist, and twisting it behind his back, slapped on a handcuff with a profound *click*. Tugging Louie's other hand behind his back, he cuffed it too. Brett examined the man's pockets, placing a fat wallet and two bucks on the table.

Eva wasted no time rifling through Louie's wallet. "U.S. Customs didn't get to search your plane. Since you hauled its contents up here, we can search everything in your apartment. Meanwhile, you'll be cuffed for your protection and ours."

"When we're done," Griff began, "you'll be taken to Miami where you will be jailed to await an appearance before a federal magistrate."

Eva pulled Brett aside. "Put Louie in that living room chair. Search it first for weapons."

"What about the suitcases?" Brett hissed.

"Check the living room first," Eva directed.

Brett went to work patting down the upholstered recliner, even searching its cushions before easing Louie into the seat. His arms still cuffed behind him, their suspect leaned awkwardly against the chair's side. He looked rather comical, but Eva resisted a snicker. Feeling no pity for the smuggler, she pulled a suitcase from Louie's bedroom to his feet.

"Anything in here gonna hurt us?" she asked the profusely-sweating suspect.

He winced with pain. "Nah."

"Sure? I'm opening this in front of you. If it goes boom, it will get us both."

"No worries." He shook his scraggly head. "You probably know. It's cigars."

Eva glanced at Griff and Brett, noting they took cover in the kitchen as they opened and clanged shut the cupboards. Neither moved a muscle to help her. Apparently, they weren't so sure they were cigars.

Trusting her instincts, she unzipped the massive zippers and gingerly opened the bag. The heady scent of expensive cigars permeated the room. Eva felt enormous relief, and a weight left her shoulders. Her partners immediately stepped closer. The trio of agents stared at packages of large Cuban cigars tightly bound with plastic wrap, each bundle roughly the size of a ten-pound bag of flour.

"Louie," Griff said, nodding toward the bedroom. "Do those nine other suitcases have cigars?"

"All nine," he muttered in despair.

"Any guns or anything illegal? 'Cause we're searching your whole place," Griff added.

Louie's head dropped low. "You'll find nothin' but cigars."

Eva straightened her spine, feeling a slight twinge. This was no time to get back pain, so she pressed forward, asking Louie, "So how did you get into this business?"

"Evelyn ... I mean ..." He wiggled his secured hands as if to make them more comfortable. "You said I don't have to talk. I could make things worse."

"Your choice."

Eva jangled a set of keys from her pocket. She grabbed Louie beneath his armpits and lifted. "Stand up here. We'll help you be more comfortable."

She spun him around and off came his cuffs. Louie sat down,

straighter this time, furiously rubbing deep pink grooves etched across his wrists. Eva arced her arm toward the Gulf.

"Louie, we tracked you to Cuba and back. We watched you drag ten bags up here. You're facing years in prison, losing bank accounts, and seizure of your plane. You don't need to say a thing. The damage is done."

He eyed her keenly before coughing out a tortured sigh.

She stood back and told him, her voice steady and strong, "By talking, you might provide information we can use. You might not think so, but what you say could allow us to tell the judge you've been cooperative. If you're especially helpful, the prosecutor might ask the judge for leniency."

Louie glanced up. A hopeful look soared across his craggy face.

Brett pounced forward. "Once I had a case where the defendant's help led to so much evidence, I convinced the prosecutor not to file charges."

Louie and Brett had talked motorcycles before he'd gone to Cuba. In the cluttered living room, the suspect studied Brett's face as though calculating if he could be trusted. Brett spoke as though he really cared about Louie, saying, "This next hour could impact your next fifteen years."

Louie's cell phone began vibrating on the kitchen table. Griff went to retrieve it, reading off the screen, "Sonya Kopanja."

"Oh, she's a snowbird widow I met last winter," Louis said, flipping his hand dismissively.

Eva noted Griff's long look at the phone before he set it down on the table. As he did, the phone emitted a brief chirp indicating Sonya had left a message. Louie raised a hand as if he was an elementary student.

"May I use the restroom? You interrupted me and I'm real uncomfortable. After that, I see no reason not to tell you what I know, which isn't much."

Brett headed for the bathroom with the shattered door, and quickly returning, he nodded at Eva. "It's safe for him to use the bathroom."

While Louie walked away, Eva unpacked the remaining cigars, smelling each package as she removed them. Brett kept watch on the bathroom door, while Griff disappeared into Louie's bedroom with the arrestee's cell phone.

At sounds of flushing, Griff scurried back to the kitchen, dropping Louie's phone in its precise spot on the table.

Chapter 31

Louie Clark wove a mournful tale. He, an American hero who had served honorably in the 82nd Airborne Division of the U.S. Army, retired as a sergeant major. His retirement years sent him spiraling into the current dilemma. A life of scuba diving and flying lessons had left him with a sporty tan and list of rich widows to fly around.

Eva took a break from copious note-taking when he stopped to wipe his forehead and sip the water she'd given him. Louie glanced at her with woeful eyes.

"The GI bill paid for me to learn to fly and all my licenses."

"Why fly cigars in from Cuba?" Eva thought it best to avoid the word "illegal."

"A couple from New Jersey wanted me to visit Cuba. On a whim, I flew them to Cuba and went shoppin' with 'em."

"So, on impulse you became a cigar smuggler." Brett didn't hide his smirk.

"Yup. I haggled with a cigar merchant to become his regular distributor in Newark for much-desired Cuban cigars."

Griff glared in disbelief. "You don't set up shop in Cuba on the spur-of-the-moment, not without greasing a few palms."

"Well, yeah. The manufacturer set me up with a Cuban Air Force officer. He lets me land at their Air Force base."

"Names." Eva snapped her fingers. "We need names."

At his feeble shrug, she led him through the story again, pressing him for specifics, including his Tampa and Newark customers. Eva drove him hard to recall details of the Cuban Air Force contact and factory. It took prodding, but eventually he admitted to raking in hefty profits.

"I took lots of flights these past few years," he added with a pained look.

Griff kicked at the cigar packages spread on the floor. "Were you bringing these bundles and the ones in the bedroom to your two customers?"

"Yup."

By now Louie had melted into the chair. Sweat beaded on his forehead and upper lip. He looked an abysmal mess.

"When did you last deliver cigars to your people?" Brett probed.

"Two months ago."

Brett leaned down, hands on his knees, to look into Louie's

bloodshot eyes. "How do we know it was only cigars? What else did you fly them? Cocaine?"

"No, no." Louie lunged forward. "Only cigars. I don't fly dope."

Brett's nostrils flared as if he smelled a rat. Eva shot a glance at Griff. He picked up the interrogation.

"Where did you really fly when you pretended it was St. Augustine?" Griff opened his hands. "You didn't go there."

"To my buyer in Newark. I didn't take him cigars."

"Straight there and back with no cargo?" Griff asked.

"Yup."

Her pen in the air, Eva opened her lips to lob another question when Griff stood up and grabbed Louie's arm. He jerked him out of the chair. With one swift move, he clamped a handcuff on one wrist, securing the other behind his back.

"Your pathetic charade is over. We're taking you to the Miami jail. I refuse to listen to any more lies."

Eva watched the scene incredulously, closing her mouth to keep from laughing. Brett rushed at Louie, ready to provide backup if Griff needed it.

"Whad'ya mean?"

"Your Sonya Kopanja is no snowbird widow. She's your daughter. You never flew to Newark. You flew to Lynchburg and met Sonya before flying her to Columbus, Ohio."

Griff hauled Louie toward the door. "I'm flying you to Miami. Eva and Brett, you process the evidence. I'll dispatch agents to arrest Sonya."

"Sorry." Louie began dragging his feet, both knees locked together. "I'm sorry. Please let me go to the bathroom."

Griff stopped dragging him mid-kitchen. "Why should I?"

"I'm telling you mostly truth. I have to protect my daughter. Let me in the bathroom and I'll tell you even more."

"Is there any reason we should cut this guy a break?" Griff growled at Eva.

"He's been in the bathroom a lot," she replied. "Once more won't hurt."

Griff asked Brett if he agreed. His reply was quick, his Southern drawl more pronounced, "Okay, y'all. I suppose thirty minutes more won't keep us from gettin' him to Miami. Let's hear him out."

After removing the handcuffs, Griff pointed to the bathroom. Louie went inside and closed the door. Eva and Brett nudged Griff into the living area.

"What happened in there?" she demanded of Griff, a smile

curving on her lips.

"I listened to Louie's voicemail. Sonya called him 'dad.' His recent calls are from her, including one before he flew to Lynchburg and one after he left Columbus."

Brett fist-bumped Griff. "Good job."

After the toilet flushed, Eva added, "He's holding back the truth. I smell it."

"Me too," Brett agreed, swiping at his chin. "I'll haul him to the plane in his bare feet. Too bad if he's scraped up a little."

"No." Griff pointed to Louie's cell phone. "He's psychologically primed now."

Eva rubbed the back of her neck and said, "Yes, I agree with Griff."

Louie finally emerged looking like he'd plastered water on his hair. It hung below his chin in long, wet pieces. Eva suggested he retake his seat in the recliner.

"You have thirty minutes before you're on a fast flight to a life behind bars," she advised him sharply. "Buddy, there's no going back."

He moaned sharply. "My neighbor Cecil warned me."

Eva ignored this, and facing Brett, issued instructions. "Go downstairs and call the agents arresting Sonya. Ask them to wait a few minutes."

No agents were about to arrest Sonya, but Louie didn't know that. If Eva could manipulate his emotions to compel him to cooperate, she'd do so.

LOUIE PLUNKED INTO HIS CHAIR with an apparent new attitude. He admitted Sonya was his daughter, claiming she wasn't into illegal stuff. That was all he'd said when Brett marched in, nodding at Eva. Louie gaped at his interrogators as if unsure what to do next. Griff leveled his eyes like a laser beam on their suspect.

"Make it short. You have twenty-seven minutes and counting."

"Up 'til three years ago," he drooped in the chair, "I didn't know my daughter."

"Why is that?" Brett leaned against the wall, his sturdy arms crossed.

"I met a gal while stationed in Kosovo. I looked into marriage. Know what I found?"

"She was already married," Griff said, pointing at his watch.

"No, her dead father was in Russia's Security Service."

Eva poised her pen in the air. "Do you mean FSB or KGB?"

"Yeah, they're about the same, right?"

Louie rubbed sweat from his reddening cheeks. Eva turned the ceiling fan on high. When Griff tapped his watch, Louie picked up the pace.

"Her father had been dead five years. She claimed she'd never seen his bio data. Blah, blah. I figured messy paperwork would torpedo my career, so I broke it off. Two months later, I came stateside."

Louie stood beneath the fan, a stream of water running down his neck. He gulped.

"Fast-forward eighteen years. Livin' the good life here in Florida, I got a weird message on my social media page. It's from Sonya in Kosovo. Her mom died. Based on things she was told, Sonya believes I'm her dad."

Brett scowled. "So you suddenly have an eighteen-year-old daughter?"

"Yer a smart one." Louie fanned the bottom of his shirt. "Sonya sent an online image of her birth certificate. Her mom's the gal I dated in Kosovo. Sonya's birth date is right for her to be mine. She knew my childhood home, and names of my folks and brothers. All things her mom and I talked about."

"What does this have to do with anything?" Griff said, stalking to the window.

Louie blinked at Eva and then Brett. They both stared back.

"Digger … er … Griff, Sonya got me involved in cigar smugglin'," he sputtered.

"Explain," Eva insisted. "You said she wasn't involved in anything illegal."

"She was gonna visit Cuba and invited me. People from Kosovo could go there. That's when I first saw her, and when I met the cigar guy who started me flyin' cigars."

"You're blaming your long-lost daughter for leading you into a life of crime?" Brett sounded doubtful.

When Louie raised both hands they trembled all the more. "Earlier I left Sonya out, protectin' her like. She doesn't know I smuggle cigars. She's a nice girl."

He coughed, holding his stomach. "I need a soda or somethin'. I'm parched."

Brett ambled to the kitchen, popped a tab, and gave Louie a can of orange soda. He took a long swig and wet his lips. Eva used the lull to write on her pad: *Why did Sonya go to Cuba?* and *Who else went along?*

Louie swiped his mouth with a hand. "After Cuba, Sonya

finished college in Kosovo. I helped her get a visa and green card. She's studyin' international law at Ohio State. When I picked her up in Lynchburg, she'd just finished her fake court practice."

"You mean 'moot court,' don't you?" Eva said.

"I guess so. Anyways, I'm proud of her."

Eva aimed the pen at him. "Does she visit you here?"

"Oh yeah, during study breaks. She brings friends once in a while."

Griff stepped toward Louie as he regained his seat. "Ever fly your daughter to Cuba to meet her friends from Kosovo or Russia?"

"Oh." Louie jerked his head at Griff. "Guess you already knew. I did a few times. Her friends could travel to Cuba, but not into the U.S."

"Are they on the terror watch list?" Eva asked.

Eyes wide, Louie shook his head.

"Bring back cigars when you flew with Sonya from Cuba?" Brett asked, tag teaming it with the other two agents.

"Sure, only she didn't know I had 'em."

Brett cranked his head toward the airstrip. "Your rear seats are gone to make room for suitcases of cigars, and your daughter couldn't tell she was in a cargo plane?"

"I mean it! She didn't know!"

Eva had heard enough. She tossed down her pen and stood. "Brett, contact the Columbus agents to arrest Sonya for cigar smuggling."

Louie jumped to his feet. Waving his arms, he splashed orange soda on the floor.

"Please, don't arrest her. If you do, Sonya won't get her law license. I'll help you anyways I can."

Griff approached him, lightly shoving him down into the chair. "Here's what you'll do. You sign a confession to everything, including how Sonya started you in the cigar organization, because that's true. Isn't it?"

Louie slumped, totally dejected. Sweat dripped into his eyes.

"Admit it, Louie. We aren't stupid. If you cooperate, we can try helping Sonya, but you must be honest with us. No lies. None."

"Okay, you got me there. Some of Sonya's friends know the head cigar guys."

"Anymore lies you'd like to correct?" Eva snatched her pen from the floor.

"Nah, that's it."

Griff had another idea. "Here's how this will work. Take me

with you, introducing me as your new partner in Cuba and to your U.S. customers."

"No. No. These people won't accept you. They'll know yer an agent."

All three agents began laughing.

"What's so funny?" Louie asked, holding his stomach.

"You look more like an undercover agent than either Griff or Brett. They accepted you," Eva pointed out.

"I suppose. We'll need a pretty good cover story."

"Oh, we have one," Griff replied with a hearty chuckle. "Listen, you haven't told us about these other folks you flew here from Cuba."

Louie's eyes rolled. "You know about them too?"

The three agents nodded their heads in unison.

"There were a few." He guzzled the soda in one gulp. "One guy lost his passport and paid me plenty to bring him in. The others were Sonya's friends from Kosovo."

Eva sat down, wiggling her pen at him. "Louie, Louie. You need to regain your memory. We shocked you a bit, jolting certain facts right out of your brain."

He shrugged, and she turned to a blank page on her legal pad. "You write and sign a statement under oath. We won't arrest you or Sonya today."

"Yup, give me a minute to get my facts straight."

"You'll be under house arrest," Griff added. "Brett's moving from the hangar to make sure you don't forget again and maybe get fleet-footed."

Brett flexed his upper arm muscles. "Too many snakes on the ground floor. You'd better make sure there are no snakes up here, including you. "

"No snakes," Louie assured him.

"Your life will be different. Expecting any visitors?" Griff probed.

"Not a one. Do I still have the right to talk to my attorney?"

"It's kinda late for that, isn't it?" Brett shot back. "You've confessed to everything. But yeah, we can still arrest and transport him to Miami, right, Griff?"

"No. No." Louie backpedaled. "I'm okay with how things are."

"Good." Eva rose. "You push your mind into high gear. Brett's going for sandwiches. After Griff and I finish the search, we'll record your truthful statement."

Eva hurried to the bathroom, noting repairs needed for the smashed door. She opened the medicine cabinet, finding something of importance. Coming back into the living room, she twirled a pink hair-bungy around her fingers.

"I found this in your bathroom. Louie, do you have a wife or girlfriend?"

He drew closer. "That's Sonya's. Pink's her favorite color."

Eva noted that interesting tidbit, and secured the hair band. At length, Brett returned with four delicious-smelling Italian subs and gave one to all but Louie.

"Hey, what about me?" he griped.

Brett smiled, handing him a sandwich. "If you eat one of our sandwiches, you become part of our team. On our team, we don't lie to each other."

"Right," Louie said, unwrapping his sub. "I won't be lyin' to you."

After eating a hurried meal, Brett and Griff tagged packages and cartons of cigars, which they loaded into the FBI's Cessna 421 for flight to Virginia. Eva fingerprinted and photographed their reluctant informant.

She swabbed inside his cheek for a DNA sample explaining, "Louie, this will stay in government files if at some point we have to book you."

He moaned, lowering his head. Did Eva see him wipe away a tear?

Chapter 32

Eva returned to Virginia with Griff and the tagged evidence. Scott picked her up in Manassas. He greeted Griff, who left to process the evidence. Scott's brief hug filled Eva with joy and zest for their future together.

She whispered in his ear, "I shouldn't be leaving again anytime soon."

"Good." He gripped her more tightly. "You light up my life."

The pull of home beckoned, so they drove straight there even though her stomach felt empty. She unpacked her bag in the bedroom while Scott helped Dutch build a trial-run volcano out of dishwashing liquid, baking soda, and vinegar for his science class.

To thumping sounds of Andy practicing drums in the basement, Eva found the makings of a sandwich. She spread mayo on rye bread, piling on ham and Swiss cheese. A few slices of sweet pickle added crunch. She took her sandwich and cup of tea to the den. She'd taken a bite when Kaley walked in, producing a sheaf of papers.

"Glad you're home, Mom. Will you read my report before I turn it in?"

"You've been one busy girl in my absence. This is about Russia?"

"Yes. I finished it last night. Dad read it."

It was then Eva realized she'd let her daughter down. She hadn't phoned Mr. Sikorski. She set down her sandwich, confessing her lapse to Kaley.

Kaley's eyes shone. "It's okay. I'm not meant to know yet what I discovered in the Vistula River. When the time is right, I'll find out."

"We'll leave it there until I wrap up my case."

"Do you have time to read my paper? If not …" Kaley's voice faltered.

Eva reached for her papers. "I'm reading your masterpiece if I stay up all night."

"Thanks, Mom." Her cheeks turned a rosy pink. "Ms. Yost told you at my party I have a conflict of interest because of the ferry seizure. Dad believes I stayed objective."

"The courage you showed on the Baltic will add depth. Let me drink my tea, and I'll get down to business."

"I value your opinion. Ms. Yost says Russia is misunderstood by Americans."

"Her ideas don't have to become yours. Did you use your own research and judgment?"

Kaley nodded, fidgeting with her hair before turning to leave. Her nervousness was palpable. Eva realized that Kaley, like her mom, strove too hard for perfection. Eva promised herself to lighten up at home around her children. A yawn released some tension, and she ate her sandwich while reading Kaley's term paper entitled, "Russia's power advances while America's wanes."

Time passed, and before Eva knew it, she'd reached Kaley's incisive conclusion. Kaley's theme paper contained such perceptive analysis Eva considered it college-level work. Last week, she'd read an article from a retired general at the War College who argued in a similar vein, how Russia was simply filling a vacuum left by recent U.S. policy of disengagement around the world.

She found Kaley lying on her purple bedspread, eyes closed as she listened through her earbuds. Eva lightly perched on the edge of the bed. Kaley's eyes fluttered open. She snapped the buds from her ears.

"Well, Mom? What do you think?"

Eva's smile exuded warmth. "Exceptional job, Kaley. I especially like how you wove in future biblical prophecy of Gog and Magog. You've given Ms. Yost important facts to consider. Your analytical skills are superb."

"It was tons of work. With you and Dad approving, I am relieved."

"Are you thinking of studying criminal justice? Or are you leaning toward medicine, like Aunt Viola?"

"Still praying about it. Glenna is too. It would be great if she and I could attend the same college and be roommates."

Eva stood up smiling. "Your dad and I would like nothing better."

SLEEP REFRESHED EVA. Firing up her G-car in the morning, she roared to the office with enormous enthusiasm for digging deeper into Louie's scheme. She was the first to arrive, and after sending some evidence to the FBI lab, she plunged into writing a report on Louie's evidence, which he so reluctantly gave. It was surprising he had any teeth left, Eva thought wryly. Her phone rang, and she said hello to Brett.

"What's new at Lime Key?" she asked, eyes riveted on her screen.

"I'm hunkered down with Louie. The guy's a mess. He's

receiving endless calls since you left. His customers insist on knowing when his next cigar shipment arrives."

Her fingers tensed and she quit typing. "We need a reason for the delay."

"Yeah, that's what I said. He's fidgety, acting guilty. Something reeks."

She spotted Griff walking toward his cubicle. "We'll talk things over up here. Meantime, use your vivid undercover imagination."

"Eva, you're brilliant. Once at DEA we seized a drug shipment where the Attorney General let us deliver a small amount to the recipients."

"That could work, except we don't want to brief the Attorney General yet."

Brett agreed to keep a sharp eye on Louie and hung up. Griff stepped into her tiny cubicle. She filled him in on Brett's idea to use Louie's cigars.

Griff wrinkled his brow. "The entire load's already in evidence. I'm uncomfortable distributing any of those cigars, aren't you?"

"Illegality is illegality. So no, even if it advances our undercover op."

"You know," he sat on her empty chair, "the chances of us being allowed to pursue this case are diminishing faster than ice on a hot stove."

Her shoulders fell. "You think so too?"

"If you were our boss, would you approve us working it further?"

"What are you saying, Griff?" She didn't much care for his opinion.

"Eva, we're neck deep in a bald-faced espionage case, not terrorism."

"How can you be so sure it isn't both?"

Griff lifted his bushy eyebrows. The two agents stared at each other. Defeat hung in the air. Eva's mind whirled to process what he'd put on the table. She had spent too much time away from family for Operation Stogie to be a bust.

"Football coaches always have plan B ready if the game plan fails," she offered.

Griff squared his chin, his next words doing nothing to relieve her angst.

"Louie can only fly in and out of Cuba with Cuban or Russian help. Holly saw that Russian passport in possession of Louie's passenger, whoever he is. We can't continue the farce Louie is helping terrorists. The Bureau will shut us down once they read our reports."

"Espionage can lead to terrorism," she snapped.

Griff groaned. "Even I'm not buying that."

Her mind churning in high gear, Eva lurched from her chair to pace by her small window. Their next move occurred to her in a flash. She whirled around.

"We act quickly. I sent Louie's DNA swab to the FBI lab with Sonya's hair band. He thinks she is his daughter. I don't. You and Louie fly to Cuba while we can still argue our case involves terrorism. We delay sending our reports."

He whistled low. "You're a genius."

"What?"

"Eva, you're such an excellent agent, you refuse to submit reports until you've proofread them several times to ensure total accuracy. Plus, we wait for DNA analysis."

"True." She grinned sheepishly. "And we delay proofing our reports."

Hoping their plan to stall the Bureau would succeed, Eva closed her file cabinet and spun the combination dial. She grabbed her purse, heavy with the Glock.

"Tomorrow we have Brett bring Louie up. And I have another plan," Griff said.

"Care to elaborate?"

"Let me piece a few things together first."

That said, Griff went to his desk, and Eva drove to Alexandria for her appointment with Holly. It was imperative she confront the woman before her sentencing. In a side office at the federal courthouse, a deputy marshal brought in Holly, looking dazed in a tan jumpsuit and handcuffs.

The defendant pitched a complaint before Eva could insist on answers.

"Agent Montanna, I sent you messages. You ignored me. What are you telling Judge Harding about keeping me from prison?" Holly arms trembled with fear.

Eva slid a chair close to her. "I have nothing to say to help you."

"I did everything you asked." Holly moaned. "You don't know anything?"

"I'm cautiously optimistic in time good will come from your assistance."

Holly's lips quivered. "My lawyer says Harding will send me to the penitentiary."

"The jury found you guilty of several crimes," Eva said evenly.

"Listen. Reporters will be in the courtroom when you are sentenced. If I tell the judge of your cooperation, he'll demand to know the benefits. I have nothing to say."

"You don't care what happens to me," Holly grumbled, sticking out her lower lip.

Not persuaded by Holly's hysterics, Eva said icily, "I'm your only chance at a reduced sentence. What I convey to the judge about your cooperation, reporters will publish in the papers or on TV. You'll be branded a snitch."

"Sticks and stones might break my bones, but names ..." Holly shrugged. "Let them call me a snitch. It's better than being locked up for an eternity."

Eva replied that in a month or two, if her assistance helped, Eva would inform her attorney, adding, "Constance Ingles can ask the judge to reconsider your sentence, and he can reduce whatever time you receive, with no reporters noticing."

A glistening tear crept slowly down Holly's cheek. "Okay."

"There is one possible problem."

"What?" Holly demanded.

"You failed to tell me about your private mailbox at Little Torch Key."

Holly's eyes sparked with panic. "I don't have one."

"Carlos gets statements at one in the name of Ulises Munoz. Did you know?"

"No." Holly tilted her head as if thinking. "Carlos put his name on his father's accounts. Bank statements quit coming to our house in West Palm. When I told Carlos, he said he cashed them in because they had so little value."

"Then why are statements going to an unknown box in Little Torch Key?"

Holly gaped at Eva with sudden awareness. "Carlos probably hid investors' money in those accounts, which he hid from me too."

"And the government. He's in big trouble."

"You believe me, right?"

Eva stood without answering. "I will contact your attorney within two months."

Though Holly agreed to keep up the charade through her sentencing, Eva felt compelled to confirm. "I won't yet divulge to the AUSA, your lawyer, or the judge anything about your cooperation."

Holly nodded gravely, and Eva left the courthouse ready to learn what else Griff had up his sleeve.

Chapter 33

Two days later, Eva found out Griff's unusual plan for Louie. In the rolling hills of Virginia's horse country, she sat with the informant in a confined examining room at a veterinary clinic. Photos of children hugging cats and dogs dotted four yellow walls. Dr. Viola Montanna, Eva's sister-in-law and pediatrician, was busy helping Eva with a doubtful look on her pretty face.

Viola had purchased a Friesian mare the second week in her new home, so she was getting to know the local vet quite well. When Eva had asked this favor, Viola pushed back with serious reservations.

"I won't risk my admitting privileges at Ryan-Gauge Hospital," she'd insisted.

So here the federal agent and doctor were using the examining room of Viola's veterinarian friend, all for a furtive reason. Eva hadn't a single qualm about what Viola was doing. Still, her sister-in-law also demanded the patient never know her name.

Louie rested his left heel on the examining table, his knee bent slightly. Viola used latex-gloved hands to smooth white plaster over the exterior of a fresh cast. Louie's tanned right leg extended from his shorts and hung down from the table.

"My leg's burnin'," he protested.

"It's temporary," Viola countered. "The plaster is curing, and when it hardens, we'll let you get down. Your leg will be cooler then."

Louie wasn't done whining. "I've got me one whale of a lawsuit. My unbroken leg's stuffed in a cast by some doc who won't say who she is. It's done in the back room of a dog hospital. I'll wreck my back from walkin' on crutches."

"Better than the alternative," Eva reminded him sharply. "How would you like being carried about in a casket because your smuggling partners did you in?"

"Hmmph," he grumped in reply.

Viola smoothed the plaster asking Eva, "Why the cast?"

"Mr. Clark here helps foreign mobsters fly contraband into the U.S. He says they will object if he tries introducing our agent as his replacement. He can't fly a plane with his leg in a cast, so he'll bring my partner along as his pilot."

Louie winced, pointing to the cast. "I had no idea you'd burn my leg so bad."

"Twenty years in a hot prison cell is worse," Eva warned. "Don't forget it."

Viola tore off the gloves. "We're done. I haven't put on a cast since I was in residency, and those were much smaller."

"I'll bet they were crybabies too." Eva snickered.

"Mr. Clark, you wait twenty minutes while it cures. Let me speak to Agent Montanna out in the hall."

The doctor left the room. On her way out, Eva gave Louie a *Hound and Country* to read. He rolled his eyes. Viola and Eva headed straight for the employee break room.

Viola gazed at Eva with worried eyes. "Am I going to be sued?"

"Don't give him another thought," Eva said firmly. "He's venting because he's become a turncoat against friends and his daughter. You are saving his life. Guys have been killed for less than what we would require him to do 'but for' the cast on his leg."

Viola washed her hands at a small sink. Drying them off on a paper towel, she asked, "Will Brett be going back to Florida right away?"

"Would you like to come for dinner before he returns to the land of sunshine?"

Viola raised her eyebrows. "I can check my calendar."

"Yes, do."

Eva smiled as she went outside the vet's office with no idea when to fit in a dinner party. Keeping it casual with pizza and salad might work. That is, if Viola wanted a ruse to spend more time with the handsome DEA agent. Eva collected crutches from the G-car, which she'd bought at a local pharmacy. Later, she and Viola checked on Louie's cast in the exam room.

"Your patient is ready to go," Viola pronounced.

Eva handed him the crutches. He slid off the examining table, standing surprisingly erect with crutches in hand. Being careful not to mention Viola's name, Eva thanked the doctor. She held the door for him to hobble out to the car.

Their drive to a Fairfax hotel, where Brett had him stashed, began with Eva asking him something that had bothered her.

"You have a swanky car and nice plane. Does cigar smuggling pay for those?"

"Eva, you already know, don't you? Every time I try lyin', you figure the truth."

"So?"

"You probably know Carlos owns 'em both."

She tried not to let her surprise show. "They're registered in your name."

"I signed a note. It looks like I borrowed money from him. I never made a loan payment. He hides ownership and I have free use of the car and plane."

"Who pays for the license tags and insurance?" Eva came to a stop at a red light.

"Bills come to me in the mail. I send 'em to Carlos and voilà, they're paid. Renewal tags appear in my mail. For such a good deal, I get to cater to his friends when they come down to use the place, or used to. Now since his arrest, I don't know what to expect."

"When you say cater, you mean you're their driver too?"

"No. Carlos had me give the BMW to friends he wanted to impress. I rode the little motorbike."

Eva recalled her crazy night ride with Griff on the Honda. Thinking of Louie doing his shopping on the dinky bike while Carlos's guests partied at the house made her wonder. What other nefarious criminal deeds could she possibly uncover with Louie's forced assistance?

A WEEK AFTER LOUIE'S LEG had been set in a cast Brett buttonholed Eva by the JTTF's tiny but well-used coffee station. The DEA agent's massive arms were pressed against his chest.

"Eva, give me some help. Louie is driving me nuts. He complains about us harassing him, about us maiming him, and about heading to jail instead."

Griff walked up interjecting, "Tell him if he doesn't clam up, you'll have Griff Topping babysit him. Then he'll know what jail is like."

"Sounds good." Brett poured a large coffee. "Come over tonight."

Griff laughed over his supposed threat. The three agents began talking seriously about when Griff should return with Louie to Florida and fly with him into Cuba.

Eva refilled her coffee mug, giving an update. "An ATF agent is checking with his headquarters to see if they want to charge the dealers selling Louie's untaxed cigars."

Their task force supervisor interrupted their impromptu huddle. Oliver's jaw muscle flexed in and out. He jangled change in his pocket as if extremely keyed up.

"The Bureau phoned," he said. "They want me and you two downtown pronto. This Clark fiasco has provoked a hornet's nest."

Griff turned to his boss. "I knew this would happen. Eva and I held off writing and sending in our reports until we had no more excuses."

Brett stepped back. "I think he's looking at you two."

Exonerated, Brett scurried out the exit, coffee in hand. Oliver grabbed his suit coat, ordering Griff to drive. Eva snatched her purse, and she brought their boss up to speed from the backseat while Griff deftly navigated the usual traffic jams into the nation's capital. He managed to reach FBI Headquarters and locate a parking spot in a record twenty minutes.

Oliver led them through security, with Eva hardly believing she was back here so soon. The ride in the elevator was again totally quiet. Their previous meeting with Director Taggart had been strange indeed, yet he had assured they had the Bureau's full support. Why were they being summoned?

The same agent behind a desk in Director Taggart's reception area consulted his computer. This time he wore a black suit over his starched white shirt. Eva noted an Army colonel in dress uniform was sitting by the door, a large file between his hands. The black-suit nodded toward Taggart's office, and pushed a button at his desk.

Taggart's lock buzzed. Oliver swung open the door, taking his puzzled team into Taggart's inner sanctum. The assistant director halted Oliver's introductions with a raised hand.

"We met earlier, when I approved this operation."

Dressed in a white shirt, blue tie, and dark blue suit, Taggart pointed to five chairs forming a semicircle in front of his impressive desk. His scowl brought his dark shaggy eyebrows low, shrouding his eyes.

"Be seated," he growled. "We need a prompt understanding of your recent activities at Lime Key. I find task forces, crammed with competing agencies and military honchos, to be a complete nuisance."

"Sir," was the beginning and ending of Oliver's defense.

Taggart silenced him by rapping his knuckles on the desk. No one said a word. Eva could almost hear a clock ticking though she didn't see a clock. Taggart cleared his throat before glaring at Griff, the FBI agent on the team.

"Agent Topping, do you realize you've ruffled the feathers of the colonel cooling his heels in my reception area? No? How could you? Well, he read your report and is steamed. More troubling is that the Bureau's Assistant Director for Espionage is lobbying for his division to take over my case."

Griff and Eva exchanged troubled looks. Oliver sat silent, like he was in a trance. Meanwhile, Taggart proceeded to give a precise summary of Operation Stogie, suggesting either he or his assistant had read and understood both reports Griff and Eva had submitted. He looked each of them in the eye.

"What you thought was a terrorism case involves espionage."

Eva girded her mind to the inevitable. Too bad she and Griff couldn't have delayed sending their reports until his return from Cuba. Taggart's smacking his knuckles on the desk simply drove her regret in deeper.

"I don't have to remind you it's customary to transfer control of espionage cases to a group specializing in spies."

"Sir, excuse me," Eva said. "I'm the ICE agent on the JTTF. As we've infiltrated a smuggling case, my agency will gladly take control."

Eva saw Griff's fingers digging into his thighs. Was he going to interject? The FBI couldn't hurt her, so Eva prepared to further protest when Taggart focused on her.

"I believe you, the ICE agent, developed the original informant."

"Yes, and Gr—"

Taggart cut her off. "This JTTF case is within my division, and since it may contain a terrorism angle, I retain control. Oliver, your group stays on the case."

"Yes, sir," their boss replied.

Taggart wasn't finished. He fixed an intense stare at Eva, telling her, "You developed the source and established a good relationship with Ms. Munoz. I want you to continue. Far be it from me to offend the director of ICE."

Tension eased from her shoulders. Eva sat more comfortably in her chair.

Taggart switched his piercing gaze to Griff. "Topping, your report states on his first Cuban flight, Louis Clark was intercepted by MiG-29s. Since then, he's gone into Cuba without incident."

"Yes, sir. He bribed a Cuban Air Force officer, though he no longer does."

"Exactly." Taggart banged his knuckles sharply on the wooden desk. "Which means someone high up in Cuba's government approves his comings and goings. It doesn't take a genius to see what's happening here."

Oliver pulled on his eyebrow. "Sir, per my instructions, Griff and Eva devised an ops plan permitting Griff and Clark to fly into Cuba and learn as much as possible."

"Excellent. That was my next request." Taggart closed his file with a dour face. "Here's a thorny issue. I noted Clark makes his trips when the DOD's surveillance blimp at Cudjoe Key is down for maintenance. The Pentagon should help us with that."

Taggart pressed a button on his intercom. When his assistant answered, he commanded, "Bring in Colonel Lou Penrod."

"Yes, sir."

In strode the colonel Eva noticed in the reception area. Colonel Penrod was introduced, and settled his thin frame into the empty chair with an air of disdain.

Taggart waved a hand at the two JTTF agents. "Your report states Clark called the blimp 'Fat Albert.' As I understand it, Colonel, when you read the report, you went ballistic. Am I right?"

Colonel Penrod twisted in his seat. His direct glare at Eva was a forceful reminder she'd written that debriefing report.

"We at the Pentagon do not admit to such a system." The colonel's neck beamed red above his collar. "Your report should not identify our Tethered Aerostat Radar System, let alone refer to it as Fat Albert. TARS and its accomplishments are classified. "

Eva bristled at the colonel's lecture as if she was a child. "We never mentioned a Tethered Aerostat Radar System. We merely described what a resident near Cudjoe Key called a tethered military blimp, as do residents in the Florida Keys."

"You make my point," Colonel Penrod objected. "You should have described it as a Tethered Aerostat Radar System. You should have 'classified' your report."

"You make my point," Eva countered. "When you read my report, you recognized what the resident called Fat Albert. Mr. Clark doesn't know a Tethered Aerostat Radar System from a pelican, let alone knowing things about it are classified."

"We prefer in the future that you describe the blimp as TARS and classify it."

"Colonel," Eva said, her eyes flashing. "'Fat Albert' are Clark's words from his debriefing."

Griff jumped in. "Sir, in the future, we will refer to Fat Albert as TARS."

"Thank you." Penrod gave a brusque nod. "I—"

Eva opened her mouth to continue blasting the colonel when Griff cut her off. "Louie Clark is a believer in what your … ah … TARS can do. It's so close to Lime Key I was forced to alter my approach when landing. Louie never heads to Cuba unless Albert is lowered for maintenance."

"Not Albert, Agent," Colonel Penrod shot a fierce look at Griff. "Even though I think your idea to fly into Cuba is foolhardy, we must work together. I'll try convincing my superiors we should lower the TARS when you make your ill-advised flight."

The colonel then leveled a bony finger at Griff. "You listen to me, Agent. Don't go getting in hot water down there. I warn you, I won't be part of starting WWIII or repeating any Cuban missile crisis."

Eva gave a sideways glance at Director Taggart, whose nostrils convulsed as he told their supervisor through clenched teeth, "Oliver, you and your team are free to finish this operation. Colonel Penrod and I have a few matters to discuss."

Penrod thrust out his chest as if to make certain the agents saw his medals. Eva loved the U.S. military; however, the colonel didn't know the first thing about the mission of law enforcement. Trusting Director Taggart would iron out any remaining difficulties, she hurried from his office. In the elevator, she took one look at Griff's contorted face and resisted the urge to break out laughing.

His flying undercover into Cuba and risking his life to stop smugglers was nothing to laugh over. When the doors opened, she walked out beside him. The first thing their boss did was yank out a cell phone and call the office.

"Can you and Dawn join us for pizza tonight?" Eva asked Griff in hushed tones. "Brett and Viola are coming."

"Appreciate the offer. I'm taking my wife for a nice dinner before leaving town. I'd like to wrap up this baby before Christmas."

Eva pondered what Griff just said. Could he or she still be stuck in the Keys over Thanksgiving? This case had more twists and turns than a roller coaster. She knew anything could happen.

Chapter 34

To Griff's profound relief, FBI Assistant Director Taggart must have talked turkey with Colonel Penrod, because Oliver told him later everything was "a go" with the Pentagon. The DOD would keep the "Albert" blimp in the air until Griff prepared to leave, and then they'd bring it down.

He obtained an official bankroll of fifty thousand dollars in fifties and hundreds from undercover funds. Louie couldn't be expected to bankroll the cigar loads they were going to buy. The one thing he didn't count on was Dawn waking up at 5:00 a.m. with a cold. They lingered together by the back door. He, dressed and ready to go, and she, wrapped in a fluffy robe and slippers, tissues in hand.

"Cold wind blew in my ears last night when we walked around Georgetown," she said, sneezing into a tissue.

Griff rubbed her upper arms with both hands. "Will you be all right?"

"Don't worry ab—"

She sneezed twice, and blew him a kiss. "Don't get sick, and come home safe."

"Okay, Sarge, and I promise to call the first chance I have."

Hustling out to his Bucar, Griff drove to the airport at Manassas. Too early to phone Eva, he instead completed the preflight check on the undercover plane. It wasn't until seven o'clock that Brett roared in full of apologies for being late with his "whining child." True to form, Louie grumbled he was "tired of his crutches."

Griff eased into the left pilot seat after Brett occupied the copilot's seat. Louie settled into the seat of his choice in the cabin behind them, bemoaning the lack of room for his cast. The trio wore headsets. That permitted them to talk over droning sounds of the plane's engines.

Brett's voice crackled into Griff's headset, "Perfect weather for flying. I've had a few lessons and want to earn my license. Until then, I get my thrills on a Harley."

"My club has a 172, we'll have to plan some trips," Griff replied, leveling off at cruising altitude. "It would be great to have this weather all the way to Florida."

Brett adjusted his headset. "The mountains over North Carolina may give us some bumps."

Louie piped in saying, "My 310 should be ready for the short flight to Cuba."

"Your 310 won't cut it," Griff replied. "I don't know how airworthy it is."

Louie sputtered, "Oh yeah? The Cubans know my plane."

"No way. We're taking this 421."

"The Cubans won't let us land in yer plane. They've never seen me in it and will shoot us down faster than you can say Fidel."

For the balance of the trip, Griff and Brett talked about their law enforcement careers, finding that as teens they had both been in police department explorer scout programs. A stop to buy fuel and sandwiches at Ft. Lauderdale cut short their conversation, which never picked back up because in no time Griff expertly landed at the Pelican's Nest.

He phoned Dawn soon after touchdown. His wife didn't answer so he left a message about landing at his first destination. He then rang Eva.

"I arranged with Colonel Penrod to lower the blimp this evening," she said. "At least you didn't have to listen to another lecture about the fat guy."

"You saved me," Griff said, forcing a chuckle. "Could you check on Dawn? She came down with the crud and didn't answer my call."

Eva sighed in his ear. "Tis the season. Scott left the house wheezing this morning. How are you?"

"Ready to rumble."

"That's our Griff. Watch your six."

He signed off as Louie shuffled up on his crutches. "I'm goin' up to check my place. Eva promised my doors are fixed."

Griff fired off an exaggerated salute. He and Brett backed the FBI undercover plane into the hangar. Later as the sun was dropping in the west, Louie hurtled back down the steps, leaning on his crutch and barging onto the deck outside Griff's second-story quarters.

"I seen it! Fat Albert's comin' down!"

Griff rubbed his hands. "We're good to go. Phone your people."

Then the FBI agent changed his mind. "No, wait."

Griff sped out to the corner deck to see for himself, looking southwest.

Brett joined him, pointing. "Sure enough, the fat blimp's nearly to the ground."

"Louie and I will leave at dawn, and return here before dusk, if all goes as planned."

"That's a big if, but there's no turning back now," Brett said.

Griff gazed at the clear blue sky with a gnawing question. What would Castro do if he knew an FBI agent was sneaking into his Communist fiefdom? Colonel Penrod's dire warning not to start World War III pulsed through Griff's mind like a hot current.

Brett slapped him on the back. "You'll be in and out in no time. Meanwhile, I'll be holding down the fort and ready for any and all contingencies."

"I'm counting on you."

Griff motioned for Louie to come with him, and they rode the elevator to the hangar. Griff walked around the undercover plane, trying to anticipate any problems. All seemed feasible.

"Okay," Griff finally said. "Make your call."

Louie pulled out his smartphone and tapped some numbers on the screen.

"Hold on," Griff interrupted. "Who you calling?"

"Ramon, my contact in their Air Force."

"Have you gone nuts? You can't just call Cuba, you don't know who is listening."

Louie leaned on his crutch, and whirled his phone around. "See? I'm callin' Miami. How do you think we've gotten away with this for so long?"

"Isn't Ramon in Cuba?"

"Yeah, but he has a Miami cell phone. If I don't call him, you and me get shot outta the air."

"What's taking you so long? Make the call."

Louie punched in numbers and waited. So did Griff. He glanced at his watch, questioning if he wasn't the one who had lost his mind, heading into Cuba with his untested informant.

To avoid jail, Louie might sabotage the deal by telling Ramon that Griff was an FBI agent. Then Griff would be languishing in a Cuban prison, and Louie would spend his life in a Cuban villa with a classic 1955 Chevy and a housekeeper.

"Hey, Ramon, it's me," Louie finally chirped into his phone. "I'm droppin' in tomorrow to pick up some things."

He scuffed the toe of his boot on the concrete.

"Yup. I got a new ride and chauffeur. Broke my leg and can't drive."

Louie hobbled to the rear of Griff's plane where he read off the tail number to Ramon. "That's his license number. It's a white 421. We arrive after sunup."

He ended the call, telling Griff, "Ramon is all set. He's

arrangin' for our order to be picked up in the mornin'."

Griff could almost picture Ramon, the Cuban Air Force officer, as some character from a comic book. Only this excursion over the Straits of Florida was no joke.

"Louie, be down here at seven, sharp. I checked. Weather looks good, as usual."

"I'll be here."

Griff gave his informant a keen appraisal as Louie ducked beneath the tail and got into the elevator. Recalling Louie's past flights, Griff removed the extra seats and loaded in the suitcases. He locked up, certain he'd considered every aspect for the coming escapade.

GRIFF SLEPT LITTLE. He dreamed Ramon blocked his takeoff to leave Cuba. Rather than keep tossing and turning, he dressed for his undercover role and brewed coffee. He was well into his second cup when Brett ambled in.

After saying good morning, his task force partner heated up frozen egg sandwiches in the microwave. The duo sipped coffee and huddled over breakfast. They reviewed the plan, talking in hushed whispers.

"So you're all set?" Brett wiped his mouth with a paper napkin.

Griff patted his pocket. "I have my undercover driver's license and no weapon."

"And no passport?" Brett asked.

"Right. The FBI plane is registered in the name of the undercover corporation that leases planes to small companies. I'd better bring it back in one piece."

"Keep your cool no matter what's thrown at you. I've worked undercover for years and would go in your place. Of course," Brett spread his hands apart, "I don't fly, except on my Harley."

Griff shifted on the chair, wanting Brett's reaction to something that happened yesterday. He finished his coffee to the last dregs before saying, "FBI Headquarters called to caution me about the prospect of Cuba detaining me and discovering I'm an FBI agent. If that happens, our government will claim I'm corrupt and acting on my own."

"That's rough." Brett rubbed his squared chin. "Remember Eva's take."

"Yeah. Someone in Cuba's regime is using Louie to their advantage, meaning they'll accept me and allow their illegal cigar ring to continue without a hitch."

"Exactly. Don't ask any questions that will make them

nervous," Brett advised.

Griff brooded over the FBI threat, recalling his abduction in Kazakhstan some years ago. He refilled his coffee, resisting thoughts that could endanger his undercover role. Besides, he'd survived that run-in with the KGB. Why should this Cuban insertion turn out any differently? Brave thoughts gave birth to brave conduct. No doubt, Brett would agree.

Brett cleared the dishes, asking Griff a probing question.

"You've searched the plane. There's nothing in it to blow your cover?"

"It's clean."

"You've got your burn phone?"

Griff double-checked his pocket for the prepaid phone he'd recently bought. "Got it. If there's an emergency, I'll call your burn phone."

"You're ready. Happy hunting."

Griff's hand paused by the button to open the hangar door. Inner resolve to succeed took over. He punched the "up" button, and the giant hangar door clattered.

"This is it," Griff said, leading Brett down the stairs from the second floor.

Heavy dew soaked the surface of Louie's plane parked to one side of the yard. Though the sun had just crested the horizon, there was plenty of light to launch. Griff took hold of a tow bar attached to the nose gear of the Cessna, and began pulling.

Brett leaned on the trailing edge of the wing. With a grunt, he helped Griff push the plane to the taxiway. Perhaps their noise caused Louie to wake because he finally appeared by the rear of the plane. His unshaven face and unbuttoned alligator-print shirt fluttering in the breeze were telltale signs he'd probably overslept.

"You're late," Griff said, straightening his back.

Louis grunted. "Let's get this dumb thing over with."

Griff removed the tow bar and handed it to Brett. He pulled down the door behind the left wing.

"Louie, make your way up the steps. See if you fit in the right seat. If not, I left one seat in the back by the suitcases."

Louie managed to squeeze up front, bellyaching all the way. Griff went about his business completing the exterior pre-flight check. Brett fist-bumped Griff. Then Griff climbed in, and raised and locked the door. He saw Louie's crutches lying flat in the cargo area. In the right seat, Louie began ranting.

"What if Ramon doesn't like you being my pilot?"

"Forget about me. Just buy your cigars as usual. I'm just flying you in, see?"

Louie gulped, and started through the checklist. The FBI agent—using his real name to keep Louie from getting confused—started one engine, the second.

Griff adjusted his headset mic. "Louie, keep your cast off the rudders and brakes."

"What if Ramon doesn't believe I broke my leg? These guys are like … you know … power crazy. In an emergency, I could try flyin' this."

"Don't even think about it," Griff warned.

What was Louie really afraid of? Griff reminded himself that Louie had made many successful trips to Cuba. This one should be no exception.

He applied power to the throttles, adrenaline spiking through his body. Turning the airplane onto the road, Griff's thoughts flew to a dark, unwanted place. What if Louie was a Cuban or Russian agent? He swallowed. This was the moment to place his total trust in God. Time alone would supply the answers.

Griff reached the runway, announcing over the radio his departure from Lime Key. He applied full power to the throttle with an unwavering hand. They steadily gained speed until the 421 lifted into the air seconds before he ran out of runway.

Griff's headset crackled with Louie cautioning, "Stay at three hundred feet. Less chance of bein' caught on radar."

Outwardly, Griff stayed cool, adjusting the throttles and fuel mixture for an efficient flight. Inwardly, his pulse fluttered. Clear skies and decent weather gradually buoyed him. To avoid dropping too near the water, he kept checking the altimeter.

When they neared Cuba, Louie's voice popped again, this time more urgently. "Quick! Climb to three thousand! We'll see company any time."

Griff pulled back on the yoke and added power. While the undercover craft slowly climbed, he geared up for what his undercover role might lead to, forcing from his mind words like "prison" and "capture."

Unexpectedly, Louie banged on Griff's arm. He glanced sideways. Louie was jabbing a finger out the port window. Griff scanned the cloudless sky. Oh wow!

His heart collided with his ribs. He gawked at the unmistakable Cuban flag painted on a twin-tailed Russian Mig-29 shadowing their flight.

Would they be shot down before ever landing in Cuba?

"Okay, we've got someone's attention," he said, trying to

remain calm.

Louie wiped a hand across his mouth. "He's checkin' the tail number to see if it matches what I gave Ramon."

The Mig-29 never left their side. Minutes ticked by. Griff's pulse raced. Then a heavily-accented voice barked the 421's tail number into Griff's headset, followed by a curt, "Announce your intentions!"

Griff swiftly called off the last digits of the plane's tail number, "Two Lima Charlie requesting vector to San Antonio field."

"Two Lima Charlie, maintain altitude and heading of one eight seven," the Cuban air traffic controller replied.

Griff came back with, "Two Lima Charlie, maintaining three thousand feet and one eight seven heading. Two Lima Charlie."

He was taking no chances. Louie slumped as if the air left him.

"Okay, Griff. All's cool. The MiG stays on us 'til we land."

Griff leaned back into his seat hoping to release his own escalating tension. What an experience. He'd just encountered his first Russian MiG in the air. He held on to his edge, fully expecting the unexpected.

Chapter 35

Following the air traffic controller's commands, Griff landed at the San Antonio de los Banos Airfield southwest of Havana. His wheels hit the concrete with a loud thud. What lay before his eyes, he refused to believe. The runway was cut in half! Some old Russian Army command car sat blocking the middle of the runway.

"Aggh!" Louie yelled in Griff's ear.

Griff's blood pressure skyrocketed. He jammed both feet against the brakes, pushing them hard to the firewall. The 421 slowed and shuddered. Somehow he stopped the airplane just before ramming the green antique car.

He recalled his earlier dream, where Louie's Cuban contact "Ramon" blocked the runway so Griff could not leave. Hair prickled on the back of his neck.

Breathing deeply, he reminded himself. He wasn't Special Agent Griff Topping, but a criminal in league with Louie Clark, another criminal. He wiped his thoughts clean of all federal agent instincts.

A Cuban Army officer dressed in an olive-green uniform waved from the doorless driver's seat in the Army command car. A fresh burst of adrenaline coursed through Griff's veins. He could have plowed that dude over with his plane. The four-door Jeep-like car with a canvas top began speeding onto the taxiway.

"Follow him!" Louie hollered. "He's takin' us to the military hangar."

"You got it."

Griff applied pressure to the left brake, adding power to the starboard engine, and the plane turned. He followed the bouncing Jeep as his energized informant shouted out instructions. Griff powered through one more turn, going onto a parallel taxiway. That's when he saw the MiG-29 touch down on the runway Griff had just left.

He fought for composure. The terrifying words "World War III" collided with his logic and reason.

Louie grinned, cranking his head to the side. "Same thing happened when I landed here the first time."

All right, Griff figured. If Louie was telling the truth, this venture into Cuba might end up okay. The command car jerked to a stop by the military hangar Louie mentioned. Score one for Griff's reluctant informant.

The green-uniformed driver hopped out. With gyrating arms, he directed Griff to spin around so the 421's nose pointed back toward the runway. Griff readily complied. After all, he might want to fly off in a hurry.

Both engines shut down, and Griff climbed from of his seat anticipating what came next. One thing he knew. The heat was already beginning to build in the plane's interior. Sweat pooled on his brow, dripped into his eyes.

He dashed moisture off with the back of his hand before opening the door, which dropped down behind the port-side engine. A towering Cuban Army officer greeted him by aiming an AK-47 right in his face. This military man flicked his weapon at Griff in command for him to walk down the steps.

Griff did so, reaching the rough concrete with his hands raised. The heavily-built officer shifted his eyes up at the door behind Griff. A look of profound relief spread across his glowering face, and he burst into startling laughter.

"Bueno, eet ees you!"

Griff craned his head over his shoulder to see what evoked such high spirits. Louie stood in the 421's doorway holding his crutches. The chuckling Cuban lowered his gun. Eerie music from the old *Twilight Show* played through Griff's mind. At the sound of a groan, he rushed to support Louie as he hopped down the steps.

For a brief moment, Griff forgot Louie's "fake" leg injury. His informant winced as if truly in pain while tucking crutches under his armpits and hobbling to the officer. It wasn't lost on Griff what a great actor Louie was. He'd bear it in mind as the operation unfolded.

Smirking, Louie tapped a crutch on his cast, and introduced Griff to Ramon as his new pilot. "I can't fly myself or my plane."

Griff was then introduced to Ramon, who nodded as if understanding. "*Si. Si.*"

"So we're all set?" Louie acted as the one in charge.

Again Ramon bobbed his head saying, "*Si, si.*"

Griff suspected Louie was putting on a show to convince Griff that he was masterful at deal-making. Ramon spun toward the soldier behind the wheel of the command car. He clapped his hands forcefully, shaking a finger at the nosewheel of Griff's plane. After a volley of Spanish between the two soldiers, the driver ran to the hangar, returning with a tow bar.

As he attached it to the front gear, Louie hissed at Griff, "Snatch your bag from the plane. We do business in Ramon's office."

Griff grabbed the strap of a canvas bag that hung around the pilot's seat. He slung it over his shoulder, hiking down the steps. The driver backed the plane into the hangar with Ramon shouting orders in Spanish.

That done, Louie whispered to Griff, "They put the empty suitcases in the command car. We pay Ramon. Don't mess up."

Griff lifted his chin a fraction, thinking things were going smoothly, maybe too smoothly. What would go down in Ramon's office? Would the Cuban military officer arrest him?

Searing heat dogged Griff as he trailed Ramon across the tarmac. His ears were attuned to the whine of the MiG's engine. He spotted it parking beside a hangar at the other side of the airport. Griff observed armed soldiers crisscrossing the tarmac, and fought to focus on his undercover role. If he played this dangerous mission right, he'd be back in the air before long.

Ramon swaggered and puffed his way into a cramped office. Griff trudged in behind him, with Louie scraping in on crutches. The filthy place bore no screens on the open windows. If possible, the room was even hotter than outside.

A flimsy wooden desk, which had seen better days thirty years ago, was shoved sideways towards a rain-streaked wall. Ramon swelled his chest as he squeezed behind the desk. He swirled a wooden cane chair around, which was as decrepit as everything else in sight. Much of the cane was busted in.

Ramon lowered himself gingerly upon the broken seat, rubbing his right thumb and finger together. "Senor, you bring da' handling fees?"

"That's yer cue." Louie stumbled up to Griff with shifting eyes. "He gets twenty thousand, you know."

"Sure thing."

Griff dug into his bag and removed bundles of one hundred dollar bills. He counted out $20,000, and with one rapid movement, handed Ramon the cash. The officer's eyes shone as he grabbed for the money. Griff watched closely while Ramon counted each stack.

Ramon mumbled an oath in Spanish, only to recount the bundles again. Griff tamped down rising concern. He knew the money was all there. Ramon eventually locked eyes with Griff and grunted, stuffing cash into his pants pockets. Waddling out of his puny office a richer man, the Cuban officer returned to the hangar.

Griff left the stifling room and wiped down his moustache with his right palm, feeling edgy. What would happen next? Louie acted content, meandering along his crutches grinding on the cement.

Clickety click, clickety click.

Ramon hustled to the old Army vehicle, which the driver had moved to the apron outside of the hangar. The motor was running. Suitcases were crowded into its back end.

As Louie maneuvered to the command car, he unloaded a ton of gripes to Griff. "The cast is baking my skin in this heat. My stomach is hollow. I could use some food."

"Where is Ramon taking us?" Griff asked under his breath.

"To the cigar factory. They'll pack the bags full. We pay him the rest when we come back here."

Ramon didn't wait for them to catch up. He climbed behind the wheel ready to leave for the factory. The other driver had disappeared. Louie struggled to sit up front, taking longer than he had getting into the cockpit.

Was he purposely causing a delay? Why would he do so, unless he'd concocted some plan Griff knew nothing of, like fingering him and seeking asylum.

Griff wiped sweat from beneath his collar. He carefully arranged himself in the backseat to avoid a spring poking through the patched leather surface. Suitcases filled the canvas-covered rear, plus two were stowed beside Griff.

Ramon popped the clutch and Griff's head snapped backwards. They blasted off at a high rate of speed.

THE DRIVE INTO HAVANA'S suburbs lasted a hair-raising forty minutes. Griff suffered through the acute heat and incessant bumps into gaping potholes. His neck ached. His empty stomach rumbled, but he forced from his mind any idea of eating. Whenever he safely reached the good ole' USA, he'd chow down a burger and fries.

He grinned, watching Louie bounce around like a bronco rider in his cast. Then he realized the Cuban people must also be suffering from the appalling conditions; however, there was nothing he could do for them. They whizzed past run-down homes where Griff saw no air conditioning. The assortment of mid-to-late twentieth-century trucks and cars along the roadway made him marvel, and he wondered where they got parts to keep these cars from the fifties running. Then it hit him: Russia.

Why hadn't the people of Cuba overthrown the Regime and the likes of Ramon? Not much had changed since the late President John F. Kennedy reneged on his promise of air support for the rebels at the Bay of Pigs.

The Jeep's right front wheel dropped into a huge pothole.

Griff's teeth collided, rattling his jaw. He shifted his weight to relieve a sharp pain in his lower back. And he reminded himself this case wasn't about lousy Cuban cigars. To him and Eva, it was all about the strangers Louie secretly flew from Cuba into the U.S.

It remained to be seen how much Ramon knew about the human smuggling scheme. Griff suddenly thought of a new snag. Ramon might ask him to fly undeclared passengers to the States. What would he do then?

Griff looked out the window. The houses they passed were becoming larger and better maintained closer to Havana, Cuba's capital city. The Army car swerved all at once to the right. Griff refocused his eyes and steadied his stomach.

They were driving along a narrow palm-tree-lined drive. An impressive white mansion with a red tile roof rose before them. Ramon maneuvered the Jeep around to a rear entrance.

Griff was reminded of the servants' entrances at all the British mansions he and Dawn had seen on her extensive DVD movie collection. He had no way of knowing who owned this beautiful home before the Communist revolution.

Ramon parked abruptly and jumped out as if impatient to rake in the rest of his fortune. He whistled a jarring tune while opening the door to the mansion.

Louie settled on his crutches and dipped his head as he started walking. He told Griff in low tones, "Ramon is payin' his people to load our suitcases with cigars. Wanna see around?"

"Don't we watch them pack and do a count?" Griff asked, amazed.

Louie tossed his balding head. "Nah. They always get it right."

Inside the multi-level mansion, Griff was greeted with a sweet and musty fragrance of tobacco. He felt like sneezing, and hoped he wasn't getting Dawn's cold. After hopping up five steps to the main floor, Louie showed Griff a tiny space where Ramon was conversing in Spanish with a man dressed in casual clothes and sandals.

"He's the plant manager." Louie didn't linger. "Come, you gotta see this."

He stopped inside a darkened room, where Griff blinked rapidly. Once his eyes adjusted to the faint light, he counted ten comfortably-dressed women sitting at wooden desks. Each was rolling cigars by hand. Not one looked up. Their intense concentration for what must be little pay resonated with Griff. He was witnessing a side of this deal he hadn't expected.

Louie drew in a lungful of air. "Ahh …That's an aroma. After the revolution this was a school. Women learned to roll cigars here in the early 1960s."

He took Griff to yet another room with ten more women toiling at desks, rolling tobacco. "This factory creates the most expensive and exquisite cigars in the world. Still rolled only by women."

"Cigars aren't my cup of tea."

Griff wiped his forehead and moistened his dry lips. Louie pointed upward, explaining there were a bunch more rooms just like these on the two upper floors.

"Want to see them?" he asked, his eyes wide in anticipation.

Griff didn't relish a hike in this heat, so answered, "How long does it take Ramon to load our cigars?"

"Not too long. I don't much like going upstairs in my dumb cast anyways."

Louie brought him instead down the opposite side of the hall. More women wound brightly-colored bands around seven-inch-long cigars. One lady had a tiny fan oscillating by her face.

What would happen if Griff stepped in front of the moving air for a moment? Would alarm bells go off? The heat was unbearable.

Louie spoke in hushed tones though no one was within earshot. "Time was, only foreign dignitaries Fidel liked got these cigars as gifts. The British royal family did. One cigar goes for $25.00 here. In the U.S., since they can't be sold, they cost much more."

"What do these women earn in a day, do you suppose?" Griff wondered aloud.

Louie shrugged like he didn't care. For his part, Griff couldn't wait to leave this sweltering "mansion." Still, it was more elaborate than the sterile warehouse he imagined. Louie the tour guide used his crutch to gesture at another room off to their right.

"Watch how they roll cigars. That's one reason they're sought after."

Griff leaned into the doorway. A woman sat behind a desk, a purple scarf wrapped about her head. Humming a merry tune, she picked up a light-colored tobacco leaf, which she laid beside a darker leaf on her desk top. Then she selected various colored leaves from different bins above her desk and tore veins from the leaves.

After crushing the leaves into small pieces, she placed them atop the longer leaves. Her hands worked quickly, rolling long leaves around short ones. In moments, she produced a nine-inch cigar. She snipped an inch off the end using a cutter, and placed the unfinished cigar in a rack at the top of her desk.

"Is the tobacco grown near here?" Griff asked his cigar-smuggling informant.

"Nah. Every leaf's grown on seven hundred acres in Vuelta Abajo, a hundred miles southwest of here. Even after it's harvested, it goes through three separate fermentations. It takes eighteen months to cure."

"So long?"

"Yup. I'm tellin' you, this stuff is primo. The blend of these tobaccos produces an unequaled flavor of coffee and chocolate."

Griff didn't smoke so he couldn't verify his claims. All he wanted was to determine if Louie was knowingly smuggling Russian operatives. One aspect he found remarkable was Louie's lively interest and demeanor in this place. He acted more purposeful than in the Keys.

Ramon's rapid-fire talking on his cell phone down the hallway ended the tour.

"Loo-eee," Ramon called in his sing-song voice.

With a flippant gesture of his hand, the Army officer motioned them out the back entrance. He marched straight to the command car loaded with suitcases, which Griff presumed were stuffed with cigars. Ramon clambered in and started the engine. With a groan, Louie got in the passenger side.

Griff eased into the same seat with the busted spring. He nudged a suitcase with his elbow to make room for his knee. When it failed to give, he knew it was full of cigars. Perhaps something else too?

Griff wouldn't relax until sitting behind the controls of his plane, and not even then. No. He'd stay on high alert until liftoff. Wait … his instincts warned, not even then. The MiG-29 might harass him in the sky toward Florida.

Agents anticipated danger when working undercover and so would Griff until he flew totally out of Cuba's airspace. The Cuban officer drove like a maniac on a wild ride back to the air base. He breezed past a guard at the entrance without stopping. Griff noted the sentry dribbled a sloppy salute.

At the hangar, the assistant unloaded suitcases from the car and shoved them into the Cessna. As a precaution, Griff rearranged the cases for optimum weight balance.

Louie called as he headed into Ramon's office, "Step in here when yer done."

Griff hustled down the 421's steps, looking for the Russian MiG. Seeing no military craft, relief filled him, and he strode into

Ramon's dirty office. Griff counted out the final $20,000 bucks, ready to roar out of this airport. He sure hoped Ramon didn't count his final fee another three times.

Things were looking good. Ramon made a cursory count before jamming reams of cash into his ample cargo pockets. How easily he accepted Griff's role as Louie's pilot. Greed made him careless.

"Yer the best," Louie praised Ramon.

The officer smiled grandly, pointing to his cast. "Soon you be feexed?"

"Before my next trip here, I hope."

Only one thing left to do and that was to leave Cuban airspace with no problems. Griff and Louie snuggled into the sweltering plane, and were being pulled back toward the taxiway the instant Griff slid into his seat. His mind said, *Go, go, go!*

The tow bar disconnected, the Cuban soldier fled for the hangar. Griff fired his engines. He zoomed through the checklist, desperate for cooler air. Once cleared by the San Antonio tower, Griff's eyes focused out the front windshield.

He inhaled, lifting up a silent prayer thanking God for getting them this far safely. Thoughts of being arrested and languishing in a Cuban jail as other Americans had done evaporated from his mind. He throttled to the runway, eager for freedom.

Freedom! What a wonderful word!

He'd never take it for granted again.

Chapter 36

Would Fat Albert sound the alarm at his plane entering Florida's airspace? Griff's expertise was about to be sorely tested when he dropped to three hundred feet on his approach to Lime Key.

He scanned the skies. The feds shouldn't chase him because DOD was cooperating. So were Customs and the DEA. Still, you never knew when a rookie didn't get the memo.

Griff changed his course, avoiding the restricted areas near Key West and Cudjoe Key. Louie's eyes remained closed. Griff couldn't begin to imagine what was swirling around in his mind. Griff was eager to phone Dawn. Finally setting the 421 down on Lime Key's strip mid-afternoon, his back was drenched in sweat.

His pulse began returning to normal as he taxied to Holly's house. A final one-eighty turn and he cut the engines. Louie looked pale and sickly. Griff climbed from his seat, pushing open and lowering the door.

Brett stood on the tarmac looking like a tourist in shorts, T-shirt, and sandals. He grinned sheepishly. "Welcome to Florida. You're in time for a late lunch."

"Great. I can eat three burgers no problem."

Griff helped Louie down a few steps, and reached back to retrieve his crutches. The sullen informant went straight to the elevator.

Brett stopped him in mid-stride. "How did it go?"

"I was surprised Ramon accepted Griff like that." Louie snapped his fingers.

"It's typical, not because I'm so persuasive. Ramon is greedy." Griff was thrilled to have put ninety miles between him and Cuba.

Louie acted dazed. He left them saying, "I'm eatin' pizza, and takin' a nap."

"Are you all right?" Griff called after him.

Louie simply continued on his crutches. Brett turned to Griff, his eyebrows raised in a question mark. "Did something happen you need to tell me about?"

"Let's get the plane inside first. We can talk over a sandwich."

The two agents pushed the aircraft into the hangar. Down rattled the large overhead door, and Griff threw the circuit breaker, locking it.

"Our evidence should be secure enough," Griff said.

"Let's head to the marina where I bought those Italian subs."

A few minutes later, Brett drove the rental car while Griff called Dawn, happy to learn she was feeling better. Inside the deli, Griff's mouth watered at the overpowering smell of food. A server hurried by with platters of shrimp po'boys. When she came for his order, Griff ordered two, with coleslaw and fries.

"Ditto," Brett chimed. "Diet colas all around."

"Bring mine with lime," Griff added.

The server hustled to the kitchen, and Griff reported in low tones about the successful op.

"Eva called while you were changing clothes," Brett told him. "She's a fount of knowledge, per usual."

"Fill me in."

After their icy drinks arrived, Brett explained how Eva wanted to bring charges against the people smuggling the Cuban cigars. Griff took time to sip his drink, the coolness refreshing him after the daring escapade into Cuba.

"I suppose she'd charge them for illegally trading with Cuba in violation of long-standing sanctions," he observed.

Brett rolled his eyes. "The State Department is against such legal steps. They're all for improving Cuban relations. The ATF agent on our task force wants to make a case against the Tampa and New Jersey cigar dealers for possessing untaxed cigars."

"ATF does have jurisdiction over that aspect," was all Griff could manage.

He'd hit the wall. His mind felt mired in thick mud. Good thing their food arrived. He waved off talking to feed his growling stomach. When he'd eaten every last bite, they dove into their next plan. Bottom line was they would fly home in the morning, ATF would seize the cigars, and Griff would head out on a whirlwind trip with Louie next week to deliver cigars to the merchants.

"Wish you had your license," Griff said. "You could fly to Cuba next time."

Brett grimaced. "Not me. Miami's close enough to the fanatical regime. Louie acted in a fog when you landed."

"Something's eating him," Griff agreed. "I wouldn't be shocked if he's been hiding assets too."

GRIFF'S EVENING TURNED OUT FAR DIFFERENT than he expected after coming back with Brett. Ten minutes into the nightly news, Brett said he was going to make phone calls in his room. Griff checked his phone and found a new voicemail message from Eva telling him to check the news. Russia was amassing troops near Poland's border, in protest to the U.S. providing them with antiaircraft missiles.

Moments later, Griff heard a light tapping on the door. Peering through the security hole, he saw Louie's receding hairline beneath the entrance light. He opened the door.

"Got a minute?" Louie lifted his shoulders in apology.

The way his lips drooped and hair hung in graying strings, Griff took pity on him. He stepped back to let him in. "I'm about to pop some corn. Interested? "

"Sounds good. I didn't eat nothin'."

Louie pulled out a kitchen chair and flopped down. He leaned his crutches against his right leg. Griff ripped open a microwave packet and started the device.

"Fridge is stocked with diets and lemonade. What's your pleasure?"

"Diet. Where's your sidekick?"

"On the phone," Griff replied, opening the fridge.

The cooking corn filled the air with a buttery smell. Griff set two cans on the table and slid out a chair. He snapped the tab on his can.

"You recovered from today's flight?" Griff asked, drinking tart lemonade while waiting for Louie's answer.

"I've been thinkin'," he finally mumbled.

"I want to hear about it. Just a sec."

Griff got up quickly, whisking the bag from the microwave before it burned. The delicious-smelling contents he poured into a big green bowl, which he set on the table. He told Louie to help himself.

The downcast man spread out a napkin, poured popcorn on it, and said in between bites, "Can you believe Ramon accepted you?"

"I predicted he would," Griff said, pouring popcorn onto a napkin.

"You did, you did." Louie's voice held respect. "Someday Ramon, whoever he is really, may go to prison."

"Right."

Louie thumped his chest. Popcorn flew from his hand.

"Because of me," he moaned.

"Right again."

He fiddled nervously with his paper napkin. "Could I end up in prison with 'em? I'll be a sittin' duck."

Aha, Griff thought. Louie's life must have flashed before his eyes on their trip into Cuba.

"We talked about that." Griff palmed his moustache, reminding Louie, "Eva and I will vouch for your cooperation, if you are ever charged."

"Is there a way you won't charge me?" Louie's voice shook.

Griff considered his heartfelt plea. Flying into Cuba and meeting his smuggling buddies with a federal agent had surely given the man a glimpse of his honorable past, crime-filled present, and bleak future. He'd become afraid of what he saw.

"I hope you hear me." Griff let go of his can. "You want me to say your sins are forgiven. The legal system doesn't hand out mercy the same way God in heaven does."

"Don't talk that way!"

"What way?"

"You sound like Cecil next door." Louie jerked his head toward the right. "He scares the daylights outta me talkin' of sin and death."

"You're scared like the scarecrow on the *Wizard of Oz*. In reality, you accepted those risks when you joined forces with criminals."

Louie banged a crutch on the floor. "No! I'm talkin' about Cecil next door, man."

"Okay, I'll bite. Who is he and why are you scared of him?"

"You didn't meet Cecil? He's a pilot for the airlines. He flies in and out of here regular in his Velocity."

"I've seen the plane. So what?"

"Cecil's okay, but …" Louie's words dropped off, his eyes opening wide. "He believes everyone's goin' to hell unless God forgives 'em."

Griff leveled a direct gaze at Louie so he wouldn't miss the truth. "Your neighbor is right. You do realize my influence for you is only with the government."

Louie picked up his crutch and thwacked it on the floor again. Griff ignored his angry outburst by getting up and tossing another packet of popcorn in the microwave.

While it sizzled and popped, he ambled back over. "Louie, rant away. It's as I said before. We inform the prosecutor of your criminal activity, advise O'Rourke how you've helped us and changed your ways. You could testify about your past dealings."

"Is O'Rourke the fed who got Holly and Carlos convicted?"

"The very one." Griff dashed over to retrieve the popped corn.

"What are the chances I'll be luckier than Carlos?"

"Hard to say."

Griff dumped hot corn in the bowl, not admitting he had no

interest in cigar smuggling. It was Louie's daughter Sonya and her foreign connections Griff and Eva were zeroing in on.

"The more we achieve in delivering cigars to your customers, the brighter your future looks," Griff said, piling corn on a new napkin.

"I might still get charged and go to jail?"

"If you are convicted, I'll testify about your help. If Judge Harding believes you helped us greatly, he could shorten your sentence or give you probation."

"You promise? Let me hear you say it agin."

Griff first ate some popcorn. Telling Louie he promised, he added, "I won't guarantee the outcome. Appointed for life, federal judges have power and authority over you. In case you hadn't noticed, God has the ultimate power over your life."

"Not mine!" Louie whipped his crutch down again. "Quit saying so!"

To calm him, Griff explained, "In some cases the prosecutor finds cooperation is so vital, no charges are filed. I could possibly make that happen."

"Okay, now yer talkin'."

"*Possibly* I said. Sometimes, despite a defendant's help, the judge sends him to prison. Take the case of Barry Seal, former TWA pilot and drug smuggler for a murderous Colombian drug cartel. Though he testified, the federal judge sentenced him to work release at a drug rehab in New Orleans. It made the news. Unfortunately for Barry, he was assassinated outside of the rehab."

"Agghh!" Louie screamed. "I could get killed double-crossin' these jerks."

"Steady on." Griff did some fast backtracking. "That was a violent drug case. I shouldn't have mentioned it. I don't see that happening to you."

"You agree with Cecil next door." Louie gulped, looking petrified. "Do you get what I'm sayin'?"

Regret filled Griff. Why had he mentioned Barry's death? Then it occurred to him perhaps Barry's case could help his informant understand the truth before it was too late.

"Okay, you said Cecil believes everyone's going to hell unless they're forgiven by God. That's what you said, right?"

Louie's bloodshot eyes darted from side to side. He wiped his hands on his slacks. Griff slid his chair forward an inch.

"You're right to fear the prosecutor and judge. You broke the law many times. But Cecil's right too, about fearing God Almighty."

"Yer tryin' to scare me, right?"

With his eyes zipping about the room, hands trembling, and left leg bobbing up and down, Louie was a wreck. This kind of opportunity didn't come too often to the FBI agent. Griff would not lose such a profound moment.

He held up a single finger. "Stand by."

Griff went to his bedroom, bringing out his Bible, which he opened on the table. He flipped pages until he found the book of Romans. He pointed a finger at a particular verse in chapter 3.

"Read this aloud," Griff said. "There at number 23."

Louie tilted the Bible so light from the ceiling fixture shone on the pages. He cleared his throat. "It says, 'All have sinned and fall short of God's glory.'"

"God's glory means His holiness," Griff explained gently. "It means you and I are sinners. We're unholy."

"I don't get what yer sayin'."

Griff took the Bible, thumbing through pages. "It's not me saying this, but God. Listen to what He says in Romans chapter 6, verse 23: 'For the wages of sin is death.' Death means separation, to be apart from God for all eternity in hell."

"Why'd I ever come up here?" Louie whacked the table leg with his crutch. "Cecil's a real my-life's-all-together guy. Okay, his is. Mine isn't. Yer tellin' me he's right and I'm wrong?"

"Louie, you're throwing questions at me. I'm doing my best to answer them. I'd rather be getting shut-eye before flying north in the morning."

"Okay," he sighed. "I'm listenin'."

"It gets better." Griff wasn't ready to give up. He wanted him to truly understand.

"Badder? As in bad news gets badder?"

Griff forced himself not to laugh. "No. The rest is, 'For the wages of sin is death, but the gift of God is eternal life in Christ Jesus our Lord.'"

"What's it mean?" Louie leaned forward to gaze at the Bible as Griff put it down.

"You once loved Sonya's mother," Griff said. "God's love for you is way beyond that. It's so big, He sent His Son Jesus Christ to earth to die on a cross for our sins. That's what Good Friday means. On the third day after His death, Christ rose from the grave. That's why we celebrate Easter. Just imagine the power in defeating death."

Louie examined his fingernails. "My mom took me to church once. It was Easter. I was eight. She died after that. It was my last church day."

"That doesn't matter." Griff tapped the Bible page with his hands. "When we believe in Christ and accept Him as God's gift to us, God forgives our sins. He washes us white as your T-shirt."

"Sounds too easy."

Griff placed a napkin between the pages at the book of John. Arguing was fruitless. "It's no skin off my nose. You're the one fretting about your future, and what Cecil told you. Read through John. It's about Jesus's miraculous life. Remember, I'll tell the prosecutor and judge why you shouldn't go to prison."

"So?"

"Read John. Know this. Jesus is in heaven representing me before God. He tells God that I asked for forgiveness of my sins and changed my ways. He tells God how I accepted God's gift of Jesus Christ, and so I'll be in heaven and not hell for eternity. He offers you the same gift. You believe or reject it. Either way, you decide."

"I don't know." Louie guzzled his can of soda and banged it on the table.

Griff picked up the cans. "By helping us, you'll have a good outcome. This matter of hell and heaven? I can't help you there. It's between you and God. I'll talk to the judge for you, but it's up to you to deal with God."

He pointed upward toward heaven. Louie snatched up his crutches and left. The whole episode gave Griff much to ponder about the real reason for and possible outcome of Operation Stogie.

Chapter 37

Griff's grueling flight from Florida to Manassas the next day was bumpy and long. With Brett going to camp out with Louie at a local safe house, Griff drove home with his mind gearing up for more flights in the coming days. He opened the back door, and Dawn fell into his arms.

"I took a vacation day from work," she told him after their tender hug. "Your supper is almost ready."

He breathed in, smelling cinnamon. Thinking she'd baked an apple pie, he washed up and joined her at the table where they shared lively conversation over a delicious meal of roasted pork with apples and whipped sweet potatoes.

"Let's eat our pie in the living room," she said with a gleam in her eye. "You put your feet up."

The second he relaxed in the recliner, his eyelids began to droop. Good thing Dawn hurried in or he would have started snoring.

She lovingly placed a tray on his lap. "Decaf coffee and homemade pie."

"This looks fabulous." Griff tried a bite of the creamy confection. "It's tart, yet sweet. What am I eating?"

"Can't you tell? It's key lime pie! In honor of my hero's return from Lime Key."

Delicate sounds of her twinkling laughter made him realize it had never felt so good to be home.

"No, honey. The truth is, you are my hero," Griff said. "Let's watch one of your British movies and enjoy this scrumptious dessert together."

GRIFF DRAGGED HIMSELF to the office the next morning. It wasn't jet lag, but it sure felt like it. Eva welcomed him with a warm smile and friendly handshake. After a few pleasantries, she briefed him on her endless haggling with the ATF.

"Our task force ATF agent's paving the way," she said. "Good thing he's on our team or this case would go nowhere."

Griff yawned. "It was a long flight up here. It's not like I could stop at rest areas."

"I am happy to see your smiling face. With Russia putting missiles into Cuba, you had me on pins and needles the entire time."

"You and me both, partner." Griff's energy began to ebb. "I

need coffee."

"You read this, and I'll fetch you a cup."

She gave him a sheet detailing names and phone numbers of ATF agents, bringing him back a steaming black coffee. Griff thanked him and got busy making calls, volleying back and forth with ATF. He needed assurance from the agents that any searches and arrests in the two states wouldn't be traced to the deliveries. That would jeopardize his and Eva's more significant espionage case.

Finally, all agencies agreed: The agents would conduct surveillance, follow the cigars, and identify buyers with no arrests leading back to Griff or Louie.

So early on Thursday, Griff reached for the skies again, a subdued Louie in tow. This time they flew to New Jersey, and not Cuba. Here they delivered half the cigar load to Louie's customer. Cigars and cash traded hands. Then Griff was up and away in a calm and clear autumn sky. The landing gear retracted, and he skillfully reached his assigned altitude.

Meanwhile, Louie removed his headset and began dozing in the right seat. To his light snores, Griff mentally recapped their progress. He was troubled about their upcoming Tampa delivery, although he couldn't pinpoint exactly why. Maybe it was the sheer proximity to Cuba's borders again that made him restless.

Louie stirred awake when they landed for fuel and lunch north of Charleston. He remained pretty quiet as they ascended into the cloudless sky.

Reaching cruising altitude, Griff said in his mic, "You slept the whole first leg."

"Not been gettin' much sleep."

"Still worried your customers will find out I'm an FBI agent?"

Louie shrugged. "Maybe."

"Ramon, your Cuba guy, bought me," Griff reminded him. "So did the buyer in Jersey. So will Dino in Tampa. They trust you, they'll trust me."

"Yer probably right."

"Tonight after we drop off the last cigar load, you should sleep better," Griff said, gesturing at the plane's cargo. "You will have completed what we asked of you."

Louie spoke loudly in the microphone. "Jail's not keepin' me awake. It's you and Cecil sayin' I could spend forever in hell."

"Do you—wait. It's air traffic control."

Griff listened in his headset, made an altitude adjustment per the controller's request, and glanced at Louie. He looked haggard and worn out from despair.

"Remember the verses from Romans the other night?" Griff asked.

"Yeah."

Griff held the yoke steady. "A few years back, I realized the truth of what Cecil's been telling you. I read those Bible verses and grew uncomfortable. A former police officer I'd worked with who became a pastor encouraged me to read John, the book I showed you in the Bible. Then I accepted God's forgiveness."

Louie fumbled with his headset, prompting Griff to ask, "Did you read John?"

"Nah, no time."

"You've had time. Read it. Believe me, it's good news."

Louie glanced down at a folded chart in his hands. "Jacksonville's below. How we doin' on our ETA at Tampa?"

"We're good."

Griff used his cell phone to make a phone call. Time passed as the Cessna soared through light cloud cover, both men nursing their private thoughts. It was late afternoon when their altitude dropped. As they flew over Leesburg, Griff calculated they'd be meeting the Tampa federal agents right on time.

He decided to tell Louie about this twist in his plan. "Two agents are meeting us at Tampa's Executive Airport when we land."

"Oh?" Louie coughed into his microphone. "Is that who you were talkin' to back there by Jacksonville?"

"It was. Tampa's delivery should be smooth like Jersey. My guys rented a van for us. We drive to your customer and do the deal. Bingo, we fly home."

"Virginia's not my home," Louis grumbled.

Griff called air traffic control, asking and receiving clearance to land on runway two three. He banked west, lowering the gear. He dropped so low over cars racing along over I-75 he could count the passengers. A smooth touchdown on runway two three with no hiccups eased his mind somewhat. Still, he'd be more relaxed once they completed this final delivery. Where the case went next remained to be seen.

Griff taxied past two corporate jets and parked close to visitor parking. He cut the 421's engines, drawing in a deep breath. He peeled off his headset and crawled from his seat. Opening the door, he was ready to assume his undercover identity once more.

Warm breezes wafted in. Louie squirmed free of the cockpit, and Griff helped him down, crutches in hand. His whining seemed louder than usual.

"When can I get rid of this stupid cast?"

"We need to find the right timing," Griff replied. He was determined to keep the cast in place, in the event Sonya's friends wanted a ride from her dad.

"Whad'ya mean? This thing's killin' me."

"Live with it."

Griff noticed a pair of ATF agents from the Tampa's JTTF waiting along the fence. They were dressed in blue jeans and brightly colored golf-style shirts. He strode over to a well-tanned, young man by the chain-link fence. Jorge Ruiz from the Tampa task force extended his hand, asking Griff if they spoke on the phone.

"Correct." Griff grabbed his hand, introducing Louie, his disadvantaged pilot.

"This is Tom, also on my task force," Jorge said. "Griff, we need to talk in the terminal. Louie, you jump in the white minivan. Tom will drive to the plane and load your cargo."

Louie jiggled his leg. "See my cast? I don't jump anywhere."

"Do your best," Griff snapped. "We'll be back in a jiffy."

He and Jorge hustled to the terminal's restroom. The Tampa agent briefly stooped down. "I see nobody's feet in the stalls. Step in this one. We'll wire you up."

Inside a bigger stall, Griff unbuttoned his shirt. Jorge handed him a transmitter.

"It's smaller than the wireless mics my pastor uses," Griff said.

Jorge snorted. "The whole idea, man. Tape it to your skin so your belt covers it."

Griff did, running the mic's fine wire up beneath his shirt. Jorge swiftly covered the mic with an adhesive shield, and stuck it on Griff's skin near his collarbone.

"This prevents your shirt from rubbing the mic and distorting the sound," he said.

Griff buttoned his shirt ready to be on his way. "These new transmitters are better than those old bulky ones, which got too warm."

"Tell me about it. Being the only Hispanic undercover agent in our group, I wore those ancient ones making gun buys from gangs."

They checked for betraying evidence, and Jorge announced Griff was good to go.

"The quickest guilty pleas come from the perp's recorded voice," Griff said, leaving the stall.

Jorge grinned, putting the tape in his pocket. "We could swap stories, if we had time."

Thankfully, no one walked in to catch their undercover preparations. Griff faced the mirror, with the man in the mirror nodding his approval. He'd gone undercover plenty of times, yet this one seemed peculiar. Louie's mood changes didn't help.

"You ready?" Jorge asked.

Griff patted the transmitter under his shirt. "I'll do what I can to get Dino's voice recorded. You know how it goes. Some guys don't talk much on these buys."

"I'll be nearby," Jorge assured him, asking, "You don't have Dino's last name?"

"No. Based on previous deliveries, his guys will take the van, unload it, and bring it back. The van's clean, right? Nothing traceable to the government? "

"Yeah. That's all cool," Jorge said.

"Okay. Lead the way."

Jorge went straight to the van. Louie sat up front, the door open. He fanned himself with a map.

Jorge handed Griff the key, asking in low tones, "And the meeting is in the usual spot?"

"I've not been to this particular restaurant," Griff replied. "Is the area safe?"

"Oh, yeah. You're in for a treat. It's one of the best eateries in Florida."

Griff shielded his eyes from the sun. "You'll have surveillance inside with me?"

"Yes." Then Jorge hesitated. "We checked the phone number Louie uses to contact Dino. The subscriber is a woman, unknown to us."

Griff opened the van door. "See you here after. I expect no problems."

Chapter 38

Griff flipped the transmitter switch to the on position while he climbed in the van. From here, the surveillance agent would hear everything Griff said with Louie and Dino. Louie called out directions in a monotone voice, and Griff was confident his informant didn't know their conversation was being recorded.

"Where did you and Dino meet?" Griff asked, taking the turn for Route 301.

"Um … my New Jersey customer. I only know he pays regular."

"Is he always from Tampa?"

"Nah. New York City."

Griff did not admit he'd been born in New York. He rarely deviated from his hard and fast rule—never mix business with personal life.

So he asked simply, "How long's he been in Tampa?"

"Um … a while."

That Griff had exhausted Louie's knowledge of Dino was highly doubtful. Informants often held back pertinent info until it proved useful. He stopped talking to Louie, not wanting any setbacks, and merged into heavy traffic on I-4. Fifteen minutes later they reached the eclectic Ybor City district of Tampa, an odd mix of renovated older homes sprinkled among vacant lots and warehouses.

At the corner of East Seventh Avenue and North Twenty Second Street, Louie started acting jittery like he'd had too much coffee, directing Griff into a parking lot gesturing with his arms. Griff sensed his informant was anxious about facing Dino. They were running five minutes late. After Louie slid out of the van, he paused on the asphalt.

"I wish you didn't have to meet Dino."

"Why?" Griff pocketed the keys. "Is he different from your Jersey contacts?"

"Well … he's deep in the cigar world and who knows what else."

Who knows what else? Griff thought.

Griff then recalled something he wished his mind had forgotten. An FBI instructor at the academy once worked undercover on a Tampa mob case. The trial revealed too much of his personal life, forcing his relocation to another state. Louie hadn't mentioned Dino had mob ties. Then again, his informant lacked truthfulness.

At least the agent monitoring the transmitter would be analyzing Louie's statements. Griff locked the expensive cargo in the van, and when the duo reached the tile-fronted restaurant, he swung open the door. The boisterous place was packed with an early dinner crowd.

Louie waved to a man at a table in the ornate bar area. He sported wavy salt-and-pepper hair and appeared to be about Louie's age. The man must be Dino, the buyer who would pay for suitcases stuffed with cigars.

Transmitter on, Griff walked behind Louie, observing other diners, being alert to his surroundings. Dino's tan skin glowed against a plum-colored shirt. Their would-be buyer shook Louie's hand friendly-like, motioning at his crutches.

"What gives, man? You had me worried when I didn't hear for so long."

"My reason for not seein' you sooner," Louie replied, wincing.

"Who's your friend?"

Griff noted Dino was eying him from head to toe.

"I'm Griff, his pilot and chauffeur due to his broken leg." He winked. "We've just returned from a trip out of the country together."

"How do you know Griff?" Dino demanded of Louie.

Griff again answered before his informant could, even though they had rehearsed the answer. "We live near each other. I fly charters whenever I can."

"Okay then." Dino put out his hand. "Any friend of Louie's is a friend of mine."

Staying true to form, Griff chose a seat with his back to the wall and next to Dino so he could position his secret microphone close by.

"You have cargo for me?" Dino tented his hands expectantly, a diamond ring flashing on his pinkie.

Griff shot back, "Wouldn't be here if we didn't."

A slim waiter clad in a black tuxedo and bow tie approached the linen-covered table. "*Bienvendo*. Let me start you with our sparkling drinks."

"I'll have another of these." Dino held his cocktail glass aloft.

Griff twisted his neck to look at the server. "I'm flying. Bring me iced tea, unsweetened."

"Louie, you're not flying." Dino swiveled his head. "What'll you have?"

"Coffee," Griff replied. "He can barely walk on those crutches without alcohol."

Louie smiled crookedly, asking for a cola with a twist of lime. Their waiter sped away. Dino checked over his shoulder before reaching beneath his chair. He snatched out a leather valise, and giving it to Louie said gruffly, "Count it. See if it's right."

Louie stuffed his hand into the case, and Griff imagined he was mentally calculating stacks of cash. Anticipation rose within Griff. The undercover meet seemed right on track after Dino's initial probing questions.

"It's all here," Louie proclaimed, zipping the bag shut.

Without missing a beat, Dino whipped out his cell phone and made a call, "Get over here. I'm in the bar."

The moment he hung up, an athletically-built guy with a blond buzz cut and a fashionable lady sat at a table across from them. Griff glanced at the couple. Though they fit in beautifully, he guessed they were the JTTF surveillance agents Jorge promised. Dino didn't seem to notice their arrival.

"My guys want your keys," he told Griff in a harsh voice. "They'll drive my cigars to my stash, and then return your ride. Nice and easy like."

"That works." Griff dug the keys from his pocket.

Dino switched his attention to Louie. "Buddy, you kept me in the lurch. Your leg and all, but come on. Next time, don't keep me waiting so long."

"Sorry. Ever break your leg? It lays you up." Louie scowled meanly at Griff.

The waiter served their drinks. Dino instantly took a sip and beamed.

"Griff, this place makes the best pressed Cuban sandwich anywhere. Roast pork, ham, Swiss cheese, and a little something extra in Tampa you won't find in Miami—Genoa salami."

"That's what I'll have," Griff told the waiter.

He hadn't realized how hungry he was after all the flying. Sitting there looking glum, Louie said he wanted the same sandwich. Dino nodded at the waiter.

"Cuban sandwich runs the table. Me too."

Their server left them to talk business. Dino had other ideas. His hand flitted around the bar area, his small pinkie ring catching the light.

"You guys fly. Me, I love this place. It's the largest Spanish restaurant in the world. If these walls could talk. Marilyn Monroe, Liza Minnelli, Fred MacMurray, they've been here. The neighborhood was cigar factories, and they made the best here."

"Do you have an ownership interest?" Griff asked. "You're a great promoter."

"The same family has owned it for generations." Dino pointed behind him. "People came to the cigar bar for a drink and cigar. They still make their own cigars."

He treated Louie to a toothy smile. "But my customers crave your Cuban ones."

A young guy in a flowery shirt and shorts rushed to the table. Dino held out his hand palm up. Griff gave him the key.

"Drive carefully," Griff admonished the young kid to alert agents monitoring the wire to expect some action. "We don't need heat on our tail."

The kid left as quickly as he'd come. Dino hardly missed a beat in bragging about his influential customers.

"The ones in D.C. are begging me for their resupply. These are the best of the best Cuban cigars. They buy me influence, which is better than money."

The sandwiches arrived, and Louie grabbed his with both hands. Dino didn't touch his. Instead, he declared to Griff that his family used to be in the cigar business.

"Before my retirement, I was a national cigar salesman. These days, I aim to please my best customers," Dino boasted. "They may think relations are warming with Cuba and they don't need me. That won't happen anytime soon."

Louie looked knowingly at Griff. The undercover FBI agent refused to become embroiled in talking about future deals. The longer Griff listened, the smaller Dino became, going from mobster to cigar salesman in ten minutes. He'd never spent so much money on such a lowlife. What a waste of time.

Wait! What about all the cigars waiting in the van?

Griff munched his Cuban sandwich realizing Dino had purchased far more cigars than he needed to maintain friendships. To get him talking again for the recording, Griff told Dino, "Louie says it's safe flying illegal stogies to Tampa from Cuba. I'm concerned about my plane and license. Should I be worried?"

"You flew into Cuba?" Dino's dark eyes glittered in respect.

"Yeah. It was a bit hairy, I tell you."

"I'd think so. The Castro brothers could lock you up for years. Not much chance of that here."

Griff laid a hand on the table. "So you have some influence then?"

"This is Tampa. Nobody cares about untaxed and smuggled cigars."

"Whew, that's good news."

The flowered-shirt runner appeared, dropping the van key next to Griff.

"Everything good?" Dino asked. He'd taken one bite out of his sandwich.

"Yes, sir."

Dino waved him off. "Okay, get outta here."

He leaned close to Griff whispering, "Louie said your plane is bigger. You guys should haul larger loads. My customers have insatiable appetites for these cigars."

The waiter came with the check. Dino dropped a hundred-dollar bill between the folds. Griff felt the man from New York nudge his leg with his hand. Unsure what he wanted, Griff put a hand beneath the tablecloth. Dino slipped a card into it and smiled.

GRIFF LEFT THE RESTAURANT, the valise of cash in one hand and Dino's card crushed in his pocket. He and Louie trudged along in silence. Griff mused how his misgivings had vanished during the meeting with the cigar smuggler. In the past, Griff had faced down gun-toting drug dealers and snuck aboard the floating headquarters of the world's leading terrorist. Dino was a petty crook, a man impressed by a lavish lifestyle.

But then again, was Griff losing his touch? The Cuban-sandwich-loving and Cuban-cigar-smoking Dino could be knee-deep into Cuba's nefarious connections with Russia. Griff would decide later how to handle the card Dino secretly handed him.

They settled into the van, and as they drove off, Griff asked Louie for the benefit of the agents listening to the transmitter, "How did it go?"

"Dino likes you."

Griff's eyebrows shot up. "What are you talking about?"

"I can tell. He trusts and feels comfortable with you. I never heard him talk so much. Maybe I'll make it out of this alive."

Traffic congealed into a heavy mass. Shrill sounds of a nearby siren prompted Griff to feel through the fabric of his shirt and turn off the transmitter. He saw no further reason to transmit the rest of his conversation with Louie.

"Maybe he wants to do business with me," Griff tested after traffic began flowing.

"No. No. I'm his connection for Cuban cigars."

"Were, Louie. You *were* his connection."

"Oh yeah."

Griff's phone whirled in his pants pocket. He fumbled to take it out. It was Jorge, the task force agent doing surveillance.

"We can talk at the airport," Griff told him. "We're on our way."

"Forget meeting me. Dino put a tail on you."

Griff's eyes darted to the rearview mirror. Things looked like normal expressway traffic.

"Are you sure?"

"The guys who took the van and unloaded it are tailing you in a Beamer. Two cars behind you, in the right lane."

Griff checked again. "Okay, I see a white Charger."

"That's me," Jorge barked. "Your tail's the black car ahead of me. It may be coincidence. Let's see if they exit when you do."

Griff slid over a lane. So did the Beamer.

Jorge spoke rapid-fire, "He's tailing you. Drop Louie and the suitcases at your plane, then drive to the rental agency. Park in front, leave the key under the floor mat, and lock it up. We have another key. Make a pretext visit to the rental office. Place the transmitter at the bottom of the trashcan in the men's room. If you walk to the plane, Dino's thugs will figure you rented the van there."

"Good idea." Griff pulled the card from his pocket. "Dino wants to do business with me. He slipped me a card with his number."

Louie flipped his head toward Griff saying, "That dirty dog."

"Why should you care?" Griff replied to Louie. "You're out of the business."

Griff cranked a few more turns before roaring through the airport's open gate. He drove Louie up to the plane with Jorge talking on the phone, his voice slightly muffled. Griff had shoved the phone into his shirt pocket so not to be seen talking on it.

"They followed you into the lot," Jorge said. "They parked behind a row of cars."

Griff scanned the parking lot, not spotting a black BMW.

"Jorge, did you see where the cargo went?"

"Sure. Our agents are watching the house where they stashed the load."

Griff put the van in park. "Maybe they wanted to verify we actually flew in. I'll be taking the proceeds with me to your headquarters in D.C."

Griff signed off with Jorge, and put Louie and the empty suitcases into the plane before taking the van to the car rental place. He continued carrying the valise to prevent Louie from flying off with the money in the FBI's plane. He ditched the transmitter in the bathroom and picked up a travel map, which he thrust into his shirt pocket pretending it was his rental receipt. Then Griff paid the fixed base operator for topping off his fuel tanks.

He completed the pre-flight check in record time, wanting to get his baby in the air while there was enough light to land. Griff climbed aboard, and Louie had the checklist at the ready.

He growled, "Dino asked you to call him? Gave you his number, did he?"

"Look at your phone." Griff handed him the card. "Is the number the same?"

"I don't have to check. It's different."

"Maybe he has other business in mind," Griff said.

Louie rattled the list in his hand. "The dirty dog had us tailed. I heard you talkin' in yer phone. What are we gonna do?"

"Simple. You call off the checklist and I fly us out of here."

Once both engines were running, Griff received taxi instructions and headed for the departure runway.

"We head to Lime Key and put the seats back in the plane," he said. "We've had a full day's work."

"Yeah. The sandwich was good, but I'm never goin' to see Dino again."

"Now you're talking."

They lifted off, vectoring toward the Florida Keys. They soared above I-75 traffic. The sun was dipping west, painting the horizon purple and gold. It wasn't too far to Lime Key by air so Griff figured he could land before total darkness. He pushed the throttle forward, giving more speed. His hands settled on the yoke with a question churning in his mind.

What were Dino's true motives in passing him the card and having him followed?

Griff's instincts in the beginning were proved right. Something still ate at him about the guy and the entire setup. He vowed to call Eva and talk the situation through when he reached the Pelican's Nest. Another set of eyes and ears never hurt, especially ones as experienced as Eva's. Too bad she wasn't on this trip.

EVA HUNG UP AFTER an all-too-brief conversation with Griff. She hurried to put dinner on the table, saying nothing to Scott about her call. The kids talked about school activities during the meal. Eva forced herself to listen, yet her mind kept wandering to Griff's request. Scott helped himself to more salad.

"Eva, you're not eating," he said, snapping the salad tongs to get her attention.

She picked up her fork. "You're right. Work is on my mind."

"The pizza tastes good, Mom." Andy reached for another

piece.

Eva ate some pizza and helped herself to the crisp veggie salad. Scott passed her the dressing, and facing Kaley, asked if she heard the news.

"No." Kaley froze her fork midair. "Is it Russia?"

Scott glanced at Eva. "When Poland's military was conducting joint exercises with our Navy in the Baltic, Russian jet fighters buzzed their ship. They recently stationed troops along Poland's border."

"Will it cause a war?" their daughter asked in a serious voice.

Scott heaped more salad in his bowl. "We conduct similar flights to test their tracking systems and those of China. Russian troops on Poland's border are more problematic."

"I am going to send Izzy a message and see how she's holding up," Kaley said, returning to her pizza.

Russia's unrelenting aggression stuck in Eva's mind like a burr. She determined to ask Scott later what he thought. The pizza gobbled up, her kids disappeared down the hall claiming they had homework. Eva tidied the kitchen before sitting across from Scott in the family room. Her ragged sigh caused him to look up from his newspaper.

"Griff phoned," Eva said. "I'm off to Florida, so you're mister mom again."

"Any closer to wrapping up your case?"

"We think so. Griff may make an undercover trip into Cuba."

He dropped the paper frowning. "No! I mean, I hope you're kidding."

His stern tone and words convinced Eva something was terribly amiss in Cuba. She recalled a new State Department directive. If she mentioned it, perhaps Scott would disclose more of what he knew.

She joined him on the sofa. "State Department deferred one of our agent's transfer to the U.S. Embassy in Havana. They warned U.S. citizens not to travel there. Have you heard anything lately?"

"Um." Scott paused. "No."

"Okay, when you say 'Um' it usually means you know things you can't say. There is truth to Kat's report on Russian missiles in Cuba, isn't there?"

"Even if I knew, I couldn't tell you."

"So she's right." Eva grabbed his hand. "Government spokespeople parse their words when answering Kat's questions, which explains recent travel restrictions by State."

"It's not a good idea for Griff to fly down there," Scott insisted.

She drew back in surprise. "I never said he was flying there. How did you know?"

"He can't drive there, can he? I just assumed."

"Hypothetically, based on your assumption, why shouldn't he go to Cuba?"

"The Cuban government may hold him as a spy. He is an FBI agent, after all."

"Without telling me what you know, can you make an informed assumption there are Russian missiles in Cuba?"

Scott's powerful glare answered her question. He didn't need to say anything more.

Chapter 39

On the following Tuesday, Kaley Montanna was daydreaming in government class. Ms. Yost was droning on about other forms of governments in the world besides the republic form in the States. Kaley was familiar with America's three branches of government.

Rather than listen, adventurous thoughts of leaving the sudden cold snap and sunning herself in warm Florida occupied her mind. Her mom had flown down there yesterday for a prolonged assignment. When her dad dropped Kaley off at school this morning, he'd mentioned they all might fly and meet Mom at a hotel for a long weekend, depending on how long she stayed in Florida.

Kaley pictured flying dragon kites with her brothers in the Keys, a place she'd never visited before, when her teacher did the unexpected.

She aimed her question at Kaley. "China has three branches of government. How does its government compare to ours, Kaley?"

"Yes, ma'am," Kaley chimed as she gathered her thoughts. She drew upon her extensive reading to explain that the People's Republic of China also divided power in the legislative, executive, and judicial branches.

"However, they have a fourth branch," Kaley said, looking beyond Austin Oaks, who sat in front of her. "Their military is controlled by the Communist Party of China. The CPC wields monopoly over government, media, and people's lives. Chinese citizens don't share our same freedoms. For example, our First Amendment gives us the right to express ourselves."

Her teacher seemed satisfied, although Kaley had more to say about the Chinese people living under authoritarianism without freedom of thought, religion, or association. Her concern for them vanished the moment she heard Austin's cell phone vibrating. He struggled to pull his phone out of his pocket.

Kaley glanced at Ms. Yost, who enforced strict rules about phones in class. The teacher didn't seem to notice Austin had his phone out. When he held the device down at his side to read a text, Kaley leaned forward and looked.

She saw it said *911* followed by lots of exclamation points.

Austin stuffed the phone into his pocket and began coughing. Next, he crammed his book in the backpack dangling on his chair.

Though Kaley hadn't talked to him much since they returned from Poland, he seemed in distress. She wanted to help. Maybe someone in his family was being rushed to the hospital.

He went out the door coughing and holding his stomach. Kaley collected her notebook and backpack. Her hand shot up.

"Ms. Yost, I think Austin is sick. May I check on him?"

"Well ... all right," her teacher said hesitantly.

Kaley rushed out before the teacher changed her mind. There was Austin's black heel disappearing around the corner at the end of the hall. She shot after him. At the intersection of the main hallway running along the front of the school, Kaley looked both ways, seeing no sign of him. She even checked the empty waiting area in the nurse's office. No Austin.

Kaley hurried to the front entrance and saw him by the door talking on his cell phone. As she walked toward him, he quickly terminated the call.

"Are you okay?" Kaley asked, out of breath. "Ms. Yost asked me to find out."

"Yeah."

His pale face and cell phone shaking in his hand hinted there was more to it.

Kaley pressed, "You left so fast. You could be busted for not getting permission."

"I don't care. It's a family emergency."

His eyes looked shrouded. Kaley sensed he was withholding something. Still, she asked how she could help.

"I called my mom," Austin replied, his icy glare radiating something more than anxiety. "She's coming to pick me up."

"Are you sure?" Kaley tried again to get to the bottom of his text.

"Yes. Go back to class."

"What should I tell our teacher?"

Austin adjusted the position of the backpack. He started down the cement steps. Looking back, he hissed, "Say you couldn't find me."

He wanted Kaley to lie! That was suspicious. Of course, she wouldn't. She stepped back into the main hallway where she watched out the large windows for Mrs. Oaks to arrive. Instead, a taxicab pulled up. Kaley glimpsed only a male driver inside, and no Austin's mom. Her rattled classmate hopped into the empty backseat.

When the yellow cab drove him away, he never looked back to see if Kaley was still there. She traipsed back to her classroom where she lifted her hands palms up, indicating to Ms. Yost that she had nothing to say. Kaley thought about Austin's strange behavior, hearing nothing else for the rest of the class.

EVA WAS NO STRANGER TO STRESS. This day was proving to be hectic, given her rushed flight to Lime Key yesterday. Though dressed in jeans and T-shirt, and sitting outdoors beneath a deck umbrella at Holly's house, Eva was not relaxed. She and her two JTTF partners were on the second-floor deck conferring about a startling development that happened at the same time Eva flew to Lime Key.

Griff's eyes appeared drained of life from all the flying he'd done back and forth. The usually-jovial Brett wore a dour expression while sitting in a canvas chair next to Eva. It was a mild October morning, but tension sizzled in the air among the agents.

"Tell me everything Sonya told Louie in her call about going to Cuba," Eva said.

Griff's voice also was low. "She called him yesterday in a panic, saying she needed a lift to Cuba."

"Her story is highly questionable," Brett added in strained tones. "She and her friends are on some kind of wait-list to attend a human rights gig in Havana."

"Is there such a conference?" Eva probed quietly.

Griff gestured wildly, as if his gyrating hands added volume to his whispers. "The UN is holding its annual retreat in Cuba. I guess they'll be teaching the entire world how to control people and rob them of their liberties."

Eva understood his angst. An assembly in Cuba on human rights was worse than absurd. The earth spun on its axis as God made it, yet the people living on it acted more haywire by the day. A thought occurred to her, and she grinned.

"At least Sonya's call will keep Louie in his cast a bit longer."

"Oh, he'll be crabby about that." Brett gave a forced chuckle. "He was bragging this morning how great he was gonna feel wiggling ten toes in the sand."

Eva sipped her tepid coffee, wanting to clear the air about Louie. "Look, our petulant informant gets no sympathy from me, not for linking his life with the Queen of Ponzi, Holly Munoz. We've arrested and unarrested him for cigar smuggling, juggled our investigations of suspected terrorists, and listened to him bellyache about permanent injuries to his body from walking in an unneeded cast."

Brett gave her a thumbs-up. "You're spot-on."

"Yeah." Griff folded his arms. "I thought things were winding down with him, but another snag erupted. The ATF agents targeting his cigar buyers in New Jersey and Tampa are impatient in the extreme."

"So? Bottom line?" Eva asked, finishing her tasteless coffee.

Griff extended his legs and crossed his feet. "I've held them off arresting Dino and the others. Sonya's call saves our hide. Still, I dread making another trip to the Communist-controlled country."

A knock sounded on the door, and Brett yelled, "We're out here on the deck."

In a few moments, Louie joined them on the deck as an unexpected voice hollered from below, "Hey up there! Is Louie around?"

Footsteps resounded on the deck's stairs. A middle-aged man with tough, leathery skin reached the top step. In khaki shorts and tank top, he had a visor strapped around his head with sunglasses perched on its bill.

"I heard sounds of celebrating, so thought I'd join you." The stranger gripped a six-pack, which now held three cans of beer.

"Rory lives on the other side of Cecil," Louie mumbled with a nod at Griff.

"Hee-re go." Rory handed Louie the beers. "You haa-ve one."

Eva noticed the man's flushed face and slurred speech. Rory obviously felt no pain for so early in the day. He sat gingerly on an empty canvas chair.

"I figure you're celebrating the recent shower of cigars."

Eva hid her surprise. Louie looked downright panicky though said nothing.

"No worries." Rory waved a hand as if swatting at a mosquito. "I know these things. Louie and I go way back."

"How far back?" Brett asked with a raised eyebrow.

Eva sensed her partner was zeroing in to make something of this unforeseen visitor. She sat back willing to give Louie's friend a few more minutes to see where this might go. For his part, Rory turned to Louie, his head swaying from side to side. "Hadn't seen you fly south lately, but then I seen you limping on crutches. How are you keeping your customers supplied?"

"Hey, Rory." Louie gestured to the agents, and stammering said, "My ... ah... friends here don't know about my part-time job."

The interloper slapped his knee. "Come on. I didn't fall off a turnip truck. I saw you both," he gave a weak salute to Griff, "fly out at dawn last week. Later, you taxied past my deck in a Golden Eagle with no seats and stuffed with suitcases."

Louie's attempts to interrupt him failed. There was no stopping Rory.

"We're among friends." He flashed them all a lopsided grin. "Louie prob'ly said how he helped me save that load of nose candy stranded in Belize."

Louie's face flushed beet red, and his shoulders heaved. Eva was ready to quiz Rory about the cocaine when the ever-alert Brett made his move. He walked over to Louie and ripped a beer can from the dwindling six-pack. Brett pulled a chair next to Rory and began talking in gentle tones.

"I don't like discussing such things in front of ladies." Brett jerked his head at Eva. "She doesn't like knowing about our work."

"Ah."

Eva jumped to her feet, motioning Louie to come inside with her. Griff promptly followed. Louie leaned on his crutches looking like a forlorn puppy.

"Don't be alarmed," Eva soothed. "We all have a past."

"Yeah, but mine's criminal. It just got mentioned in front of federal agents who are tryin' to put me away."

"Don't worry." Griff sauntered up beside him. "Brett's making friends with Rory. You can imagine he'll give us more to impress Judge Harding on your behalf."

A light flickered in Louie's eyes. "Eva, do you agree?"

"I do. Rory can't claim you set him up. He confessed to it."

Outside, Brett's arm was draped over Rory's shoulder as if they were lifelong friends. A slow smile formed at the corner of Louie's mouth.

"At this rate, I won't have nothin' left to confess to the man upstairs," he said, pointing up.

What else might Louie confess? Eva knew this was the time for her to make her move.

"Rory spilled your secrets out there. What secret is Sonya going to tell Griff about you?"

"You mean about going to Cuba?" Louie's eyes searched Griff's for help. "Looks like we'll get another excuse to pick up more cigars?"

LATER, BRETT AND RORY AMBLED IN with Rory asking Louie about his good-looking daughter. That's when Griff's phone whirled in his pocket. He pulled it out, and glancing sideways, saw it was the FBI duty agent from northern Virginia.

"Hello," was Griff's answer in front of Rory.

"I'm calling for Agent Topping."

"Oh, hi, baby." Griff looked intently at Eva. "I miss you too."

He hurried to the bedroom with the duty agent demanding to speak to Agent Topping.

A safe distance from the criminals, Griff explained, "It's me. I'm in Lime Key in the midst of an undercover meeting with a corrupt businessman and drug smuggler."

"Sir, forgive the interruption. I'll move on down my list."

"What's going on?"

"We're rounding up agents here in D.C. for a problem involving espionage."

Griff's mental gears activated. "Well, it would be hard to assist from Florida."

"Understood, Agent Topping. Carry on."

The line clicked off in his ear. Back in the living room, Griff motioned Eva to the deck where they huddled before the crooks came back out.

"The FBI duty agent asked me to join a D.C. roundup in an espionage case," Griff told her. "I can't, because I'm down here."

"Does it involve Cuba?" Eva wondered aloud.

He hadn't asked. With a grimace, he offered to phone back for details. Before he made the call, Louie hobbled out with sorrowful eyes. "Rory's braggin' about his past deals. What's gonna become of me?"

"We shall see, my friend," Griff replied ominously.

To Louie's loud groans, Eva went inside, returning to the deck with her notepad and pen telling Louie, "Brett's taking Rory to the canal for their talk. If you're ready to tell us everything else you've hidden from us, I'm ready to write."

Chapter 40

Griff and his partners grilled Louie in the living room about Rory's admissions after Brett had taken the talkative man home. Eva wrote furiously while Griff and Brett alternated questioning Louie, who lamented his fate. When they wrapped up, Louie's tired face bore dark rings under his eyes.

Looking distressed, he gaped at Griff. "Will Rory's confessin' change the amnesty you and Eva offered me for introducin' you to Ramon?"

"Grandmother Topping warned me growing up, 'Griffin lad, be sure your sins will find you out.'"

Griff didn't mean to grind salt into the wound, but their informant was living proof her warning had come true. Louie gave no reply because his cell phone barked out the "U.S. Army Caisson Song." He snatched it from his pocket.

"Sonya, what's up?" Louie pressed the phone against his ear. "Ah … did you forget my broken leg?"

Her voice rose through the phone, but with her accent, Griff couldn't discern her words. Louie told Sonya in a rush, "Griff is here. We flew down south together, remember?"

Louie covered the microphone on his cell phone. "She needs to fly to Cuba tomorrow."

Griff yanked the phone from his hand, saying hello to Sonya.

"Oh Griff." Her voice gushed sweetness in his ear. "Daddy's probably told you that I'm his daughter."

"Told me? Louie's done nothing but brag how you're clever and smart."

"He is sweet. My friends and I are in Virginia and discovered they have openings for us at the human rights conference in Havana. Daddy promised you'd fly us there."

"To Cuba?" Griff tried to sound incredulous.

Sonya giggled in his ear. "Yes! Daddy says you fly him to bring back smokes."

Griff paused, wishing their conversation was being recorded. "Sonya, my plane is larger and burns more fuel. You can imagine how expensive it is to fly."

"Oh Griff," she giggled again, "we'll pool our cash. Can you carry five people?"

"For three thousand each. I can collect you all tomorrow morning."

"Three thousand each? My, that seems like a lot."

Griff stared at Eva, raising his eyebrows. "Sonya, you could legally fly to Havana from Miami. You're asking me to do something worse than cigar smuggling."

"Okay …" she sputtered. "Three thousand each. Pick us up in Fredericksburg."

"Virginia, right?" he asked to clarify. "What time?"

Louie leaned on his crutches, hovering by Griff's ear. Meanwhile, Griff mentally reviewed the myriad of decisions. He walked out to the deck, gaping at the Fat Albert blimp in the southwest, telling Sonya he didn't think it was a good time for him to fly.

"I'm looking at the fat guy in the sky. We usually wait for him to disappear."

Louie began pulling on Griff's sleeve.

"Hold on." Griff covered the microphone.

"Don't worry about the blimp goin' south," Louie hissed. "We come back empty and land at Lauderdale like we're from the Bahamas. We clear customs no sweat."

Louie sure was willing to go the extra mile to help Sonya. Griff put Louie's phone back to his ear. "Sonya, your dad reminds me there's a way to make it happen."

"Oh, you are both absolute dears," she squealed.

After ironing out details, Griff warned, "You each bring one small bag. That's it."

When they hung up, Griff began issuing orders, "We fly to Fredricksburg in an hour. Get ready. Tomorrow we'll take Sonya and four friends to Cuba."

"Thanks for helpin' like this." Louie gripped his crutches, his knuckles turning white. "I'll phone Ramon and tell him we're flyin' in yer plane late tomorrow afternoon."

He ascended in the elevator with Griff calling up, "Tell him we're bringing Sonya and not picking up anything."

"Oh yeah," Louie shouted back.

Griff gave a long look at Eva and Brett. "This is what we've been waiting for. I'll get airborne. Meantime, you two work on John Oliver's approval."

EVA'S CELL PHONE WHIRLED AGAINST HER WAIST. She looked at the caller, her heart contracting when she saw it was Kaley.

"Mom, can you talk?" Her voice sounded worried.

Eva steadied her mind, hastening to her bedroom at the Nest.

"What happened?"

"A bizarre thing occurred earlier at school. Austin got a text in government class and tried concealing it. Though the way he held the phone at his side, I could read it."

"Are you okay?" Eva asked, unsure what to think.

"Yes," Kaley said softly. "His text was 911 and tons of exclamation marks."

"Was someone in an accident?"

"I thought so at first. Then he acted sick, running from the room. Ms. Yost let me check so I followed Austin. In front of the school, he was talking on the phone. He told me his mom was coming. Next thing I know, he jumped in a taxi and took off."

"Do you know what happened?"

"No. What's weird is Glenna and I drove to his house over lunch. No one answered the door. Everything was closed up. Maybe he's in the hospital."

"Have you talked with your teacher?"

"She wasn't in class when Glenna and I went back to see her about Austin. I don't know where she is."

It was clear to Eva that whatever had happened to Austin was disturbing to Kaley. Her daughter had great instincts. Eva searched for the right words and tone to be help from this far away.

"You might learn more at school tomorrow. It's right to be concerned and to pray for Austin."

"Oh, I have. Love you, Mom."

"Me too, Kaley. And I'll be praying as well."

Eva ended their call to the chirp of a text alert on her phone. Was something else amiss with her family? She noticed Scott had just sent a new text.

He'd written: *... new problem ... kat digging into it and also what you and I talked of before you left ... beware to griff ...*

Her heart skipped a beat at the implication. Scott was taking a huge chance in warning Griff. She hurried onto the deck, passing Griff's travel bag by the door. He and Brett were in the middle of strategizing.

Eva held up her phone. "I received a text. Can't say from whom or what it says, but Griff, you must not fly into Cuba. I won't let you."

"That's what Brett and I were just chewing over." Griff's eyes burned with intensity. "But it may be our last chance to rip the veil off Sonya and Louie's criminal enterprise."

Brett interjected, his voice rising, "Why take risks for Sonya and her pals when we have no idea what they're doing in Cuba?

It's not cigars, I can tell you."

Eva dropped her eyes again to Scott's text, trying to perceive everything her husband meant. "Griff, things are happening ninety miles from Florida I simply can't explain. Let's figure out an alternate plan before Louie shows up."

"Okay, I believe you," Griff said, sounding relieved. "The 421 has to stop for fuel when loaded with five extra people. Even Louie should realize that."

Brett swiped at his unshaven jaw. "How about landing in Miami?"

"Marathon!" Eva cried. "You and I flew there several times."

"That's it." Tension vanished from Griff's taut face. "I'll land there for fuel after I pick up the passengers in Virginia. Once I know who the others are, I can text Eva. Brett, you reach out to Miami's JTTF for help."

Griff stood up, stretching his arms about his head. "I'll be so thankful to see Dawn for more than an hour, and to get Louie out of that cast."

"Buddy, wait just a minute," Brett objected. "He's stays in the cast until I infiltrate the drug smuggling group Rory just spilled his guts about."

Although Eva voiced her agreement with Brett, Griff urged patience. "Let's wait and see what transpires in the morning. If our op isn't exposed when we confront Sonya, then we'll go after Rory's drug cartel."

"This doesn't sound right to me," Brett said. "If we arrest Sonya, Louie will refuse to help us."

Eva posed a different take. "Louie has no choice, not after Rory's admissions. Besides, I plan to have a talk with him, which will change his whole attitude."

A knock at the door, and Louie hobbled in, his face a portrait of happiness.

"Mates, I'm ready to go airborne. Griff, wait 'til you meet my daughter. She is one special lady."

With a flurry of activity getting Louie and their bags down to the plane, it wasn't more than fifteen minutes before Griff achieved liftoff. Only then did Brett call JTTF Miami and Eva messaged Scott: *trip changed ... new destination ... you're the best ...*

Hunger drove Eva to buy deli sandwiches at a local store. She and Brett sat on the deck within reach of their phones. He didn't talk until he'd consumed the ham and Swiss sub.

"Viola sure helped with Louie," Brett said, crushing the wrapper into a ball.

Eva waddled up her paper plate with a wide grin. "Her setting his leg in a cast brought us where we are today. She is one terrific friend and doctor. You have her number. Anything come of that?"

"We spoke once." His eyes drifted to his phone. "She was at the hospital and sounded busy. Is that why she isn't married?"

"In part. Did she explain her husband-to-be died of cancer before their wedding?"

Brett looked up sharply. "No. My wife died just before our fourth anniversary. That was five years ago. I didn't know about Viola ..."

Eva left him alone to his thoughts and checked her phone. Still no text from Griff, though she didn't expect one for hours yet, not until he landed in Virginia.

Chapter 41

Griff refueled and spent the night at an express hotel in Culpeper, Virginia. After the sun rose warming the plane, he and Louie flew a short distance to Shannon Airport at Fredericksburg. The forty-degree October day meant no frost, which was a plus. And the light breeze wouldn't hinder their flight to Marathon.

Upon landing he taxied to the aviation terminal, scanning the area for his passengers. Griff spotted an attractive lady with shoulder-length auburn hair in a pink coat and scarf and black slacks waiting beneath an overhang. Two other women stood with her, one blonde in a short navy coat, and a brown-haired lady bundled in a long camel-colored coat. Two men wore jackets and hovered behind the women. Griff couldn't see their faces.

He hit the brakes to stop the plane. Then he shut down the engines. Louie pointed out Griff's side window, and over the fading engine sounds, said with a lilt in his voice, "See the pretty woman? That's my Sonya."

"I see three ladies," Griff replied. "Which one is Sonya?"

"Tall with auburn hair. Remember I said she likes pink?"

"Who are the others and where are they from?" Griff was eager to know more.

"Colleagues, I guess."

Griff noted Louie's shrug as if he knew nothing about the passengers, and removed his headset. He opened the cabin door and climbed down. Sonya's face glowed as she waved to Louie in the doorway.

"Daddy, thanks for coming."

She threw her arms around Griff at the bottom of the steps, telling him, "I am Sonya." Then she handed him a bulky envelope, adding, "My legal associates are also attending the conference. Your fifteen thousand is all in there."

Her Eastern European accent was thick, Griff observed, shoving the envelope in his back pocket. She'd provided no names, although Sonya and friends each carried a small bag per his instructions.

Griff reached for her pink bag, saying firmly, "Let me. I need to distribute weight equally in the plane."

After feeling the weight of her bag, he returned it, telling her to stow it behind the last seat, and to sit wherever she wanted, adding, "Not in the copilot seat. That's for your dad."

He took the bag from the blond woman, thinking she was more striking than Sonya with high cheekbones and sparkling blue eyes.

"Is anything in this case flammable or explosive?" he intoned.

The lady's answer, "Just clothes and makeup," gave away her faint accent, as if she'd lived in the U.S. for many years.

Griff lifted her case up to Sonya, who stood in the doorway hugging Louie.

"Put this in the back by yours," Griff told Sonya before turning back to the blonde. Upon closer examination, she was older than he first thought and most likely colored her hair. She accepted Griff's hand and help onto the first step. That's when he noticed the glittering rock on her left hand, an expensive wedding and diamond ring set.

He repeated the same routine with the last lady. This brown-haired beauty seemed classier than Sonya and the blonde in a mature way. She spoke perfect American English and wore no rings. Once her small bag was aboard, Griff faced the two men.

The taller of the two boasted salt-and-pepper hair, and wore a wedding band. Though dressed casually in a Red Sox jacket, he walked erect with a professional bearing. Griff imagined he might be a CEO of a large company. The last man standing was closer to Louie's height. His light brown hair curled along the collar of his golf jacket.

Griff secured the door, and as he resumed his seat, he realized Sonya's friends did appear to be legal professionals. Coming to the States three years ago from Kosovo, she had assimilated well.

Still, he nursed his doubts over their claimed reason for traveling to Cuba. The hefty sums of cash they paid, which was several times greater than a legal flight, persuaded him that their mission was nefarious. He turned his gaze to the cramped cabin where each passenger was buckled into their seats as if raring to go.

Griff told them, "We'll be in the air four plus hours."

"Yup," Louie chimed. "Then we're stoppin' for fuel in Marathon. For comfort's sake, avoid drinkin' anything."

Louie held up the checklist wearing an expansive grin.

Griff waved him off. "Forget that for now. We'll be on our way."

He fired up the engine. As his undercover plane turned onto the runway, Griff's mind became engrossed by the identities of the well-to-do people and why they were heading to Cuba in such a covert fashion. None of them looked like terrorists, but Griff wished he could have patted them down for weapons before ascending into the clouds.

THAT SAME MORNING, EVA SAT BENEATH PALM FRONDS on the Lime Key deck looking down the canal and out to sea. She sipped freshly brewed coffee and watched news on the TV, which she'd adjusted so it faced the open French doors. Brett had not come from his room. She assumed he'd slept in.

Last night over their fish baskets at the local marina, he'd said in casual tones, "I called Viola. We're having dinner when I get back. Know any terrific places?"

She'd laughed good-naturedly, suggesting two special restaurants he might try. One in Georgetown served a dish Viola enjoyed, Chilean sea bass, and a Chinese restaurant in Alexandria had remarkable Peking duck. At Brett's diligent note-making in his phone, Eva had smiled with pleasure. How fun for them to make a fresh start.

A plane landing on the strip behind the house spurred Eva's mind to the present, and she wondered if Griff had left Fredericksburg yet. Gentle breezes tossed her long hair. The sun low in the eastern sky warmed her back. Eva enjoyed the calm respite, and she imagined her family visiting her in Keys.

Her daydream burst when the TV announcer blared, "We bring you Kat Kowicki reporting outside FBI Headquarters on Pennsylvania Avenue."

Eva shot out of her chair. The screen switched to Kat, who appeared tired, her hair disheveled.

"Forgive my appearance. I've been up all night. I just received a briefing about an incident that's developed through the wee hours. Yesterday, Baltimore FBI agents arrested an aeronautical engineer from Seattle. The man sought to deliver secrets to Russian agents about America's development of the next generation of our B-2 bomber."

Eva hurried in and cranked up the sound. Kat's eyes burned with indignation as she told viewers, "The engineer is detained in Baltimore. He refuses to talk and demands a lawyer. FBI agents searched all night in hopes of disrupting a cell of Russian spies operating in the D.C. area. My source, who isn't authorized to speak, has confirmed these spies and their handlers have all vanished."

Kat ended her live report from FBI Headquarters. Eva sat stunned, recalling her recent meeting with CIA Agent Bo Rider at

Nottaway Park. In that park, Bo warned that Russia had created a personal dossier not only on him, but Eva as well. Sitting here in the Pelican's Nest away from family, it unnerved her to learn how aggressive Russia was in infiltrating America. Their military power might be a day away with their missiles installed in Cuba, ninety miles from America's shores.

What else did Scott know? Eva sped to the kitchen where she consulted her phone. Scott hadn't written anything about Kat's report so she began typing him a message with her thumbs. At that moment, the phone alerted Eva to an incoming text.

This from Griff: *heading south ... sonya & two woman & two men aboard ...*

Eva texted him back: *kat broke story ... fbi searching for russian spies ... are they on your plane ...*

Could it be? Without hesitating, and based on her law-enforcement instincts honed through the years, Eva called Miami's JTTF informing the supervisor that Griff was flying to Marathon with five passengers. Without missing a beat, she urged, "I think they are terrorists or the Russian spies the FBI's searching for in D.C."

After more discussion, the supervisor agreed to dispatch agents to meet Eva and Brett in Marathon. Eva hung up, recalling a recent conversation and a big fat clue. Was it possible?

Kaley had seen Austin's 911 alert in class. And hadn't her daughter also heard him talking with Russian soldiers while Kaley hid in the lifeboat?

Eva's phone chirped. She read Griff's text *... whats status on help...*

She responded swiftly *... miami sending help ... is teen boy on board ...*

Griff replied *... no ...*

Eva texted *... b-2 bomber expert arrested ... Russian handlers escaped ...*

Griff came back with *... woohoo ... i bet we got em ...*

The French door opened, and Eva whirled around to see Brett come hurrying in from the deck, wearing shorts and T-shirt. Sweat beaded on his face beneath a sweatband.

"I thought you'd slept in," Eva said, quickly muting the TV.

His chest heaved, and he managed in between breaths, "Nope. Just ran six miles."

"Get cleaned up. I have loads to tell you."

"Heard from Griff?"

"Yes." Eva tapped her phone. "He has five others on the flight.

Could be Russkies."

Brett's jaw dropped. "Do I have time for a fast shower?"

"Make it snappy. We have to brief agents rushing to Marathon from Miami."

He left Eva to zoom through pictures on her phone. When she reached those from Kaley's trip, she slowed to scrutinize each one. She stopped and backed up. There it was. The day the kids left for Poland, Eva had taken a photo of Austin and his mother.

Eva sent Griff the photo via text, typing a message *... is she on board ...*

A moment later he answered *... bingo ... that's her ...*

Eva's fingers shook typing *... her son austin went on kaley's Poland trip ... tight w/ russian soldiers ... disappeared from class yesterday ...*

Chapter 42

Eva would leave for Marathon in roughly twenty minutes. First, she needed coffee and set it to brew, only it seemed to take forever making its popping sounds and sending steam into the air. Time was of the essence, yet they didn't know when Griff's plane would arrive with Sonya and the four others. Brett paced by the counter, checking his watch and acting tense.

"Would you shut and lock the doors?" Eva hoped to buy another minute for her coffee to finish.

He was gone in a flash and she heard the distant click of the lock. She checked the TV news, which was still on mute. Instantly, Brett was back in the kitchen watching her pour hot java into a travel mug.

Eva headed for the TV. "Let me turn this off, then let's go hunt us some moles."

To her ears, that sounded both exciting and dangerous. What if they were armed? Griff wouldn't have searched them. Eva twisted shut the top to her mug. Brett was antsy, snapping his cell phone in and out of its holder.

She put her hands on her hips. "I've known you long enough to know you have something on your mind. Out with it."

"You're right. I want the deal to work out for me to infiltrate Rory's smuggling operation. Who knows where it might lead."

Eva grabbed her coffee mug. "When he mentioned cocaine, I knew you'd nail him. You're chomping to bring down drug cartels, and you'll get your chance. Today plays out first."

Brett objected, "Louie is the lynchpin. If Sonya is arrested, he'll clam up tight."

"I disagree," Eva said. "We already talked about this. With Rory's admissions, Louie has to cooperate. Wait and see."

Snagging her purse from the table, she went to turn off the TV. What she saw made her call, "Brett, come in here."

He hustled into the living room. She pointed at the bedraggled reporter gripping a microphone. "That's Kat Kowicki. I warned you about talking to her."

"Oh yeah. Turn it up."

Eva raised the sound as Kat told viewers, "Metro Police were called here to the Russian Embassy yesterday by a taxi driver over a fare dispute. The cab picked up a young man at a northern Virginia high school and drove him to the Russian Embassy."

Brett grunted, checking his watch as if anxious to be going.

"Wait one minute," Eva said. "This might be important to our case."

"How so?"

"Sshh."

Kat gestured to Russia's embassy behind her. "The student appeared to be an American citizen. When he arrived here, he had no money to pay the fare."

The camera focused on Kat's gaunt face as she said, "Embassy personnel paid the fare for the twenty-one-year-old man who was seeking asylum. Police let him enter the embassy with Russian officials."

"Stay with me." Kat consulted her spiral notepad. "With yesterday's arrest of the American aeronautical engineer and the FBI's fruitless hunt for Russian spy handlers, this young man seeking refuge at Russia's embassy is significant. All available FBI agents are assigned to the case, vacations cancelled. Sources admit the FBI visited the student's Virginia home, but no one was there. Agents are applying for a search warrant as I sign off."

Eva and Brett stared at each other, their mouths gaping open.

"Twenty-one? He was in my daughter's class!" Eva cried, righteous anger rising in her chest. "His mother is on Griff's plane."

Brett grabbed his keys. "You and I are outta here."

Five minutes later, Brett's rented car blasted north on Overseas Highway straight for Marathon. Eva talked with him nonstop about the latest bombshell implicating Austin Oaks and his mother.

"She must be the Russian spy the FBI is searching for. She or Austin may have targeted Kaley's ferry as a way to seize children of U.S. officials. It's unbelievable. If I was on that plane with her ..."

Brett interjected with, "You'd be in her face, making her talk, I'm sure. The gritty tone in your voice is proof. I had a case where a teen's dope-dealing dad used the son as a courier. I wanted to smack his old man."

"Course you didn't," Eva said, digging her fingers into the armrest.

"Not in the way you mean. I made sure he went to prison for a long time."

"Yes! That's gotta happen to Mrs. Oaks. If she reaches Russia's embassy in Cuba, or anywhere on Cuban soil, she'll never pay for her crimes."

They were roughly ten minutes from the Marathon airport when Eva's phone alerted to a text. She read Griff's message aloud, "40 minutes out ... full bladders ... bathroom best place to isolate men and women … graying male in red sox jacket could be corporate or military … segregate him first … sonya in pink."

Eva texted they were on their way, adding, … *austin oaks hiding at russian embassy in dc* …

TEN MINUTES LATER, Brett and Eva wheeled into the General Aviation area of Marathon's compact airport. As they bounded from their rental, a woman emerged from a Toyota van and approached them asking, "Are you Eva Montanna?"

The lanky African-American woman held up a gold badge. She was FBI Agent Shirley Dobbs from Miami. Eva flashed her badge in return, as did Brett.

"I hope you brought more help," Brett said, pocketing his badge. "We have three females and two males to arrest."

"Five additional agents are in the terminal building checking the layout and using the bathroom," answered Agent Dobbs.

"Good," Eva said with a terse nod. "That's where Griff's passengers will likely flock when the flight lands. Let's head inside, and we'll explain."

Brett barreled inside after Eva, adrenaline pumping through him. This could be his biggest catch, if the men and women with Griff were truly escaping spies. On the other hand, they could simply be mopes like Rory.

Once the manager on duty learned of their operation, he offered them a small conference room as well as an empty office. FBI Agent Dobbs rounded up the other agents, introducing everyone in the bright room. Sunlight streamed in the large windows.

Brett tried ignoring the heat as Eva took the lead, describing Griff and Louie, and passing around Eva's phone with Mrs. Oaks' photo. She filled in what else she knew of the passengers as well as a strategy to detain them all in one fell swoop. Brett observed in awe how quickly the six FBI agents agreed with her plan.

It turned out one FBI agent was good buddies with Brett's former DEA colleague. He took the agent's card, stowing it in his wallet. He hoped Rory's drug operation would connect back to Miami, where Brett knew the ropes.

After checking his watch, he excused himself saying, "Time for me to prepare."

"Ask the manager if you don't find what you need," Eva instructed, a stern glint in her eyes.

"Eva, I'm new on your team," Brett said. "But you can count on me."

"I have no doubt you're one terrific agent. Let's catch these dirtbags."

Brett grinned and put in motion her plan to segregate the male passengers. Armed with a piece of copy paper, a marker, and tape, he entered the men's room. Here he taped an "out of order" sign on the lone stall. Three simple words were the key to snaring the man that Griff wanted most of all. At least Brett hoped it would be so.

He went in the stall and threw the door lock from inside. Then he crawled underneath the partition, which was no easy feat given his strapping frame. Brett dusted his clothes off, then spotting the second bathroom in the attached hangar, he rummaged through the janitor's closet nearby. Soon he was wearing an apron and carrying a plunger.

His tasks complete, he joined Eva and the FBI agents outside the conference room. From a speaker mounted near the ceiling, he heard Griff's voice intone, "Two Lima Charlie on final approach to Marathon runway two five."

Eight zealous agents gathered at the window, watching intently as the Cessna expertly touched down on the runway and made a short turn. Brett's eyes never left the plane. Griff taxied closer to the General Aviation terminal.

When he shut off both engines, Eva twirled one finger in the air. "That's our cue, everyone. Remember, our informant is on crutches and Agent Topping has a moustache."

The Cessna's door swung open. An instant later, the two male passengers headed for the bathroom. Three women followed one at a time down the plane's steps.

This was it! Brett shot to the men's room where he'd posted his sign.

The stockier man with curly brown hair hustled toward the bathroom and Brett held the door for him. Then holding the plunger, Brett blocked the door as the gray-haired man wearing a Red Sox jacket walked up with a scowl.

"Got a broken toilet in here," Brett told him in a gruff tone. He pointed down the hall. "There's another bathroom in the hangar."

Mr. Red Sox ran for it like he was about to explode. Brett spun around toward the ladies' room to where Sonya and two other females were making a beeline. He stepped clear, letting two male FBI agents rush into the men's room with the broken toilet.

A minute later, they escorted out their "curly-haired" prisoner in handcuffs. The FBI agents were walking him by the ladies' room when Curly hollered, "You'll be sorry!"

That was the precise moment when Sonya and her friends opened their restroom door. The sight of their friend being hauled off in handcuffs made them duck back in and close the door.

Eva waited for these agents to take their prisoner away. A split second later, she and two female FBI agents barged in the ladies' room to grab Sonya.

"No!" Brett heard reverberating in the hall.

Figuring Eva and her team could handle the three women, Brett was primed to nab Mr. Red Sox before he got wind of his compatriots being arrested. But where was Griff? Brett might have to go it alone.

He went to the large front windows to see what was amiss. There was Griff ambling along with Louie toward the entrance. Oh yeah. In the excitement Brett forgot Louie even used crutches. Their slow-walking informant passed by Brett as if not recognizing him in the janitor's gear. Louie shuffled into the men's room.

Brett hissed in Griff's ear, "I sent the gray-haired suspect to the hangar's john. Let's grab him."

"Only for my country," Griff said, puckering his brow. "It's been a long flight, but hey, I can hold it."

Brett marched stride-for-stride with Griff, catching sight of Eva and two FBI agents leaving the ladies' room with Sonya and her two friends all in handcuffs. One woman was yelling loudly at Eva, but Brett didn't stick around to hear what she said.

He and Griff had their own arrest to make in a hurry.

Chapter 43

Griff felt behind his back for the gun beneath his shirt as he approached the men's john in the hangar. Brett stood outside, his muscular arms folded across his chest telling Griff, "Red Sox is in there finishing what he's doing."

"You got cuffs?" Griff snapped.

Brett touched his cargo pants' side pocket. "Right here and all ready."

"Okay." Griff reached for the door. "Let's go talk to him."

Griff yanked open the door. Red Sox washed his hands, so the agents waited for him to dry them on a paper towel. Then Griff stepped beside the man flashing his badge.

"FBI. We'd like you to answer questions out in the hangar."

The man's entire body lurched in surprise. "I'm sorry. You must be mistaken. I'm here to rent a car."

"No, I'm not mistaken," Griff growled. "You were on that plane out there."

"I was not." His hands clung to the wet paper towel.

Griff smiled and said easily, "Sorry, sport. I piloted the plane bringing you here from Fredericksburg. You're trying to reach Cuba."

The well-built guy began walking out. Griff grabbed his elbow. Red Sox wrenched his arm away. With both hands, Griff muscled him through the door and into the hangar.

"Brett, go ahead and search him."

"Put your arms up," Brett snarled as he stepped up to the guy's face. "You don't want to resist, I can tell you that."

Red Sox kicked at the floor, but lifted his hands slowly. Brett started patting him down under the arms beneath his Red Sox jacket, and ending at his ankles. Then he straightened his back. Brett put a hand into the man's right front pocket, his fingers grasping something like metal.

"What's this?" Brett demanded, pulling out a thumb drive.

The man shook his head. "You're wrong. I can explain. I'm a Navy captain on an undercover mission to infiltrate a group suspected of stealing our secrets."

Griff glanced at Brett trying to regain his footing. Had he seriously messed up?

"Got ID?" Griff asked. "Put down your hands long enough to show me."

Their suspect removed a wallet from his back pocket,

displaying a Maryland driver's license in the name of Calum Wentworth. Brett reached inside the captain's left front pants pocket.

"What have we here?" Brett tugged out an external hard drive.

Wentworth blinked. "Those aren't what you think they are. It's critical I rejoin my group before they become suspicious." He pointed to the hard drive Brett held. "That's filled with fake documents … you know … decoys for Russian intelligence. So is the thumb drive."

Griff's mind processed Calum's assertions at the speed of light. It was possible Sonya had stumbled into a CIA or Pentagon operation. Maybe she was being deceived into thinking she'd actually co-opted a high-ranking Naval officer.

Visions of his career being torpedoed by his own cleverness danced through Griff's head. How to douse the pending flames that could torch his career?

He gazed at Brett whose eyes had narrowed to slits. His look of disbelief was enough for Griff to act.

"Cuff Captain Wentworth," Griff told his partner. "Retain his hard and thumb drives. Take him to the conference room."

Questions peppering his mind like so many blows from a prizefighter, Griff hurried to find Eva. She met him in the hallway by the restrooms.

"Griff, we have a problem."

"You're telling me! The tall guy claims to be Navy Captain Calum Wentworth who is working to feed false intelligence to the Russians."

Eva pulled Griff into the woman's john and lodged her booted toe against the door. She stepped close whispering, "The couple with Sonya is Mr. and Mrs. Oaks. They claim to be Russian diplomats. They showed me their diplomatic passports to prove it."

"Oh great." Griff's head started swimming and his pulse racing. "The Russians have done that before. They give their spies diplomatic passports so they can't be arrested. What does Sonya say?"

"She's not claiming diplomatic immunity and isn't talking. Do you think it's time to call your headquarters?"

"I will," he said, scarcely believing this awful turn of events. "First, who else do we have in custody?"

Her foot still against the door, Eva said, "I think they're handlers in a spy network, even Austin's mother, Mrs. Oaks. She insists she has diplomatic immunity. The blonde with the fancy diamond ring goes with Mr. Red Sox. She's not talking either."

"She must be married to Captain Wentworth," Griff replied. "He's carrying a thumb drive and external hard drive in his pockets. He claims they're phony to confuse the Russians."

"This is messed up." Griff stepped back, reality sinking in like a bad stench.

Eva covered her mouth with her hand. "Have we scrambled some other agency's counterespionage sting? I was on the way to advise you about their passports."

"Get Brett's keys. He's in the conference room with Captain Wentworth. You and I will adjourn to the car and call Washington."

In short order, the car engine on and air conditioning blasting, Griff consulted his phone and dialed. "I'm calling Director Taggart about the captain."

"You have guts." Eva pulled down her bottom lip.

"What else can I do? If we go through Oliver at JTTF and up the chain of command, we'll be sitting here until the sun rises in the morning."

Eva tilted her head at him. "I agree, but this could be the end of us and Stogie."

Griff punched in numbers, holding up his finger to pause further talk. He gave his name, telling the duty agent at FBI HQ that he must speak to Director Taggart ASAP.

"It's a matter of extreme urgency," he insisted, and then switched his phone to speaker and mouthed to Eva, "He's coming."

"Topping, you're breaching protocol," Taggart barked. "Report to me through channels."

"Sir, you'll want to know this. Agent Montanna and I are at the Marathon, Florida, airport. We've arrested five people we believe could be Russian spies. One claims he is a U. S. Navy captain."

Taggart gulped loudly. "Did I hear correctly? You stopped the spies we're combing the country for?"

"This catches us by surprise, sir. We were trying to stop the smuggling case we previously briefed you about."

"You arrested a Navy captain?" Taggart's voice echoed in the car. "Who is he?"

Rolling his eyes at Eva, Griff replied, "Calum Wentworth says he's a U.S. Navy captain. He's carrying an external hard drive and a thumb drive. His story is that these contain fake documents to bamboozle Russian intelligence agents."

"To be clear," Taggart boomed, "he professes to be working for us on a secret intelligence-gathering mission?"

The consequences of what he was about to say made

torrents of sweat pour down Griff's sides. "Sir, Wentworth won't divulge for whom. We may have done irreparable damage to another agency's stealth operation."

"Topping, you babysit that clown, and sit tight on whoever else you've snagged down there. I've a few important calls to make."

Griff furnished his cell number, which would have come in as a blocked call. He also promised Taggart to keep the suspects separated. The call over, Griff leaned back against the headrest.

"Eva, can you get me a job at ICE if I'm fired?"

She dismissed his concern with a wave of her hand. "That will never happen. Captain Wentworth has gone rogue. You know I'm rarely wrong."

"Why didn't we just take these jerks to federal court in Miami? Let the federal prosecutors untangle this muddle."

"And give up our jurisdiction over Mrs. Oaks? Never!" Eva's voice conveyed power and authority.

In spite of the air conditioning, sweat continued to pool beneath Griff's armpits. "Easy for you to have bravado. You don't work directly for Taggart. He may order us off the case in the next five minutes. Then we'll have no choice."

"Maybe," Eva said, until a light sparked in her eyes. "I need to check on Louie."

She sprang from the car as Griff turned it off. He eased out, asking her to have the attendant refuel their plane, adding in a hushed voice, "I want to peek inside their luggage in the plane."

"That's smart. Then join me with Louie. He's not going to like what I tell him."

"Oh? What do you know?"

Eva grinned sheepishly. "You'll find out *after* you do your snooping."

EVA WAS CONSOLING LOUIE when Griff entered the side office. Their sad-looking informant blotted his eyes with a hankie.

"He knows Sonya's been arrested," Eva told Griff bleakly.

"Louie, had you seen any of these people before?" Griff pulled a chair across from him. "Don't even think of messing with us."

Their snitch blew his nose into a crumpled hankie sounding like a honking goose.

"Yeah. The stocky guy with curled hair and the brown-haired gal are Sonya's colleagues. I think they're married, tho' they don't wear rings. I flew 'em in from Cuba once. Red Sox jacket guy and his blonde? I never seen 'em."

Griff shook his head slowly. Louie would melt when he knew the whole truth.

"Eva, did you tell Louie why Sonya was arrested?"

"Not yet."

In his steeliest voice, Griff told him point-blank, "Sonya's a Russian intelligence agent spying against the U.S. Those other folks are working with her."

"No. No." Louie began sobbing as if in sharp pain. "That can't be. She's unfortunate. She never had a dad's influence. I would'a done the right thing. I never knew I got her mom pregnant."

Eva lobbed an intense look at Griff while she removed a folded paper from her pocket. Griff prepared himself for the next blow, whatever that might be, wishing she'd confided in him.

"Louie, remember when we arrested you at the house," Eva said. "And I asked you to give me a DNA swab?"

He swallowed, his hands trembling and wringing the hankie.

"You said the pink hair bungy was Sonya's."

"Yeah. So?"

Eva jiggled the paper before his eyes. "I sent her bungy for DNA testing along with your sample to the FBI lab. This report proves my suspicions. The hairs from Sonya's bungy and your DNA do not match. Not even close. You are *not* her father. The hair in the bungy is from a Russian woman. Sonya told you she is from Kosovo."

"She is my daughter!"

"These tests do not lie, but Sonya has lied to you from day one. She's a Russian spy and deceived you. You unknowingly helped her commit espionage against America."

Louie's face dropped into his hands. He groaned miserably. Griff's cell phone began vibrating.

"Excuse me," he told Eva. "This is the call we are waiting for."

She trailed behind him, with Griff whispering to her in the hall, "It's a 202 area code." Then he spoke into the phone, answering, "This is Griff Topping."

They walked outside, and stopped beneath a palm tree. Griff set his phone on speaker so Eva could hear.

"Taggart here. Captain Wentworth is AWOL. The Pentagon has no idea where he is. Worse, he's assigned to the Navy Submarine Warfare Command. He has access to things I can't discuss on this line."

He cleared his throat before continuing, "I've dispatched one of our jets to Marathon. When it arrives, turn Wentworth and his wife over to agents on board. They will handle the matter from here on. Turn the other three, including the alleged diplomats, over to the agents from Miami. Let them authenticate any diplomatic immunity."

"One more thing, sir." Griff raised his eyebrows at Eva. "I've combed through their untagged luggage. Some have handwritten notes in Russian. Three bags are crammed with USB and external hard drives."

Taggart's tone turned softer. "Good job. No names on the luggage, Topping?"

"That's right, sir."

"Good! Hand the luggage over to the Miami agents. It will take time to identify the owners of lost luggage, if you get my gist. Tell them I said so."

"Sir," Griff grimaced, "so we remain on site until the Miami agents take the three and the D.C. jet arrives for the captain and his wife?"

"Correct. Your instincts are superb. Have John Oliver call me. Your conduct deserves an award and he may not think of it. From here, say nothing about the captain. You'll be told how and when to write your reports."

"Yes, sir."

Griff ended the call feeling sorry for Eva. "You heard him. Mrs. Oaks heads to Miami. You won't be handling her case."

"I'll deal with that somehow," Eva quipped rather quickly. "What do you make of his order to delay writing our reports?"

"I hadn't thought about it yet."

Eva clasped his forearm. "Griff, we've gathered plenty of evidence. Why don't they want a record? Meanwhile, Mrs. Oaks is still my prisoner. Leave her to me."

IT DIDN'T TAKE LONG FOR EVA AND GRIFF to brief several Miami agents about Taggart's instructions. After arranging for their departure with Sonya and the two fake diplomats for Miami, Eva stepped into the office, where FBI Agent Dobbs guarded the three women suspects.

Eva asked, "Which of you is Mrs. Wentworth?"

The fashionable blonde tried raising her hands cuffed behind her. "I am."

Her reply, though brief, revealed a slight Eastern European accent.

"You come with me," Eva said, helping to lift the stylish lady from her chair.

From there, Eva brought her into the conference room where

Brett kept her husband under scrutiny. By bringing the couple together, Eva hoped to confirm her suspicions. Brett stepped out and as he did, Eva noticed husband and wife lock eyes for an instant.

"Mrs. Wentworth, do you know why you are under arrest?"

"I want to consult with an attorney," she said, holding her head up high.

"That is your choice."

Eva dropped all further questioning. It was apparent the wife was the bait to entrap the Navy captain into committing who knew what kind of treason. When Brett strode back into the room, ready to assume command of the prisoners, Eva walked up and cautioned him in low tones, "They're married. Don't let them talk to each other while we await their transport."

"Any idea how long?" he asked, his tone barely audible.

"Just sit tight for now."

She left him to watch the Navy spy and his wife, disgust mounting in Eva's mind for the entire lousy deal. Could she sit by and let Mrs. Oaks get whisked away to Miami without confronting her? Eva could not. She would not.

The FBI agents were gathering with Sonya and the Oaks by the side entrance. In a quick maneuver, Eva intercepted them on the way to the FBI van. Sonya stopped in her tracks though a female agent tugged on her arm.

Sonya turned to Mrs. Oaks demanding, "Show them my diplomatic passport."

The entire group of agents and spies came to a halt by Eva. Agent Dobbs asked Mrs. Oaks, "Do you have this woman's diplomatic passport?"

"I have no idea what she is talking about. I met her today on the plane." Austin's mother turned her face away.

Sonya was having none of her rude treatment. She screamed at her, "You told me that I would have diplomatic immunity."

Mr. Oaks still hadn't said one word. One of the FBI agents led him away quietly. Not so with Sonya. While the agent wrenched her arm toward the van, Sonya shouted all the way. Eva was glad Louie wasn't out here to witness the spectacle.

"Hold on a second, please," Eva called out to Agent Dobbs.

The tall FBI agent drew up short with Mrs. Oaks nearly colliding with her back.

"Agent Montanna, do you have new instructions?" Dobbs asked.

"Yes, I have something to say." Eva squared her body to face

Mrs. Oaks. The woman's hands remained cuffed behind her back.

"Do you recognize me?" Eva snarled.

"Not at all."

"I think you do. In fact, I suspect you've communicated intelligence about me and my family."

Austin's mother stood rigidly, without looking at Eva. "You know I have diplomatic immunity."

Eva noticed a surprising flaw. The woman's right eye twitched ever so slightly.

"You are no more a diplomat than I am Minnie Mouse," Eva countered, venom dripping in her voice.

Mrs. Oaks pressed her lips together so tightly they became white.

"Is Austin even your son?" Eva lobbed. "Did you co-opt him into spying on classmates? And what is he doing in high school when he is twenty-one years old?"

When there was no response, just an icy chill from Mrs. Oaks' cold shoulder, Eva felt it her sworn duty to warn the agent in charge. "Agent Dobbs, be especially careful of this woman. She's treacherous."

"I hear you," Agent Dobbs said, her face stoic.

Eva stepped behind Mrs. Oaks to examine her handcuffs saying, "Let me check if she's secure. Oh, would you look at these? They're loose."

With a *click, click*, Eva tightened the cuffs until they pushed against the woman's wrist bone.

"That's much better," Eva intoned. "We don't want anyone getting hurt on your long drive to Miami."

She eyeballed Mrs. Oaks staggering next to Agent Dobbs, who was herding her to the idling van. The heel of her one shoe wobbled as if about to fall off. Eva hoped her claim of immunity would turn out to be unfounded. This was one Russian spy who needed all the justice American courts could muster. Austin's mother had messed with the wrong agent.

Eva intended to contact the federal prosecutor ASAP to ensure Mrs. Oaks was formally charged with the highest crimes possible. Yet, the words "diplomatic immunity" hounded Eva like a yapping dog on her jog back to the terminal. What would Griff and Brett say about this debacle?

Chapter 44

Night had erased all pink from the sky by the time the FBI jet left the Marathon airport with the enigmatic Captain Wentworth and his wife. Outside the manager's office, Eva was debating with Griff over their options going forward. Inside, Brett and Louie were embroiled in a hushed conversation.

Eva turned her mind to what they should do next. "The sun is down. Flying to Lime Key is out. We could get hotel rooms for the night."

"I'm in no mood for Louie's lip. We leave the Cessna here and return at sunrise."

To the rumble of her hollow stomach, Eva smiled wanly at her partner. "At least Taggart sees the value of what we've done here."

"Your silver lining may soon become tarnished just like everything else in this case." Griff crushed an empty foam cup in his hands. "This coffee without food leaves a bitter taste."

Eva wrinkled her nose. "I threw mine out if you can believe it. And that's not the only bitter pill we're swallowing. I begin to doubt that Sonya and the Oaks will be processed, fingerprinted, and jailed in Miami."

"The diplomatic issue complicates things, right? They'll probably have initial appearances in the morning to hear what charges, if any, will be lodged against them."

"You doubt it too, right?" Eva demanded.

Griff swiped his forehead. "I can hope, can't I? Let's get out of here. Let Brett drive with Louie up front. I'm so beat my eyes refuse to stay open."

Eva was too wound up to be tired. She thanked the manager on duty, and off they drove to Lime Key in the heart of night. Eva found one bright side; she was in a car this time and not on the back of a run-down motorbike. They were well south of the Seven Mile Bridge when Louie's question punctured Eva's glum thoughts about the havoc Mrs. Oaks had created.

"What's gonna happen to me?" he piped softly from the front seat.

Eva leaned forward telling him, "You're flying back to D.C. with us."

"We have questions for you," Griff added, waking up from his catnap.

"And something important remains to be done." Eva put a hand on Louie's shoulder. "We need to have your cast taken off."

"Finally! What a relief!"

In the glare of a passing car's lights, Eva saw Louie glance back toward Griff.

His voice gentle and without guile, he said, "Last night in the motel, I read John in the Bible like you said. I made my peace with God, and now with you guys."

Soon, sounds of his snoring drifted from the front seat.

"Wow, that makes the muddle worth it," Griff observed with a contented sigh. "He's sleeping with a clear conscience, and I couldn't be happier for him."

Eva grinned, more for her sake as it was too dark for Griff to see. "I suspect there's a story behind his decision, and he'll be eternally thankful to you."

They tore down the road with Eva reflecting on the day's dramatic events. They passed an occasional dimly-lit parking lot; otherwise, she saw only blackness on each side of the road. Then up ahead a streak of lightning blazed white and blue across the sky. Seconds later, thunder rumbled off in the distance. A nighttime storm was brewing offshore.

Not relishing being buffeted by rain on a narrow road surrounded by water, Eva forced her mind to the positive realm.

"Griff," she whispered. "Things will come together, you'll see. With our arrests today, you should notify ATF to arrest Louie's cigar dealers."

"Valid point. In the end something good came from helping Sonya."

"I second that," Brett chimed from the driver's seat. "I'll always remember this day. What a hoot. A narc busting spies. Go figure."

With Louie snorting as if waking up, Griff told Eva quietly, "You were right to remind me and Taggart didn't fire me." He paused. "I'll contact the ATF first thing."

"Anything else we need to wrap up?" she asked him.

"A good night's sleep will reveal that answer. My brain is fried."

Eva's brain was the opposite, revving ultra-fast. She gazed out the window agreeing Louie's change of heart was the best prize. Besides, it was gratifying to know she and her task force partners had captured five Russian spies! Five traitors were caught—five traitors who were no longer a threat to America.

Bright mercury lights from a hotel parking lot and restaurant shone into the car. They were fast approaching Lime Key. Huge raindrops began plastering the windshield. Louie snorted once more, and Eva's phone whirled on her waistband. She plucked it from its holder. A 305 area code suggested a southern Florida caller.

She answered with a vague, "Hello."

"Eva … it's Agent Dobbs. I've an update on our Marathon arrests."

"Yes, Shirley. Fill me in please."

Dobbs sounded tentative as she began, "Um … Eva … You should know we've encountered an ugly rub here in Miami."

"I'm listening," Eva replied, suspecting a jurisdictional snafu.

"Before we lodged our three as federal prisoners for the night, the U.S. Attorney's office called. No espionage charges will be filed against them. We don't know what that means, or if they will be charged."

"Perhaps they don't want the media discovering the true reason."

Dobbs was adamant. "No, the U.S. Attorney's office rarely makes such calls."

"You're right." Eva deflated like a popped balloon. "What reason did they give?"

"That's all I know."

Eva's blood pressure soared. All she could manage was, "Why?"

"Between you and me," Dobbs's voice fell to a whisper, "I think State exerted influence so no one will know these spies were trying to escape to Russia through Cuba."

Eva was steaming. Still, she thanked Shirley for the heads-up and asked, "Are you delivering them to court tomorrow?"

"No. We're told Immigration will handle any appearance. You can guess what will happen. I'll let you know if I learn anything else."

Eva hung up and faced Griff, whispering, "It's worse than you can imagine."

Brett was rolling to a stop at Pelican's Nest, and Eva flung her door open. It wasn't raining here yet.

"You guys go in," she declared. "I need to clear my head."

Griff grasped her forearm. "I understand. Brett and I will handle Louie."

"Do you have your burn phone on you?"

As Griff thumped his jeans' pocket, Eva crooked her finger for him to turn over the phone. Louie wrestled out of the car with his crutches, and she stomped around the house to the canal's edge.

Tree toads chirped a nocturnal melody while Eva fumed. How could the U.S. government take such risks? They were allowing three Russian spies to escape to the motherland rather than let Americans discover they were passing through Cuba. Worse than insane, State's position insulted the dangerous and hard work of every agent.

Pulse pounding in her ears, Eva found the contact on her cell phone, then punched the number on the burn phone. She hesitated ... should she? Yes!

She made the call, hoping to reach voicemail. Three rings and a computer voice answered, "Please leave a message after the tone."

Speaking clearly, Eva said, "You know my voice, but don't contact me. I'll deny talking with you because I'm not talking with you. Erase the message. I know your interest in Russian spies. At Marathon Florida's airport today, five people were arrested fleeing to Cuba. A Russian woman recruited the aeronautical engineer. Sonya Kopanja may be in Miami Immigration Court tomorrow, or released as an illegal rather than involve Cuba.

"A Russian couple named Oaks recruited Navy Captain Calum Wentworth and his foreign wife who the FBI spirited to D.C. The Oaks claim to be Russian diplomats. Their son Austin took refuge at Russia's embassy. You play this right, and you'll get another exclusive interview."

Eva ended the call, and fastening the phone on her belt, raced up the steps to Holly's second-floor home. Griff wasn't to be seen, so she figured he and Brett were plotting upstairs with Louie about inserting Brett into the drug-smuggling scheme.

Kicking off her boots, Eva felt no regrets over her call. She leaned on the kitchen counter, typing Scott a text ... *home tomorrow ... love you ...*

Chapter 45

Northern Virginia

It was pitch-dark in Eva's bedroom except for the obnoxious tiny red light emitting from the TV. She heard Scott's deep breathing and the grandfather clock *tick tocking* in the living room. Sleep seemed as distant as Lime Key.

Adrenalin from the preceding week, the arrests, and long flight home this morning kept her mental gears churning. She thought of Agent Dobbs and colleagues who had dashed from Miami to help capture what they thought might be terrorists in Marathon, only to learn they disrupted the largest spy ring of their time. As happened to Eva before, the Miami agents returned home never able to tell anyone what they'd done.

There was one good result. The Florida drug case was coming together for Brett. Eva's heart lightened recalling him going off whistling to babysit Louie at an area hotel. The two were conniving, and Louie would vouch for Brett with Rory and his drug-smuggling pals. In a few hours, Brett would take Louie to the vet to saw off his cast.

Eva flipped onto her side, but Louie didn't budge from her mind. His teary eyes rose before her, how he pleaded for her and Griff to ask federal prosecutors not to indict him for past mistakes in smuggling cigars and Russian spies. Listening to Scott's breathing next to her, she felt confident Louie would go free. Well, he had endured the inconvenience of a month-long fake broken leg.

Scott's breathing turned discordant as if caught in a bad dream. She jostled his foot with hers, and he returned to a steady rhythm. Scott's fingers touched hers.

"Are you awake?" he whispered.

"I can't sleep."

Scott sat up. "You can tell me all about it."

He plodded down the hall in pjs while Eva nestled into her robe. By the time she reached the family room, he had the TV on low. He patted the sofa beside him.

"Look who is on," Scott told her. "The station is replaying breaking news."

Eva sat down in disbelief. There was Kat with the sun setting behind her.

"I want to hear this. Turn it up," Eva said.

Kat told viewers she was at the Marathon Airport in Florida, adding with a fierce glare, "I'm not reporting news, but lack of news. An employee named Shane said that yesterday five people arrived on a propeller aircraft and were arrested as spies. Federal officials in Miami will confirm nothing. Recently, I announced the arrest of a Seattle aeronautical engineer accused of selling Russia plans for our next B-2 bomber."

The camera panned the airport as Kat continued, "Sources tell me that yesterday a high-ranking American military officer was arrested here. Shane informs me the propeller plane sat here over night, departing this morning. I have numbers from the tail. It's owned by a mysterious leasing agency."

Scott clasped Eva's hand as the scene changed to an executive jet behind Kat's face. She gazed sternly into the camera.

"Shane reports an FBI jet landed here last night. Agents took into custody the officer and a woman also arrested as part of the five. It flew out last night, heading for D.C., and I will keep digging for you."

The screen image showed the Ft. Lauderdale Executive Airport with Kat breathlessly reporting beside a private jet. "I've just learned Sonya Kopanya, the spymaster who controlled the aeronautical engineer and who was herself arrested last night in Marathon, was today released on bond in Miami for entering the country illegally. Also released in Miami were Stuart and Trudy Oaks, believed to be Russian spies carrying diplomatic passports. The Oaks were trying to smuggle a U.S. Navy captain and his wife to Cuba."

She paused for the diminishing sound of a departing jet. "I tried to get here in time, but as you can hear, the three Russian spies just left on a chartered jet, like the one behind me. They are destined for Mexico City. Officials are staying mum. I will stay on the case. That's all for now."

"Unbelievable!" Eva snorted.

He shut off the TV and squeezed her hand. "You have been through the pepper grinder, love. I can tell by the furious gleam in your beautiful blue eyes."

"If you only knew what I know," Eva said. "You heard Kat. The Oaks are the parents of Kaley's friend Austin Oaks."

He leaned his head back and sighed. "I should have told you before now. Kaley told me that kids in her government class were talking how Austin was the Russian spy who escaped to Russia's embassy two days ago. Ms. Yost admonished them, refusing to let them speak about it."

"Kaley called me in the Keys, saying Austin fled her class. Did she tell you?"

"I guess she mentioned it. I was up to my eyeballs cooking spaghetti, and never followed up. I should have."

Eva leaned on her husband's solid shoulder. "You and I will have time later to sort out what we should do differently."

"I love you, do you know that?"

She touched his cheek. "Sweetheart, my love grows and deepens for you by the day. You are the most wonderful blessing to me."

"A slice of apple pie in the fridge has your name on it. Interested?"

"Try and stop me."

A BUSY TWO WEEKS LATER, Eva drove her G-car to Alexandra's federal courthouse. She planned to arrive early for a two o'clock appointment with AUSA O'Rourke and Judge Harding, if traffic cooperated. Griff looked tense over in the passenger seat, jiggling their file folder on his knee.

He asked her, "Do you think the judge will accept our recommendations?"

"You know Harding's as unpredictable as the nor'easter that blew through last week. At least we aren't driving in snow."

Eva cranked a turn onto the highway, glancing in the rearview mirror. Brett and Louie were talking in the backseat.

"Louie," she said. "How does it feel having enough room for your legs without the cast?"

"I'd feel better if I knew I wasn't goin' to prison. So what about Dino and the cigar guys?"

Brett beat Eva to the punch, saying, "They're in custody, which is why you're coming with us. After Eva and Griff talk to the judge, you meet Mr. O'Rourke. He's agreed to not charge you. He'll have you sign an immunity letter he's already signed."

"What does that get me?"

Griff gazed over his shoulder telling Louie, "You agree to testify in court about Sonya, her associates, and the cigar dealers."

"Do I have to?"

"No!" Eva barked, her patience worn thin. "Go to prison if you'd rather."

Brett joined the chorus. "Hear that? It's a super deal for you. Quit complaining."

She'd heard enough from Louie, and flipped on the car radio to a talk show host beginning his rant.

"My warning of our government harassing citizens rather than plugging the holes in our national security has come true. Nameless suits in D.C. have released Russian spies, one for being an undocumented immigrant, and two as diplomats. We're awash with Russian spies being kicked out of the country. How absurd!"

Eva agreed, but what could she do? Her pulse rose as the talk show host blared, "To add insult to injury, Americans are being arrested, all so our government can protect the environment from tobacco smoke. Listen up."

He paused to rattle paper. "I'm holding a news release. The nameless suits proudly proclaimed agents spread across the nation seizing cigar aficionados. Dealers in Newark and Tampa were selling untaxed and illegally-imported cigars from Cuba. Folks, this gets interesting.

"These expensive and choice Cuban cigars are smoked behind closed doors by politicians and judges. Past presidents have gifted them to foreign dignitaries. I'm waiting to see if the government finds a trial judge who hasn't smoked one of these dangerous and unlawful cigars."

Eva switched off the radio. "There you have it, Louie. We told the AUSA you are the key to those arrests, as well as Sonya's arrest and deportation."

"That's nice, but if Holly gets out early, I have no place to go."

Griff crooked his head toward the backseat. "You may have a chance to talk with her about future living arrangements."

In the mirror, Eva saw a puzzled look pass over Louie's beleaguered face.

"I might see her at the court?" he asked.

Eva rolled the Fusion into a parking garage, and killing the engine promised, "We'll try to make it happen for you."

Chapter 46

Eva and Griff entered the judge's reception area while Brett stayed in the hall with Louie. Being in a federal judge's chambers was something agents wished to avoid. This time, the secretary brought them into the judge's inner sanctum where Eva and Griff would inform the judge of Holly's cooperation, the details of which couldn't be said in open court.

Judge Harding rose from his chair to greet them, admonishing the defense attorney to get her show moving. "Ingles, my jury's due back from lunch soon."

He motioned to several empty chairs. AUSA Patrick O'Rourke's wheelchair already faced the judge's desk, a file resting on his lap. Defense Attorney Constance Ingles slid her chair closer to the judge's giant desk to make room. Her client, Holly Munoz, was handcuffed and perched clumsily on a chair to the other side of Constance.

The defense attorney's cheeks blazed crimson as she addressed the judge. "I am outraged, which is why I demanded this in-camera meeting prior to my client's sentence reduction hearing. Agents negotiated a deal with Holly without my knowledge."

"Is it true?" The judge fixed a piercing gaze upon Eva. "You contacted Ms. Munoz?"

O'Rourke interjected, "Your Honor, Ms. Munoz requested the contact."

"Why did she ask to meet without her attorney?" Harding asked Eva.

She wasn't intimidated by his stony glare. "Because she didn't trust her attorney."

"I object!" Constance jumped to her feet. "Agent Montanna can't speak for Holly."

"You're not in court showing off for the jury," Harding lectured. "Sit down."

Constance sat down in a huff.

O'Rourke lifted his file, offering the judge a copy of the signed statement. "Ms. Munoz signed a statement asking no one know of her meeting with Agent Montanna until this reduction hearing. Agent Montanna has the original. You will see it was signed and witnessed by Deputy Marshal Cheri Duggan. Ms. Munoz is here as well."

The judge waggled his finger at Eva. "Let me read this

missive."

She handed it over. Everyone sat quietly as he read, except Constance kept sighing. Some moments later, he laid the paper on his desk with a flourish.

"Ms. Munoz, did you read this before you signed it?"

"Yes, sir." Holly coughed, unable to cover her mouth with her cuffed hands. "Agent Montanna made me read out loud so she knew I could read."

"Fine. Ingles, get over it. Your client didn't trust you, but don't feel like the Lone Ranger. She didn't trust Mr. O'Rourke or Yours Truly either."

His grin was fleeting and he handed Constance the statement for review. "Now that we're clear the agents weren't sneaking behind your back, let's learn how your client helped them. I want to hear what's so important it can't be said in open court."

"The agents will provide an unclassified version," O'Rourke intoned, shuffling papers into his file.

During ten raucous minutes, with Constance constantly objecting and the judge admonishing her, Eva and Griff alternated, telling about the Munoz home on Lime Key. That led to details about cigar smuggling from the home, and the eventual discovery of a foreign government using Holly's caretaker to shuttle foreign agents into the country from Cuba in the Munoz airplane.

"Like a house of cards, the caretaker's cooperation led to the dismantling of the smuggling organization," Eva said in conclusion.

Judge Harding demanded, "So you're saying Ms. Munoz was critical to the success of your case?"

"Yes, Your Honor," Eva replied. "Holly introduced me and Agent Topping to the caretaker, which resulted in his vital assistance. Without it we would never have known."

Judge Harding shifted his probing eyes to Griff. "Do you agree there is sufficient reason to reduce this woman's sentence?"

"Yes. Here's why." Griff straightened his back. "Have you heard about recent arrests of an aeronautical engineer and high-ranking military officer?"

At the judge's nod, Griff added, "Then you have learned of the case."

"Oh?" Harding's eyebrows arched. "Oh! Well in that case, does the government object to Ms. Munoz's sentence being reduced to time served?"

The agents and O'Rourke joined in a chorus of "No."

"So be it. We reconvene in the courtroom," Harding ordered.

O'Rourke put his hands on his wheels to turn when Eva

leaned down and whispered in his ear. Then he addressed the judge respectfully about the Munoz assets.

"Your Honor, everything from the Ponzi case has been auctioned and victims compensated minus one. Her name is Thelma King. Two newly discovered assets, a car and airplane, have been recently seized and sold. Ms. King is the only claimant, and I have an order for you to sign compensating her with these proceeds."

Again the judge motioned with his finger. "Give it to me."

"Oh no! How will I get around?" Holly instantly objected.

Eva was shocked a prisoner in handcuffs dared to interrupt a federal judge.

Harding glared at Constance. "Care to comment on the behalf of your client, Ingles?"

Constance and her client hurriedly whispered, and the lawyer assured the judge, "My client appreciates her reduction in sentence, Your Honor. She's lamenting her only home is on Lime Key and she has no way to get around."

Eva knew better, and told Harding the truth. "Your Honor, two motorbikes are kept at the residence. We used them during the undercover operation. Her caretaker is in your reception area, hoping to speak with her. I'm sure he'll keep the bikes running."

The judge gazed in surprise as Holly spoke up. "Good. I hoped Louie would agree to stay. I'd like to talk with him."

"That's it then." Judge Harding signed the order allowing Thelma to receive all sums from the Cessna 310 and the BMW. They headed out toward the courtroom to record Holly's sentence as time served.

Eva glanced at Holly, her once dyed hair a dull gray. What a picture Eva had of Holly zooming around Lime Key on the tiny blue motorbike.

She pulled Griff aside. "Good job, partner. You make sure there are no more interruptions of the judge by Holly. I'm calling Thelma to share the great news."

Chapter 47

The Florida Keys

A month later, life brought wonderful blessings to Eva and her family. Here they all were laughing and kicking up sand on their long-delayed Florida vacation. Friends from across the Atlantic had joined them at the Marathon Key resort to celebrate the Thanksgiving holiday.

Last week, Stanislaw Sikorski arrived at Dulles International Airport from Poland along with his wife Gita and daughter Izzy. From their home in Fairfax, Eva and Kaley made an impromptu visit with the Sikorskis to a private university in southern Virginia. Kaley was determined to attend the college next fall. Izzy drew encouragement from an advisor who urged her to apply for a scholarship reserved for students from former Communist countries.

Happiness filled Eva from her head, covered with a white floppy hat, to her wiggling bare toes as she soaked up warm sunshine. A lovely breeze blowing off the ocean was great for kite flying. Eva hooted and hollered watching Scott, Stanislaw, and the boys make their acrobatic kites swoop and dive above the sugary sands. When the kite lines crossed during a dogfight, the colorful kites would spiral to the beach, amidst groans from their handlers.

On towels spread next to Eva, Kaley and Izzy were busy planning their future as roommates with Glenna and the fun they expected as first-year college students.

Kaley giggled. "Who knows? Maybe you'll find an American husband and remain here as a citizen."

"I could never leave my papa."

"Oh, you'd sponsor your family," Kaley explained. "You can all move here, and leave horrible Russia behind."

Izzy sighed. "Papa is sorry he forgot to bring your relics. The university said you could have some of the Soviet kopeks, and he forgot to pick them up."

"That's okay, Izzy. I think the school should keep those Soviet Union coins. I don't care if they're nearly a century old. They remind me too much of Russia, and you know how I feel about their constant harassment of you in Poland."

Eva's vibrating cell phone ended her eavesdropping. She decided it must be important because Griff and Brett wouldn't interrupt her vacation otherwise. The display revealed she'd missed a call from Griff. The incoming call was from CIA Agent Bo

Rider.

"It's Eva," she answered, lowering the wide brim of her hat.

"Sorry to bother you." Bo's voice sounded rushed. "Has Griff called you?"

A sense of dread enveloped Eva. "I just saw he left me a voicemail. I'm at the beach and missed his call. Is something wrong?"

"Not wrong, just noteworthy. Thought I'd bring you up-to-date on the latest news, but you catch it on the TV. Enjoy your rays."

Click.

Eva checked her phone. Bo had hung up on her. She instantly punched in the last call, which rang once before he answered.

"What's the big idea?" Eva snapped. "You serve me an appetizer, then hang up."

Bo laughed jovially. "I was testing to see if you're ever on vacation, or if you're always working like me."

"I'm not leaving this beautiful beach to find a TV. What do you know?"

"Here's the TV synopsis so we don't have to worry about security."

Eva grew impatient. "Enough! Tell me."

"According to Kat Kowicki, a Navy captain from Submarine Warfare Command at the Pentagon was arrested for furnishing secrets to a Russian spy network. One Russian spy handler was arrested and released as an undocumented person by Immigration, your agency, Eva. Two others were released as Russian diplomats."

"I had heard something about that," she said cryptically, unable to admit her involvement in the espionage case.

Bo kept talking in her ear. "The FBI found reams of documents in their luggage, which identified other Americans furnishing information to the Russians. Amazingly, Kat's exclusive interview of the FBI director airs tonight."

Eva thought back to the five suitcases, external hard drives, and USB drives Sonya's spies brought to the airport mere blocks from where Eva now enjoyed the sun with family and friends.

"Did you hear anything else about Russia, Bo?"

"Yes, and I scarcely believe it myself. It probably won't be included in Kat's recorded interview, as it just happened. Seventeen more Americans were arrested coast to coast. One is Ms. Yost, Glenna and Kaley's government teacher."

Eva's mind reeled. She jumped to her feet. "No way! For

what?"

"Here's where I need to be careful and circumspect." He paused. "She was dead-dropping documents to a Russian named Sonya, leaving them in a Maryland park."

"Like Hanssen did at Nottoway Park?"

"Well … being a teacher, she identified students whose parents held important jobs in our government."

To say Eva was stunned was an understatement. Anger gripped her, and she wanted to confront that miserable wretch of a teacher face-to-face. Gita looked at Eva curiously, so she walked up the path to the palm trees where she could talk privately.

In a soft voice she told Bo, "You and I wondered if the ferry to Sweden was targeted because of our girls."

"It was," Bo growled in her ear. "Through God's intervention, their plans were foiled."

"It's truly miraculous. Obviously this Sonya had managed to get info about our daughters to Moscow."

"Eva, they had stuff not only about us and our daughters, but other students and dossiers on government families. After your much-deserved vacation, we need to talk about the impact on our families and what precautions to take."

"Your call makes me realize the extent of God's protection for us and our families. I'll catch Kat's interview tonight."

"Eva, can you believe she nailed an exclusive? How does she do it?"

"I wish I knew." Eva didn't like fibbing, but circumstances demanded she say nothing more. She could never admit to calling Kat. "Say hello to Julia for me."

Bo promised he would, adding, "Don't hang up. The news broadcast said Captain Wentworth married a Russian woman, but no one knew. It wasn't caught because his top-secret background investigation was never brought up-to-date."

"Right," Eva quipped. "They're too busy checking on you and me, the good guys."

Eva walked over to her lounge chair after Bo signed off. Reclining, her cheeks were greeted by heavenly sunshine. Her mind soon returned to the five suitcases. When they were within her reach weeks ago in Marathon, Eva never imagined that her and her family's names were inside of them screaming to be found.

It was unbelievable. So was Kaley's teacher being a Russian spy. Would Ms. Yost be convicted or would she, too, claim immunity and skip to Russia? After all, Kaley's teacher had arranged the class trip to Poland in the first place.

Eva gaped over at Gita Sikorski, searing doubts rattling in her brain. Could this Polish family also be fooling Eva and Scott? In their minds, Eva and her husband had totally exonerated them from any wrongdoing. She rose to sit on a vacant chair beside Gita to learn the truth once and for all. Izzy's mother turned a page in a book she was reading.

"We are so glad you are here," Eva soothed, trying to see if the book was Russian.

"The blue sea is so tranquil. No Russian tanks." Gita treated Eva to a delicate smile. "Thanks you for inviting."

Eva stiffened. The Polish woman's reference to Russia might be a ploy to catch her off guard. What did she mean about Russian tanks? Who could Eva trust?

A gust of wind caught her floppy hat. Eva clamped a hand on the brim to keep it from blowing away. She gestured to Gita's leather-bound book asking, "What captures your interest?"

"The most precious book I own. My Bible."

She turned it so Eva could see, her finger resting on red letters. "Jesus is in boat with disciples. A bad storm scares them. Jesus calms the storm by telling waves, 'Quiet!' That is what I must say to my heart about Izzy going to American college."

Regret clenched at Eva's heart. How could she think this dear family spied for Russia? She reached for Gita's hand. "That's how I felt when Kaley visited you. God showed me that He cared for her thousands of miles from my eyesight."

"We mothers pray for much faith," Gita said. "Nothing separates us from God's pure love."

It was Eva's turn to smile. "You are right. No matter how dark or how cold or how scary, God calms every one of our looming storms."

"You are wise woman," Gita said, hugging her Bible.

Eva returned to her chair, where holding her hat, she shut her eyes, thanking God Almighty for the heights and depths of His mercy and love. A moment later, she heard Kaley shout, "Look, Mom!"

Eva's eyes opened in a flash. Looking up, she expected to see a Russian jet flying over. Instead, a formidable bald eagle lofted toward the shore, its grand wings spread in flight.

Yet America's national symbol of freedom soared away, and she was overwhelmed with a sense the eagle was protecting the land Eva loved so strongly. Watching the magnificent eagle in flight, Eva realized she and her team had run and not grown weary, and had worked hard without fainting. There on the Florida sandy beach, Eva was inspired to place all her trust in her Heavenly Father to care for her family and their future.

ABOUT THE AUTHORS

ExFeds, Diane and David Munson write High Velocity Suspense novels reviewers compare to John Grisham. The Munsons call their novels "factional fiction" because they write books based on their exciting and dangerous careers.

Diane Munson has been an attorney for more than thirty years. She has served as a Federal Prosecutor in Washington, D.C., and with the Reagan Administration appointed by Attorney General Edwin Meese as Deputy Administrator/Acting Administrator of the Office of Juvenile Justice and Delinquency Prevention. She worked with the Justice Department, U.S. Congress, and White House on policy and legal issues. More recently she has been in a general law practice.

David Munson served as a Special Agent with the Naval Investigative Service (now NCIS), and U.S. Drug Enforcement Administration over a twenty-seven year career. As an undercover agent, he infiltrated international drug smuggling organizations, and traveled with drug dealers. He met their suppliers in foreign countries, helped fly their drugs to the U.S., feigning surprise when shipments were seized by law enforcement. Later his true identity was revealed when he testified against group members in court. While assigned to DEA headquarters in Washington, D.C., David served two years as a Congressional Fellow with the Senate Permanent Subcommittee on Investigations.

As Diane and David research and write, they thank the Lord for the blessings of faith and family. They are collaborating on their next novel and traveling the country speaking/appearing at various venues.
Check out their critiques of the popular TV show found on their NCIS blog at their website below:

www.DianeAndDavidMunson.com

THE MUNSONS' STAND-ALONE THRILLERS MAY BE READ IN ANY ORDER.

Facing Justice

Diane and David Munson draw on their true-life experiences in this suspense novel about Special Agent Eva Montanna, whose twin sister died at the Pentagon on 9/11. Eva dedicates her career to avenge her death while investigating Emile Jubayl, a member of Eva's church and CEO of Helpers International, who is accused of using his aid organization to funnel money to El Samoud, head of the Armed Revolutionary Cause, and successor to Al Qaeda. Family relationships are tested in this fast-paced, true-to-life legal thriller about the men and women who are racing to defuse the ticking time bomb of international terrorism.
ISBN-13: 978-0982535509
352 pages, trade paper
Christian Fiction / Mystery and Suspense
14.99

Confirming Justice

In Confirming Justice, the second thriller by ExFeds, Diane/David Munson (Ex-Federal Prosecutor/Ex-Federal undercover agent), all eyes are on Federal Judge Dwight Pendergast, secretly in line for nomination to the Supreme Court, who is presiding over a bribery case involving a cabinet secretary's son. When the key prosecution witness disappears, FBI agent Griff Topping risks his life to save the case while powerful enemies seek to entangle the judge in a web of corruption and deceit. Diane and David Munson masterfully create plot twists and fast-paced intrigue in this family friendly portrayal of what transpires behind the scenes at the center of power. The Munsons' thrillers are companion books, with characters reappearing in other novels, but each begins and ends a new story.

The Camelot Conspiracy

"The Camelot Conspiracy" rocks with a sinister plot even more menacing than the headlines. Former DC insiders Diane and David Munson feature a brash TV reporter, Kat Kowicki, who receives an ominous email that throws her into the high stakes conspiracy of John F. Kennedy's assassination. When Kat uncovers evidence Lee Harvey Oswald did not act alone, she turns for help to Federal Special Agents Eva Montanna and Griff Topping who uncover the chilling truth: A shadow government threatens to tear down the very foundation of the American justice system. The Munsons' thrillers are companion books, with characters reappearing in other novels, but each begins and ends a new story.
ISBN-13: 978-0982535523
352 pages, trade paper
Christian Fiction / Mystery and Suspense
14.99

Hero's Ransom

Could Chinese espionage disrupt your home town? CIA Agent Bo Rider (The Camelot Conspiracy) and Federal Agents Eva Montanna and Griff Topping (Facing Justice, Confirming Justice, The Camelot Conspiracy) return in Hero's Ransom, the Munsons' fourth family-friendly adventure. When archeologist Amber Worthing uncovers a two-thousand-year-old mummy and witnesses a secret rocket launch at a Chinese missile base, she is arrested in China for espionage. Her imprisonment sparks a custody battle between grandparents over her young son, Lucas. Caught between sinister world powers, Amber's faith is tested in ways she never dreamed possible. Danger escalates as Bo races to stop China's killer satellite from destroying America, and with Eva and Griff's help, to rescue Amber using a unexpected ransom.
ISBN-13: 978-0982535530
320 pages, trade paper
Christian Fiction / Mystery and Suspense
14.99

Redeeming Liberty

In this timely thriller by ExFeds Diane and David Munson (former Federal Prosecutor and Federal Agent), parole officer Dawn Ahern is shocked to witness her friend Liberty, the chosen bride of Wally (former "lost boy" from Sudan) being kidnapped by modern-day African slave traders. Dawn tackles overwhelming danger head-on in her quest to redeem Liberty. When she reaches out to FBI agent Griff Topping and CIA agent Bo Rider, her life is changed forever. Suspense soars as Bo launches a clandestine rescue effort for Liberty only to discover a deadly Iranian secret threatening the lives of millions of Americans and Israelis. Glimpse tomorrow's startling headlines in this captivating story of faith and freedom under fire. The Munsons' thrillers are companion books, with characters reappearing in other novels, but each begins and ends a new story.
ISBN-13: 978-0982535547
320 Pages, trade paper
Fiction / Mystery and Suspense
14.99

Joshua Covenant

CIA agent Bo Rider moves to Israel after years of clandestine spying around the world. He takes his family, wife Julia, and teens, Glenna and Gregg while serving in America's Embassy using his real name. While Glenna and Gregg face danger while exploring Israel's treasures, their father is shocked to uncover a menacing plot jeopardizing them all. A Bible scholar helps Bo in amazing ways. He discovers the truth about the Joshua Covenant and battles evil forces that challenge his true identity. Will Bo survive the greatest threat ever to his career, his family, and his life? Glimpse tomorrow's startling headlines as risks it all to stop an enemy spy.
ISBN-13: 978-0-983559009
336 Pages, trade paper
Christian Fiction / Mystery and Suspense
14.99

Night Flight

When CIA Agent Bo Rider adopts a retired law enforcement dog for his family, teenagers Glenna and Gregg are surprised to discover Blaze's special skills. They put the dog to work solving crimes, but a captured criminal seeks revenge forcing the kids to hide out at their grandparents' Florida home. In Skeleton Key powerful villains connive to stop the teens from discovering their criminal enterprise. As Glenna and Gregg face high stakes, they find courage to keep pursuing justice. In Night Flight, the Rider family learns the true meaning of loving your neighbor as yourself. This is the debut thriller for young adults and grand parents by these best-selling ExFeds who write factional fiction based on their careers.
ISBN-13: 978-0983559023
224 Pages, trade paper
Fiction / Mystery and Suspense
9.99

Stolen Legacy

Stolen Legacy, by Diane and David Munson, tells the daunting tale of Germany invading Holland, and the heroes who dare to resist by hiding Jews. Federal agent Eva Montanna stops protecting America long enough to visit her grandfather's farm and help write a memoir of his dangerous time under Nazi control. Eva is shocked to uncover a plot to harm Grandpa Marty. Memories are tested as secrets from Marty's time in the Dutch resistance and later service in the Monuments Men of the U.S. Army fuel this betrayal. The Munsons' eighth thriller unveils priceless relics and a stolen legacy, forever changing Eva's life and her faith.
ISBN-13: 978-0983559047
336 pages, trade paper
Christian Fiction / Mystery and Suspense
14.99

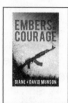

Embers of Courage

ICE Special Agent Eva Montanna discovers the world is ablaze with danger when militants capture her task force teammate, NCIS Special Agent Raj Pentu, during a CIA operation in Egypt. She risks her life to defeat tyrants oppressing Christians, and is plunged into a daring rescue mission. Eva's faith is tested like never before as mysterious ashes, her ancient family Bible, and fifteenth century religious persecution collide with modern-day courage under fire. This riveting novel, the ninth by ExFeds Diane and David Munson, is their third linking true historical events with their signature High Velocity Suspense.

ISBN-13: 978-0983559061
336 pages, trade paper
Christian Fiction / Mystery and Suspense
14.99